The Mysterious Stranger and Other Curious Tales

Mark Twain

The Mysterious Stranger

and Other Curious Tales

Mark Twain

GRAMERCY BOOKS
New York

This edition is published by Gramercy Books,
a division of Random House Value Publishing, Inc.
201 East 50th Street, New York, New York 10022.

Gramercy Books and colophon are trademarks of
Random House Value Publishing, Inc.

Random House
New York • Toronto • London • Sydney • Auckland

Printed and bound in the United States of America

COMPILED, EDITED, AND COMPOSITED BY FRANK J. FINAMORE

A CIP catalog record for this book is available from the Library of Congress.

The Mysterious Stranger and Other Curious Tales / by Mark Twain
ISBN 0-517-15073-5

8 7 6 5 4 3 2 1

Editor's Note. Certain characterizations and language of the author should be viewed as arising from the context of the time in which these stories were written. Any offense to modern sensibilities is unintended and does not reflect the attitudes of the editor or publisher of the current edition.

CONTENTS

Introduction

Mark Twain was born Samuel Langhorne Clemens on November 20, 1835, in Florida, Missouri. When he was four his family moved to the larger town of Hannibal—with a population of about five hundred—located on the mighty Mississippi River.

Clemens's childhood was spent in the rough and tumble life of the American frontier, which at first glance would hardly seem a conducive environment for the beginnings of a major literary career. But the town of Hannibal, the Mississippi River, and the expanding frontier of the youthful American Republic left an indelible mark upon Clemens's imagination. The writer and critic William Dean Howells accurately assessed Clemens as "the Lincoln of our literature."

When Samuel Clemens was twelve his father died and he was apprenticed to a local printer. Later the young man worked for his older brother Orion's local Hannibal newspaper, where he began to write short humorous pieces. When he was eighteen he left Hannibal; among his most notable stops were St. Louis, Cincinnati, and New York—where he practiced his trade as a printer and newspaperman. A major turning point in his life came in 1857 as he was journeying down to New Orleans on his way to South America: he met Horace Bixby, a riverboat pilot, who cast a spell over Clemens with his colorful and exciting stories of his adventures on the Mississippi. Clemens was soon apprenticed to become a steamboat pilot, and by 1859 he had his license. He would later describe these years in *Life on the Mississippi*, writing that "a pilot in those days was the only unfettered and entirely independent human being that lived on the earth." His carefree adventures on the Mississippi, however, were cut short by the Civil War. By 1861 he was with his brother in Nevada, where he tried his hand at prospecting and gambling. His lack of success in these questionable professions forced him back to work on newspapers.

In 1864, Clemens was in California, writing mostly freelance for papers like the *San Francisco Call.* However, he considered newspaper work "fearful drudgery, an awful employment for a lazy man." He was by this time using the pseudonym "Mark Twain"—a term from his steamboat days that leadsmen would utter indicating the water ahead was safe, but barely so. In December 1866 he signed with the *Alta California*, a prominent western paper, as its "traveling correspondent . . . not stinted to place, time or direction." This job paid his way for travels to New York, the Mediterranean, and the Near East. His letters of the account of his travels—published by the *Alta California* and the New York *Tribune*—and the book that grew from these pieces, *The Innocents Abroad; or, The New Pilgrim's Progress* (1869), made Clemens a popular literary sensation. It was hailed as "fresh, racy, and sparkling as a glass of champagne." It was a hilarious exploration of the collision between the decaying Old World and the uncultivated, unstudied, and often impudent views of no-nonsense Americans.

The next twenty years would mark the humorist's most productive and creative years as well as his happiest. In 1870, he married Olivia Langdon, the daughter of a wealthy New York industrialist, and settled down in Hartford, Connecticut, where they raised three daughters. His two finest and most famous books, *The Adventures of Tom Sawyer* (1876) and *Huckleberry Finn* (1885), were written during this period. In addition to his lucrative success as a writer he was also a very popular lecturer—both of which combined with his wife's fortune to make him a very wealthy man. However, bad investments—such as his own unsuccessful mechanical typesetter—and the failure of his own publishing company forced him into bankruptcy by the mid-1890s.

Twain soon undertook a very successful worldwide lecture tour, through which he was able to pay off his debts. However, his beloved eldest daughter Susy died suddenly while he was on tour, a blow that would profoundly alter Clemens's view of life and that marked the beginning of the tragedy that would plague him the remainder of his life. His wife's health, always frail, declined rapidly; she died in 1904. Until his death in 1910, Clemens would be wracked by profound bitterness and pessimism, which was clearly reflected in his writings, which became much darker.

The humorous Mark Twain that the public had become accustomed to and adulated seemed to have disappeared. But the darker side was always there, as in his famous description of man "as a museum of diseases, a home of impurities who begins as dirt and departs as stench" clearly shows. While undoubtedly funny, the meaning is grotesquely dark. Clemens wrote, "The secret source of Humor itself is not joy but sorrow. There is no humor in Heaven." It also must be remembered that "Mark Twain"—writer and lecturer—was an invention of Clemens, a persona used as a crowd-pleaser, a joker and clown. He thought of humor as a selling device, writing, "Humor is only a fragrance, a decoration." Near the end of his life, Clemens did not see the need to be merely entertaining.

The works collected in this volume are all late works that reveal the darker side of Clemens's genius. Eight months before his death he wrote to a friend, "I am full of malice, saturated with malignity." His finest works from this period mercilessly attack mankind and what Clemens considered its evil flaws. In what is probably his greatest short story, "The Man That Corrupted Hadleyburg" (1899), Clemens shows the dishonesty and greed that lie within the hearts of even the most respectable and upstanding citizens of an idyllic American small town, the supposed backbone of American moral integrity and fortitude. In "The $30,000 Bequest" (1904) he shows the devastating effect money has upon a married couple. "Extract from Captain Stormfield's Visit to Heaven" (1908) is a comic satire of mankind's misguided traditional view of the afterlife that ridicules its delusion that it is the center of the universe. Clemens called *What Is Man?* (1906) his "wicked book." It is a philosophical treatise that paints man as a mechanism that is at the mercy of chance and whose brain is "so constructed that it can originate nothing."

His greatest work from this period is his last, posthumous novel, *The Mysterious Stranger* (1916). Set in 1590, it is the story of an Austrian boy who encounters an angel called Satan who reveals to him the true nature of existence. Near the end, Satan tells the youth, "There is no God, no universe, no human race, . . . no heaven, no hell. It is all a dream—a grotesque and foolish dream. Nothing exists but you." It is a nihilistic but fascinating and thought-provoking book that stands as the final testament of Clemens's art.

FRANK JAMES FINAMORE

New York, 1996

The Man That Corrupted Hadleyburg

I

It was many years ago. Hadleyburg was the most honest and upright town in all the region round about. It had kept that reputation unsmirched during three generations, and was prouder of it than of any other of its possessions. It was so proud of it, and so anxious to insure its perpetuation, that it began to teach the principles of honest dealing to its babies in the cradle, and made the like teachings the staple of their culture thenceforward through all the years devoted to their education. Also, throughout the formative years temptations were kept out of the way of the young people, so that their honesty could have every chance to harden and solidify, and become a part of their very bone. The neighboring towns were jealous of this honorable supremacy, and affected to sneer at Hadleyburg's pride in it and call it vanity; but all the same they were obliged to acknowledge that Hadleyburg was in reality an incorruptible town; and if pressed they would also acknowledge that the mere fact that a young man hailed from Hadleyburg was all the recommendation he needed when he went forth from his natal town to seek for responsible employment.

But at last, in the drift of time, Hadleyburg had the ill luck to offend a passing stranger—possibly without knowing it, certainly without caring, for Hadleyburg was sufficient unto itself, and cared not a rap for strangers or their opinions. Still, it would have been well to make an exception in this one's case, for he was a bitter man and revengeful. All through his wanderings during a whole year he kept his injury in mind, and gave all his leisure moments to trying to invent a compensating satisfaction for it. He contrived many plans, and all of them were good, but none of them was quite sweeping enough; the poorest of them would hurt a great many individuals, but what he wanted was a plan which would comprehend the entire town, and not let so much as one person escape unhurt. At last he had a fortunate idea, and when it fell into his brain it lit up his whole head with an evil joy. He began to form a plan at once, saying to himself, "That is the thing to do—I will corrupt the town."

Six months later he went to Hadleyburg, and arrived in a buggy at the house of the old cashier of the bank about ten at night. He got a sack out of the buggy, shouldered it, and staggered with it through the cottage yard, and knocked at the door. A woman's voice said "Come in," and he entered, and set his sack behind the stove in the parlor, saying politely to the old lady who sat reading the *Missionary Herald* by the lamp:

"Pray keep your seat, madam, I will not disturb you. There—now it is pretty well concealed; one would hardly know it was there. Can I see your husband a moment, madam?"

No, he was gone to Brixton, and might not return before morning.

"Very well, madam, it is no matter. I merely wanted to leave that sack in his care, to be delivered to the rightful owner when he shall be found. I am a stranger; he does not know me; I am merely passing through the town tonight to discharge a matter which has been long in my mind. My errand is now completed, and I go pleased and a little proud, and you will never see me again. There is a paper attached to the sack which will explain everything. Good-night, madam."

The old lady was afraid of the mysterious big stranger, and was glad to see him go. But her curiosity was roused, and she went straight to the sack and brought away the paper. It began as follows:

> "To be Published; or, the right man sought out by private inquiry—either will answer. This sack contains gold coin weighing a hundred and sixty pounds four ounces—"

"Mercy on us, and the door not locked!"

Mrs. Richards flew to it all in a tremble and locked it, then pulled down the window-shades and stood frightened, worried and wondering if there was anything else she could do toward making herself and the money more safe. She listened awhile for burglars, then surrendered to curiosity and went back to the lamp and finished reading the paper:

"I am a foreigner, and am presently going back to my own country, to remain there permanently. I am grateful to America for what I have received at her hands during my long stay under her flag; and to one of her citizens—a citizen of Hadleyburg—I am especially grateful for a great kindness done me a year or two ago. Two great kindnesses, in fact. I will explain. I was a gambler. I say I *was.* I was a ruined gambler. I arrived in this village at night, hungry and without a penny. I asked for help—in the dark; I was ashamed to beg in the light. I begged of the right man. He gave me twenty dollars—that is to say, he gave me life, as I considered it. He also gave me fortune; for out of that money I have made myself rich at the gaming-table. And finally, a remark which he made to me has remained with me to this day, and has at last conquered me; and in conquering has saved the remnant of my morals: I shall gamble no more. Now I have no idea who that man was, but I want him found, and I want him to have this money, to give away, throw away, or keep, as he pleases. It is merely my way of testifying my gratitude to him. If I could stay, I would find him myself; but no matter, he will be found. This is an honest town, an incorruptible town, and I know I can trust it without fear. This man can be identified by the remark which he made to me; I feel persuaded that he will remember it.

"And now my plan is this: If you prefer to conduct the inquiry privately, do so. Tell the contents of this present writing to any one who is likely to be the right man. If he shall answer, 'I am the man; the remark I made was so-and-so,' apply the test—to wit: Open the sack, and in it you will find a sealed envelope containing that remark. If the remark mentioned by the candidate tallies with it, give him the money, and ask no further questions, for he is certainly the right man.

"But if you shall prefer a public inquiry, then publish this present writing in the local paper—with these instructions added, to wit: Thirty days from now, let the candidate appear at the town hall at eight in the evening (Friday), and hand his remark, in a sealed envelope, to the Rev. Mr. Burgess (if he will be kind enough to act); and let Mr. Burgess there and then destroy the seals of the sack, open it, and see if the remark is correct; if correct, let the money be delivered, with my sincere gratitude, to my benefactor thus identified."

Mrs. Richards sat down, gently quivering with excitement, and was soon lost in thinkings—after this pattern: "What a strange thing it is! . . . And what a fortune for that kind man who set his bread afloat upon the waters! . . . If it had only been my husband that did it!—for we are so poor, so old and poor! . . ." Then, with a sigh—"But it was not my Edward; no, it was not he that gave a stranger twenty dollars. It is a pity too; I see it now . . . ." Then, with a shudder— "But it is *gambler's* money! the wages of sin; we couldn't take it; we couldn't touch it. I don't like to be near it; it seems a defilement." She moved to a farther chair . . . . "I wish Edward would come, and take it to the bank; a burglar might come at any moment; it is dreadful to be here all alone with it."

At eleven Mr. Richards arrived, and while his wife was saying, "I am *so* glad you've come!" he was saying, "I'm so tired—tired clear out; it is dreadful to be poor, and have to make these dismal journeys at my time of life. Always at the grind, grind, grind, on a salary—another man's slave, and he sitting at home in his slippers, rich and comfortable."

"I am so sorry for you, Edward, you know that; but be comforted; we have our livelihood; we have our good name—"

"Yes, Mary, and that is everything. Don't mind my talk—it's just a moment's irritation and doesn't mean anything. Kiss me—there, it's all gone now, and I am not complaining any more. What have you been getting? What's in the sack?"

Then his wife told him the great secret. It dazed him for a moment; then he said:

"It weighs a hundred and sixty pounds? Why, Maw, it's for-ty thou-sand dollars—think of it—a whole fortune! Not ten men in this village are worth that much. Give me the paper."

He skimmed through it and said:

"Isn't it an adventure! Why, it's a romance; it's like the impossible things one reads about in books, and never sees in life." He was well stirred up now; cheerful, even gleeful. He tapped his old wife on the cheek, and said, humorously, "Why, we're rich, Mary, rich; all we've got to do is to bury the money and burn the papers. If the gambler ever comes to inquire, we'll merely look coldly upon him and say: 'What is this nonsense you are talking? We have never heard of you and your sack of gold before;' and then he would look foolish, and—"

"And in the mean time, while you are running on with your jokes, the money is still here, and it is fast getting along toward burglar-time."

"True. Very well, what shall we do—make the inquiry private? No, not that; it would spoil the romance. The public method is better. Think what a noise it will make! And it will make all the other towns jealous; for no stranger would trust such a thing to any town but Hadleyburg, and they know it. It's a great card for us. I must get to the printing office now, or I shall be too late."

"But stop—stop—don't leave me here alone with it, Edward?

But he was gone. For only a little while, however. Not far from his own house he met the editor-proprietor of the paper, and gave him the document, and said, "Here is a good thing for you, Cox—put it in."

"It may be too late, Mr. Richards, but I'll see."

At home again he and his wife sat down to talk the charming mystery over; they were in no condition for sleep. The first question was, Who could the citizen have been who gave the stranger the twenty dollars? It seemed a simple one; both answered it in the same breath—

"Barclay Goodson."

"Yes," said Richards, "he could have done it, and it would have been like him, but there's not another in the town."

"Everybody will grant that, Edward—grant it privately, anyway. For six months, now, the village has been its own proper self once more—honest, narrow, self-righteous, and stingy."

"It is what he always called it, to the day of his death—said it right out publicly, too."

"Yes, and he was hated for it."

"Oh, of course; but he didn't care. I reckon he was the best-hated man among us, except the Reverend Burgess."

"Well, Burgess deserves it—he will never get another congregation here. Mean as the town is, it knows how to estimate *him*. Edward, doesn't it seem odd that the stranger should appoint Burgess to deliver the money?"

"Well, yes—it does. That is—that is—"

"Why so much that-*is*-ing? Would *you* select him?"

"Mary, maybe the stranger knows him better than this village does."

"Much *that* would help Burgess!"

The husband seemed perplexed for an answer; the wife kept a steady eye upon him, and waited. Finally Richards said, with the hesitancy of one who is making a statement which is likely to encounter doubt,

"Mary, Burgess is not a bad man."

His wife was certainly surprised.

"Nonsense!" she exclaimed.

"He is not a bad man. I know. The whole of his unpopularity had its foundation in that one thing—the thing that made so much noise."

"That 'one thing,' indeed! As if that 'one thing' wasn't enough, all by itself."

"Plenty. Plenty. Only he wasn't guilty of it."

"How you talk! Not guilty of it! Everybody knows he *was* guilty."

"Mary, I give you my word—he was innocent."

"I can't believe it, and I don't. How do you know?"

"It is a confession. I am ashamed, but I will make it. I was the only man who knew he was innocent. I could have saved him, and—and—well, you know how the town was wrought up—I hadn't the pluck to do it. It would have turned everybody against me. I felt mean, ever so mean; but I didn't dare; I hadn't the manliness to face that."

Mary looked troubled, and for a while was silent. Then she said, stammeringly:

"I—I don't think it would have done for you to—to—One mustn't—er—public opinion—one has to be so careful—so—" It was a difficult road, and she got mired; but after a little she got started again. "It was a great pity, but—Why, we couldn't afford it, Edward—we couldn't indeed. Oh, I wouldn't have had you do it for anything!"

"It would have lost us the good-will of so many people, Mary; and then—and then—"

"What troubles me now is, what *he* thinks of us, Edward."

"He? *He* doesn't suspect that I could have saved him."

"Oh," exclaimed the wife, in a tone of relief, "I am glad of that.

As long as he doesn't know that you could have saved him, he—he—well, that makes it a great deal better. Why, I might have known he didn't know, because he is always trying to be friendly with us, as little encouragement as we give him. More than once people have twitted me with it. There's the Wilsons, and the Wilcoxes, and the Harknesses, they take a mean pleasure in saying, '*Your friend* Burgess,' because they know it pesters me. I wish he wouldn't persist in liking us so; I can't think why he keeps it up."

"I can explain it. It's another confession. When the thing was new and hot, and the town made a plan to ride him on a rail, my conscience hurt me so that I couldn't stand it, and I went privately and gave him notice, and he got out of the town and staid out till it was safe to come back."

"Edward! If the town had found it out—"

"*Don't!* It scares me yet, to think of it. I repented of it the minute it was done; and I was even afraid to tell you, lest your face might betray it to somebody. I didn't sleep any that night, for worrying. But after a few days I saw that no one was going to suspect me, and after that I got to feeling glad I did it. And I feel glad yet, Mary—glad through and through."

"So do I, now, for it would have been a dreadful way to treat him. Yes, I'm glad; for really you did owe him that, you know. But, Edward, suppose it should come out yet, some day!"

"It won't."

"Why?"

"Because everybody thinks it was Goodson."

"Of course they would!"

"Certainly. And of course *he* didn't care. They persuaded poor old Sawlsberry to go and charge it on him, and he went blustering over there and did it. Goodson looked him over, like as if he was hunting for a place on him that he could despise the most, then he says, 'So you are the Committee of Inquiry, are you?' Sawlsberry said that was about what he was. 'Hm. Do they require particulars, or do you reckon a kind of a *general* answer will do?' 'If they require particulars, I will come back, Mr. Goodson; I will take the general answer first.' 'Very well, then, tell them to go to hell—I reckon that's general enough. And I'll give you some advice, Sawlsberry: when you come back for the particulars, fetch a basket to carry the relics of yourself home in.'"

"Just like Goodson; it's got all the marks. He had only one vanity; he thought he could give advice better than any other person."

"It settled the business, and saved us, Mary. The subject was dropped."

"Bless you, I'm not doubting *that.*"

Then they took up the gold-sack mystery again, with strong interest. Soon the conversation began to suffer breaks—interruptions caused by absorbed thinkings. The breaks grew more and more frequent. At last Richards lost himself wholly in thought. He sat long, gazing vacantly at the floor, and by-and-by he began to punctuate his thoughts with little nervous movements of his hands that seemed to indicate vexation. Meantime his wife too had relapsed into a thoughtful silence, and her movements were beginning to show a troubled discomfort. Finally Richards got up and strode aimlessly about the room, plowing his hands through his hair, much as a somnambulist might do who was having a bad dream. Then he seemed to arrive at a definite purpose; and without a word he put on his hat and passed quickly out of the house. His wife sat brooding, with a drawn face, and did not seem to be aware that she was alone. Now and then she murmured, "Lead us not into t . . . . but—but—we are so poor, so poor! . . . . Lead us not into . . . . Ah, who would be hurt by it?—and no one would ever know . . . . Lead us . . . ." The voice died out in mumblings. After a little she glanced up and muttered in a half-frightened, half-glad way—

"He is gone! But, oh dear, he may be too late—too late. . . . Maybe not—maybe there is still time." She rose and stood thinking, nervously clasping and unclasping her hands. A slight shudder shook her frame, and she said, out of a dry throat, "God forgive me—it's awful to think such things—but . . . . Lord, how we are made—how strangely we are made!"

She turned the light low, and slipped stealthily over and kneeled down by the sack and felt of its ridgy sides with her hands, and fondled them lovingly; and there was a gloating light in her poor old eyes. She fell into fits of absence; and came half out of them at times to mutter, "If we had only waited! —oh, if we had only waited a little, and not been in such a hurry!"

Meantime Cox had gone home from his office and told his wife all about the strange thing that had happened, and they had talked it over eagerly, and guessed that the late Goodson was the only man in the town who could have helped a suffering stranger with so noble a sum as twenty dollars. Then there was a pause, and the two became thoughtful and silent. And by-and-by nervous and fidgety. At last the wife said, as if to herself,

"Nobody knows this secret but the Richardses . . . . and us . . . . nobody."

The husband came out of his thinkings with a slight start, and gazed wistfully at his wife, whose face was become very pale; then he hesitatingly rose, and glanced furtively at his hat, then at his wife—a sort of mute inquiry. Mrs. Cox swallowed once or twice, with her hand at her throat, then in place of speech she nodded her head. In a moment she was alone, and mumbling to herself.

And now Richards and Cox were hurrying through the deserted streets, from opposite directions. They met, panting, at the foot of the printing office stairs; by the night-light there they read each other's face. Cox whispered,

"Nobody knows about this but us?"

The whispered answer was,

"Not a soul—on honor, not a soul!"

"If it isn't too late to—"

The men were starting upstairs; at this moment they were overtaken by a boy, and Cox asked,

"Is that you, Johnny?"

"Yes, sir."

"You needn't ship the early mail—nor *any* mail; wait till I tell you."

"It's already gone, sir."

"*Gone?*" It had the sound of an unspeakable disappointment in it.

"Yes, sir. Timetable for Brixton and all the towns beyond changed today, sir—had to get the papers in twenty minutes earlier than common. I had to rush; if I had been two minutes later—"

The men turned and walked slowly away, not waiting to hear the rest. Neither of them spoke during ten minutes; then Cox said, in a vexed tone,

"What possessed you to be in such a hurry, *I* can't make out."

The answer was humble enough:

"I see it now, but somehow I never thought, you know, until it was too late. But the next time—"

"Next time be hanged! It won't come in a thousand years."

Then the friends separated without a good-night, and dragged themselves home with the gait of mortally stricken men. At their homes their wives sprang up with an eager "Well?"—then saw the answer with their eyes and sank down sorrowing, without waiting for it to come in words. In both houses a discussion followed of a heated sort—a new thing; there had been discussions before, but not heated ones, not ungentle ones. The discussions tonight were a sort of seeming plagiarisms of each other. Mrs. Richards said,

"If you had only waited, Edward—if you had only stopped to think; but no, you must run straight to the printing office and spread it all over the world."

"It *said* publish it."

"That is nothing; it also said do it privately, if you liked. There, now—is that true, or not?"

"Why, yes—yes, it is true; but when I thought what a stir it would make, and what a compliment it was to Hadleyburg that a stranger should trust it so—"

"Oh, certainly, I know all that; but if you had only stopped to think, you would have seen that you *couldn't* find the right man, because he is in his grave, and hasn't left chick nor child nor relation behind him; and as long as the money went to somebody that awfully needed it, and nobody would be hurt by it, and—and—"

She broke down, crying. Her husband tried to think of some comforting thing to say, and presently came out with this:

"But after all, Mary, it must be for the best—it *must* be; we know that. And we must remember that it was so ordered—"

"Ordered! Oh, everything's *ordered*, when a person has to find some way out when he has been stupid. Just the same, it was *ordered* that the money should come to us in this special way, and it was you that must take it on yourself to go meddling with the designs of Providence—and who gave you the right. It was wicked, that is what it was—just blasphemous presumption, and no more becoming to a meek and humble professor of—"

"But, Mary, you know how we have been trained all our lives

long, like the whole village, till it is absolutely second nature to us to stop not a single moment to think when there's an honest thing to be done—"

"Oh, I know it, I know it—it's been one everlasting training and training and training in honesty—honesty shielded, from the very cradle, against every possible temptation, and so it's *artificial* honesty, and weak as water when temptation comes, as we have seen this night. God knows I never had shade nor shadow of a doubt of my petrified and indestructible honesty until now—and now, under the very first big and real temptation, I—Edward, it is my belief that this town's honesty is as rotten as mine is; as rotten as yours is. It is a mean town, a hard, stingy town, and hasn't a virtue in the world but this honesty it is so celebrated for and so conceited about; and so help me, I do believe that if ever the day comes that its honesty falls under great temptation, its grand reputation will go to ruin like a house of cards. There, now, I've made confession, and I feel better; I am a humbug, and I've been one all my life, without knowing it. Let no man call me honest again—I will not have it."

"I— Well, Mary, I feel a good deal as you do; I certainly do. It seems strange, too, so strange. I never could have believed it—never."

A long silence followed; both were sunk in thought. At last the wife looked up and said,

"I know what you are thinking, Edward."

Richards had the embarrassed look of a person who is caught.

"I am ashamed to confess it, Mary, but—"

"It's no matter, Edward, I was thinking the same question myself."

"I hope so. State it."

"You were thinking, if a body could only guess out *what the remark was* that Goodson made to the stranger."

"It's perfectly true. I feel guilty and ashamed. And you?"

"I'm past it. Let us make a pallet here; we've got to stand watch till the bank vault opens in the morning and admits the sack . . . . Oh, dear, oh, dear—if we hadn't made the mistake!"

The pallet was made, and Mary said:

"The open sesame—what could it have been? I do wonder what that remark could have been? But come; we will get to bed now."

"And sleep?"

"No; think."

"Yes, think."

By this time the Coxes too had completed their spat and their reconciliation, and were turning in—to think, to think, and toss, and fret, and worry over what the remark could possibly have been which Goodson made to the stranded derelict: that golden remark; that remark worth forty thousand dollars, cash.

The reason that the village telegraph office was open later than usual that night was this: The foreman of Cox's paper was the local representative of the Associated Press. One might say its honorary representative, for it wasn't four times a year that he could furnish thirty words that would be accepted. But this time it was different. His dispatch stating what he had caught got an instant answer:

"*Send the whole thing—all the details—twelve hundred words.*"

A colossal order! The foreman filled the bill; and he was the proudest man in the State. By breakfast-time the next morning the name of Hadleyburg the Incorruptible was on every lip in America, from Montreal to the Gulf, from the glaciers of Alaska to the orange-groves of Florida; and millions and millions of people were discussing the stranger and his money-sack, and wondering if the right man would be found, and hoping some more news about the matter would come soon—right away.

II

Hadleyburg village woke up world-celebrated—astonished —happy—vain. Vain beyond imagination. Its nineteen principal citizens and their wives went about shaking hands with each other, and beaming, and smiling, and congratulating, and saying *this* thing adds a new word to the dictionary—*Hadleyburg*, synonym for *incorruptible*—destined to live in dictionaries forever! And the minor and unimportant citizens and their wives went around acting in much the same way. Everybody ran to the bank to see the gold-sack; and before noon grieved and envious crowds began to flock in from Brixton and all neighboring towns; and that afternoon and next day reporters began to arrive from everywhere to verify the sack and its history and write the whole thing up anew, and make dashing freehand pictures of the sack, and of Richards's house, and the bank, and the Presbyterian church, and the Baptist church, and the public square, and the town hall where the test would be applied and the money delivered; and damnable portraits of the Richardses, and Pinkerton the banker, and Cox, and the foreman, and Reverend Burgess, and the postmaster—and even of Jack Halliday, who was the loafing, good-natured, no-account, irreverent fisherman, hunter, boys' friend, stray-dogs' friend, typical "Sam Lawson" of the town. The little mean, smirking, oily Pinkerton showed the sack to all comers, and rubbed his sleek palms together pleasantly, and enlarged upon the town's fine old reputation for honesty and upon this wonderful endorsement of it, and hoped and believed that the example would now spread far and wide over the American world, and be epoch-making in the matter of moral regeneration. And so on, and so on.

By the end of a week things had quieted down again; the wild intoxication of pride and joy had sobered to a soft, sweet, silent delight—a sort of deep, nameless, unutterable content. All faces bore a look of peaceful, holy happiness.

Then a change came. It was a gradual change: so gradual that its beginnings were hardly noticed; maybe were not noticed at all, except by Jack Halliday, who always noticed everything; and always made fun of it, too, no matter what it was. He began to throw out charting remarks about people not looking quite so happy as they did a day or two ago; and next he claimed that the new aspect was deepening to positive sadness; next, that it was taking on a sick look; and finally he said that everybody was become so moody, thoughtful, and absent-minded that he could rob the meanest man in town of a cent out of the bottom of his breeches pocket and not disturb his reverie.

At this stage—or at about this stage—a saying like this was dropped at bedtime—with a sigh, usually—by the head of each of the nineteen principal households:

"Ah, what *could* have been the remark that Goodson made!"

And straightway—with a shudder—came this, from the man's wife:

"Oh, *don't!* What horrible thing are you mulling in your mind? Put it away from you, for God's sake!"

But that question was wrung from those men again the next night—and got the same retort. But weaker.

And the third night the men uttered the question yet again—with anguish, and absently. This time—and the following night—the wives fidgeted feebly, and tried to say something. But didn't.

And the night after that they found their tongues and responded—longingly,

"Oh, if we *could* only guess!"

Halliday's comments grew daily more and more sparklingly disagreeable and disparaging. He went diligently about, laughing at the town, individually and in mass. But his laugh was the only one left in the village: it fell upon a hollow and mournful vacancy and emptiness. Not even a smile was findable anywhere. Halliday carried a cigar-box around on a tripod, playing that it was a camera, and halted all passers and aimed the thing and said, "Ready!—now look pleasant, please," but not even this capital joke could surprise the dreary faces into any softening.

So three weeks passed—one week was left. It was Saturday evening—after supper. Instead of the aforetime Saturday evening flutter and bustle and shopping and larking, the streets were empty and desolate. Richards and his old wife sat apart in their little parlor—miserable and thinking. This was become their evening habit now: the life-long habit which had preceded it, of reading, knitting, and contented chat, or receiving or paying neighborly calls, was dead and gone and forgotten, ages ago—two or three weeks ago; nobody talked now, nobody read, nobody visited—the whole village sat at home, sighing, worrying, silent. Trying to guess out that remark.

The postman left a letter. Richards glanced listlessly at the superscription and the postmark—unfamiliar, both—and tossed the letter on the table and resumed his might-have-beens and his hopeless dull miseries where he had left them off. Two or three hours later his wife got wearily up and was going away to bed without a good-night—custom now—but she stopped near the letter and eyed it awhile with a dead interest, then broke it open, and began to skim it over. Richards, sitting there with his chair tilted back against the wall and his chin between his knees, heard something fall. It was his wife. He sprang to her side, but she cried out:

"Leave me alone, I am too happy. Read the letter—read it!" He did. He devoured it, his brain reeling. The letter was from a distant State, and it said:

> "I am a stranger to you, but no matter: I have something to tell. I have just arrived home from Mexico, and learned about that episode. Of course you do not know who made that remark, but I know, and I am the only person living who does know. It was *Goodson.* I knew him well, many years ago. I passed through your village that very night, and was his guest till the midnight train came along. I overheard him make that remark to the stranger in the dark—it was in Hale Alley. He and I talked of it the rest of the way home, and while smoking in his house. He mentioned many of your villagers in the course of his talk—most of them in a very uncomplimentary way, but two or three favorably: among these latter yourself. I say 'favorably'—nothing stronger. I remember his saying he did not actually *like* any person in the town—not one; but that you—I *think* he said you—am almost sure—had done him a very great service once, possibly without knowing the full value of it, and he wished he had a fortune, he would leave it to you when he died, and a curse apiece for the rest of the citizens. Now, then, if it was you that did him that service, you are his legitimate heir, and entitled to the sack of gold. I know that I can trust to your honor and honesty, for in a citizen of Hadleyburg these virtues are an unfailing inheritance, and so I am going to reveal to you the remark, well satisfied that if you are not the right man you will seek and find the right one and see that poor Goodson's debt of gratitude for the service referred to is paid. This is the remark: '*You are far from being a bad man: go, and reform.*'
>
> HOWARD L. STEPHENSON."

"Oh, Edward, the money is ours, and I am so grateful, *oh*, so grateful—kiss me, dear, it's forever since we kissed—and we needed it so—the money—and now you are free of Pinkerton and his bank, and nobody's slave any more; it seems to me I could fly for joy."

It was a happy half-hour that the couple spent there on the settee caressing each other; it was the old days come again—days that had begun with their courtship and lasted without a break till the stranger brought the deadly money. By-and-by the wife said:

"Oh, Edward, how lucky it was you did him that grand service, poor Goodson! I never liked him, but I love him now. And it was fine and beautiful of you never to mention it or brag about it." Then, with a touch of reproach, "But you ought to have told *me*, Edward, you ought to have told your wife, you know."

"Well, I—er—well, Mary, you see—"

"Now stop hemming and hawing, and tell me about it, Edward. I always loved you, and now I'm proud of you. Everybody believes there was only one good generous soul in this village, and now it turns out that you— Edward, why don't you tell me?"

"Well—er—er— Why, Mary, I can't!"

"You *can't? Why* can't you?"

"You see, he—well, he—he made me promise I wouldn't." The wife looked him over, and said, very slowly,

"Made—you—promise? Edward, what do you tell me that for?"

"Mary, do you think I would lie?"

She was troubled and silent for a moment, then she laid her hand within his and said:

"No . . . no. We have wandered far enough from our bearings—God spare us that! In all your life you have never uttered a lie. But now—now that the foundations of things seem to be crumbling from under us, we—we—" She lost her voice for a moment, then said, brokenly, "Lead us not into temptation . . . . I think you made the promise, Edward. Let it rest so. Let us keep away from that ground. Now—that is all gone by; let us be happy again; it is no time for clouds."

Edward found it something of an effort to comply, for his mind kept wandering—trying to remember what the service was that he had done Goodson.

The couple lay awake most of the night, Mary happy and busy, Edward busy, but not so happy. Mary was planning what she would do with the money. Edward was trying to recall that service. At first his conscience was sore on account of the lie he had told Mary—if it *was* a lie. After much reflection—suppose it was a lie? What then? Was it such a great matter? Aren't we always *acting* lies? Then why not *tell* them? Look at Mary—look what she had done. While he was hurrying off on his honest errand, what was she doing? Lamenting because the papers hadn't been destroyed and the money kept! Is theft better than lying?

That point lost its sting—the lie dropped into the background and left comfort behind it. The next point came to the front: *had* he rendered that service? Well, here was Goodson's own evidence as reported in Stephenson's letter; there could be no better evidence than that—it was even *proof* that he had rendered it. Of course. So that point was settled . . . . No, not quite. He recalled with a wince that this unknown Mr. Stephenson was just a trifle unsure as to whether the performer of it was Richards or some other—and, oh dear, he had put Richards on his honor! He must himself decide whither that money must go—and Mr. Stephenson was not doubting that if he was the wrong man he would go honorably and find the right one. Oh, it was odious to put a man in such a situation—ah, why couldn't Stephenson have left out that doubt! What did he want to intrude that for?

Further reflection. How did it happen that *Richards's* name remained in Stephenson's mind as indicating the right man, and not some other man's name? That looked good. Yes, that looked very good. In fact, it went on looking better and better, straight along—until by-and-by it grew into positive *proof*. And then Richards put the matter at once out of his mind, for he had a private instinct that a proof once established is better left so.

He was feeling reasonably comfortable now, but there was still one other detail that kept pushing itself on his notice: of course he had done that service—that was settled; but what *was* that service? He must recall it—he would not go to sleep till he had recalled it; it would make his peace of mind perfect. And so he thought and thought. He thought of a dozen things—possible services, even probable services—but none of them seemed adequate, none of them seemed large enough, none of them seemed worth the money—worth the fortune Goodson had wished he could leave in his will. And besides, he couldn't remember having done them, anyway. Now, then—now, then—what *kind* of a service would it be that would make a man so inordinately grateful? Ah—the saving of his soul! That must be it. Yes, he could remember, now, how he once set himself the task of converting Goodson, and labored at it as much as—he was going to say three months; but upon closer examination it shrunk to a month, then to a week, then to a day, then to nothing. Yes, he remembered, now, and with unwelcome vividness, that Goodson had told him to go to thunder and mind his own business—*he* wasn't hankering to follow Hadleyburg to heaven!

So that solution was a failure—he hadn't saved Goodson's soul. Richards was discouraged. Then after a little came another idea: had he saved Goodson's property? No, that wouldn't do—he hadn't any. His life? That is it! Of course. Why, he might have thought of it before. This time he was on the right track, sure. His imagination-mill was hard at work in a minute, now.

Thereafter during a stretch of two exhausting hours he was busy saving Goodson's life. He saved it in all kinds of difficult and perilous ways. In every case he got it saved satisfactorily up to a certain point; then, just as he was beginning to get well persuaded that it had really happened, a troublesome detail would turn up which made the whole thing impossible. As in the matter of drowning, for instance. In that case he had swum out and tugged Goodson ashore in an unconscious state with a great crowd looking on and applauding, but when he had got it all thought out and was just beginning to remember all about it a whole swarm of disqualifying details arrived on the ground: the town would have known of the circumstance, Mary would have known of it, it would glare like a limelight in his own memory instead of being an inconspicuous service which he had possibly rendered "without knowing its full value." And at this point he remembered that he couldn't swim, anyway.

Ah—*there* was a point which he had been overlooking from the start: it had to be a service which he had rendered "possibly without knowing the full value of it." Why, really, that ought to be an easy hunt—much easier than those others. And sure enough, by-and-by he found it. Goodson, years and years ago, came near marrying a very sweet and pretty girl, named Nancy Hewitt, but in some way or other the match had been broken off; the girl died, Goodson remained a bachelor, and by-and-by became a soured one and a flank despiser of the human species. Soon after the girl's death the village found out, or thought it had found out, that she carried a spoonful of negro blood in her veins. Richards worked at these details a good while, and in the end he thought he remembered things concerning them which must have gotten mislaid in his memory through long neglect. He seemed to dimly remember that it was *he* that found out about the negro blood; that it was he that told the village; that the village told Goodson where they got it; that he thus saved Goodson from marrying the tainted girl; that he had done him this great service "without knowing the full value of it," in fact without knowing that he *was* doing it; but that Goodson knew the value of it, and what a narrow escape he had had, and so went to his grave grateful to his benefactor and wishing he had a fortune to leave him. It was all clear and simple now, and the more he went over it the more luminous and certain it grew; and at last, when he nestled to sleep satisfied and happy, he remembered the whole thing just as if it had been yesterday. In fact, he dimly remembered Goodson's *telling* him his gratitude once. Meantime Mary had spent six thousand dollars on a new house for herself and a pair of slippers for her pastor, and then had fallen peacefully to rest.

That same Saturday evening the postman had delivered a letter to each of the other principal citizens—nineteen letters in all. No two of the envelopes were alike, and no two of the superscriptions were in the same hand, but the letters inside were just like each other in every detail but one. They were exact copies of the letter received by Richards—handwriting and all—and were all signed by Stephenson, but in place of Richards's name each receiver's own name appeared.

All night long eighteen principal citizens did what their caste-brother Richards was doing at the same time—they put in their energies trying to remember what notable service it was that they had unconsciously done Barclay Goodson. In no case was it a holiday job; still they succeeded.

And while they were at this work, which was difficult, their wives put in the night spending the money, which was easy. During that one night the nineteen wives spent an average of seven thousand dollars each out of the forty thousand in the sack—a hundred and thirty-three thousand altogether.

Next day there was a surprise for Jack Halliday. He noticed that the faces of the nineteen chief citizens and their wives bore that expression of peaceful and holy happiness again. He could not understand it, neither was he able to invent any remarks about it that could damage it or disturb it. And so it was his turn to be dissatisfied with life. His private guesses at the reasons for the happiness failed in all instances, upon examination. When he met Mrs. Wilcox and noticed the placid ecstasy in her face, he said to himself, "Her cat has had kittens"—and went and asked the cook; it was not so; the cook had detected the happiness, but did not know the cause. When Halliday found the duplicate ecstasy in the face of "Shadbelly" Billson (village nickname), he was sure some neighbor of Billson's had broken his leg, but inquiry showed that this had not happened. The subdued ecstasy in Gregory Yates's face could mean but one thing—he was a mother-in-law short; it was another mistake. "And Pinkerton—Pinkerton—he has collected ten cents that he thought he was going to lose." And so on, and so on. In some cases the guesses had to remain in doubt, in the others they proved distinct errors. In the end Halliday said to himself, "Anyway it foots up that there's nineteen Hadleyburg families temporarily in heaven; I don't know how it happened; I only know Providence is off duty today."

An architect and builder from the next State had lately ventured to set up a small business in this unpromising village, and his sign had now been hanging out a week. Not a customer yet; he was a discouraged man, and sorry he had come. But his weather changed suddenly now. First one and then another chief citizen's wife said to him privately:

"Come to my house Monday week—but say nothing about it for the present. We think of building."

He got eleven invitations that day. That night he wrote his daughter and broke off her match with her student. He said she could marry a mile higher than that.

Pinkerton the banker and two or three other well-to-do men planned countryseats—but waited. That kind don't count their chickens until they are hatched.

The Wilsons devised a grand new thing—a fancy-dress ball. They made no actual promises, but told all their acquaintanceship in confidence that they were thinking the matter over and thought they should give it—"and if we do, you will be invited, of course." People were surprised, and said, one to another, "Why, they are crazy, those poor Wilsons, they can't afford it." Several among the nineteen said privately to their husbands, "It is a good idea; we will keep still till their cheap thing is over, then *we* will give one that will make it sick."

The days drifted along, and the bill of future squanderings rose higher and higher, wilder and wilder, more and more foolish and reckless. It began to look as if every member of the nineteen would not only spend his whole forty thousand dollars before receiving-day, but be actually in debt by the time he got the money. In some cases light-headed people did not stop with planning to spend, they really spent—on credit. They bought land, mortgages, farms, speculative stocks, fine clothes, horses, and various other things, paid down the bonus, and made themselves liable for the rest—at ten days. Presently the sober second thought came, and Halliday noticed that a ghastly anxiety was beginning to show up in a good many faces. Again he was puzzled, and didn't know what to make of it. "The Wilcox kittens aren't dead, for they weren't born; nobody's broken a leg; there's no shrinkage in mother-in-laws; *nothing* has happened—it is an insolvable mystery."

There was another puzzled man, too—the Rev. Mr. Burgess. For days, wherever he went, people seemed to follow him or to be watching out for him; and if he ever found himself in a retired spot, a member of the nineteen would be sure to appear, thrust an envelope privately into his hand, whisper "To be opened at the town hall Friday evening," then vanish away like a guilty thing. He was expecting that there might be one claimant for the sack—doubtful, however, Goodson being dead—but it never occurred to him that all this crowd might be claimants. When the great Friday came at last, he found that he had nineteen envelopes.

III

The town hall had never looked finer. The platform at the end of it was backed by a showy draping of flags; at intervals along the walls were festoons of flags; the gallery fronts were clothed in flags;

the supporting columns were swathed in flags; all this was to impress the stranger, for he would be there in considerable force, and in a large degree he would be connected with the press. The house was full. The 412 fixed seats were occupied; also the 68 extra chairs which had been packed into the aisles; the steps of the platform were occupied; some distinguished strangers were given seats on the platform; at the horseshoe of tables which fenced the front and sides of the platform sat a strong force of special correspondents who had come from everywhere. It was the best-dressed house the town had ever produced. There were some tolerably expensive toilets there, and in several cases the ladies who wore them had the look of being unfamiliar with that kind of clothes. At least the town thought they had that look, but the notion could have arisen from the town's knowledge of the fact that these ladies had never inhabited such clothes before.

The gold-sack stood on a little table at the front of the platform where all the house could see it. The bulk of the house gazed at it with a burning interest, a mouth-watering interest, a wistful and pathetic interest; a minority of nineteen couples gazed at it tenderly, lovingly, proprietarily, and the male half of this minority kept saying over to themselves the moving little impromptu speeches of thankfulness for the audience's applause and congratulations which they were presently going to get up and deliver. Every now and then one of these got a piece of paper out of his vest pocket and privately glanced at it to refresh his memory.

Of course there was a buzz of conversation going on—there always is; but at last when the Rev. Mr. Burgess rose and laid his hand on the sack he could hear his microbes gnaw, the place was so still. He related the curious history of the sack, then went on to speak in warm terms of Hadleyburg's old and well-earned reputation for spotless honesty, and of the town's just pride in this reputation. He said that this reputation was a treasure of priceless value; that under Providence its value had now become inestimably enhanced, for the recent episode had spread this fame far and wide, and thus had focused the eves of the American world upon this village, and made its name for all time, as he hoped and believed, a synonym for commercial incorruptibility. (*Applause.*) "And who is to be the guardian of this noble treasure—the community as a whole? No! The responsibility is individual, not communal. From this day forth each and every one of you is in his own person its special guardian, and individually; responsible that no harm shall come to it. Do you—does each of you—accept this great trust? [*Tumultuous assent.*] Then all is well. Transmit it to your children and to your children's children. Today your purity is beyond reproach—see to it that it shall remain so. Today there is not a person in your community who could be beguiled to touch a penny not his own—see to it that you abide in this grace. [*"We will! We will!"*] This is not the place to make comparisons between ourselves and other communities—some of them ungracious toward us; they have their ways, we have ours; let us be content. [*Applause.*] I am done. Under my hand, my friends, rests a stranger's eloquent recognition of what we are; through him the world will always henceforth know what we are. We do not know who he is, but in your name I utter your gratitude, and ask you to raise your voices in endorsement."

The house rose in a body and made the walls quake with the thunders of its thankfulness for the space of a long minute. Then it sat down, and Mr. Burgess took an envelope out of his pocket. The house held its breath while he slit the envelope open and took from it a slip of paper. He read its contents—slowly and impressively—the audience listening with tranced attention to this magic document, each of whose words stood for an ingot of gold:

" '*The remark which I made to the distressed stranger was this: "You are very far from being a bad man; go, and reform."* ' " Then he continued: "We shall know in a moment now whether the remark here quoted corresponds with the one concealed in the sack; and if that shall prove to be so—and it undoubtedly will—this sack of gold belongs to a fellow-citizen who will henceforth stand before the nation as the symbol of the special virtue which has made our town famous throughout the land—Mr. Billson!"

The house had gotten itself all ready to burst into the proper tornado of applause; but instead of doing it, it seemed stricken with a paralysis; there was a deep hush for a moment or two, then a wave of whispered murmurs swept the place—of about this tenor: "*Billson!* oh, come, this is *too* thin! Twenty dollars to a stranger—or *anybody—Billson!* Tell it to the marines? And now at this point the house caught its breath all of a sudden in a new access of astonishment, for it discovered that whereas in one part of the hall Deacon Billson was standing up with his head meekly bowed, in another part of it Lawyer Wilson was doing the same. There was a wondering silence now for a while. Everybody was puzzled, and nineteen couples were surprised and indignant.

Billson and Wilson turned and stared at each other. Billson asked, bitingly,

"Why do *you* rise, Mr. Wilson?"

"Because I have a right to. Perhaps you will be good enough to explain to the house why *you* rise?"

"With great pleasure. Because I wrote that paper."

"It is an impudent falsity! I wrote it myself."

It was Burgess's turn to be paralyzed. He stood looking vacantly at first one of the men and then the other, and did not seem to know what to do. The house was stupefied. Lawyer Wilson spoke up, now, and said,

"I ask the Chair to read the name signed to that paper."

That brought the Chair to itself, and it read out the name, "'John Wharton *Billson.*'"

"There!" shouted Billson, "what have you got to say for yourself, now? And what kind of apology are you going to make to me and to this insulted house for the imposture which you have attempted to play here?"

"No apologies are due, sir; and as for the rest of it, I publicly charge you with pilfering my note from Mr. Burgess and substituting a copy of it signed with your own name. There is no other way by which you could have gotten hold of the test-remark; I alone, of living men, possessed the secret of its wording."

There was likely to be a scandalous state of things if this went on; everybody noticed with distress that the shorthand scribes were scribbling like mad; many people were crying "Chair, Chair! Order! Order!" Burgess rapped with his gavel, and said:

"Let us not forget the proprieties due. There has evidently been a mistake somewhere, but surely that is all. If Mr. Wilson gave me an envelope—and I remember now that he did—I still have it."

He took one out of his pocket, opened it, glanced at it, looked surprised and worried, and stood silent a few moments. Then he waved his hand in a wandering and mechanical way, and made an effort or two to say something, then gave it up, despondently. Several voices cried out:

"Read it! read it! What is it?"

So he began in a dazed and sleepwalker fashion:

"'*The remark which I made to the unhappy stranger was this: "You are far from being a bad man.* [The house gazed at him, marveling.] *Go, and reform.*"' [*Murmurs:* "Amazing! what can this mean?"] This one," said the Chair, "is signed Thurlow G. Wilson."

"There!" cried Wilson, "I reckon that settles it! I knew perfectly well my note was purloined."

"Purloined!" retorted Billson. "I'll let you know that neither you nor any man of your kidney must venture to—"

The Chair. "Order, gentlemen, order! Take your seats, both of you, please."

They obeyed, shaking their heads and grumbling angrily. The house was profoundly puzzled; it did not know what to do with this curious emergency. Presently Thompson got up. Thompson was the hatter. He would have liked to be a Nineteener; but such was not for him; his stock of hats was not considerable enough for the position. He said:

"Mr. Chairman, if I may be permitted to make a suggestion, can both of these gentlemen be right? I put it to you, sir, can both have happened to say the very same words to the stranger? It seems to me—"

The tanner got up and interrupted him. The tanner was a disgruntled man; he believed himself entitled to be a Nineteener, but he couldn't get recognition. It made him a little unpleasant in his ways and speech. Said he:

"Sho, *that's* not the point! *That* could happen—re, ice in a hundred years—but not the other thing. *Neither* of them gave the twenty dollars? (*A ripple of applause.*)

Billson. "*I* did!"

Wilson. "*I* did!"

Then each accused the other of pilfering.

The Chair. "Order! Sit down, if you please—both of you. Neither of the notes has been out of my possession at any moment."

A Voice. "Good—that settles *that!*"

The Tanner. "Mr. Chairman, one thing is now plain: one of these men has been eavesdropping under the other one's bed, and filching family secrets. If it is not unparliamentary to suggest it, I will remark that both are equal to it. [The Chair. "Order! order!"] I withdraw the remark, sir, and will confine myself to suggesting that if one of them has overheard the other reveal the test-remark to his wife, we shall catch him now."

A Voice. "How?"

The Tanner. "Easily. The two have not quoted the remark in exactly the same words. You would have noticed that, if there hadn't been a considerable stretch of time and an exciting quarrel inserted between the two readings."

A Voice. "Name the difference."

The Tanner. "The word very is in Billson's note, and not in the other."

Many Voices. "That's so—he's right?

The Tanner. "And so, if the Chair will examine the test-remark in the sack, we shall know which of these two frauds—[*The Chair.* "Order!"—which of these two adventurers—[*The Chair.* "Order! order!"]—which of these two gentlemen—[*laughter and applause*]—is entitled to wear the belt as being the first dishonest blatherskite ever bred in this town—which he has dishonored, and which will be a sultry place for him from now out!" (*Vigorous applause.*)

Many Voices. "Open it! —open the sack!"

Mr. Burgess made a slit in the sack, slid his hand in and brought out an envelope. In it were a couple of folded notes. He said:

"One of these is marked, 'Not to be examined until all written communications which have been addressed to the Chair—if any—shall have been read.' The other is marked '*The Test.*' Allow me. It is worded—to wit:

" 'I do not require that the first half of the remark which was made to me by my benefactor shall be quoted with exactness, for it was not striking, and could be forgotten; but its closing fifteen words are quite striking, and I think easily rememberable; unless *these* shall be accurately reproduced, let the applicant be regarded as an impostor. My benefactor began by saying he seldom gave advice to any one, but that it always bore the hallmark of high value when he did give it. Then he said this—and it has never faded from my memory: "*You are far from being a bad man—*" ' "

Fifty Voices. "That settles it—the money's Wilson's! Wilson! Wilson! Speech! Speech?

People jumped up and crowded around Wilson, wringing his hand and congratulating fervently—meantime the Chair was hammering with the gavel and shouting:

"Order, gentlemen! Order! Order! Let me finish reading, please." When quiet was restored, the reading was resumed—as follows:

" ' "*Go, and reform —or, mark my words —wine day, for your sins, you will die and go to hell or Hadleyburg*—TRY AND MAKE IT THE FORMER." ' "

A ghastly silence followed. First an angry cloud began to settle darkly upon the faces of the citizenship; after a pause the cloud began to rise, and a tickled expression tried to take its place; tried so hard that it was only kept under with great and painful difficulty; the reporters, the Brixtonites, and other strangers bent their heads down and shielded their faces with their hands, and managed to hold in by main strength and heroic courtesy. At this most inopportune time burst upon the stillness the roar of a solitary voice—Jack Halliday's:

"*That's* got the hallmark on it!"

Then the house let go, strangers and all. Even Mr. Burgess's gravity broke down presently, then the audience considered itself officially absolved from all restraint, and it made the most of its privilege. It was a good long laugh, and a tempestuously whole-hearted one, but it ceased at last—long enough for Mr. Burgess to try to resume, and for the people to get their eves partially wiped; then it broke out again; and afterward yet again; then at last Burgess was able to get out these serious words:

"It is useless to try to disguise the fact—we find ourselves in the presence of a matter of grave import. It involves the honor of your town, it strikes at the town's good name. The difference of a single word between the test-remarks offered by Mr. Wilson and Mr. Billson was itself a serious thing, since it indicated that one or the other of these gentlemen had committed a theft—"

The two men were sitting limp, nerveless, crushed; but at these words both were electrified into movement, and started to get up—

"Sit down!" said the Chair, sharply, and they obeyed. "That, as I have said, was a serious thing. And it was—but for only one of them. But the matter has become graver; for the honor of *both* is now in formidable peril. Shall I go even further, and say in inextricable peril? *Both* left out the crucial fifteen words." He paused. During several moments he allowed the pervading stillness to gather and deepen its impressive effects, then added: "There would seem to be but one way whereby this could happen. I ask these gentlemen—Was there *collusion?—agreement?*"

A low murmur sifted through the house; its import was, "He's got them both."

Billson was not used to emergencies; he sat in a helpless collapse. But Wilson was a lawyer. He struggled to his feet, pale and worried, and said:

"I ask the indulgence of the house while I explain this most painful matter. I am sorry to say what I am about to say, since it must inflict irreparable injury upon Mr. Billson, whom I have always esteemed and respected until now, and in whose invulnerability to temptation I entirely believed—as did you all. But for the preservation of my own honor I must speak—and with frankness. I confess with shame—and I now beseech your pardon for it—that I said to the ruined stranger all of the words contained in the test-remark, including the disparaging fifteen. [*Sensation.*] When the late publication was made I recalled them, and I resolved to claim the sack of coin, for by every right I was entitled to it. Now I will ask you to consider this point, and weigh it well: that stranger's gratitude to me that night knew no bounds; he said himself that he could find no words for it that were adequate, and that if he should ever be able he would repay me a thousandfold. Now, then, I ask you this: could I expect—could I believe—could I even remotely imagine—that, feeling as he did, he would do so ungrateful a thing as to add those quite unnecessary fifteen words to his test?—set a trap for me?—expose me as a slanderer of my own town before my own people assembled in a public hall? It was preposterous; it was impossible. His test would contain only the kindly opening clause of my remark. Of that I had no shadow of doubt. You would have thought as I did. You would not have expected a base betrayal from one whom you had befriended and against whom you had committed no offense. And so, with perfect confidence, perfect trust, I wrote on a piece of paper the opening words—ending with 'Go, and reform,'—and signed it. When I was about to put it in an envelope I was called into my back office, and without thinking I left the paper lying open on my desk." He stopped, turned his head slowly toward Billson, waited a moment, then added: "1 ask you to note this: when I returned, a little later, Mr. Billson was retiring by my street door." (*Sensation.*)

In a moment Billson was on his feet and shouting:

"It's a lie! It's an infamous lie?

The Chair. "Be seated, sir! Mr. Wilson has the floor."

Billson's friends pulled him into his seat and quieted him, and Wilson went on:

"Those are the simple facts. My note was now lying in a different place on the table from where I had left it. I noticed that, but attached no importance to it, thinking a draught had blown it there. That Mr. Billson would read a private paper was a thing which could not occur to me; he was an honorable man, and he would be above that. If you will allow me to say it, I think his extra word '*very*' stands explained; it is attributable to a defect of memory. I was the only man in the world who could furnish here any detail of the test-mark—by *honorable* means. I have finished."

There is nothing in the world like a persuasive speech to fuddle the mental apparatus and upset the convictions and debauch the emotions of an audience not practiced in tricks and delusions of oratory. Wilson sat down victorious. The house submerged him in tides of approving applause; friends swarmed to him and shook him by the hand and congratulated him, and Billson was shouted down and not allowed to say a word. The Chair hammered and hammered with its gavel, and kept shouting,

"But let us proceed, gentlemen, let us proceed!"

At last there was a measurable degree of quiet, and the hatter said,

"But what is there to proceed with, sir, but to deliver the money?"

Voices. "That's it! That's it! Come forward, Wilson!"

The Hatter. "I move three cheers for Mr. Wilson, Symbol of the special virtue which—"

The cheers burst forth before he could finish; and in the midst of them—and in the midst of the clamor of the gavel also—some enthusiasts mounted Wilson on a big friend's shoulder and were going to fetch him in triumph to the platform. The Chair's voice now rose above the noise—

"Order! To your places! You forget that there is still a document to be read." When quiet had been restored he took up the document, and was going to read it, but laid it down again, saying, "I forgot; this is not to be read until all written communications received by me have first been read." He took an envelope out of his pocket, removed its enclosure, glanced at it—seemed astonished—held it out and gazed at it—stared at it.

Twenty or thirty voices cried out:

"What is it? Read it! read it!"

And he did—slowly, and wondering:

"'The remark which I made to the stranger—[*Voices.* "Hello! how's this?"]—was this: "You are far from being a bad man. [*Voices.* "Great Scott!"] Go, and reform."' [*Voice.* "Oh, saw my leg off!"] Signed by Mr. Pinkerton the banker."

The pandemonium of delight which turned itself loose now was of a sort to make the judicious weep. Those whose withers were unwrung laughed till the tears ran down; the reporters, in throes of laughter, set down disordered pothooks which would never in the world be decipherable; and a sleeping dog jumped up, scared out of its wits, and barked itself crazy at the turmoil. All manner of cries were scattered through the din: "We're getting rich—*two* Symbols of Incorruptibility!—without counting Billson!" "*Three!*—count Shadbelly in—we can't have too many!" "All right—Billson's elected!"' "Alas, poor Wilson—victim of *two* thieves!"

A Powerful Voice. "Silence! The Chair's fished up something more out of its pocket."

Voices. "Hurrah! Is it something fresh? Read it! read! read!"

The Chair (reading). " 'The remark which I made,' etc. 'You are far from being a bad man. Go,' etc. Signed, 'Gregory Yates.' "

Tornado of Voices. "Four Symbols!" " 'Rah for Yates!" "Fish again!"

The house was in a roaring humor now, and ready to get all the fun out of the occasion that might be in it. Several Nineteeners, looking pale and distressed, got up and began to work their way toward the aisles, but a score of shouts went up:

"The doors, the doors—close the doors; no Incorruptible shall leave this place! Sit down, everybody!"

The mandate was obeyed.

"Fish again! Read! read!"

The Chair fished again, and once more the familiar words began to fall from its lips— " 'You are far from being a bad man—' "

"Name! name! What's his name?"

" 'L. Ingoldsby Sargent.' "

"Five elected! Pile up the Symbols! Go on, go on!"

" 'You are far from being a bad—' "

"Name! name!"

"'Nicholas Whitworth.'"

"Hooray! hooray! it's a symbolical day!"

Somebody wailed in, and began to sing this rhyme (leaving out "it's") to the lovely *Mikado* tune of "When a man's afraid of a beautiful maid"; the audience joined in, with joy; then, just in time, somebody contributed another line—

"And don't you this forget—"

The house roared it out. A third line was at once furnished—

"Corruptibles far from Hadleyburg are—"

The house roared that one too. As the last note died Jack Halliday's voice rose high and clear, freighted with a final line—

"But the Symbols are here, you bet!"

That was sung, with booming enthusiasm. Then the happy house started in at the beginning and sang the four lines through twice, with immense swing and dash, and finished up with a crashing three-times-three and a tiger for "Hadleyburg the Incorruptible and all Symbols of it which we shall find worthy to receive the hallmark tonight."

Then the shoutings at the Chair began again, all over the place:

"Go on! go on! Read! read some more! Read all you've got!"

"That's it—go on! We are winning eternal celebrity!"

A dozen men got up now and began to protest. They said that this farce was the work of some abandoned joker, and was an insult to the whole community. Without a doubt these signatures were all forgeries—

"Sit down! sit down! Shut up! You are confessing. We'll find *your* names in the lot."

"Mr. Chairman, how many of those envelopes have you got?"

The Chair counted.

"Together with those that have been already examined, there are nineteen."

A storm of derisive applause broke out.

"Perhaps they all contain the secret. I move that you open them all and read every signature that is attached to a note of that sort—and read also the first eight words of the note."

"Second the motion!"

It was put and carried—uproariously. Then poor old Richards got up, and his wife rose and stood at his side. Her head was bent down, so that none might see that she was crying. Her husband gave her his arm, and so supporting her, he began to speak in a quavering voice:

"My friends, you have known us two—Mary and me—all our lives, and I think you have liked us and respected us—"

The Chair interrupted him:

"Allow me. It is quite true—that which you are saying, Mr. Richards; this town *does* know you two; it *does* like you; it *does* respect you; more—it honors you and *loves* you—"

Halliday's voice rang out:

"That's the hallmarked truth, too! If the Chair is right, let the house speak up and say it. Rise! Now, then—hip! hip! hip!—all together!"

The house rose in mass, faced toward the old couple eagerly, filled the air with a snowstorm of waving handkerchiefs, and delivered the cheers with all its affectionate heart. The Chair then continued:

"What I was going to say is this: We know your good heart, Mr. Richards, but this is not a time for the exercise of charity toward offenders. [Shouts of "Right! right!"] I see your generous purpose in your face, but I cannot allow you to plead for these men—"

"But I was going to—"

"Please take your seat, Mr. Richards. We must examine the rest of these notes—simple fairness to the men who have already been exposed requires this. As soon as that has been done—I give you my word for this—you shall be heard."

Many Voices. "Right!—the Chair is right—no interruption can be permitted at this stage! Go on!—the names! the names! —according to the terms of the motion!"

The old couple sat reluctantly down, and the husband whispered to the wife, "It is pitifully hard to have to wait; the shame will be greater than ever when they find we were only going to plead for *ourselves.*"

Straightway the jollity broke loose again with the reading of the names.

" 'You are far from being a bad man—' Signature, 'Robert J. Titmarsh.'

" 'You are far from being a bad man—' Signature, 'Eliphalet Weeks.'

" 'You are far from being a bad man—' Signature, 'Oscar B. Wilder.' "

At this point the house lit upon the idea of taking the eight words out of the Chairman's hands. He was not unthankful for that. Thenceforward he held up each note in its turn, and waited. The house droned out the eight words in a massed and measured and musical deep volume of sound (with a daringly close resemblance to a well-known church chant)— " 'You are f-a-r from being a b-a-a-a-d man.' " Then the Chair said, "Signature, 'Archibald Wilcox.' " And so on, and so on, name after name, and everybody had an increasingly and gloriously good time except the wretched Nineteen. Now and then, when a particularly shining name was called, the house made the Chair wait while it chanted the whole of the test-remark from the beginning to the closing words, "And go to hell or Hadleyburg—try and make it the for-or-m-e-r!" and in these special cases they added a grand and agonized and imposing "A-a-a-a-*men!*"

The list dwindled, dwindled, dwindled, poor old Richards keeping tally of the count, wincing when a name resembling his own was pronounced, and waiting in miserable suspense for the time to come when it would be his humiliating privilege to rise with Mary and finish his plea, which he was intending to word thus: ". . . for until now we have never done any wrong thing, but have gone our humble way unreproached. We are very poor, we are old, and have no chick nor child to help us; we were sorely tempted, and we fell. It was my purpose when I got up before to make confession and beg that my name might not be read out in this public place, for it seemed to us that we could not bear it; but I was prevented. It was just; it was our place to suffer with the rest. It has been hard for us. It is the first time we have ever heard our name fall from any one's lips—sullied. Be merciful—for the sake of the better days; make our shame as light to bear as in your charity, you can." At this point in his reverie Mary nudged him, perceiving that his mind was absent. The house was chanting, "You are f-a-r," etc.

"Be ready," Mary whispered. "Your name comes now; he has read eighteen."

The chant ended.

"Next! next! next!" came volleying from all over the house.

Burgess put his hand into his pocket. The old couple, trembling, began to rise. Burgess fumbled a moment, then said,

"I find I have read them all."

Faint with joy and surprise, the couple sank into their seats, and Mary whispered,

"Oh, bless God, we are saved!—he has lost ours—I wouldn't give this for a hundred of those sacks!"

The house burst out with its *Mikado* travesty, and sang it three times with ever-increasing enthusiasm, rising to its feet when it reached for the third time the closing line—

"But the Symbols are here, you bet!"

and finishing up with cheers and a tiger for "Hadleyburg purity and our eighteen immortal representatives of it."

Then Wingate, the saddler, got up and proposed cheers "for the cleanest man in town, the one solitary important citizen in it who didn't try to steal that money—Edward Richards."

They were given with great and moving heartiness; then somebody proposed that Richards be elected sole Guardian and Symbol of the now Sacred Hadleyburg Tradition, with power and right to stand up and look the whole sarcastic world in the face.

Passed, by acclamation; then they sang the *Mikado* again, and ended it with,

"And there's *one* Symbol left, you bet!"

There was a pause; then—

A Voice. "Now, then, who's to get the sack?"

The Tanner (with bitter sarcasm). "That's easy. The money has to be divided among the eighteen Incorruptibles. They gave the suffering stranger twenty dollars apiece—and that remark—each in his turn—it took twenty-two minutes for the procession to move past. Staked the stranger—total contribution, $360. All they want is just the loan back—and interest—forty thousand dollars altogether."

Many Voices (derisively). "That's it! Divvy! divvy! Be kind to the poor—don't keep them waiting!"

The Chair. "Order! I now offer the stranger's remaining document. It says: 'If no claimant shall appear [*grand chorus of groans*], I desire that you open the sack and count out the money to the principal citizens of your town, they to take it in trust [*Cries of "Oh! Oh! Oh!"*], and use it in such ways as to them shall seem best for the propagation and preservation of your community's noble reputation for incorruptible honesty [*more cries*]—a reputation to which their names and their efforts will add a new and far-reaching luster.' [Enthusiastic outburst of sarcastic applause.] That seems to be all. No—here is a postscript:

" 'P.S.—CITIZENS OF HADLEYBURG: There *is* no test remark—nobody made one. [*Great sensation.*] There wasn't any pauper stranger, nor any twenty-dollar contribution, nor any accompanying benediction and compliment—these are all inventions. [*General buzz and hum of astonishment and delight.*] Allow me to tell my story—it will take but a word or two. I passed through your town at a certain time, and received a deep offense which I had not earned. Any other man would have been content to kill one or two of you and call it square, but to me that would have been a trivial revenge, and inadequate; for the dead do not *suffer.* Besides, I could not kill you all—and, anyway, made as I am, even that would not have satisfied me. I wanted to damage every man in the place, and every woman—and not in their bodies or in their estate, but in their vanity—the place where feeble and foolish people are most vulnerable. So I disguised myself, and came back and studied you. You were easy game. You had an old and lofty reputation for honesty, and naturally you were proud of it—it was your treasure of treasures, the very apple of your eye. As soon as I found out that you carefully and vigilantly kept yourselves and your children *out of temptation*, I knew how to proceed. Why, you simple creatures, the weakest of all weak things is a virtue which has not been tested in the fire. I laid a plan, and gathered a list of names. My project was to corrupt Hadleyburg the Incorruptible. My idea was to make liars and thieves of nearly half a hundred smirchless men and women who had never in their lives uttered a lie or stolen a penny. I was afraid of Goodson. He was neither born nor reared in Hadleyburg. I was afraid that if I started to operate my scheme by getting my letter laid before you, you would say to yourselves, "Goodson is the only man among us who would give away twenty dollars to a poor devil"—and then you might not bite at my bait. But Heaven took Goodson; then I knew I was safe, and I set my trap and baited it. It may be that I shall not catch all the men to whom I mailed the pretended test secret, but I shall catch the most of them, if I know Hadleyburg nature. [*Voices.* "Right—he got every last one of them."] I believe they will even steal ostensible *gamble*-money, rather than miss, poor, tempted, and mistrained fellows. I am hoping to eternally and everlastingly squelch your vanity and give Hadleyburg a new renown—one that will stick—and spread far. If I have succeeded, open the sack and summon the Committee on Propagation and Preservation of the Hadleyburg Reputation.' "

A Cyclone of Voices. "Open it! Open it! The Eighteen to the front! Committee on Propagation of the Tradition! Forward—the Incorruptibles!"

The Chair ripped the sack wide, and gathered up a handful of bright, broad, yellow coins, shook them together, then examined them—

"Friends, they are only gilded disks of lead!"

There was a crashing outbreak of delight over this news, and when the noise had subsided, the tanner called out:

"By right of apparent seniority in this business, Mr. Wilson is Chairman of the Committee on Propagation of the Tradition. I suggest that he step forward on behalf of his pals, and receive in trust the money."

A Hundred Voices. "Wilson! Wilson! Wilson! Speech! Speech!"

Wilson (*in a voice trembling with anger*). "You will allow me to say, and without apologies for my language, *damn* the money!"

A Voice. "Oh, and him a Baptist!"

A Voice. "Seventeen Symbols left! Step up, gentlemen, and assume your trust!"

There was a pause—no response.

The Saddler. "Mr. Chairman, we've got *one* clean man left, anyway, out of the late aristocracy; and he needs money, and deserves it. I move that you appoint Jack Halliday to get up there and auction off that sack of gilt twenty-dollar pieces, and give the result to the right man—the man whom Hadleyburg delights to honor—Edward Richards."

This was received with great enthusiasm, the dog taking a hand again; the saddler started the bids at a dollar, the Brixton folk and Barnum's representative fought hard for it, the people cheered every jump that the bids made, the excitement climbed moment by moment higher and higher, the bidders got on their mettle and grew steadily more and more daring, more and more determined, the jumps went from a dollar up to five, then to ten, then to twenty, then fifty, then to a hundred, then—

At the beginning of the auction Richards whispered in distress to his wife: "Oh, Mary, can we allow it? It—it—you see, it is an honor-reward, a testimonial to purity of character, and—and—can we allow it? Hadn't I better get up and—Oh, Mary, what ought we to do? —what do you think we—" (*Halliday's voice. "Fifteen I'm bid!—fifteen for the sack!—twenty!—ah, thanks!—thirty—thanks again! Thirty, thirty, thirty!—do I hear forty?—forty it is! Keep the ball rolling, gentlemen, keep it rolling!—fifty!—thanks, noble Roman!—going at fifty, fifty, fifty,—seventy!—ninety!—splendid!—a hundred!—pile it up, pile it up!—hundred and twenty—forty!—just in time!—hundred and fifty!*—Two *hundred!—superb! Do I hear two h—thanks!—two hundred fifty!—"*)

"It is another temptation, Edward—I'm all in a tremble—but, oh, we've escaped one temptation, and that ought to warn us, to—[*"Six did I hear?—thanks!—six fifty, six f*—SEVEN *hundred!"*] And yet, Edward, when you think—nobody susp— [*"Eight hundred dollars!—hurrah!—make it nine!—Mr. Parsons, did I hear you say—thanks!—nine!—this noble sack of virgin lead going at only nine hundred dollars, gilding and all—come! do I hear—a thousand!—gratefully yours!—did some one say eleven?—a sack which is going to be the most celebrated in the whole Uni—"*] Oh, Edward" (beginning to sob), "we are *so* poor!—but—but—do as you think best—do as you think best."

Edward fell—that is, he sat still; sat with a conscience which was not satisfied, but which was overpowered by circumstances.

Meantime a stranger, who looked like an amateur detective gotten up as an impossible English earl, had been watching the evening's proceedings with manifest interest, and with a contented expression in his face; and he had been privately commenting to himself. He was now soliloquizing somewhat like this: "None of the Eighteen are bidding; that is not satisfactory; I must change that—the dramatic unities require it; they must buy the sack they tried to steal; they must pay a heavy price, too—some of them are rich. And another thing, when I make a mistake in Hadleyburg nature the man that puts that error upon me is entitled to a high honorarium, and some one must pay it. This poor old Richards has brought my judgment to shame; he is an honest man: —I don't understand it, but I acknowledge it. Yes, he saw my deuces-*and* with a straight flush, and by rights the pot is his. And it shall be a jack-pot, too, if I can manage it. He disappointed me, but let that pass."

He was watching the bidding. At a thousand, the market broke; the prices tumbled swiftly. He waited—and still watched. One competitor dropped out; then another, and another. He put in a bid or two, now. When the bids had sunk to ten dollars, he added a five; some one raised him a three; he waited a moment, then flung in a fifty-dollar jump, and the sack was his—at $1282. The house broke out in cheers—then stopped; for he was on his feet, and had lifted his hand. He began to speak.

"I desire to say a word, and ask a favor. I am a speculator in rarities, and I have dealings with persons interested in numismatics all over the world. I can make a profit on this purchase, just as it stands; but there is a way, if I can get your approval, whereby I can make every one of these leaden twenty-dollar pieces worth its face in gold, and perhaps more. Grant me that approval, and I will give part of my gains to your Mr. Richards, whose invulnerable probity you have so justly and so cordially recognized tonight; his share shall be ten thousand dollars, and I will hand him the money tomorrow. [*Great applause from the house.* But the "invulnerable probity" made the Richardses blush prettily; however, it went for modesty, and did no harm.] If you will pass my proposition by a good majority—I would like a two-thirds vote—I will regard that as the town's consent, and that is all I ask. Rarities are always helped by any device which will rouse curiosity and compel remark. Now if I may have your permission to stamp upon the faces of each of these ostensible coins the names of the eighteen gentlemen who—"

Nine-tenths of the audience were on their feet in a moment—dog and all—and the proposition was carried with a whirlwind of approving applause and laughter.

They sat down, and all the Symbols except "Dr." Clay Harkness got up, violently protesting against the proposed outrage, and threatening to—

"I beg you not to threaten me," said the stranger, calmly. "I know my legal rights, and am not accustomed to being frightened at bluster." (*Applause.*) He sat down. "Dr." Harkness saw an opportunity here. He was one of the two very rich men of the place, and Pinkerton was the other. Harkness was proprietor of a mint; that is to say, a popular patent medicine. He was running for the Legislature on one ticket, and Pinkerton on the other. It was a close race and a hot one, and getting hotter every day. Both had strong appetites for money; each had bought a great tract of land, with a purpose: there was going to be a new railway, and each wanted to be in the Legislature and help locate the route to his own advantage; a single vote might make the decision, and with it two or three fortunes. The stake was large, and Harkness was a daring speculator. He was sitting close to the stranger. He leaned over while one or another of the other Symbols was entertaining the house with protests and appeals, and asked, in a whisper,

"What is your price for the sack?"

"Forty thousand dollars."

"I'll give you twenty."

"No."

"Twenty-five."

"No."

"Say thirty."

"The price is forty thousand dollars; not a penny less."

"All right, I'll give it. I will come to the hotel at ten in the morning. I don't want it known; will see you privately."

"Very good." Then the stranger got up and said to the house:

"I find it late. The speeches of these gentlemen are not without merit, not without interest, not without grace; yet if I may be excused I will take my leave. I thank you for the great favor which you have shown me in granting my petition. I ask the Chair to keep the sack for me until tomorrow, and to hand these three five-hundred dollar notes to Mr. Richards." They were passed up to the Chair. "At nine I will call for the sack, and at eleven will deliver the rest of the ten thousand to Mr. Richards in person, at his home. Goodnight."

Then he slipped out, and left the audience making a vast noise, which was composed of a mixture of cheers, the *Mikado* song, dog-disapproval, and the chant, "You are f-a-r from being a b-a-a-d man—a-a-a-a-men!"

IV

At home the Richardses had to endure congratulations and compliments until midnight. Then they were left to themselves. They looked a little sad, and they sat silent and thinking. Finally Mary sighed and said,

"Do you think we are to blame, Edward—*much* to blame?" and her eyes wandered to the accusing triplet of big banknotes lying on the table, where the congratulators had been gloating over them and reverently fingering them. Edward did not answer at once; then he brought out a sigh and said, hesitatingly:

"We—we couldn't help it, Mary. It—well, it was ordered. *All* things are."

Mary glanced up and looked at him steadily, but he didn't return the look. Presently she said:

"I thought congratulations and praises always tasted good. But—it seems to me, now—Edward?"

"Well?"

"Are you going to stay in the bank?"

"N-no."

"Resign?"

"In the morning—by note."

"It does seem best."

Richards bowed his head in his hands and muttered:

"Before, I was not afraid to let oceans of people's money pour through my hands, but— Mary, I am so tired, so tired—"

"We will go to bed."

At nine in the morning the stranger called for the sack and took it to the hotel in a cab. At ten Harkness had a talk with him privately. The stranger asked for and got five checks on a metropolitan bank—drawn to "Bearer,"—four for $1,500 each, and one for $34,000. He put one of the former in his pocketbook, and the remainder, representing $38,500, he put in an envelope, and with these he added a note, which he wrote after Harkness was gone. At eleven he called at the Richards house and knocked. Mrs. Richards peeped through the shutters, then went and received the envelope, and the stranger disappeared without a word. She came back flushed and a little unsteady on her legs, and gasped out:

"I am sure I recognized him! Last night it seemed to me that maybe I had seen him somewhere before."

"He is the man that brought the sack here?"

"I am almost sure of it."

"Then he is the ostensible Stephenson too, and sold every important citizen in this town with his bogus secret. Now if he has sent checks instead of money, we are sold too, after we thought we had escaped. I was beginning to feel fairly comfortable once more, after my night's rest, but the look of that envelope makes me sick.

It isn't fat enough; $8500 in even the largest banknotes makes more bulk than that."

"Edward, why do you object to checks?"

"Checks signed by Stephenson! I am resigned to take the $8500 if it could come in banknotes—for it does seem that it was so ordered, Mary—but I have never had much courage, and I have not the pluck to try to market a check signed with that disastrous name. It would be a trap. That man tried to catch me; we escaped somehow or other; and now he is trying a new way. If it is checks—"

"Oh, Edward, it is *too* bad? and she held up the checks and began to cry.

"Put them in the fire! quick! we mustn't be tempted. It is a trick to make the world laugh at *us*, along with the rest, and— Give them to *me*, since you can't do it!" He snatched them and tried to hold his grip till he could get to the stove; but he was human, he was a cashier, and he stopped a moment to make sure of the signature. Then he came near to tainting.

"Fan me, Mary, fan me! They are the same as gold!"

"Oh, how lovely, Edward! Why?"

"Signed by Harkness. What can the mystery of that Mary?"

"Edward, do you think—"

"Look here—look at this! Fifteen—fifteen—fifteen—thirty-four. Thirty-eight thousand five hundred! Mary, the sack isn't worth twelve dollars, and Harkness—apparently—has paid about par for it."

"And does it all come to us, do you think—instead of the ten thousand?"

"Why, it looks like it. And the checks are made to 'Bearer,' too."

"Is that good, Edward? What is it for?"

"A hint to collect them at some distant bank, I reckon. Perhaps Harkness doesn't want the matter known. What is that—a note?"

"Yes. It was with the checks."

It was in the "Stephenson" handwriting, but there was no signature. It said:

> "I am a disappointed man. Your honesty is beyond the reach of temptation. I had a different idea about it, but I wronged you in that, and I beg pardon, and do it sincerely. I honor you—and

that is sincere, too. This town is not worthy to kiss the hem of your garment. Dear sir, I made a square bet with myself that there were nineteen debauchable men in your self-righteous community. I have lost. Take the whole pot, you are entitled to it."

Richards drew a deep sigh, and said:

"It seems written with fire—it burns so. Mary—I am miserable again."

"I, too. Ah, dear, I wish—"

"To think, Mary—he *believes* in me."

"Oh, don't, Edward—I can't bear it."

"If those beautiful words were deserved, Mary—and God knows I believed I deserved them once—I think I could give the forty thousand dollars for them. And I would put that paper away, as representing more than gold and jewels, and keep it always. But now—We could not live in the shadow of its accusing presence, Mary."

He put it in the fire.

A messenger arrived and delivered an envelope. Richards took from it a note and read it; it was from Burgess.

"You saved me, in a difficult time. I saved you last night. It was at cost of a lie, but I made the sacrifice freely, and out of a grateful heart. None in this village knows so well as I know how brave and good and noble you are. At bottom you cannot respect me, knowing as you do of that matter of which I am accused, and by the general voice condemned; but I beg that you will at least believe that I am a grateful man; it will help me to bear my burden.

[Signed] *Burgess.*"

"Saved, once more. And on such terms!" He put the note in the fire. "I—I wish I were dead, Mary, I wish I were out of it all."

"Oh, these are bitter, bitter days, Edward. The stabs, through their very generosity, are so deep—and they come so fast!"

Three days before the election each of two thousand voters suddenly found himself in possession of a prized memento—one of the renowned bogus double-eagles. Mound one of its faces was stamped these words: "THE REMARK I MADE TO THE POOR STRANGER

WAS—" Around the other face was stamped these: "GO, AND REFORM. (SIGNED) PINKERTON." Thus the entire remaining refuse of the renowned joke was emptied upon a single head, and with calamitous effect. It revived the recent vast laugh and concentrated it upon Pinkerton; and Harkness's election was a walk-over.

Within twenty-four hours after the Richardses had received their checks their consciences were quieting down, discouraged; the old couple were learning to reconcile themselves to the sin which they had committed. But they were to learn, now, that a sin takes on new and real terrors when there seems a chance that it is going to be found out. This gives it a fresh and most substantial and important aspect. At church the morning sermon was of the usual pattern; it was the same old things said in the same old way; they had heard them a thousand times and found them innocuous, next to meaningless, and easy to sleep under; but now it was different: the sermon seemed to bristle with accusations; it seemed aimed straight and specially at people who were concealing deadly sins. After church they got away from the mob of congratulators as soon as they could, and hurried homeward, chilled to the bone at they did not know what—vague, shadowy, indefinite fears. And by chance they caught a glimpse of Mr. Burgess as he turned a corner. He paid no attention to their nod of recognition! he hadn't seen it; but they did not know that. What could his conduct mean? It might mean—it might mean—oh, a dozen dreadful things. Was it possible that he knew that Richards could have cleared him of guilt in that bygone time, and had been silently waiting for a chance to even up accounts? At home, in their distress they got to imagining that their servant might have been in the next room listening when Richards revealed the secret to his wife that he knew of Burgess's innocence; next, Richards began to imagine that he *had* heard the swish of a gown in there at that time; next, he was sure he had heard it. They would call Sarah in, on a pretext, and watch her face; if she had been betraying them to Mr. Burgess, it would show in her manner. They asked her some questions—questions which were so random and incoherent and seemingly purposeless that the girl felt sure that the old people's minds had been affected by their sudden good fortune; the sharp and watchful gaze which they bent upon her frightened her, and that completed the business. She blushed, she became nervous and confused, and to the old people these were plain signs of guilt—guilt of some fearful sort or other—without doubt she was a spy and a traitor. When they were alone again they began to piece many unrelated things together and get horrible results out of the combination. When things had got about to the worst, Richards was delivered of a sudden gasp, and his wife asked,

"Oh, what is it? —what is it?"

"The note—Burgess's note! Its language was sarcastic, I see it now." He quoted: "'At bottom you cannot respect me, *knowing*, as you do, of *that matter* of which I am accused'—oh, it is perfectly plain, now, God help me! he knows that I know! You see the ingenuity, of the phrasing. It was a trap—and like a fool, I walked into it. And Mary—?"

"Oh, it is dreadful—I know what you are going to say—he didn't return your transcript of the pretended test-remark."

"No—kept it to destroy us with. Mary, he has exposed us to some already. I know it—I know it well. I saw it in a dozen faces after church. Ah, he wouldn't answer our nod of recognition—*he* knew what he had been doing!"

In the night the doctor was called. The news went around in the morning that the old couple were rather seriously ill—prostrated by the exhausting excitement growing out of their great windfall, the congratulations, and the late hours, the doctor said. The town was sincerely distressed; for these old people were about all it had left to be proud of, now.

Two days later the news was worse. The old couple were delirious, and were doing strange things. By witness of the nurses, Richards had exhibited checks—for $8500? No—for an amazing sum—$38,500! What could be the explanation of this gigantic piece of luck?

The following day the nurses had more news—and wonderful. They had concluded to hide the checks, lest harm come to them; but when they searched they were gone from under the patient's pillow—vanished away. The patient said:

"Let the pillow alone; what do you want?"

"We thought it best that the checks—"

"You will never see them again—they are destroyed. They came from Satan. I saw the hell-brand on them, and I knew they were sent to betray me to sin." Then he fell to gabbling strange and dreadful things which were not clearly understandable, and which the doctor admonished them to keep to themselves.

Richards was right; the checks were never seen again.

A nurse must have talked in her sleep, for within two days the forbidden gabblings were the property of the town; and they were of a surprising sort. They seemed to indicate that Richards had been a claimant for the sack himself, and that Burgess had concealed that fact and then maliciously betrayed it.

Burgess was taxed with this and stoutly denied it. And he said it was not fair to attach weight to the chatter of a sick old man who was out of his mind. Still, suspicion was in the air, and there was much talk.

After a day or two it was reported that Mrs. Richards's delirious deliveries were getting to be duplicates of her husband's. Suspicion flamed up into conviction, now, and the town's pride in the purity of its one undiscredited important citizen began to dim down and flicker toward extinction.

Six days passed, then came more news. The old couple were dying. Richards's mind cleared in his latest hour, and he sent for Burgess. Burgess said:

"Let the room be cleared. I think he wishes to say something in privacy."

"No!" said Richards; "I want witnesses. I want you all to hear my confession, so that I may die a man, and not a dog. I was clean—artificially—like the rest; and like the rest I fell when temptation came. I signed a lie, and claimed the miserable sack. Mr. Burgess remembered that I had done him a service, and in gratitude (and ignorance) he suppressed my claim and saved me. You know the thing that was charged against Burgess years ago. My testimony, and mine alone, could have cleared him, and I was a coward, and left him to suffer disgrace—"

"No—no—Mr. Richards, you—"

"My servant betrayed my secret to him—"

"No one has betrayed anything to me—"

—"and then he did a natural and justifiable thing; he repented of the saving kindness which he had done me, and he *exposed* me—as I deserved—"

"Never! —I make oath—"

"Out of my heart I forgive him."

Burgess's impassioned protestations fell upon deaf ears; the dying man passed away without knowing that once more he had done poor Burgess a wrong. The old wife died that night.

The last of the sacred Nineteen had fallen a prey to the fiendish sack; the town was stripped of the last rag of its ancient glory. Its mourning was not showy, but it was deep.

By act of the Legislature—upon prayer and petition—Hadleyburg was allowed to change its name to (never mind what—I will not give it away), and leave one word out of the motto that for many generations had graced the town's official seal.

It is an honest town once more, and the man will have to rise early that catches it napping again.

The Death Disk

I

This was in Oliver Cromwell's time. Colonel Mayfair was the youngest officer of his rank in the armies of the Commonwealth, he being but thirty years old. But young as he was, he was a veteran soldier, and tanned and war-worn, for he had begun his military life at seventeen; he had fought in many battles, and had won his high place in the service and in the admiration of men, step by step, by valor in the field. But he was in deep trouble now; a shadow had fallen upon his fortunes.

The winter evening was come, and outside were storm and darkness; within, a melancholy silence; for the Colonel and his young wife had talked their sorrow out, had read the evening chapter and prayed the evening prayer, and there was nothing more to do but sit hand in hand and gaze into the fire, and think—and wait. They would not have to wait long; they knew that, and the wife shuddered at the thought.

They had one child—Abby, seven years old, their idol. She would be coming presently for the good-night kiss, and the Colonel spoke now, and said:

"Dry away the tears and let us seem happy, for her sake. We must forget, for the time, that which is to happen."

"I will. I will shut them up in my heart, which is breaking."

"And we will accept what is appointed for us, and bear it in patience, as knowing that whatsoever He doeth is done in righteousness and meant in kindness—"

"Saying, His will be done. Yes, I can say it with all my mind and soul—I would I could say it with my heart. Oh, if I could! if this dear hand which I press and kiss for the last time—"

"Sh! sweetheart, she is coming!"

A curly-headed little figure in nightclothes glided in at the door and ran to the father, and was gathered to his breast and fervently kissed once, twice, three times.

"Why, papa, you mustn't kiss me like that: you rumple my hair."

"Oh, I am so sorry—so sorry: do you forgive me, dear?"

"Why, of course, papa. But *are* you sorry?—not pretending, but real, fight down sorry?"

"Well, you can judge for yourself, Abby," and he covered his face with his hands and made believe to sob. The child was filled with remorse to see this tragic thing which she had caused, and she began to cry herself, and to tug at the hands, and say:

"Oh, don't, papa, please don't cry; Abby didn't mean it; Abby wouldn't ever do it again. Please, papa!" Tugging and straining to separate the fingers, she got a fleeting glimpse of an eye behind them, and cried out: "Why, you naughty papa, you are not crying at all! You are only fooling! And Abby is going to mamma, now: you don't treat Abby right."

She was for climbing down, but her father wound his arms about her and said: "No, stay with me, dear: papa *was* naughty, and confesses it, and is sorry—there, let him kiss the tears away—and he begs Abby's forgiveness, and will do anything Abby says he must do, for a punishment; they're all kissed away now, and not a curl rumpled—and whatever Abby commands—"

And so it was made up; and all in a moment the sunshine was back again and burning brightly in the child's face, and she was patting her father's cheeks and naming the penalty—"A story! a story!"

Hark!

The elders stopped breathing, and listened. Footsteps! faintly caught between the gusts of wind. They came nearer, nearer—louder, louder—then passed by and faded away. The elders drew deep breaths of relief, and the papa said: "A story, is it? A gay one?"

"No, papa: a dreadful one."

Papa wanted to shift to the gay kind, but the child stood by her rights—as per agreement, she was to have anything she commanded. He was a good Puritan soldier and had passed his word—he saw that he must make it good. She said:

"Papa, we mustn't always have gay ones. Nurse says people don't always have gay times. Is that true, papa? She *says* so."

The mamma sighed, and her thoughts drifted to her troubles again. The papa said, gently: "It is true, dear. Troubles have to come; it is a pity, but it is true."

"Oh, then tell a story about them, papa—a dreadful one, so that we'll shiver, and feel just as if it was *us.* Mamma, you snuggle up close, and hold one of Abby's hands, so that if it's too dreadful it'll be easier for us to bear it if we are all snuggled up together, you know. Now you can begin, papa."

"Well, once there were three Colonels—"

"Oh, goody! *I* know Colonels, just as easy! It's because you are one, and I know the clothes. Go on, papa."

"And in a battle they had committed a breach of discipline."

The large words struck the child's ear pleasantly, and she looked up, full of wonder and interest, and said:

"Is it something good to eat, papa?

The parents almost smiled, and the father answered:

"No, quite another matter, dear. They exceeded their orders."

"Is *that* someth—"

"No; it's as uneatable as the other. They were ordered to feign an attack on a strong position in a losing fight, in order to draw the enemy about and give the Commonwealth's forces a chance to retreat; but in their enthusiasm they overstepped their orders, for they turned the feint into a fact, and carried the position by storm, and won the day and the battle. The Lord General was very angry at their disobedience, and praised them highly, and ordered them to London to be tried for their lives."

"Is it the great General Cromwell, papa?"

"Yes."

"Oh, I've seen *him*, papa! and when he goes by our house so grand on his big horse, with the soldiers, he looks so—so—well, I don't know just how, only he looks as if he isn't satisfied, and you can see the people are afraid of him; but *I'm* not afraid of him, because he didn't look like that at me."

"Oh, you dear prattler! Well, the Colonels came prisoners to London, and were put upon their honor, and allowed to go and see their families for the last—"

Hark!

They listened. Footsteps again; but again they passed by. The mamma leaned her head upon her husband's shoulder to hide her paleness.

"They arrived this morning."

The child's eyes opened wide.

"Why, papa! is it a *true* story?"

"Yes, dear."

"Oh, how good! Oh, it's ever so much better! Go on, papa. Why, mamma!—*dear* mamma, are you crying?"

"Never mind me, dear—I was thinking of the—of the—the poor families."

"But *don't* cry, mamma: it'll all come out right—you'll see; stories always do. Go on, papa, to where they lived happy ever after; then she won't cry any more. You'll see, mamma. Go on, papa."

"First, they took them to the Tower before they let them go home."

"Oh, *I* know the Tower! We can see it from here. Go on, papa."

"I am going on as well as I can, in the circumstances. In the Tower the military court tried them for an hour, and found them guilty, and condemned them to be shot."

"*Killed*, papa?"

"Yes."

"Oh, how naughty! Dear mamma, you are crying again. Don't, mamma; it'll soon come to the good place—you'll see. Hurry, papa, for mamma's sake; you don't go fast enough."

"I know I don't, but I suppose it is because I stop so much to reflect."

"But you mustn't *do* it, papa; you must go fight on."

"Very well, then. The three Colonels—" "Do you know them, papa?"

"Yes, dear."

"Oh, I wish I did! I love Colonels. Would they let me kiss them, do you think?" The Colonel's voice was a little unsteady when he answered:

"*One* of them would, my darling! There kiss me for him."

"There, papa—and these two are for the others. I think they would let me kiss them, papa; for I would say, 'My papa is a Colonel, too, and brave, and he would do what you did; so it *can't* be wrong, no matter what those people say, and you needn't be the least bit ashamed'; then they would let me—wouldn't they, papa?"

"God knows they would, child!"

"Mamma!—oh, mamma, you mustn't. He's soon coming to the happy place; go on, papa."

"Then, some were sorry—they all were; that military court, I mean; and they went to the Lord General, and said they had done their duty—for it *was* their duty, you know—and now they begged that two of the Colonels might be spared, and only the other one shot. One would be sufficient for an example for the army, they thought. But the Lord General was very stern, and rebuked them forasmuch as, having done *their* duty and cleared their consciences, they would beguile him to do less, and so smirch his soldierly honor. But they answered that they were asking nothing of him that they would not do themselves if they stood in his great place and held in their hands the noble prerogative of mercy. That struck him, and he paused and stood thinking, some of the sternness passing out of his face. Presently he bid them wait, and he retired to his closet to seek counsel of God in prayer; and when he came again, he said: 'They shall cast lots. That shall decide it, and two of them shall live.' "

"And did they, papa, did they? And which one is to die?—ah, that poor man!"

"No. They refused."

"They wouldn't do it, papa?"

"No."

"Why?"

"They said that the one that got the fatal bean would be sentencing himself to death by his own voluntary act, and it would be but suicide, call it by what name one might. They said they were Christians, and the Bible forbade men to take their own lives. They sent back that word, and said they were ready—let the court's sentence be carried into effect."

"What does that mean, papa?"

"They—they will all be shot."

Hark!

The wind? No. Tramp—tramp—tramp—r-r-r-umble-dumdum, r-r-rumble-dumdum—

"Open—in the Lord General's name!"

"Oh, goody, papa, it's the soldiers!—I love the soldiers! Let me let them in, papa, let *me!*"

She jumped down, and scampered to the door and pulled it open, crying joyously: "Come in! come in! Here they are, papa! Grenadiers! I know the Grenadiers!"

The file marched in and straightened up in line at shoulder arms; its officer saluted, the doomed Colonel standing erect and returning the courtesy, the soldier wife standing at his side, white, and with features drawn with inward pain, but giving no other sign of her misery, the child gazing on the show with dancing eyes. . . .

One long embrace, of father, mother, and child; then the order, "To the Tower—forward!" Then the Colonel marched forth from the house with military step and bearing, the file following; then the door closed.

"Oh, mamma, didn't it come out beautiful! I *told* you it would; and they're going to the Tower, and he'll *see* them! He—"

"Oh, come to my arms, you poor innocent thing!". . .

II

The next morning the stricken mother was not able to leave her bed; doctors and nurses were watching by her, and whispering together now and then; Abby could not be allowed in the room; she was told to run and play—mamma was very ill. The child, muffled in winter wraps, went out and played in the street awhile; then it struck her as strange, and also wrong, that her papa should be allowed to stay at the Tower in ignorance at such a time as this. This must be remedied; she would attend to it in person.

An hour later the military court were ushered into the presence of the Lord General. He stood grim and erect, with his knuckles resting upon the table, and indicated that he was ready to listen. The spokesman said: "We have urged them to reconsider; we have implored them: but they persist. They will not cast lots. They are willing to die, but not to defile their religion."

The Protector's face darkened, but he said nothing. He remained a time in thought, then he said: "They shall not all die; the lots shall be cast *for* them." Gratitude shone in the faces of the court. "Send for them. Place them in that room there. Stand them side by side with their faces to the wall and their wrists crossed behind them. Let me have notice when they are there."

When he was alone he sat down, and presently gave this order to an attendant: "Go, bring me the first little child that passes by."

The man was hardly out at the door before he was back again—leading Abby by the hand, her garments lightly powdered with snow. She went straight to the Head of the State, that formidable personage at the mention of whose name the principalities and powers of the earth trembled, and climbed up in his lap, and said:

"I know *you*, sir: you are the Lord General; I have seen you; I have seen you when you went by my house. Everybody was afraid; but I wasn't afraid, because you didn't look cross at *me;* you remember, don't you? I had on my red frock—the one with the blue things on it down the front. Don't you remember that?

A smile softened the austere lines of the Protector's face, and he began to struggle diplomatically with his answer:

"Why, let me see I—"

"I was standing right by the house—*my* house, you know."

"Well, you dear little thing, I ought to be ashamed, but you know—"

The child interrupted, reproachfully.

"Now you *don't* remember it. Why, I didn't forget *you.*"

"Now *I* am ashamed: but I will never forget you again, dear; you have my word for it. You will forgive me now, won't you, and be good friends with me, always and forever?

"Yes, indeed I will, though I don't know how you came to forget it; you must be very forgetful: but I am too, sometimes. I can forgive you without any trouble, for I think you *mean* to be good and do right, and I think you are just as kind—but you must snuggle me better, the way papa does—it's cold."

"You shall be snuggled to your heart's content, little new friend of mine, always to be *old* friend of mine hereafter, isn't it? You mind me of my little girl—not little any more, now—but she was dear, and sweet, and daintily made, like you. And she had your charm, little witch—your all-conquering sweet confidence in friend and stranger alike, that wins to willing slavery any upon whom its precious compliment falls. She used to lie in my arms, just as you are doing now; and charm the weariness and care out of my heart and give it peace, just as you are doing now; and we were comrades, and equals, and playfellows together. Ages ago it was, since that pleasant heaven faded away and vanished, and you have brought it back again;—take a burdened man's blessing for it, you tiny creature, who are carrying the weight of England while I rest!"

"Did you love her very, very, *very* much?"

"Ah, you shall judge by this: she commanded and I obeyed!"

"I think you are lovely! Will you kiss me?"

"Thankfully—and hold it a privilege, too. There—this one is for you; and there—this one is for her. You made it a request; and you could have made it a command, for you are representing her, and what you command I must obey."

The child clapped her hands with delight at the idea of this grand promotion—then her ear caught an approaching sound: the measured tramp of marching men.

"Soldiers!—soldiers, Lord General! Abby wants to see them!"

"You shall, dear; but wait a moment, I have a commission for you."

An officer entered and bowed low, saying, "They are come, your Highness," bowed again, and retired.

The Head of the Nation gave Abby three little disks of sealing-wax: two white, and one a ruddy red—for this one's mission was to deliver death to the Colonel who should get it.

"Oh, what a lovely red one! Are they for me?"

"No, dear; they are for others. Lift the corner of that curtain, there, which hides an open door; pass through, and you will see three men standing in a row, with their backs toward you and their hands behind their backs—so—each with one hand open, like a cup. Into each of the open hands drop one of those things, then come back to me."

Abby disappeared behind the curtain, and the Protector was alone. He said, reverently: "Of a surety that good thought came to me in my perplexity from Him who is an ever-present help to them that are in doubt and seek His aid. He knoweth where the choice should fall, and has sent His sinless messenger to do His will. Another would err, but He cannot err. Wonderful are His ways, and wise blessed be His holy Name!"

The small fairy dropped the curtain behind her and stood for a moment coming with alert curiosity the appointments of the chamber of doom, and the rigid figures of the soldiery and the prisoners; then her face lighted merrily, and she said to herself: "Why, one of them is papa! I know his back. He shall have the prettiest one!" She tripped gaily forward and dropped the disks into the open hands, then peeped around under her father's arm and lifted her laughing face and cried out:

"Papa! papa! look what you've got. I gave it to you!"

He glanced at the fatal gift, then sunk to his knees and gathered his innocent little executioner to his breast in an agony of love and pity. Soldiers, officers, released prisoners, all stood paralyzed, for a moment, at the vastness of this tragedy, then the pitiful scene smote their hearts, their eyes filled, and they wept unashamed. There was deep and reverent silence during some minutes, then the officer of the guard moved reluctantly forward and touched his prisoner on the shoulder, saying, gently:

"It grieves me, sir, but my duty commands."

"Commands what?" said the child.

"I must take him away. I am so sorry."

"Take him away? Where?"

"To—to—God help me!—to another part of the fortress."

"Indeed you can't. My mamma is sick, and I am going to take him home." She released herself and climbed upon her father's back and put her arms around his neck. "Now Abby's ready, papa—come along."

"My poor child, I can't. I must go with them." The child jumped to the ground and looked about her, wondering. Then she ran and stood before the officer and stamped her small foot indignantly and cried out:

"I told you my mamma is sick, and you might have listened. Let him go—you *must!*"

"Oh, poor child, would God I could, but indeed I must take him away. Attention, guard! . . . . fall in! . . . shoulder arms!" . . .

Abby was gone—like a flash of light. In a moment she was back, dragging the Lord Protector by the hand. At this formidable apparition all present straightened up, the officers saluting and the soldiers presenting arms.

"Stop them, sir! My mamma is sick and wants my papa, and I *told* them so, but they never even listened to me, and are taking him away."

The Lord General stood as one dazed.

"*Your* papa, child? Is he your papa?"

"Why, of course—he was *always* it. Would I give the pretty red one to any other, when I love him so? No!"

A shocked expression rose in the Protector's face, and he said:

"Ah, God help me! through Satan's wiles I have done the cruelest thing that ever man did—and there is no help, no help! What can I do?"

Abby cried out, distressed and impatient: "Why you can make them let him go," and she began to sob. "Tell them to do it! You told me to command, and now the very first time I tell you to do a thing you don't do it!"

A tender light dawned in the rugged old face, and the Lord General laid his hand upon the small tyrant's head and said: "God be thanked for the saving accident of that unthinking promise; and you, inspired by Him, for reminding me of my forgotten pledge, O incomparable child! Officer, obey her command—she speaks by my mouth. The prisoner is pardoned; set him free!"

The Belated Russian Passport

One fly makes a summer.—*Pudd'nhead Wilson's Calendar.*

I

A great beer saloon in the Friedrichstrasse, Berlin, toward mid-afternoon. At a hundred round tables gentlemen sat smoking and drinking; flitting here and there and everywhere were white-aproned waiters bearing foaming mugs to the thirsty. At a table near the main entrance were grouped half a dozen lively young fellows—American students—drinking good-bye to a visiting Yale youth on his travels, who had been spending a few days in the German capital.

"But why do you cut your tour short in the middle, Parrish?" asked one of the students. "I wish I had your chance. What do you want to go home for?"

"Yes," said another, "what is the idea? You want to explain, you know, because it looks like insanity. Homesick?"

A girlish blush rose in Parrish's fresh young face, and after a little hesitation he confessed that that was his trouble.

"I was never away from home before," he said, "and every day I get more and more lonesome. I have not seen a friend for weeks, and it's been horrible. I meant to stick the trip through, for pride's sake, but seeing you boys has finished me. It's been heaven to me, and I can't take up that companionless dreariness again. If I had company—but I haven't, you know, so it's no use. They used to call me Miss Nancy when I was a small chap, and I reckon I'm that yet—girlish and timorous, and all that. I ought to have *been* a girl! I can't stand it; I'm going home."

The boys rallied him good-naturedly, and said he was making the mistake of his life; and one of them added that he ought at least to see St. Petersburg before turning back.

"Don't!" said Parrish, appealingly. "It was my densest dream, and

I'm throwing it away. Don't say a word more on that head, for I'm made of water, and can't stand out against anybody's persuasion. I *can't* go alone; I think I should die." He slapped his breast pocket, and added: "Here is my protection against a change of mind; I've bought ticket and sleeper for Paris, and I leave tonight. Drink, now—this is on me bumpers—this is for home!"

The good-byes were said, and Alfred Parrish was left to his thoughts and his loneliness. But for a moment only. A sturdy middle-aged man with a brisk and businesslike bearing, and an air of decision and confidence suggestive of military training, came bustling from the next table, and seated himself at Parrish's side, and began to speak, with concentrated interest and earnestness. His eyes, his face, his person, his whole system, seemed to exude energy. He was full of steam—racing pressure—one could almost hear his gauge-cocks sing. He extended a frank hand, shook Parrish's cordially, and said, with a most convincing air of strenuous conviction:

"Ah, but you *mustn't;* really you mustn't; it would be the greatest mistake; you would always regret it. Be persuaded, I beg you; don't do it—don't!"

There was such a friendly note in it, and such a seeming of genuineness, that it brought a sort of uplift to the youth's despondent spirits, and a telltale moisture betrayed itself in his eyes, an unintentional confession that he was touched and grateful. The alert stranger noted that sign, was quite content with that response, and followed up his advantage without waiting for a spoken one:

"No, don't do it; it would be a mistake. I have heard everything that was said—you will pardon that—I was so close by that I couldn't help it. And it troubled me to think that you would cut your travels short when you really *want* to see St. Petersburg, and are right here almost in sight of it! Reconsider it—ah, you *must* reconsider it. It is such a short distance it is very soon done and very soon over—and think what a memory it will be!"

Then he went on and made a picture of the Russian capital and its wonders, which made Alfred Parrish's mouth water and his roused spirits cry out with longing. Then—

"Of course you must see St. Petersburg—you *must!* Why, it will be a joy to you—a joy! I know, because I know the place as familiarly as I know my own birthplace in America. Ten years—I've known it ten years. Ask anybody there; they'll tell you; they all know me Major Jackson. The very dogs know me. Do go; oh, you must go; you must, indeed."

Alfred Parrish was quivering with eagerness now. He would go. His face said it as plainly as his tongue could have done it. Then—the old shadow fell, and he said, sorrowfully:

"Oh, no—no, it's no use; I can't. I should die of the loneliness."

The Major said, with astonishment: "The loneliness! Why, I'm going *with* you!"

It was startlingly unexpected. And not quite pleasant. Things were moving too rapidly. Was this a trap? Was this stranger a sharper? Whence all this gratuitous interest in a wandering and unknown lad? Then he glanced at the Major's frank and winning and beaming face, and was ashamed; and wished he knew how to get out of this scrape without hurting the feelings of its contriver. But he was not handy in matters of diplomacy, and went at the difficulty with conscious awkwardness and small confidence. He said, with a quite overdone show of unselfishness:

"Oh no, no, you are too kind; I couldn't—I couldn't allow you to put yourself to such an inconvenience on my—"

"Inconvenience? None in the world, my boy; I was going tonight, anyway; I leave in the express at nine. Come! we'll go together. You sha'n't be lonely a single minute. Come along—say the word!"

So that excuse had failed. What to do now? Parrish was disheartened; it seemed to him that no subterfuge which his poor invention could contrive would ever rescue him from these toils. Still, he must make another effort, and he did; and before he had finished his new excuse he thought he recognized that it was unanswerable:

"Ah, but most unfortunately luck is against me, and it is impossible. Look at these "—and he took out his tickets and laid them on the table. "I am booked through to Paris, and I couldn't get these tickets and baggage coupons changed for St. Petersburg, of course, and would have to lose the money; and if I could afford to lose the money I should be rather short after I bought the new tickets—for there is all the cash I've got about me"—and he laid a five-hundred mark banknote on the table.

In a moment the Major had the tickets and coupons and was on his feet, and saying, with enthusiasm:

"Good! It's all right, and everything safe. They'll change the tickets and baggage pasters for *me;* they all know me everybody knows me. Sit right where you are; I'll be back right away." Then he reached for the banknote, and added, "I'll take this along, for there will be a little extra pay on the new tickets, maybe"—and the next moment he was flying out at the door.

II

Alfred Parrish was paralyzed. It was all so sudden. So sudden, so daring, so incredible, so impossible. His mouth was open, but his tongue wouldn't work; he tried to shout "Stop him," but his lungs were empty; he wanted to pursue, but his legs refused to do anything but tremble; then they gave way under him and let him down into his chair. His throat was dry, he was gasping and swallowing with dismay, his head was in a whirl. What must he do? He did not know. One thing seemed plain, however—he must pull himself together, and try to overtake that man. Of course the man could not get back the ticket-money, but would he throw the tickets away on that account? No; he would certainly go to the station and sell them to someone at half-price; and today, too, for they would be worthless tomorrow, by German custom. These reflections gave him hope and strength, and he rose and started. But he took only a couple of steps, then he felt a sudden sickness, and tottered back to his chair again, weak with a dread that his movement had been noticed—for the last round of beer was at his expense; it had not been paid for, and he hadn't a pfennig. He was a prisoner—Heaven only could know what might happen if he tried to leave the place. He was timid, scared, crushed; and he had not German enough to state his case and beg for help and indulgence.

Then his thoughts began to persecute him. How could he have been such a fool? What possessed him to listen to such a manifest adventurer? *And here comes the waiter!* He buried himself in the newspaper—trembling. The waiter passed by. It filled him with thankfulness. The hands of the clock seemed to stand still, yet he could not keep his eyes from them.

Ten minutes dragged by. The waiter again! Again he hid behind the paper. The waiter paused—apparently a week—then passed on.

Another ten minutes of misery—once more the waiter; this time he wiped off the table, and seemed to be a month at it; then paused two months, and went away.

Parrish felt that he could not endure another visit; he must take the chances: he must run the gantlet; he must escape. But the waiter stayed around about the neighborhood for five minutes—months and months seemingly, Parrish watching him with a despairing eye, and feeling the infirmities of age creeping upon him and his hair gradually turning gray.

At last the waiter wandered away—stopped at a table, collected a bill, wandered farther, collected another bill, wandered farther—Parrish's praying eye riveted on him all the time, his heart thumping, his breath coming and going in quick little gasps of anxiety mixed with hope.

The waiter stopped again to collect, and Parrish said to himself, it is now or never! and started for the door. One step—two steps—three—four—he was nearing the door—five his legs shaking under him—was that a swift step behind him?—the thought shriveled his heart—six steps—seven, and he was out!—eight—nine—ten—eleven—twelve. There is a pursuing step!—he turned the corner, and picked up his heels to fly—a heavy hand fell on his shoulder, and the strength went out of his body.

It was the Major. He asked not a question, he showed no surprise. He said, in his breezy and exhilarating fashion:

"Confound those people, they delayed me; that's why I was gone so long. New man in the ticket office, and he didn't know me, and wouldn't make the exchange because it was irregular; so I had to hunt up my old friend, the great mogul—the stationmaster, you know—hi, there, cab! cab! jump in, Parrish!—Russian consulate, cabby, and let them fly!—so, as I say, that all cost time. But it's all right now, and everything straight; your luggage reweighed, rechecked, fare-ticket and sleeper changed, and I've got the documents for it in my pocket; also the change I'll keep it for you.

Whoop along, cabby, whoop along; don't let them go to sleep!"

Poor Parrish was trying his best to get in a word edgeways, as the cab flew farther and farther from the bilked beer hall, and now at last he succeeded, and wanted to return at once and pay his little bill.

"Oh, never mind about that," said the Major, placidly; "that's all right, they know me, everybody knows me. I'll square it next time I'm in Berlin—push along, cabby, push along—no great lot of time to spare, now."

They arrived at the Russian consulate, a moment after-hours, and hurried in. No one there but a clerk. The Major laid his card on the desk, and said, in the Russian tongue, "Now, then, if you'll visé this young man's passport for Petersburg as quickly as—"

"But, dear sir, I'm not authorized, and the consul has just gone."

"Gone where?"

"Out in the country, where he lives."

"And he'll be back—"

"Not till morning."

"Thunder! Oh, well, look here, I'm Major Jackson—he knows me, everybody knows me. You visé it yourself; tell him Major Jackson asked you; it'll be all right."

But it would be desperately and fatally irregular; the clerk could not be persuaded; he almost fainted at the idea.

"Well, then, I'll tell you what you do," said the Major. "Here's stamps and the fee—visé it in the morning, and start it along by mail."

The clerk said, dubiously, "He well, he may perhaps do it, and so—"

"May? He *will!* He knows me—everybody knows me."

"Very well," said the clerk, "I will tell him what you say." He looked bewildered, and in a measure subjugated; and added, timidly: "But—but—you know you will beat it to the frontier twenty-four hours. There are no accommodations there for so long a wait."

"Who's going to *wait?* Not I, if the court knows herself."

The clerk was temporarily paralyzed, and said, "Surely, sir, you don't wish it sent to Petersburg!"

"And why not?"

"And the owner of it tarrying at the frontier, twenty-five miles away? It couldn't do him any good, in those circumstances."

"Tarry—the mischief! Who said he was going to do any tarrying?"

"Why, you know, of course, they'll stop him at the frontier if he has no passport."

"Indeed they won't! The Chief Inspector knows me— everybody does. I'll be responsible for the young man. You send it straight through to Petersburg—Hotel de l'Europe, care Major Jackson: tell the consul not to worry, I'm taking all the risks myself."

The clerk hesitated, then chanced one more appeal:

"You must bear in mind, sir, that the risks are peculiarly serious, just now. The new edict is in force."

"What is it?"

"Ten years in Siberia for being in Russia without a passport."

"Mm—damnation!" He said it in English, for the Russian tongue is but a poor standby in spiritual emergencies. He mused a moment, then brisked up and resumed in Russian: "Oh, it's all right—label her St. Petersburg and let her sail! I'll fix it. They all know me there all the authorities everybody."

III

The Major turned out to be an adorable traveling companion, and young Parrish was charmed with him. His talk was sunshine and rainbows, and lit up the whole region around, and kept it gay and happy and cheerful; and he was full of accommodating ways, and knew all about how to do things, and when to do them, and the best way. So the long journey was a fairy dream for that young lad who had been so lonely and forlorn and friendless so many homesick weeks. At last, when the two travelers were approaching the frontier, Parrish said something about passports; then started, as if recollecting something, and added:

"Why, come to think, I don't remember your bringing my passport away from the consulate. But you did, didn't you?"

"No; it's coming by mail," said the Major, comfortably.

"C—coming—by—mail!" gasped the lad; and all the dreadful

things he had heard about the terrors and disasters of passportless visitors to Russia rose in his frightened mind and turned him white to the lips. "Oh, Major—oh, my goodness, what will become of me! How *could* you do such a thing?"

The Major laid a soothing hand upon the youth's shoulder and said:

"Now, don't you worry, my boy, don't you worry a bit. I'm taking care of you, and I'm not going to let any harm come to you. The Chief Inspector knows me, and I'll explain to him, and it'll be all right—you'll see. Now don't you give yourself the least discomfort—I'll fix it all up, easy as nothing."

Alfred trembled, and felt a great sinking inside, but he did what he could to conceal his misery, and to respond with some show of heart to the Major's kindly pettings and reassurings.

At the frontier he got out and stood on the edge of the great crowd, and waited in deep anxiety while the Major plowed his way through the mass to "explain to the Chief Inspector." It seemed a cruelly long wait, but at last the Major reappeared. He said, cheerfully, "Damnation, it's a new inspector, and I don't know him!"

Alfred fell up against a pile of trunks, with a despairing, "Oh, dear, dear, I might have known it!" and was slumping limp and helpless to the ground, but the Major gathered him up and seated him on a box, and sat down by him, with a supporting arm around him, and whispered in his ear:

"Don't worry, laddie, don't—it's going to be all right; you just trust to me. The sub-inspector's as nearsighted as a shad. I watched him, and I know it's so. Now I'll tell you how to do. I'll go and get my passport chalked, then I'll stop right yonder inside the grille where you see those peasants with their packs. You be there, and I'll back up against the grille, and slip my passport to you through the bars, then you tag along after the crowd and hand it in, and trust to Providence and that shad. Mainly the shad. You'll pull through all right—now don't you be afraid."

"But, oh dear, dear, *your* description and *mine* don't tally any more than—"

"Oh, that's all right—difference between fifty-one and nineteen—just entirely imperceptible to that shad—don't you fret, it's going to come out as right as nails."

Ten minutes later Alfred was tottering toward the train, pale, and in a collapse, but he had played the shad successfully, and was as grateful as an untaxed dog that has evaded the police.

"I told you so," said the Major, in splendid spirits. "I knew it would come out all right if you trusted in Providence like a little trusting child and didn't try to improve on His ideas—it always does."

Between the frontier and Petersburg the Major laid himself out to restore his young comrade's life, and work up his circulation, and pull him out of his despondency, and make him feel again that life was a joy and worth living. And so, as a consequence, the young fellow entered the city in high feather and marched into the hotel in fine form, and registered his name. But instead of naming a room, the clerk glanced at him inquiringly, and waited. The Major came promptly to the rescue, and said, cordially:

"It's all right—you know me—set him down, I'm responsible." The clerk looked grave, and shook his head. The Major added: "It's all right, it'll be here in twenty-four hours—it's coming by mail. Here's mine, and his is coming, right along."

The clerk was full of politeness, full of deference, but he was firm. He said, in English:

"Indeed, I wish I could accommodate you, Major, and certainly I would if I could; but I have no choice, I must ask him to go; I cannot allow him to remain in the house a moment."

Parrish began to totter, and emitted a moan; the Major caught him and stayed him with an arm, and said to the clerk, appealingly:

"Come, you know me—everybody does—just let him stay here the one night, and I give you my word—"

The clerk shook his head, and said:

"But, Major, you are endangering me, you are endangering the house. I—I hate to do such a thing, but I—I *must* call the police."

"Hold on, don't do that. Come along, my boy, and don't you fret—it's going to come out all right. Hi, there, cabby! Jump in, Parrish. Palace of the General of the Secret Police turn them loose, cabby! Let them go! Make them whiz! Now we're off, and don't you give yourself any uneasiness. Prince Bossloffsky knows me, knows me like a book; he'll soon fix things all right for us."

They tore through the gay streets and arrived at the palace, which was brilliantly lighted. But it was half past eight; the Prince was about going in to dinner, the sentinel said, and couldn't receive any one.

"But he'll receive *me*," said the Major, robustly, and handed his card. "I'm Major Jackson. Send it in; it'll be all right."

The card was sent in, under protest, and the Major and his waif waited in a reception room for some time. At length they were sent for, and conducted to a sumptuous private office and confronted with the Prince, who stood there gorgeously arrayed and frowning like a thundercloud. The Major stated his case, and begged for a twenty-four-hour stay of proceedings until the passport should be forthcoming.

"Oh, impossible!" said the Prince, in faultless English. "I marvel that you should have done so insane a thing as to bring the lad into the country without a passport, Major, I marvel at it; why, it's ten years in Siberia, and no help for it—catch him! support him!" for poor Parrish was making another trip to the floor. "Here—quick, give him this. There take another draught; brandy's the thing, don't you find it so, lad? Now you feel better, poor fellow. Lie down on the sofa. How stupid it was of you, Major, to get him into such a horrible scrape." The Major eased the boy down with his strong arms, put a cushion under his head, and whispered in his ear:

"Look as damned sick as you can! Play it for all it's worth; he's touched, you see; got a tender heart under there somewhere; fetch a groan, and say, 'Oh, mamma, mamma'; it'll knock him out, sure as guns."

Parrish was going to do these things anyway, from native impulse, so they came from him promptly, with great and moving sincerity, and the Major whispered: "Splendid! Do it again; Bernhardt couldn't beat it."

What with the Major's eloquence and the boy's misery, the point was gained at last; the Prince struck his colors, and said:

"Have it your way; though you deserve a sharp lesson and you ought to get it. I give you exactly twenty-four hours. If the passport is not here then, don't come near me; it's Siberia without hope of pardon."

While the Major and the lad poured out their thanks, the Prince rang in a couple of soldiers, and in their own language he ordered them to go with these two people, and not lose sight of the younger one a moment for the next twenty-four hours; and if, at the end of that term, the boy could not show a passport, impound him in the dungeons of St. Peter and St. Paul, and report.

The unfortunates arrived at the hotel with their guards, dined under their eyes, remained in Parrish's room until the Major went off to bed, after cheering up the sad Parrish, then one of the soldiers locked himself and Parrish in, and the other one stretched himself across the door outside and soon went off to sleep.

So also did not Alfred Parrish. The moment he was alone with the solemn soldier and the voiceless silence his machine-made cheerfulness began to waste away, his medicated courage began to give off its supporting gases and shrink toward normal, and his poor little heart to shrivel like a raisin. Within thirty minutes he struck bottom; grief, misery, fright, despair, could go no lower. Bed? Bed was not for such as he; bed was not for the doomed, the lost! Sleep? He was not the Hebrew children, he could not sleep in the fire! He could only walk the floor. And not only could, but must. And did, by the hour. And mourned, and wept, and shuddered, and prayed.

Then all-sorrowfully he made his last dispositions, and prepared himself, as well as in him lay, to meet his fate. As a final act, he wrote a letter:

"My Darling Mother—When these sad lines shall have reached you your poor Alfred will be no more. No; worse than that, far worse! Through my own fault and foolishness I have fallen into the hands of a sharper or a lunatic; I do not know which, but in either case I feel that I am lost. Sometimes I think he is a sharper, but most of the time I think he is only mad, for he has a kind, good heart, I know, and he certainly seems to try the hardest that ever a person tried to get me out of the fatal difficulties he has gotten me into.

"In a few hours I shall be one of a nameless horde plodding the snowy solitudes of Russia, under the lash, and bound for that land of mystery and misery and termless oblivion, Siberia! I shall not live to see it; my heart is broken and I shall die. Give my picture to *her*, and ask her to keep it in memory of me, and to so live that in the appointed time she may join me in that better world where there is no marriage nor giving in marriage, and where there are no more separations, and troubles never come. Give my yellow dog to Archy Hale, and the other one to Henry Taylor; my blazer I give to brother Will, and my fishing-things and Bible.

"There is no hope for me. I cannot escape; the soldier stands there with his gun and never takes his eyes off me, just blinks; there is no other movement, any more than if he was dead. I cannot bribe him, the maniac has my money. My letter of credit is in my trunk, and may never come—*will* never come, I know. Oh, what is to become of me! Pray for me, darling mother, pray for your poor Alfred. But it will do no good."

IV

In the morning Alfred came out looking scraggy and worn when the Major summoned him to an early breakfast. They fed their guards, they lit cigars, the Major loosened his tongue and set it going, and under its magic influence Alfred gradually and gratefully became hopeful, measurably cheerful, and almost happy once more.

But he would not leave the house. Siberia hung over him black and threatening, his appetite for sights was all gone, he could not have borne the shame of inspecting streets and galleries and churches with a soldier at each elbow and all the world stopping and staring and commenting—no, he would stay within and wait for the Berlin mail and his fate. So, all day long the Major stood gallantly by him in his room, with one soldier standing stiff and motionless against the door with his musket at his shoulder, and the other one drowsing in a chair outside; and all day long the faithful veteran spun campaign yarns, described battles, reeled off explosive anecdotes, with unconquerable energy and sparkle and resolution, and kept the scared student alive and his pulses functioning. The long day wore to a close, and the pair, followed by their guards, went down to the great dining room and took their seats.

"The suspense will be over before long, now," sighed poor Alfred.

Just then a pair of Englishmen passed by, and one of them said, "So we'll get no letters from Berlin tonight."

Parrish's breath began to fail him. The Englishmen seated themselves at a nearby table, and the other one said:

"No, it isn't as bad as that." Parrish's breathing improved. "There is later telegraphic news. The accident did detain the train formidably, but that is all. It will arrive here three hours late tonight."

Parrish did not get to the floor this time, for the Major jumped for him in time. He had been listening, and foresaw what would happen. He patted Parrish on the back, hoisted him out of his chair, and said, cheerfully:

"Come along, my boy, cheer up, there's absolutely nothing to worry about. I know a way out. Bother the passport; let it lag a week if it wants to, we can do without it."

Parrish was too sick to hear him; hope was gone, Siberia present; he moved off on legs of lead, upheld by the Major, who walked him to the American legation, heartening him on the way with assurances that on his recommendation the minister wouldn't hesitate a moment to grant him a new passport.

"I had that card up my sleeve all the time," he said. "The minister knows me knows me familiarly—chummed together hours and hours under a pile of other wounded at Cold Harbor; been chummies ever since, in spirit, though we haven't met much in the body. Cheer up, laddie, everything's looking splendid! By gracious! I feel as cocky as a buck angel. Here we are, and our troubles are at an end! If we ever really had any."

There, alongside the door, was the trademark of the richest and freest and mightiest republic of all the ages: the pine disk, with the planked eagle spread upon it, his head and shoulders among the stars, and his claws full of out-of-date war material; and at that sight the tears came into Alfred's eyes, the pride of country rose in his heart, Hail Columbia boomed up in his breast, and all his fears and sorrows vanished away; for here he was safe, safe! not all the powers of the earth would venture to cross that threshold to lay a hand upon him!

For economy's sake the mightiest republic's legations in Europe consist of a room and a half on the ninth floor, when the tenth is occupied, and the legation furniture consists of a minister or an ambassador with a brakeman's salary, a secretary of legation who sells matches and mends crockery for a living, a hired girl for interpreter and general utility, pictures of the American liners, a chromo of the reigning President, a desk, three chairs, kerosene lamp, a cat, a clock, and a cuspidor with the motto, "In God We Trust."

The party climbed up there, followed by the escort. A man sat at the desk writing official things on wrapping paper with a nail. He rose and faced about; the cat climbed down and got under the desk; the hired girl squeezed herself up into the corner by the vodka jug to make room; the soldiers squeezed themselves up against the wall alongside of her, with muskets at shoulder arms. Alfred was radiant with happiness and the sense of rescue.

The Major cordially shook hands with the official, rattled off his case in easy and fluent style, and asked for the desired passport.

The official seated his guests, then said: "Well, I am only the secretary of legation, you know, and I wouldn't like to grant a passport while the minister is on Russian soil. There is far too much responsibility."

"All right, send for him."

The secretary smiled, and said: "That's easier said than done. He's away up in the wilds, somewhere, on his vacation."

"Ger-reat Scott?' ejaculated the Major.

Alfred groaned; the color went out of his face, and he began to slowly collapse in his clothes. The secretary said, wonderingly:

"Why, what are you Great-Scotting about, Major? The Prince gave you twenty-four hours. Look at the clock; you're all right; you've half an hour left; the train is just due; the passport will arrive in time."

"Man, there's news! The train is three hours behind time! This boy's life and liberty are wasting away by minutes, and only thirty of them left! In half an hour he's the same as dead and damned to all eternity! By God, we *must* have the passport!"

"Oh, I am dying, I know it!" wailed the lad, and buried his face in his arms on the desk. A quick change came over the secretary, his placidity vanished away, excitement flamed up in his face and eyes, and he exclaimed:

"I see the whole ghastliness of the situation, but, Lord help us, what can I do? What can you suggest?"

"Why, hang it, give him the passport!"

"Impossible! Totally impossible! You know nothing about him; three days ago you had never heard of him; there's no way in the world to identify him. He is lost, lost—there's no possibility of saving him!"

The boy groaned again, and sobbed out, "Lord, Lord, it's the last of earth for Alfred Parrish!"

Another change came over the secretary.

In the midst of a passionate outburst of pity, vexation, and hopelessness, he stopped short, his manner calmed down, and he asked, in the indifferent voice which one uses in introducing the subject of the weather when there is nothing to talk about, "Is that your name?"

The youth sobbed out a yes. "Where are you from?"

"Bridgeport."

The secretary shook his head—shook it again—and muttered to himself. After a moment:

"Born there?"

"No; New Haven."

"Ah-h." The secretary glanced at the Major, who was listening intently, with blank and unenlightened face, and indicated rather than said, "There is vodka there, in case the soldiers are thirsty." The Major sprang up, poured for them, and received their gratitude. The questioning went on.

"How long did you live in New Haven?"

"Till I was fourteen. Came back two years ago to enter Yale."

"When you lived there, what street did you live on?"

"Parker Street."

With a vague half-light of comprehension dawning in his eye, the Major glanced an inquiry at the secretary. The secretary nodded, the Major poured vodka again.

"What number?"

"It hadn't any."

The boy sat up and gave the secretary a pathetic look which said, "Why do you want to torture me with these foolish things, when I am miserable enough without it?"

The secretary went on, unheeding: "What kind of a house was it?

"Brick—two-story."

"Flush with the sidewalk?"

"No, small yard in front."

"Iron fence?"

"No, palings."

The Major poured vodka again—without instructions—poured brimmers this time; and his face had cleared and was alive now.

"What do you see when you enter the door?"

"A narrow hall; door at the end of it, and door at your right."

"Anything else?"

"Hat-rack."

"Room at the right?"

"Parlor."

"Carpet?"

"Yes."

"Kind of carpet?"

"Old-fashioned Wilton."

"Figures?"

"Yes—hawking-party, horseback."

The Major cast an eye at the clock—only six minutes left! He faced about with the jug, and as he poured he glanced at the secretary, then at the clock—inquiringly. The secretary nodded; the Major covered the clock from view with his body a moment, and set the hands back half an hour; then he refreshed the men—double rations.

"Room beyond the hall and hat-rack?"

"Dining room."

"Stove?"

"Grate."

"Did your people own the house?"

"Yes."

"Do they own it yet?"

"No; sold it when we moved to Bridgeport."

The secretary paused a little, then said, "Did you have a nickname among your playmates?"

The color slowly rose in the youth's pale cheeks, and he dropped his eyes. He seemed to struggle with himself a moment or two, then he said, plaintively, "They called me Miss Nancy."

The secretary mused awhile, then he dug up another question: "Any ornaments in the dining room?"

"Well, y—no."

"*None?* None at *all?*"

"No."

"The mischief! Isn't that a little odd? Think!" The youth thought and thought; the secretary waited, slightly punting. At last the imperiled waif looked up sadly and shook his head.

"Think—*think!*" cried the Major, in anxious solicitude; and poured again.

"Come!" said the secretary, "not even a *picture?*"

"Oh, certainly! but you said ornament."

"Ah! What did your father think of it?"

The color rose again. The boy was silent.

"Speak," said the secretary.

"Speak," cried the Major, and his trembling hand poured more vodka outside the glasses than inside.

"I—I can't tell you what he said," murmured the boy.

"Quick! quick!" said the secretary; "out with it; there's no time to lose home and liberty or Siberia and death depend upon the answer."

"Oh, have pity! he is a clergyman, and—"

"No matter; out with it, or—"

"He said it was the hell-firedest nightmare he ever struck!"

"Saved!" shouted the secretary, and seized his nail and a blank passport. "*I* identify you; I've lived in the house, and I painted the picture myself!"

"Oh, come to my arms, my poor rescued boy!" cried the Major. "We will always be grateful to God that He made this artist!—if He did."

A Double-Barreled Detective Story

Chapter 1

The first scene is in the country, in Virginia; the time, 1880. There has been a wedding, between a handsome young man of slender means and a rich young girl—a case of love at first sight and a precipitate marriage; a marriage bitterly opposed by the girl's widowed father.

Jacob Puller, the bridegroom, is twenty-six years old, is of an old but unconsidered family which had by compulsion emigrated from Sedgemoor, and for King James's purse's profit, so everybody said—some maliciously, the rest merely because they believed it. The bride is nineteen and beautiful. She is intense, high-strung, romantic, immeasurably proud of her Cavalier blood, and passionate in her love for her young husband. For its sake she braved her father's displeasure, endured his reproaches, listened with loyalty unshaken to his warning predictions, and went from his house without his blessing, proud and happy in the proofs she was thus giving of the quality of the affection which had made its home in her heart.

The morning after the marriage there was a sad surprise for her. Her husband put aside her proffered caresses, and said:

"Sit down. I have something to say to you. I loved you. That was before I asked your father to give you to me. His refusal is not my grievance—I could have endured that. But the things he said of me to you—that is a different matter. There—you needn't speak; I know quite well what they were; I got them from authentic sources.

Among other things he said that my character was written in my face; that I was treacherous, a dissembler, a coward, and a brute without sense of pity or compassion: the 'Sedgemoor trademark,' he called it—and 'white-sleeve badge.' Any other man in my place would have gone to his house and shot him down like a dog. I wanted to do it, and was minded to do it, but a better thought came to me: to put him to shame; to break his heart; to kill him by inches. How to do it? Through my treatment of you, his idol! I would marry you; and then—Have patience. You will see."

From that moment onward, for three months, the young wife suffered all the humiliations, all the suits, all the miseries that the diligent and inventive mind of the husband could contrive, save physical injuries only. Her strong pride stood by her, and she kept the secret of her troubles. Now and then the husband said, "Why don't you go to your father and tell him?" Then he invented new tortures, applied them; and asked again. She always answered, "He shall never know by my mouth," and taunted him with his origin; said she was the lawful slave of a scion of slaves, and must obey, and would—up to that point, but no further; he could kill her if he liked, but he could not break her; it was not in the Sedgemoor breed to do it. At the end of the three months he said, with a dark significance in his manner, "I have tried all things but one "—and waited for' her reply. "Try that," she said, and curled her lip in mockery.

That night he rose at midnight and put on his clothes, then said to her:

"Get up and dress!"

She obeyed—as always, without a word. He led her half a mile from the house, and proceeded to lash her to a tree by the side of the public road; and succeeded, she screaming and struggling. He gagged her then, struck her across the face with his cowhide, and set his bloodhounds on her. They tore the clothes off her, and she was naked. He called the dogs off, and said:

"You will be found—by the passing public. They will be dropping along about three hours from now, and will spread the news—do you hear? Good-bye. You have seen the last of me."

He went away then. She moaned to herself:

"I shall bear a child—to *him!* God grant it may be a boy!"

The farmers released her by and by—and spread the news, which was natural. They raised the country with lynching intentions, but the bird had flown. The young wife shut herself up in her father's house; he shut himself up with her, and thenceforth would see no one. His pride was broken, and his heart; so he wasted away, day by day, and even his daughter rejoiced when death relieved him.

Then she sold the estate and disappeared.

Chapter 2

In 1886 a young woman was living in a modest house near a secluded New England village, with no company but a little boy about five years old. She did her own work, she discouraged acquaintanceships, and had none. The butcher, the baker, and the others that served her could tell the villagers nothing about her further than that her name was Stillman, and that she called the child Archy. Whence she came they had not been able to find out, but they said she talked like a Southerner. The child had no playmates and no comrade, and no teacher but the mother. She taught him diligently and intelligently, and was satisfied with the results—even a little proud of them. One day Archy said:

"Mamma, am I different from other children?"

"Well, I suppose not. Why?"

"There was a child going along out there and asked me if the postman had been by and I said yes, and she said how long since I saw him and I said I hadn't seen him at all, and she said how did I know he'd been by, then, and I said because I smelt his track on the sidewalk, and she said I was a dumb fool and made a mouth at me. What did she do that for?"

The young woman turned white, and said to herself, "It's a birthmark! The gift of the bloodhound is in him." She snatched the boy to her breast and hugged him passionately, saying, "God has appointed the way!" Her eyes were burning with a fierce light, and her breath came short and quick with excitement. She said to herself: "The puzzle is solved now; many a time it has been a mystery to me, the impossible things the child has done in the dark, but it is all clear to me now."

She set him in his small chair, and said:

"Wait a little till I come, dear; then we will talk about the matter."

She went up to her room and took from her dressing table several small articles and put them out of sight: a nail-file on the floor under the bed; a pair of nail-scissors under the bureau; a small ivory paper-knife under the wardrobe. Then she returned, and said:

"There! I have left some things which I ought to have brought down." She named them, and said, "Run up and bring them, dear."

The child hurried away on his errand and was soon back again with the things.

"Did you have any difficulty, dear?"

"No, mamma; I only went where you went."

During his absence she had stepped to the bookcase, taken several books from the bottom shelf, opened each, passed her hand over a page, noting its number in her memory, then restored them to their places. Now she said:

"I have been doing something while you have been gone, Archy. Do you think you can find out what it was?"

The boy went to the bookcase and got out the books that had been touched, and opened them at the pages which had been stroked.

The mother took him in her lap, and said:

"I will answer your question now, dear. I have found out that in one way you are quite different from other people. You can see in the dark, you can smell what other people cannot, you have the talents of a bloodhound. They are good and valuable things to have, but you must keep the matter a secret. If people found it out, they would speak of you as an odd child, a strange child, and children would be disagreeable to you, and give you nicknames. In this world one must be like everybody else if he doesn't want to provoke scorn or envy or jealousy. It is a great and fine distinction which has been born to you, and I am glad; but you will keep it a secret, for mamma's sake, won't you?"

The child promised, without understanding.

All the rest of the day the mother's brain was busy with excited thinkings; with plans, projects, schemes, each and all of them uncanny, grim, and dark. Yet they lit up her face; lit it with a fell light of their own; lit it with vague fires of hell. She was in a fever of unrest; she could not sit, stand, read, sew; there was no relief for her but in movement. She tested her boy's gift in twenty ways, and kept saying to herself all the time, with her mind in the past: "He broke my father's heart, and night and day all these years I have tried, and all in vain, to think out a way to break his. I have found it now—I have found it now."

When night fell, the demon of unrest still possessed her. She went on with her tests; with a candle she traversed the house from garret to cellar, hiding pins, needles, thimbles, spools, under pillows, under carpets, in cracks in the walls, under the coal in the bin; then sent the little fellow in the dark to find them; which he did, and was happy and proud when she praised him and smothered him with caresses.

From this time forward life took on a new complexion for her. She said, "The future is secure I can wait, and enjoy the waiting." The most of her lost interests revived. She took up music again, and languages, drawing, painting, and the other long-discarded delights of her maidenhood. She was happy once more, and felt again the zest of life. As the years drifted by she watched the development of her boy, and was contented with it. Not altogether, but nearly that. The soft side of his heart was larger than the other side of it. It was his only defect, in her eyes. But she considered that his love for her and worship of her made up for it. He was a good hater—that was well; but it was a question if the materials of his hatreds were of as tough and enduring a quality as those of his friendships—and that was not so well.

The years drifted on. Archy was to become a handsome, shapely, athletic youth, courteous, dignified, companionable, pleasant in his ways, and looking perhaps a trifle older than he was, which was sixteen. One evening his mother said she had something of grave importance to say to him, adding that he was old enough to hear it now, and old enough and possessed of character enough and stability enough to carry out a stern plan which she had been for years contriving and maturing. Then she told him her bitter story, in all its naked atrociousness. For a while the boy was paralyzed; then he said:

"I understand. We are Southerners; and by our custom and nature there is but one atonement. I will search him out and kill him."

"Kill him? No! Death is release, emancipation; death is a favor. Do I owe him favors? You must not hurt a hair of his head."

The boy was lost in thought awhile; then he said:

"You are all the world to me, and your desire is my law and my pleasure. Tell me what to do and I will do it."

The mother's eyes beamed with satisfaction, and she said:

"You will go and find him. I have known his hiding-place for eleven years; it cost me five years and more of inquiry, and much money, to locate it. He is a quartz-miner in Colorado, and well-to-do. He lives in Denver. His name is Jacob Fuller. There—it is the first time I have spoken it since that unforgettable night. Think! That name could have been yours if I had not saved you that shame and furnished you a cleaner one. You will drive him from that place; you will hunt him down and drive him again; and yet again, and again, and again, persistently, relentlessly, poisoning his life, filling it with mysterious terrors, loading it with weariness and misery, making him wish for death, and that he had a suicide's courage; you will make of him another Wandering Jew; he shall know no rest any more, no peace of mind, no placid sleep; you shall shadow him, cling to him, persecute him, till you break his heart, as he broke my father's and mine."

"I will obey, mother."

"I believe it, my child. The preparations are all made; everything is ready. Here is a letter of credit; spend freely, there is no lack of money. At times you may need disguises. I have provided them; also some other conveniences." She took from the drawer of the type-writer-table several squares of paper. They all bore these typewritten words:

$10,000 REWARD

> It is believed that a certain man who is wanted in an Eastern state is sojourning here. In 1880, in the night, he tied his young wife to a tree by the public road, cut her across the face with a cowhide, and made his dogs tear her clothes from her, leaving her naked. He left her there, and fled the country. A blood-relative of hers has searched for him for seventeen years. Address . . . . . ., ..., Post Office. The above reward will be paid in cash to the person who will furnish the seeker, in a personal interview, the criminal's address.

"When you have found him and acquainted yourself with his scent, you will go in the night and placard one of these upon the building he occupies, and another one upon the post office or in some other prominent place. It will be the talk of the region. At first you must give him several days in which to force a sale of his belongings at something approaching their value. We will ruin him by and by, but gradually; we must not impoverish him at once, for that could bring him to despair and injure his health, possibly kill him."

She took three or four more typewritten forms from the drawer—duplicates—and read one:

. . . . , ..., 18 . . . .

To Jacob Fuller:

You have . . . . . . days in which to settle your affairs. You will not be disturbed during that limit, which will expire at . . . . . . M., on the . . . . . . of . . . . . . You must then MOVE ON. If you are still in the place after the named hour, I will placard you on all the dead walls, detailing your crime once more, and adding the date, also the scene of it, with all names concerned, including your own. Have no fear of bodily injury—it will in no circumstances ever be inflicted upon you. You brought misery upon an old man, and ruined his life and broke his heart. What he suffered, you are to suffer.

"You will add no signature. He must receive this before he learns of the reward placard—before he rises in the morning—lest he lose his head and fly the place penniless,"

"I shall not forget."

"You will need to use these forms only in the beginning—once may be enough. Afterward, when you are ready for him to vanish out of a place, see that he gets a copy of *this* form, which merely says:

MOVE ON. You have . . . . . . days.

"He will obey. That is sure."

Chapter 3

Extracts from letters to the mother:

DENVER, April 3, 1897.

I have now been living several days in the same hotel with Jacob Puller. I have his scent; I could track him through ten divisions of infantry and find him. I have often been near him and heard him talk. He owns a good mine, and has a fair income from it; but he is not rich. He learned mining in a good way—by working at it for wages. He is a cheerful creature, and his forty-three years sit lightly upon him; he could pass for a younger man—say thirty-six or thirty-seven. He has never married again—passes himself off for a widower. He stands well, is liked, is popular, and has many friends. Even I feel a drawing toward him—the paternal blood in me making its claim. How blind and unreasoning and arbitrary are some of the laws of nature—the most of them, in fact! My task is become hard now—you realize it? you comprehend, and make allowances?—and the fire of it has cooled, more than I like to confess to myself. But I will carry it out. Even with the pleasure paled, the duty remains, and I will not spare him.

And for my help, a sharp resentment rises in me when I reflect that he who committed that odious crime is the only one who has not suffered by it. The lesson of it has manifestly reformed his character, and in the change he is happy. He, the guilty party, is absolved from all suffering; you, the innocent, are borne down with it. But be comforted—he shall harvest his share.

SILVER GULCH, May 19.

I placarded Form No. 1 at midnight of April 3; an hour later I slipped Form No. 2 under his chamber door, notifying him to leave Denver at or before 11.50 the night of the 14th.

Some late bird of a reporter stole one of my placards, then hunted the town over and found the other one, and stole that. In this manner he accomplished what the profession call a "scoop"—that is, he got a valuable item, and saw to it that no other paper got it. And so his paper—the principal one in the town—had it in glaring type on the editorial page in the morning, followed by a Vesuvian opinion of our wretch a column long, which wound up by adding a thousand dollars to our reward on the *paper's* account! The journals out here know how to do the noble thing—when there's business in it.

At breakfast I occupied my usual seat—selected because it afforded a view of papa Fuller's face, and was near enough for me to hear the talk that went on at his table. Seventy-five or a hundred people were in the room, and all discussing that item, and saying they hoped the seeker would find that rascal and remove the pollution of his presence from the town—with a rail, or a bullet, or something.

When Fuller came in he had the Notice to Leave—folded up in one hand, and the newspaper in the other; and it gave me more than half a pang to see him. His cheerfulness was all gone, and he looked old and pinched and ashy. And then—only think of the things he had to listen to! Mamma, he heard his own unsuspecting friends describe him with epithets and characterizations drawn from the very dictionaries and phrase-books of Satan's own authorized editions down below. And more than that, he had to *agree* with the verdicts and applaud them. His applause tasted bitter in his mouth, though; he could not disguise that from me; and it was observable that his appetite was gone; he only nibbled; he couldn't eat. Finally a man said:

"It is quite likely that that relative is in the room and hearing what this town thinks of that unspeakable scoundrel. I hope so."

Ah, dear, it was pitiful the way Fuller winced, and glanced around scared! He couldn't endure any more, and got up and left.

During several days he gave out that he had bought a mine in Mexico, and wanted to sell out and go down there as soon as he could, and give the property his personal attention. He played his cards well; said he would take $40,000—a quarter in cash, the rest in safe notes; but that as he greatly needed money on account of his new purchase, he would diminish his terms for cash in full. He sold out for $30,000. And then, what do you think he did? He asked for greenbacks, and took them, saying the man in Mexico was a New-Englander, with a head full of crotchets, and preferred greenbacks to gold or drafts. People thought it queer, since a draft on New York could produce *greenbacks* quite conveniently. There was talk of this odd thing, but only for a day; that is as long as any topic lasts in Denver.

I was watching, all the time. As soon as the sale was completed and the money paid—which was on the 11th—I began to stick to Puller's track without dropping it for a moment. That night—no, 12th, for it was a little past midnight—I tracked him to his room, which was four doors from mine in the same hall; then I went back and put on my muddy day-laborer disguise, darkened my complexion, and sat down in my room in the gloom, with a gripsack handy, with a change in it, and my door ajar. For I suspected that the bird would take wing now. In half an hour an old woman passed by, carrying a grip: I caught the familiar whiff, and followed with my grip, for it was Puller. He left the hotel by a side entrance, and at the corner he turned up an unfrequented street and walked three blocks in a light rain and a heavy darkness, and got into a two-horse hack, which of course was waiting for him by appointment. I took a seat (uninvited) on the trunk platform behind, and we drove briskly off. We drove ten miles, and the hack stopped at a way station and was discharged. Fuller got out and took a seat on a barrow under the awning, as far as he could get from the light; I went inside, and watched the ticket office. Fuller bought no ticket; I bought none. Presently the train came along, and he boarded a car; I entered the same car at the other end, and came down the aisle and took the seat behind him. When he paid the conductor and named his objective point, I dropped back several seats, while the conductor was changing a bill, and when he came to me I paid to the same place—about a hundred miles westward.

From that time for a week on end he led me a dance. He traveled here and there and yonder—always on a general westward trend—but he was not a woman after the first day. He was a laborer, like myself, and wore bushy false whiskers. His outfit was perfect, and he could do the character without thinking about it, for he had served the trade for wages. His nearest friend could not have recognized him. At last he located him self here, the obscurest little mountain camp in Montana; he has a shanty, and goes out prospecting daily; is gone all day, and avoids society. I am living at a miner's boardinghouse, and it is an awful place: the bunks, the food, the dirt—everything.

We have been here four weeks, and in that time I have seen him but once; but every night I go over his track and post myself. As soon as he engaged a shanty here I went to a town fifty miles away and telegraphed that Denver hotel to keep my baggage till I should send for it. I need nothing here but a change of army shirts, and I brought that with me.

SILVER GULCH, June 12.

The Denver episode has never found its way here, I think. I know most of the men in camp, and they have never referred to it, at least in my hearing. Puller doubtless feels quite safe in these conditions. He has located a claim, two miles away, in an out-of-the-way place in the mountains; it promises very well, and he is working it diligently. Ah, but the change in him! He never smiles, and he keeps quite to himself, consorting with no one—he who was so fond of company and so cheery only two months ago. I have seen him passing along several times recently—drooping, forlorn, the spring gone from his step, a pathetic figure. He calls himself David Wilson.

I can trust him to remain here until we disturb him. Since you insist, I will banish him again, but I do not see how he can be unhappier than he already is. I will go back to Denver and treat myself to a little season of comfort, and edible food, and endurable beds, and bodily decency; then I will fetch my things, and notify poor papa Wilson to move on.

DENVER, June 19.

They miss him here. They all hope he is prospering in Mexico, and they do not say it just with their mouths, but out of their hearts. You know you can always tell. I am loitering here overlong, I confess it. But if you were in my place you would have charity for me. Yes, I know what you will say, and you are right: if I were in your place, and carried *your* scalding memories in my heart—

I will take the night train back tomorrow.

DENVER, June 20.

God forgive us, mother, we are hunting the *wrong man!* I have not slept any all night. I am now waiting, at dawn, for the *morning* train—and how the minutes drag, how they drag!

This Jacob Puller is a *cousin* of the guilty one. How stupid we have been not to reflect that the guilty one would never again wear his own name after that fiendish deed! The Denver Puller is four years younger than the other one; he came here a young widower in '79, aged twenty-one—a year before you were married; and the documents to prove it are innumerable. Last night I talked with familiar friends of his who have known him from the day of his arrival. I said nothing, but a few days from now I will land him in this town again, with the loss upon his mine made good; and there will be a banquet, and a torchlight procession, and there will not be any expense on anybody but me. Do you call this "gush"? I am only a boy, as you well know; it is my privilege. By and by I shall not be a boy any more.

Silver Gulch, July 3.

Mother, he is gone! Gone, and left no trace. The scent was cold when I came. Today I am out of bed for the first time since. I wish I were not a boy; then I could stand shocks better. They all think he went west. I start tonight, in a wagon—two or three hours of that, then I get a train. I don't know where I'm going, but I must go; to try to keep still would be torture.

Of course he has effaced himself with a new name and a disguise. This means that *I may have to search the whole globe to find him.* Indeed it is what I expect. Do you see, mother? It is *I* that am the Wandering Jew. The irony of it! We arranged that for another.

Think of the difficulties! And there would be none if I only could advertise for him. But if there is any way to do it that would not frighten him, I have not been able to think it out, and I have tried till my brains are addled. "If the gentleman who lately bought a mine in Mexico and sold one in Denver will send his address to" (to whom, mother!), "it will be explained to him that it was all a mistake; his forgiveness will be asked, and full reparation made for a loss which he sustained in a certain matter." Do you see? He would think it a trap. Well, any one would. If I should say, "It is now known that he was not the man wanted, but another man—a man who once bore the same name, but discarded it for good reasons"—would that answer? But the Denver people would wake up then and say "Oho!" and they would remember about the suspicious greenbacks, and say, "Why did he run away if he wasn't the right man?—it is too thin." If I failed to find him he would be ruined there—there where there is no taint upon him now. You have a better head than mine. Help me.

I have one clue, and only one. I know his handwriting. If he puts his new false name upon a hotel register and does not disguise it too much, it will be valuable to me if I ever run across it.

SAN FRANCISCO, June 28, 1898.

You already know how well I have searched the states from Colorado to the Pacific, and how nearly I came to getting him once. Well, I have had another close miss. It was here, yesterday. I struck his trail, *hot*, on the street, and followed it on a run to a cheap hotel. That was a costly mistake; a dog would have gone the other way. But I am only part dog, and can get very humanly stupid when excited. He had been stopping in that house ten days; I almost know, now, that he stops long nowhere, the past six or eight months, but is restless and has to keep moving. I understand that feeling! and I know what it is to feel it. He still uses the name he had registered when I came so near catching him nine months ago—"James Walker"; doubtless the same he adopted when he fled from Silver Gulch. An unpretending man, and has small taste for fancy names. I recognized the hand easily, through its slight disguise. A square man, and not good at shams and pretenses.

They said he was just gone, on a journey; left no address; didn't say where he was going; looked frightened when asked to leave his address; had no baggage but a cheap valise; carried it off on foot—a "stingy old person, and not much loss to the house." "*Old!*" I suppose he is, now. I hardly heard; I was there but a moment. I rushed along his trail, and it led me to a wharf. Mother, the smoke of the steamer he had taken was just fading out on the horizon! I should have saved half an hour if I had gone in the right direction at first. I could have taken a fast tug, and should have stood a chance of catching that vessel. She is bound for Melbourne.

HOPE CAÑON, CALIFORNIA, October 3, 1900.

You have a fight to complain. "A letter a year" *is* a paucity; I freely acknowledge it; but how can one write when there is nothing to write about but failures? No one can keep it up; it breaks the heart.

I told you—it seems ages ago, now—how I missed him at Melbourne, and then chased him all over Australasia for months on end.

Well, then, after that I followed him to India; almost saw him in Bombay; traced him all around—to Baroda, Rawal-Pindi, Lucknow, Lahore, Cawnpore, Allahabad, Calcutta, Madras—oh, everywhere; week after week, month after month, through the dust and swelter—always approximately on his track, sometimes close upon him, yet never catching him. And down to Ceylon, and then to—Never mind; by and by I will write it all out.

I chased him home to California, and down to Mexico, and back again to California. Since then I have been hunting him about the state from the first of last January down to a month ago. I feel almost sure he is not far from Hope Cañon; I traced him to a point thirty miles from here, but there I lost the trail; some one gave him a lift in a wagon, I suppose.

I am taking a rest, now—modified by searchings for the lost trail. I was tired to death, mother, and low-spirited, and sometimes coming uncomfortably near to losing hope; but the miners in this little camp are good fellows, and I am used to their sort this long time back; and their breezy ways freshen a person up and make him forget his troubles. I have been here a month. I am cabining with a young fellow named "Sammy" Hillyer, about twenty-five, the only son of his mother—like me—and loves her dearly, and writes to her every week—part of which is like me. He is a timid body, and in the matter of intellect—well, he cannot be depended upon to set a river on fire; but no matter, he is well liked; he is good and fine, and it is meat and bread and rest and luxury to sit and talk with him and have a comradeship again. I wish "James Walker" could have it. He had friends; he liked company. That brings up that picture of him, the time that I saw him last. The pathos of it! It comes before me often and often. At that very time, poor thing, I was girding up my conscience to make him move on again!

Hillyer's heart is better than mine, better than anybody's in the community, I suppose, for he is the one friend of the black sheep of the camp—Flint Buckner—and the only man Flint ever talks with or allows to talk with him. He says he knows Flint's history, and that it is trouble that has made him what he is, and so one ought to be as charitable toward him as one can. Now none but a pretty large heart could find space to accommodate a lodger like Flint Buckner, from all I hear about him outside. I think that this one detail will give you a better idea of Sammy's character than any labored-out description I could furnish you of him. In one of our talks he said something about like this: "Flint is a kinsman of mine, and he pours out all his troubles to me empties his breast from time to time, or I reckon it would burst. There couldn't be any unhappier man, Archy Stillman; his life had been made up of misery of mind—he isn't near as old as he looks. He has lost the feel of reposefulness and peace oh, years and years ago! He doesn't know what good luck is—never has had any; often says he wishes he was in the other hell, he is so tired of this one."

Chapter 4

No real gentleman will tell the naked truth in the presence of ladies.

It was a crisp and spicy morning in early October. The lilacs and laburnums, lit with the glory-fires of autumn, hung burning and flashing in the upper air, a fairy bridge provided by kind Nature for the wingless wild things that have their homes in the treetops and would visit together; the latch and the pomegranate flung their purple and yellow flames in brilliant broad splashes along the slanting sweep of the woodland; the sensuous fragrance of innumerable deciduous flowers rose upon the swooning atmosphere; far in the empty sky a solitary esophagus* slept upon motionless wing; everywhere brooded stillness, serenity, and the peace of God.

---

* From the Springfield *Republican*, April 12, 1902.

To the Editor of the Republican:

One of your citizens has asked me a question about the "esophagus," and I wish to answer him through you. This in the hope that the answer will get around, and save me some penmanship, for I have already replied to the same question more than several times, and am not getting as much holiday as I ought to have.

I published a short story lately, and it was in that that I put the esophagus. I will say privately that I expected it to bother some people—in fact, that was the intention—but the harvest has been larger than I was calculating upon. The esophagus has gathered in the guilty and the innocent alike, whereas I was only fishing for the innocent—the innocent and confiding. I knew a few of these would write and ask me; that would give me but little trouble; but I was not expecting that the wise and the learned would call upon me for succor. However, that has happened, and it is time for me to speak up and stop the inquiries if I can, for letter-writing is not restful to me, and I am not having so much fun out of this thing as I counted on. That you may understand the situation, I will insert a couple of sample inquiries. The first is from a public instructor in the Philippines:

Santa Cruz, Ilocos, Stir, P.I.
February 13, 1902.

My Dear Sir,—I have just been reading the first part of your latest story, entitled "A Double-barreled Detective Story," and am very much delighted with it. In Part IV, page 264,

October is the time—1900; Hope Cañon is the place, a silver-mining camp away down in the Esmeralda region. It is a secluded spot, high and remote; recent as to discovery; thought by its occupants to be rich in metal—a year or two's prospecting will decide that matter one way or the other. For inhabitants, the camp has about two hundred miners, one white woman and child, several Chinese washermen, five squaws, and a dozen vagrant buck Indians in rabbit-skin robes, battered plug hats, and tin-can necklaces. There are no mills as yet; no church, no newspaper. The camp has existed but two years; it has made no big strike; the world is ignorant of its name and place.

On both sides of the canon the mountains rise wall-like, three thousand feet, and the long spiral of straggling huts down in its narrow bottom gets a kiss from the sun only once a day, when he

Harper's Magazine for January, occurs this passage: "far in the empty sky a solitary 'esophagus' slept upon motionless wing; everywhere brooded stillness, serenity, and the peace of God." Now, there is one word I do not understand, namely, "esophagus." My only work of reference is the *Standard Dictionary*, but that fails to explain the meaning. If you can spare the time, I would be glad to have the meaning cleared up, as I consider the passage a very touching and beautiful one. It may seem foolish to you, but consider my lack of means away out in the northern part of Luzon.

Yours very truly.

Do you notice? Nothing in the paragraph disturbed him but that one word. It shows that that paragraph was most ably constructed for the deception it was intended to put upon the reader. It was my intention that it should read plausibly, and it is now plain that it does; it was my intention that it should be emotional and touching, and you see, yourself, that it fetched this public instructor. Alas, if I had but left that one treacherous word out, I should have scored! scored everywhere; and the paragraph would have slidden through every reader's sensibilities like oil, and left not a suspicion behind.

The other sample inquiry is from a professor in a New England university. It contains one naughty word (which I cannot bear to suppress), but he is not in the theological department, so it is no harm:

Dear Mr. Clemens: "Far in the empty sky a solitary esophagus slept upon motionless wing."

It is not often I get a chance to read much periodical literature, but I have just gone through at this belated period, with much gratification and edification, your "Double-barreled Detective Story."

But what in hell is an esophagus? I keep one myself, but it never sleeps in the air or anywhere else. My profession is to deal with words, and esophagus interested me the moment I lighted upon it. But as a companion of my youth used to say, "I'll be eternally, co-eternally cussed" if I can make it out. Is it a joke, or I an ignoramus?

Between you and me, I was almost ashamed of having fooled that man, but for pride's sake I was not going to say so. I wrote and told him it was a joke—and that is what I am now saying to my Springfield inquirer. And I told him to carefully read the whole paragraph, and he would find not a vestige of sense in any detail of it. This also I commend to my Springfield inquirer.

sails over at noon. The village is a couple of miles long; the cabins stand well apart from each other. The tavern is the only "frame" house the only house, one might say. It occupies a central position, and is the evening resort of the population. They drink there, and play seven-up and dominoes; also billiards, for there is a table, crossed all over with torn places repaired with court-plaster; there are some cues, but no leathers; some chipped balls which clatter when they run, and do not slow up gradually, but stop suddenly and sit down; there is a part of a cube of chalk, with a projecting jag of flint in it; and the man who can score six on a single break can set up the drinks at the bar's expense.

Flint Buckner's cabin was the last one of the village, going south; his silver-claim was at the other end of the village, northward, and a little beyond the last hut in that direction. He was a sour creature,

I have confessed. I am sorry—partially. I will not do so any more—for the present. Don't ask me any more questions; let the esophagus have a rest—on his same old motionless wing.

Mark Twain.

New York City, April 10, 1902.

(Editorial)

The "Double-barreled Detective Story," which appeared in *Harper's Magazine* for January and February last, is the most elaborate of burlesques on detective fiction, with striking melodramatic passages in which it is difficult to detect the deception, so ably is it done. But the illusion ought not to endure even the first incident in the February number. As for the paragraph which has so admirably illustrated the skill of Mr. Clemens's ensemble and the carelessness of readers, here it is:

"It was a crisp and spicy morning in early October. The lilacs and laburnums, lit with the glory-fires of autumn, hung burning and flashing in the upper air, a fairy bridge provided by kind nature for the wingless wild things that have their home in the treetops and would visit together; the latch and the pomegranate flung their purple and yellow flames in brilliant broad splashes along the slanting sweep of the woodland; the sensuous fragrance of innumerable deciduous flowers rose upon the swooning atmosphere; far in the empty sly a solitary esophagus slept upon motionless wings; everywhere brooded stillness, serenity, and the peace of God.

The success of Mark Twain's joke recalls to mind his story of the petrified man in the cavern, whom he described most punctiliously, first giving a picture of the scene, its impressive solitude, and all that; then going on to describe the majesty of the figure, casually mentioning that the thumb of his right hand rested against the side of his nose; then after further description observing that the fingers of the right hand were extended in a radiating fashion; and, recurring to the dignified attitude and position of the man, incidentally remarked that the thumb of the left hand was in contact with the little finger of the right—and so on. But was it so ingeniously written that Mark, relating the history years later in an article which appeared in that excellent magazine of the past, the Galaxy, declared that no one ever found out the joke, and, if we remember aright, that that astonishing old mockery was actually looked for in the region where he, as a Nevada newspaper editor, had located it. It is certain that Mark Twain's jumping frog has a good many more "pints" than any other frog.

unsociable, and had no companionships. People who had tried to get acquainted with him had regretted it and dropped him. His history was not known. Some believed that Sammy Hillyer knew it; others said no. If asked, Hillyer said no, he was not acquainted with it. Flint had a meek English youth of sixteen or seventeen with him, whom he treated roughly, both in public and in private; and of course this lad was applied to for information, but with no success. Fetlock Jones—name of the youth—said that Flint picked him up on a prospecting tramp, and as he had neither home nor friends in America, he had found it wise to stay and take Buckner's hard usage for the sake of the salary, which was bacon and beans. Further than this he could offer no testimony.

Fetlock had been in this slavery for a month now, and under his meek exterior he was slowly consuming to a cinder with the insults and humiliations which his master had put upon him. For the meek suffer bitterly from these hurts; more bitterly, perhaps, than do the manlier sort, who can burst out and get relief with words or blows when the limit of endurance has been reached. Good-hearted people wanted to help Fetlock out of his trouble, and tried to get him to leave Buckner; but the boy showed fright at the thought, and said he "dasn't." Pat Riley urged him, and said:

"You leave the damned hunks and come with me; don't you be afraid. I'll take care of *him.*"

The boy thanked him with tears in his eyes, but shuddered and said he "dasn't risk it"; he said Flint would catch him alone, some time, in the night, and then—"Oh, it makes me sick, Mr. Riley, to think of it."

Others said, "Run away from him; we'll stake you; skip out for the coast some night." But all these suggestions failed; he said Flint would hunt him down and fetch him back, just for meanness.

The people could not understand this. The boy's miseries went steadily on, week after week. It is quite likely that the people would have understood if they had known how he was employing his spare time. He slept in an out-cabin near Flint's; and there, nights, he nursed his bruises and his humiliations, and studied and studied over a single problem—how he could murder Flint Buckner and not be found out. It was the only joy he had in life; these hours were the only ones in the twenty-four which he looked forward to with eagerness and spent in happiness.

He thought of poison. No—that would not serve; the inquest would reveal where it was procured and who had procured it. He thought of a shot in the back in a lonely place when Flint would be homeward bound at midnight—his unvarying hour for the trip. No—somebody might be near, and catch him. He thought of stabbing him in his sleep. No—he might strike an inefficient blow, and Flint would seize him. He examined a hundred different ways—none of them would answer; for in even the very obscurest and secretest of them there was always the fatal defect of a *risk*, a chance, a possibility that he might be found out. He would have none of that.

But he was patient, endlessly patient. There was no hurry, he said to himself. He would never leave Flint till he left him a corpse; there was no hurry—he would find the way. It was somewhere, and he would endure shame and pain and misery until he found it. Yes, somewhere there was a way which would leave not a trace, not even the faintest clue to the murderer—there was no hurry—he would find that way, and then—oh, then, it would just be good to be alive! Meantime he would diligently keep up his reputation for meekness; and also, as always theretofore, he would allow no one to hear him say a resentful or offensive thing about his oppressor.

Two days before the before-mentioned October morning Flint had bought some things, and he and Fetlock had brought them home to Flint's cabin: a fresh box of candles, which they put in the corner; a tin can of blasting-powder, which they placed upon the candle-box; a keg of blasting-powder, which they placed under Flint's bunk; a huge coil of fuse, which they hung on a peg. Fetlock reasoned that Flint's mining operations had outgrown the pick, and that blasting was about to begin now. He had seen blasting done, and he had a notion of the process, but he had never helped in it. His conjecture was right—blasting-time had come. In the morning the pair carried fuse, drills, and the powder-can to the shaft; it was now eight feet deep, and to get into it and out of it a short ladder was used. They descended, and by command Fetlock held the drill—without any instructions as to the right way to hold it—and Flint proceeded to strike. The sledge came down; the drill sprang out of Fetlock's hand, almost as a matter of course.

"You mangy son of a nigger, is that any way to hold a drill? Pick it up! Stand it up! There hold fast. D—— you! *I'll* teach you!"

At the end of an hour the drilling was finished.

"Now, then, charge it."

The boy started to pour in the powder.

"Idiot!"

A heavy bat on the jaw laid the lad out.

"Get up! You can't lie sniveling there. Now, then, stick in the fuse *first. Now* put in the powder. Hold on, hold on! Are you going to fill the hole *all* up? Of all the sap-headed milksops I—Put in some dirt! Put in some gravel! Tamp it down! Hold on, hold on! Oh, great Scott! get out of the way!" He snatched the iron and tamped the charge himself, meantime cursing and blaspheming like a fiend. Then he fired the fuse, climbed out of the shaft, and ran fifty yards away, Fetlock following. They stood waiting a few minutes, then a great volume of smoke and rocks burst high into the air with a thunderous explosion; after a little there was a shower of descending stones; then all was serene again.

"I wish to God you'd been in it!" remarked the master.

They went down the shaft, cleaned it out, drilled another hole, and put in another charge.

"Look here! How much fuse are you proposing to waste? Don't you know how to time a fuse?"

"No, sir."

"You *don't!* Well, if you don't beat anything *I* ever saw!"

He climbed out of the shaft and spoke down:

"Well, idiot, are you going to be all day? Cut the fuse and light it!"

The trembling creature began:

"If you please, sir, I—"

"You talk back to *me?* Cut it and light it!"

The boy cut and lit.

"Ger-reat Scott! a one-minute fuse! I wish you were in—"

In his rage he snatched the ladder out of the shaft and ran. The boy was aghast.

"Oh, my God! Help! Help! Oh, save me!" he implored. "Oh, what can I do! What *can* I do!"

He backed against the wall as tightly as he could; the sputtering fuse frightened the voice out of him; his breath stood still; he stood gazing and impotent; in two seconds, three seconds, four he would be flying toward the sky torn to fragments. Then he had an inspiration. He sprang at the fuse; severed the inch of it that was left above ground, and was saved.

He sank down limp and half lifeless with fright, his strength gone; but he muttered with a deep joy:

"He has learnt me! I knew there was a way, if I would wait."

After a matter of five minutes Buckner stole to the shaft, looking worried and uneasy, and peered down into it. He took in the situation; he saw what had happened. He lowered the ladder, and the boy dragged himself weakly up it. He was very white. His appearance added something to Buckner's uncomfortable state, and he said, with a show of regret and sympathy which sat upon him awkwardly from lack of practice:

"It was an accident, you know. Don't say anything about it to anybody; I was excited, and didn't notice what I was doing. You're not looking well; you've worked enough for today; go down to my cabin and eat what you want, and rest. It's just an accident, you know, on account of my being excited."

"It scared me," said the lad, as he started away; "but I learnt something, so I don't mind it."

"Damned easy to please!" muttered Buckner, following him with his eye. "I wonder if he'll tell? Mightn't he? . . . I wish it *had* killed him."

The boy took no advantage of his holiday in the matter of resting; he employed it in work, eager and feverish and happy work. A thick growth of chaparral extended down the mountainside clear to Flint's cabin; the most of Fetlock's labor was done in the dark intricacies of that stubborn growth; the rest of it was done in his own shanty. At last was complete, and he said:

"If he's got any suspicions that I'm going to tell on him, he won't keep them long, tomorrow. He will see that I am the same milksop as I always was—all day and the next. And the day after tomorrow night there'll be an end of him; nobody will ever guess who finished him up nor how it was done. He dropped me the idea his own self, and that's odd."

Chapter 5

The next day came and went.

It is now almost midnight, and in five minutes the new morning will begin. The scene is in the tavern billiard room. Rough men in rough clothing, slouch-hats, breeches stuffed into boot-tops, some with vests, none with coats, are grouped about the boiler-iron stove, which has ruddy cheeks and is distributing a grateful warmth; the billiard balls are clucking; there is no other sound—that is, within; the wind is fitfully moaning without. The men look bored; also expectant. A hulking broad-shouldered miner, of middle age, with grizzled whiskers, and an unfriendly eye set in an unsociable face, rises, slips a coil of fuse upon his arm, gathers up some other personal properties, and departs without word or greeting to anybody. It is Flint Buckner. As the door closes behind him a buzz of talk breaks out.

"The regularest man that ever was," said Jake Parker, the blacksmith: "you can tell when it's twelve just by him leaving, without looking at your Waterbury."

"And it's the only virtue he's got, as far as I know," said Peter Hawes, miner.

"He's just a blight on this society," said Wells-Fargo's man, Ferguson. "If I was running this shop I'd make him say something, *some* time or other, or vamos the ranch." This with a suggestive glance at the barkeeper, who did not choose to see it, since the man under discussion was a good customer, and went home pretty well set up, every night, with refreshments furnished from the bar.

"Say," said Ham Sandwich, miner, "does any of you boys ever recollect of him asking you to take a drink?"

"*Him? Flint Buckner?* Oh, Laura!"

This sarcastic rejoinder came in a spontaneous general outburst in one form of words or another from the crowd. After a brief silence, Pat Riley, miner, said:

"He's the 15-puzzle, that cuss. And his boy's another one. *I* can't make them out."

"Nor anybody else," said Ham Sandwich; "and if they are 15-puzzles, how are you going to rank up that other one? When it comes to A 1 right-down solid mysteriousness, he lays over both of them. *Easy*—don't he?"

"You bet!"

Everybody said it. Every man but one. He was the newcomer—Peterson. He ordered the drinks all round, and asked who No. 3 might be. All answered at once, "Archy Stillman!"

"Is he a mystery?" asked Peterson.

"Is *he* a mystery? Is Archy *Stillman* a mystery?" said Wells-Fargo's man, Ferguson. "Why, the fourth dimension's foolishness to *him*."

For Ferguson was learned.

Peterson wanted to hear all about him; everybody wanted to tell him; everybody began. But Billy Stevens, the barkeeper, called the house to order, and said one at a time was best. He distributed the drinks, and appointed Ferguson to lead. Ferguson said:

"Well, he's a boy. And that is just about all we know about him. You can pump him till you are tired; it ain't any use; you won't get anything. At least about his intentions, or line of business, or where he's from, and such things as that. And as for getting at the nature and get-up of his main big chief mystery, why, he'll just change the subject, that's all. You can *guess* till you're black in the face—it's your privilege but suppose you do, where do you arrive at? Nowhere, as near as I can make out."

"What *is* his big chief one?"

"Sight, maybe. Hearing, maybe. Instinct, maybe. Magic, maybe. Take your choice grownups, twenty-five; children and servants, half price. Now I'll tell you what he can do. You can start here, and just disappear; you can go and hide wherever you want to, I don't care where it is, nor how far—and he'll go straight and put his finger on you."

"You don't mean it!"

"I just do, though. Weather's nothing to him—elemental conditions is nothing to him—he don't even take notice of them."

"Oh, come! Dark? Rain? Snow? Hey?"

"It's all the same to *him.* He don't give a damn."

"Oh, *say*—including *fog,* per'aps?"

"*Fog!* he's got an eye 't can plunk through it like a bullet."

"Now, boys, honor bright, what's he giving me?"

"It's a fact!" they all shouted. "Go on, Wells-Fargo."

"Well, sir, you can leave him here, chatting with the boys, and you can slip out and go to any cabin in this camp and open a book—yes, sir, a dozen of them—and take the page in your memory, and he'll start out and go straight to that cabin and open every one of them books at the right page, and call it off, and never make a mistake."

"He must be the devil!"

"More than one has thought it. Now I'll tell you a perfectly wonderful thing that he done. The other night he—"

There was a sudden great murmur of sounds outside, the door flew open, and an excited crowd burst in, with the camp's one white woman in the lead and crying:

"My child! my child! she's lost and gone! For the love of God help me to find Archy Stillman; we've hunted everywhere!"

Said the barkeeper:

"Sit down, sit down, Mrs. Hogan, and don't worry. He asked for a bed three hours ago, tuckered out tramping the trails the way he's always doing, and went upstairs. Ham Sandwich, run up and roust him out; he's in No. 14."

The youth was soon downstairs and ready. He asked Mrs. Hogan for particulars.

"Bless you, dear, there ain't any; I wish there was. I put her to sleep at seven in the evening, and when I went in there an hour ago to go to bed myself, she was gone. I rushed for your cabin, dear, and you wasn't there, and I've hunted for you ever since, at every cabin down the gulch, and now I've come up again, and I'm that distracted and scared and heartbroke; but, thanks to God, I've found you at last, dear heart, and you'll find my child. Come on! come quick!"

"Move right along, I'm with you, madam. Go to your cabin first."

The whole company streamed out to join the hunt. All the southern half of the village was up, a hundred men strong, and waiting outside, a vague dark mass sprinkled with twinkling lanterns. The mass fell into columns by threes and fours to accommodate itself to the narrow road, and strode briskly along southward in the wake of the leaders. In a few minutes the Hogan cabin was reached.

"There's the bunk," said Mrs. Hogan; "there's where she was; it's where I laid her at seven o'clock; but where she is now, God only knows."

"Hand me a lantern," said Archy. He set on the hard earth floor and knelt by it, pretending to examine the ground closely. "Here's her track," he said, touching the ground here and there and yonder with his finger. "Do you see?"

Several of the company dropped upon their knees and did their best to see. One or two thought they discerned something like a track; the others shook their heads and confessed that the smooth hard surface had no marks upon it which their eyes were sharp enough to discover. One said, "Maybe a child's foot could make a mark on it, but I don't see how."

Young Stillman stepped outside, held the light to the ground, turned leftward, and moved three steps, closely examining; then said, "I've got the direction—come along; take the lantern, somebody."

He strode off swiftly southward, the files following, swaying and bending in and out with the deep curves of the gorge. Thus a mile, and the mouth of the gorge was reached; before them stretched the sagebrush plain, dim, vast, and vague. Stillman called a halt, saying, "We mustn't start wrong, now; we must take the direction again."

He took a lantern and examined the ground for a matter of twenty yards; then said, "Come on; it's all right," and gave up the lantern. In and out among the sagebushes he marched, a quarter of a mile, bearing gradually to the right; then took a new direction and made another great semicircle; then changed again and moved due west nearly half a mile and stopped.

"She gave it up, here, poor little chap. Hold the lantern. You can see where she sat."

But this was in a slick alkali flat which was surfaced like steel, and no person in the party was quite hardy enough to claim an eyesight that could detect the track of a cushion on a veneer like that. The bereaved mother fell upon her knees and kissed the spot, lamenting.

"But where is she, then?" some one said. "She didn't stay here. We can see *that* much, anyway."

Stillman moved about in a circle around the place, with the lantern, pretending to hunt for tracks.

"Well!" he said presently, in an annoyed tone, "I don't understand it." He examined again. "No use. She was here that's certain; she never *walked* away from here and that's certain. It's a puzzle; I can't make it out."

The mother lost heart then.

"Oh, my God! oh, blessed Virgin! some flying beast has got her. I'll never see her again!"

"Ah, *don't* give up," said Archy. "We'll find her—don't give up."

"God bless you for the words, Archy Stillman? and she seized his hand and kissed it fervently.

Peterson, the newcomer, whispered satirically in Ferguson's ear: "Wonderful performance to find this place, wasn't it? Hardly worth while to come so far, though; any other supposititious place would have answered just as well—hey?"

Ferguson was not pleased with the innuendo. He said, with some warmth:

"Do you mean to insinuate that the child hasn't been here? I tell you the child has been here! Now if you want to get yourself into as tidy a little fuss as—"

"All right!" sang out Stillman. "Come, everybody, and look at this! It was right under our noses all the time, and we didn't see it."

There was a general plunge for the ground at the place where the child was alleged to have rested, and many eyes tried hard and hopefully to see the thing that Archy's finger was resting upon. There was a pause, then a several-barreled sigh of disappointment. Pat Riley and Ham Sandwich said, in the one breath:

"What is it, Archy? There's nothing here."

"Nothing? Do you call *that* nothing?" and he swiftly traced upon the ground a form with his finger. "There—don't you recognize it now? It's Injun Billy's track. He's got the child."

"God be praised!" from the mother.

"Take away the lantern. I've got the direction. Follow!"

He started on a run, racing in and out among the sagebushes a matter of three hundred yards, and disappeared over a sand-wave; the others struggled after him, caught him up, and found him waiting. Ten steps away was a little wickiup, a dim and formless shelter of rags and old horse-blankets, a dull light showing through its chinks.

"You lead, Mrs. Hogan," said the lad. "It's your privilege to be first."

All followed the sprint she made for the wickiup, and saw, with her, the picture its interior afforded. Injun Billy was sitting on the ground; the child was asleep beside him. The mother hugged it with a wild embrace, which included Archy Stillman, the grateful tears running down her face, and in a choked and broken voice she poured out a golden stream of that wealth of worshipping endearments which has its home in full richness nowhere but in the Irish heart.

"I find her bymeby it is ten o'clock," Billy explained. "She 'sleep out yonder, ve'y tired—face wet, been cryin', 'spose; fetch her home, feed her, she heap much hungry—go 'sleep 'gin."

In her limitless gratitude the happy mother waived rank and hugged him too, calling him "the angel of God in disguise." And he probably was in disguise if he was that kind of an official. He was dressed for the character.

At half past one in the morning the procession burst into the village singing, "When Johnny Comes Marching Home," waving its lanterns, and swallowing the drinks that were brought out all along its course. It concentrated at the tavern, and made a night of what was left of the morning.

Chapter 6

The next afternoon the village was electrified with an immense sensation. A grave and dignified foreigner of distinguished bearing and appearance had arrived at the tavern, and entered this formidable name upon the register:

SHERLOCK HOLMES

The news buzzed from cabin to cabin, from claim to claim; tools were dropped, and the town swarmed toward the center of interest. A man passing out at the northern end of the village shouted it to Pat Riley, whose claim was the next one to Flint Buckner's. At that time Fetlock Jones seemed to turn sick. He muttered to himself:

"Uncle *Sherlock!* The mean luck of it!—that he should come just when. . ." He dropped into a reverie, and presently said to himself: "But what's the use of being afraid of *him?* Anybody that knows him the way I do knows he can't detect a crime except where he plans it all out beforehand and arranges the clues and hires some fellow to commit it according to instructions. . . . Now there ain't going to *be* any clues this time so, what show has he got? None at all. No, sir; everything's ready. If I was to risk putting it off—. . . No, I won't run any risk like that. Flint Buckner goes out of this world tonight, for sure." Then another trouble presented itself. "Uncle Sherlock 'll be wanting to talk home matters with me this evening, and how am I going to get rid of him? for I've *got* to be at my cabin a minute or two about eight o'clock." This was an awkward matter, and cost him much thought. But he found a way to beat the difficulty. "We'll go for a walk, and I'll leave him in the road a minute, so that he won't see what it is I do: the best way to throw a detective off the track, anyway, is to have him along when you are preparing the thing. Yes, that's the safest—I'll take him with me."

Meantime the road in front of the tavern was blocked with villagers waiting and hoping for a glimpse of the great man. But he kept his room, and did not appear. None but Ferguson, Jake Parker the blacksmith, and Ham Sandwich had any luck. These enthusiastic admirers of the great scientific detective hired the tavern's detained-baggage lockup, which looked into the detective's room across a little alleyway ten or twelve feet wide, ambushed themselves in it, and cut some peep-holes in the window-blind. Mr. Holmes's blinds were down; but by and by he raised them. It gave the spies a hair-lifting but pleasurable thrill to find themselves face to face with the Extraordinary Man who had filled the world with the fame of his more than human ingenuities. There he sat—not a myth, not a shadow, but real, alive, compact of substance, and almost within touching distance with the hand.

"Look at that head!" said Ferguson, in an awed voice. "By gracious! *that's* a head!"

"You bet!" said the blacksmith, with deep reverence. "Look at his nose! look at his eyes! Intellect? Just a battery of it!"

"And that paleness," said Ham Sandwich. "Comes from thought—that's what it comes from. Hell! duffers like us don't know what real thought *is*."

"No more we don't," said Ferguson. "What we take for thinking is just blubber-and-slush."

"Right you are, Wells-Fargo. And look at that frown—that's *deep* thinking—away down, down, forty fathom into the bowels of things. He's on the track of something."

"Well, he is, and don't you forget it. Say—look at that awful gravity—look at that pallid solemnness—there ain't any corpse can lay over it."

"No, sir, not for dollars! And it's his'n by hereditary rights, too; he's been dead four times a'ready, and there's history for it. Three times natural, once by accident. I've heard say he smells damp and cold, like a grave. And he—"

"'Sh! Watch him! There he's got his thumb on the bump on the near corner of his forehead, and his forefinger on the off one. His think-works is just a-*grinding* now, you bet your other shirt."

"That's so. And now he's gazing up toward heaven and stroking his mustache slow, and—"

"Now he has rose up standing, and is putting his clues together on his left fingers with his right finger. See? he touches the fore-finger—now middle finger—now ring-finger—"

"Stuck!"

"Look at him scowl! He can't seem to make out *that* clue. So he—"

"See him smile!—like a tiger—and tally off the other fingers like nothing! He's got it, boys; he's got it sure!"

"Well, I should *say!* I'd hate to be in that man's place that he's after."

Mr. Holmes drew a table to the window, sat down with his back to the spies, and proceeded to write. The spies withdrew their eyes from the peep-holes, lit their pipes, and settled themselves for a comfortable smoke and talk. Ferguson said, with conviction:

"Boys, it's no use talking, he's a wonder! He's got the signs of it all over him."

"You hain't ever said a truer word than that, Wells-Fargo," said Jake Parker. "Say, wouldn't it 'a' been nuts if he'd a-been here last night?"

"Oh, by George, but wouldn't it!" said Ferguson. "Then we'd have seen *scientific* work. Intellect—just pure intellect—away up on the upper levels, dontchuknow. Archy is all right, and it don't become anybody to belittle *him*, I can tell you. But his gift is only just eyesight, sharp as an owl's, as near as I can make it out just a grand natural animal talent, no more, no less, and prime as far as it goes, but no intellect in it, and for awfulness and marvelousness no more to be compared to what this man does than—than—Why, let me tell you what *he'd* have done. He'd have stepped over to Hogan's and glanced—just glanced, that's all—at the premises, and that's enough. See everything? Yes, sir, to the last little detail; and he'd know more about that place than the Hogans would know in seven years. Next, he would sit down on the bunk, just as ca'm, and say to Mrs. Hogan—*Say*, Ham, consider that you are Mrs. Hogan. I'll ask the questions; you answer them."

"All right; go on."

" 'Madam, if you please attention—do not let your mind wander. Now, then—sex of the child?'

" 'Female, your Honor.'

" 'Um—female. Very good, very good. Age?'

" 'Turned six, your Honor.'

" 'Um—young, weak—two miles. Weariness will overtake it then. It will sink down and sleep. We shall find it two miles away, or less. Teeth?'

" 'Five, your Honor, and one a-coming.'

" 'Very good, very good, *very* good, indeed. 'You see, boys, *he* knows a clue when he sees it, when it wouldn't mean a dern thing to anybody else. 'Stockings, madam? Shoes?'

" 'Yes, your Honor—both.'

" 'Yarn, perhaps? Morocco?'

" 'Yarn, your Honor. And kip.'

" 'Um—kip. This complicates the matter. However, let it go—we shall manage. Religion?'

" 'Catholic, your Honor.'

" 'Very good. Snip me a bit from the bed blanket, please. Ah, thanks. Part wool—foreign make. Very well. A snip from some garment of the child's, please. Thanks. Cotton. Shows wear. An excellent clue, excellent. Pass me a pallet of the floor dirt, if you'll be so kind. Thanks, many thanks. Ah, admirable, admirable! *Now* we know where we are, I think.' You see, boys, he's got all the clues he wants now; he don't need anything more. Now, then, what does this Extraordinary Man do? He lays those snips and that dirt out on the table and leans over them on his elbows, and puts them together side by side and studies them—mumbles to himself, 'Female'; changes them around—mumbles, 'Six years old'; changes them this way and that—again mumbles: 'Five teeth—one a-coming—Catholic—yarn—cotton—kip—damn that kip.' Then he straightens up and gazes toward heaven, and plows his hands through his hair—plows and plows, muttering, 'Damn that kip!' Then he stands up and frowns, and begins to tally off his clues on his fingers—and gets stuck at the ring-finger. But only just a minute then his face glares all up in a smile like a house afire, and he straightens up stately and majestic, and says to the crowd, 'Take a lantern, a couple of you, and go down to Injun Billy's and fetch the child—

the rest of you go 'long home to bed; good-night, madam; good-night, gents.' And he bows like the Matterhorn, and pulls out for the tavern. That's *his* style, and the *Only*—scientific, intellectual—all over in fifteen minutes—no poking around all over the sage-brush range an hour and a half in a mass-meeting crowd for *him*, boys—you hear *me!*"

"By Jackson, it's grand!" said Ham Sandwich.

"Wells-Fargo, you've got him down to a dot. He ain't painted up any exacter to the life in the books. By George, I can juse *see* him—can't you, boys?"

"You bet you! It's just a photograft, that's what it is."

Ferguson was profoundly pleased with his success, and grateful. He sat silently enjoying his happiness a little while, then he murmured, with a deep awe in his voice,

"I wonder if God made him?"

There was no response for a moment; then Ham Sandwich said, reverently:

"Not all at one time, I reckon."

Chapter 7

At eight o'clock that evening two persons were groping their way past Flint Buckner's cabin in the frosty gloom. They were Sherlock Holmes and his nephew.

"Stop here in the road a moment, uncle," said Fetlock, "while I run to my cabin; I won't be gone a minute."

He asked for something—the uncle furnished it—then he disappeared in the darkness, but soon returned, and the talking-walk was resumed. By nine o'clock they had wandered back to the tavern. They worked their way through the billiard room, where a crowd had gathered in the hope of getting a glimpse of the Extraordinary Man. A royal cheer was raised. Mr. Holmes acknowledged the compliment with a series of courtly bows, and as he was passing out his nephew said to the assemblage:

"Uncle Sherlock's got some work to do, gentlemen, that'll keep him till twelve or one; but he'll be down again then, or earlier if he can, and hopes some of you'll be left to take a drink with him."

"By George, he's just a duke, boys! Three cheers for Sherlock Holmes, the greatest man that ever lived!" shouted Ferguson. "Hip, hip, hip—"

"Hurrah! hurrah! hurrah! Tiger?"

The uproar shook the building, so hearty was the feeling the boys put into their welcome. Upstairs the uncle reproached the nephew gently, saying:

"What did you get me into that engagement for?"

"I reckon you don't want to be unpopular, do you, uncle? Well, then, don't you put on any exclusiveness in a mining-camp, that's all. The boys admire you; but if you was to leave without taking a drink with them, they'd set you down for a snob. And besides, you said you had home talk enough in stock to keep us up and at it half the night."

The boy was right, and wise the uncle acknowledged it. The boy was wise in another detail which he did not mention—except to himself: "Uncle and the others will come handy—in the way of nailing an *alibi* where it can't be budged."

He and his uncle talked diligently about three hours. Then, about midnight, Fetlock stepped downstairs and took a position in the dark a dozen steps from the tavern, and waited. Five minutes later Flint Buckner came rocking out of the billiard room and almost brushed him as he passed.

"I've *got* him!" muttered the boy. He continued to himself, looking after the shadow form: "Good-bye—good-bye for good, Flint Buckner; you called my mother a—well, never mind what: it's all right, now; you're taking your last walk, friend."

He went musing back into the tavern. "From now till one is an hour. We'll spend it with the boys: it's good for the *alibi*."

He brought Sherlock Holmes to the billiard room, which was jammed with eager and admiring miners; the guest called the drinks, and the fun began. Everybody was happy; everybody was complimentary; the ice was soon broken, songs, anecdotes, and more drinks followed, and the pregnant minutes flew. At six minutes to one, when the jollity was at its highest—

Boom!

There was silence instantly. The deep sound came rolling and rumbling from peak to peak up the gorge, then died down, and ceased. The spell broke, then, and the men made a rush for the door, saying:

"Something's blown up!"

Outside, a voice in the darkness said, "It's away down the gorge; I saw the flash."

The crowd poured down the canon—Holmes, Fetlock, Archy Stillman, everybody. They made the mile in a few minutes. By the light of a lantern they found the smooth and solid dirt floor of Flint Buckner's cabin; of the cabin itself not a vestige remained, not a rag nor a splinter. Nor any sign of Flint. Search parties sought here and there and yonder, and presently a cry went up.

"Here he is!"

It was true. Fifty yards down the gulch they had found him—that is, they had found a crushed and lifeless mass which represented him. Fetlock Jones hurried thither with the others and looked.

The inquest was a fifteen-minute affair. Ham Sandwich, foreman of the jury, handed up the verdict, which was phrased with a certain unstudied literary grace, and closed with this finding, to wit:! that "deceased came to his death by his own act or some other person or persons unknown to this jury not leaving any family or similar effects behind but his cabin which was blown away and God have mercy on his soul amen."

Then the impatient jury rejoined the main crowd, for the storm-center of interest was there Sherlock Holmes. The miners stood silent and reverent in a half-circle, enclosing a large vacant space which included the front exposure of the site of the late premises. In this considerable space the Extraordinary Man was moving about, attended by his nephew with a lantern. With a tape he took measurements of the cabin site; of the distance from the wall of chaparral to the road; of the height of the chaparral bushes; also various other measurements. He gathered a rag here, a splinter there, and a pinch of earth yonder, inspected them profoundly, and preserved them. He took the "lay" of the place with a pocket-compass, allowing two seconds for magnetic variation. He took the time (Pacific) by his watch, correcting it for local time. He paced off the distance from the cabin site to the corpse, and corrected that for tidal differentiation. He took the altitude with a pocket-aneroid, and the temperature with a pocket-thermometer. Finally he said, with a stately bow:

"It is finished. Shall we return, gentlemen?"

He took up the line of march for the tavern, and the crowd fell into his wake, earnestly discussing and admiring the Extraordinary Man, and interlarding guesses as to the origin of the tragedy and who the author of it might be.

"My, but it's grand luck having him here hey, boys?" said Ferguson.

"It's the biggest thing of the century," said Ham Sandwich. "It'll go all over the world; you mark my words."

"*You* bet!" said Jake Parker, the blacksmith. "It'll boom this camp. Ain't it so, Wells-Fargo?"

"Well, as you want my opinion—if it's any sign of how I think about it, *I* can tell you this: yesterday I was holding the Straight Plush claim at two dollars a foot; I'd like to see the man that can get it at sixteen today."

"Right you are, Wells-Fargo! It's the grandest luck a new camp ever struck. Say, did you see him collar them little rags and dirt and things? What an eye! He just can't overlook a clue 'tain't *in* him."

"That's so. And they wouldn't mean a thing to anybody else; but to him, why, they're just a book—large print at that."

"Sure's you're born! Them odds and ends have got their little old secret, and they think there ain't anybody can pull it; but, land! when he sets his grip there they've got to squeal, and don't you forget it."

"Boys, I ain't sorry, now, that he wasn't here to roust out the child; this is a bigger thing, by a long sight. Yes, sir, and more tangled up and scientific and intellectual."

"I reckon we're all of us glad it's turned out this way. Glad? George! it ain't any name for it. Dontchuknow, Archy could've learnt something if he'd had the nous to stand by and take notice of how that man works the system. But no; he went poking up into the chaparral and just missed the whole thing."

"It's true as gospel; I seen it myself. Well, Archy's young. He'll know better one of these days."

"Say, boys, who do you reckon done it?"

That was a difficult question, and brought out a world of unsatisfying conjecture. Various men were mentioned as possibilities, but one by one they were discarded as not being eligible. No one but young Hillyer had been intimate with Flint Buckner; no one had really had a quarrel with him; he had affronted every man who had tried to make up to him, although not quite offensively enough to require bloodshed. There was one name that was upon every tongue from the start, but it was the last to get utterance—Fetlock Jones's. It was Pat Riley that mentioned it.

"Oh, well," the boys said, "of course we've all thought of him, because he had a million rights to kill Flint Buckner, and it was just his plain duty to do it. But all the same there's two things we can't get around: for one thing, he hasn't got the sand; and for another, he wasn't anywhere near the place when it happened."

"I know it," said Pat. "He was there in the billiard room with us when it happened."

"Yes, and was there all the time for an hour before it happened."

"It's so. And lucky for him, too. He'd have been suspected in a minute if it hadn't been for that."

Chapter 8

The tavern dining room had been cleared of all its furniture save one six-foot pine table and a chair. This table was against one end of the room; the chair was on it; Sherlock Holmes, stately, imposing, impressive, sat in the chair. The public stood. The room was full. The tobacco smoke was dense, the stillness profound.

The Extraordinary Man raised his hand to command additional silence; held it in the air a few moments; then, in brief, crisp terms he put forward question after question, and noted the answers with "Um-ums," nods of the head, and so on. By this process he learned all about Flint Buckner, his character, conduct, and habits, that the people were able to tell him. It thus transpired that the Extraordinary Man's nephew was the only person in the camp who had a killing-grudge against Flint Buckner. Mr. Holmes smiled compassionately upon the witness, and asked, languidly:

"Do any of you gentlemen chance to know where the lad Fetlock Jones was at the time of the explosion?"

A thunderous response followed:

"In the billiard room of this house!"

"Ah. And had he just come in?"

"Been there all of an hour!"

"Ah. It is about—about—well, about how far might it be to the scene of the explosion?"

"All of a mile!"

"Ah. It isn't *much* of an alibi, 'tis true, but—"

A storm-burst of laughter, mingled with shout of "By jimmy, but he's chain-lightning!" and "Ain't you sorry you spoke, Sandy?" shut off the rest of the sentence, and the crushed witness drooped his blushing face in pathetic shame. The inquisitor resumed:

"The lad Jones's somewhat *distant* connection with the case" (*laughter*) "having been disposed of let us now call the eyewitnesses of the tragedy, and listen to what they have to say."

He got out his fragmentary clues and arranged them on a sheet of cardboard on his knee. The house held its breath and watched.

"We have the longitude and the latitude, corrected for magnetic variation, and this gives us the exact location of the tragedy. We have the altitude, the temperature, and the degree of humidity prevailing—inestimably valuable, since they enable us to estimate with precision the degree of influence which they would exercise upon the mood and disposition of the assassin at that time of the night."

(*Buzz of admiration; muttered remark, "By George, but he's deep!"*) He fingered his clues. "And now let us ask these mute witnesses to speak to us.

"Here we have an empty linen shot-bag. What is its message? This: that robbery was the motive, not revenge. What is its further message? This: that the assassin was of inferior intelligence shall we say light-witted, or perhaps approaching that? How do we know this? Because a person of sound intelligence would not have proposed to rob the man Buckner, who never had much money with him. But the assassin might have been a stranger? Let the bag speak again. I take from it this article. It is a bit of silver-bearing quartz. It is peculiar. Examine it, please—you—and you—and you. Now pass it back, please. There is but one lode on this coast which produces just that character and color of quartz; and that is a lode which crops out for nearly two miles on a stretch, and in my opinion is destined, at no distant day, to confer upon its locality a globe-girdling celebrity, and upon its two hundred owners riches beyond the dreams of avarice. Name that lode, please."

"The Consolidated Christian Science and Mary Ann!" was the prompt response.

A wild crash of hurrahs followed, and every man reached for his neighbor's hand and wrung it, with tears in his eyes; and Wells-Fargo Ferguson shouted, "The Straight Plush is on the lode, and up she goes to a hundred and fifty a foot—you hear *me!*"

When quiet fell, Mr. Holmes resumed:

"We perceive, then, that three facts are established, to wit: the assassin was approximately light-witted; he was not a stranger; his motive was robbery, not revenge. Let us proceed. I hold in my hand a small fragment of fuse, with the recent smell of fire upon it. What is its testimony? Taken with the corroborative evidence of the quartz, it reveals to us that the assassin was a miner. What does it tell us further? This, gentlemen: that the assassination was consummated by means of an explosive. What else does it say? This: that the explosive was located against the side of the cabin nearest the road—the front side—for within six feet of that spot I found it.

"I hold in my fingers a burnt Swedish match—the kind one rubs on a safety-box. I found it in the road, six hundred and twenty-two feet from the abolished cabin. What does it say? This: that the train was fired from that point. What further does it tell us? This: that the assassin was left-handed. How do I know this? I should not be able to explain to you, gentlemen, how I know it, the signs being so subtle that only long experience and deep study can enable one to detect them. But the signs are here, and they are reinforced by a fact which you must have often noticed in the great detective narratives that *all* assassins are left-handed."

"By Jackson, *that's* so!" said Ham Sandwich, bringing his great hand down with a resounding slap upon his thigh; "blamed if I ever thought of it before."

"Nor I!" "Nor I!" cried several. "Oh, there can't anything escape *him*—look at his eye!"

"Gentlemen, distant as the murderer was from his doomed victim, he did not wholly escape injury. This fragment of wood which I now exhibit to you struck him. It drew blood. Wherever he is, he bears the telltale mark. I picked it up where he stood when he fired the fatal train." He looked out over the house from his high perch, and his countenance began to darken; he slowly raised his hand, and pointed:

"There stands the assassin!"

For a moment the house was paralyzed with amazement; then twenty voices burst out with:

"Sammy Hillyer? Oh, *hell*, no! *Him!* It's pure foolishness!"

"Take care, gentlemen—be not hasty. Observe—he has the blood-mark on his brow."

Hillyer turned white with fright. He was near to crying. He turned this way and that, appealing to every face for help and sympathy; and held out his supplicating hands toward Holmes and began to plead:

"*Don't,* oh, don't! I never did it; I give my word I never did it. The way I got this hurt on my forehead was—"

"Arrest him, constable!" cried Holmes. "I will swear out the warrant."

The constable moved reluctantly forward—hesitated—stopped.

Hillyer broke out with another appeal. "Oh, Archy, don't let them do it; it would kill mother! *You* know how I got the hurt. Tell them, and save me, Archy; save me!"

Stillman worked his way to the front, and said:

"Yes, I'll save you. Don't be afraid." Then he said to the house, "Never mind how he got the hurt; it hasn't anything to do with this case, and isn't of any consequence."

"God bless you, Archy, for a true friend!"

"Hurrah for Archy! Go in, boy, and play 'em a knock-down flush to their two pair 'n' a jack!" shouted the house, pride in their home talent and a patriotic sentiment of loyalty to it rising suddenly in the public heart and changing the whole attitude of the situation.

Young Stillman waited for the noise to cease; then he said:

"I will ask Tom Jeffries to stand by that door yonder, and Constable Harris to stand by the other one here, and not let anybody leave the room."

"Said and done. Go on, old man!"

"The criminal is present, I believe. I will show him to you before long, in case I am right in my guess. Now I will tell you all about the tragedy, from start to finish. The motive *wasn't* robbery; it was revenge. The murderer *wasn't* light-witted. He *didn't* stand six hundred and twenty-two feet away. He *didn't* get hit with a piece of wood. He *didn't* place the explosive against the cabin. He *didn't* bring a shot-bag with him, and he *wasn't* left-handed. With the exception of these errors, the distinguished guest's statement of the case is substantially correct."

A comfortable laugh rippled over the house; friend nodded to friend, as much as to say, "That's the word, with the bark *on* it. Good lad, good boy. *He* ain't lowering his flag any!"

The guest's serenity was not disturbed. Stillman resumed:

"I also have some witnesses; and I will presently tell you where you can find some more." He held up a piece of coarse wire; the crowd craned their necks to see. "It has a smooth coating of melted tallow on it. And here is a candle which is burned half-way down. The remaining half of it has marks cut upon it an inch apart. Soon I will tell you where I found these things. I will now put aside reasonings, guesses, the impressive hitchings of odds and ends of clues together, and the other show theatricals of the detective trade, and tell you in a plain, straightforward way just how this dismal thing happened."

He paused a moment, for effect—to allow silence and suspense to intensify and concentrate the house's interest; then he went on:

"The assassin studied out his plan with a good deal of pains. It was a good plan, very ingenious, and showed an intelligent mind, not a feeble one. It was a plan which was well calculated to ward off all suspicion from its inventor. In the first place, he marked a candle into spaces an inch apart, and lit it and timed it. He found it took three hours to burn four inches of it. I tried it myself for half an hour, awhile ago, upstairs here, while the inquiry into Flint Buckner's character and ways was being conducted in this room, and I arrived in that way at the rate of a candle's consumption when sheltered from the wind. Having proved his trial candle's rate, he blew it out—I have already shown it to you—and put his inch-marks on a fresh one.

"He put the fresh one into a tin candlestick. Then at the five-hour mark he bored a hole through the candle with a red-hot wire. I have already shown you the wire, with a smooth coat of tallow on it—tallow that had been melted and had cooled.

"With labor—very hard labor, I should say—he struggled up through the stiff chaparral that clothes the steep hillside back of Flint Buckner's place, tugging an empty flour-barrel with him. He placed it in that absolutely secure hiding-place, and in the bottom of it he set the candlestick. Then he measured off about thirty-five feet of fuse—the barrel's distance from the back of the cabin. He bored a hole in the side of the barrel—here is the large gimlet he did it with. He went on and finished his work; and when it was done, one end of the fuse was in Buckner's cabin, and the other end, with a notch chipped in it to expose the powder, was in the hole in the candle—timed to blow the place up at one o'clock this morning, provided the candle was lit about eight o'clock yesterday evening—which I am betting it was—and provided there was an explosive in the cabin and connected with that end of the fuse—which I am also betting there was, though I can't prove it. Boys, the barrel is there in the chaparral, the candle's remains are in it in the tin stick; the burnt-out fuse is in the gimlet-hole, the other end is down the hill where the late cabin stood. I saw them all an hour or two ago, when the Professor here was measuring off unimplicated vacancies and collecting relics that hadn't anything to do with the case."

He paused. The house drew a long, deep breath, shook its strained cords and muscles free and burst into cheers. "Dang him!" said Ham Sandwich, "that's why he was snooping around in the chaparral, instead of picking up points out the P'fessor's game. Looky here—he ain't no fool, boys."

"No, sir! Why, great Scott—"

But Stillman was resuming:

"While we were out yonder an hour or two ago, the owner of the gimlet and the trial candle took them from a place where he had concealed them—it was not a good place—and carried them to what he probably thought was a better one, two hundred yards up in the pine woods, and hid them there, covering them over with pine needles. It was there that I found them. The gimlet exactly fits the hole in the barrel. And now—"

The Extraordinary Man interrupted him. He said, sarcastically:

"We have had a very pretty fairy tale, gentlemen—very pretty indeed. Now I would like to ask this young man a question or two."

Some of the boys winced, and Ferguson said: "I'm afraid Archy's going to catch it now."

The others lost their smiles and sobered down. Mr. Holmes said:

"Let us proceed to examine into this fairy tale in a consecutive and orderly way—by geometrical progression, so to speak—linking detail to detail in a steadily advancing and remorselessly consistent and unassailable march upon this tinsel toy fortress of error, the dream fabric of a callow imagination. To begin with, young sir, I desire to ask you but three questions at present—*at present.* Did I understand you to say it was your opinion that the supposititious candle was lighted at about eight o'clock yesterday evening?"

"Yes, sir—about eight."

"Could you say exactly eight?"

"Well, no, I couldn't be that exact."

"Um. If a person had been passing along there just about that time, he would have been almost sure to encounter that assassin, do you think?"

"Yes, I should think so."

"Thank you, that is all. For the present. I say, all *for the present.*"

"Dern him! he's lying for Archy," said Ferguson.

"It's so," said Ham Sandwich. "I don't like the look of it."

Stillman said, glancing at the guest, "I was along there myself at half-past eight—no, about nine."

"In-deed? This is interesting—this is very interesting. Perhaps you encountered the assassin?"

"No, I encountered no one."

"Ah. Then—if you will excuse the remark—I do not quite see the relevancy of the information."

"It has none. At present. I say it has none at present."

He paused. Presently he resumed: "I did not encounter the assassin, but I am on his track, I am sure, for I believe he is in this room. I will ask you all to pass one by one in front of me here, where there is a good light—so that I can see your feet."

A buzz of excitement swept the place, and the march began, the guest looking on with an iron attempt at gravity which was not an unqualified success. Stillman stooped, shaded his eyes with his hand, and gazed down intently at each pair of feet as it passed. Fifty men tramped monotonously by—with no result. Sixty. Seventy. The thing was beginning to look absurd. The guest remarked, with suave irony:

"Assassins appear to be scarce this evening."

The house saw the humor of it, and refreshed itself with a cordial laugh. Ten or twelve more candidates tramped by—no, danced by, with airy and ridiculous capers which convulsed the spectators—then suddenly Stillman put out his hand and said:

"This is the assassin!"

"Fetlock Jones, by the great Sanhedrim!" roared the crowd; and at once let fly a pyrotechnic explosion and dazzle and confusion of stirring remarks inspired by the situation.

At the height of the turmoil the guest stretched out his hand, commanding peace. The authority of a great name and a great personality laid its mysterious compulsion upon the house, and it obeyed. Out of the panting calm which succeeded, the guest spoke, saying, with dignity and feeling:

"*This* is serious. It strikes at an innocent life. Innocent beyond suspicion! Innocent beyond peradventure! Hear me *prove* it; observe how simple a fact can brush out of existence this witless lie. Listen. My friends, that lad was never out of my sight yesterday evening at *any* time!"

It made a deep impression. Men turned their eyes upon Stillman with grave inquiry in them. His face brightened, and he said:

"I *knew* there was another one!" He stepped briskly to the table and glanced at the guest's feet, then up at his face, and said: "You were *with* him! You were not fifty steps from him when he lit the candle that by and by fired the powder!" (*Sensation.*) "And what is more, you furnished the matches yourself!"

Plainly the guest seemed hit; it looked so to the public. He opened his mouth to speak; the words did not come freely.

"This—er—this is insanity—this—"

Stillman pressed his evident advantage home. He held up a charred match.

"Here is one of them. I found it in the barrel—and there's *another* one there."

The guest found his voice at once.

"*Yes*—and put them there yourself!"

It was recognized a good shot. Stillman retorted.

"It is *wax*—a breed unknown to this camp. I am ready to be searched for the box. Are you?"

The guest was staggered this time the dullest eye could see it. He fumbled with his hands; once or twice his lips moved, but the words did not come. The house waited and watched, in tense suspense, the stillness adding effect to the situation. Presently Stillman said, gently:

"We are waiting for your decision."

There was silence again during several moments; then the guest answered, in a low voice:

"I refuse to be searched."

There was no noisy demonstration, but all about the house one voice after another muttered:

"That settles it! He's Archy's meat."

What to do now? Nobody seemed to know. It was an embarrassing situation for the moment—merely, of course, because matters had taken such a sudden and unexpected turn that these unpracticed minds were not prepared for it, and had come to a standstill, like a stopped clock, under the shock. But after a little the machinery began to work again, tentatively, and by twos and threes the men put their heads together and privately buzzed over this and that and the other proposition. One of these propositions met with much favor; it was, to confer upon the assassin a vote of thanks for removing Flint Buckner, and let him go. But the cooler heads opposed it, pointing out that addled brains in the Eastern states would pronounce it a scandal, and make no end of foolish noise about it. Finally the cool heads got the upper hand, and obtained general consent to a proposition of their own; their leader then called the house to order and stated it—to this effect: that Fetlock Jones be jailed and put upon trial.

The motion was carried. Apparently there was nothing further to do now, and the people were glad, for, privately, they were impatient to get out and rush to the scene of the tragedy, and see whether that barrel and the other things were really there or not.

But no—the breakup got a check. The surprises were not over yet. For a while Fetlock Jones had been silently sobbing, unnoticed in the absorbing excitements which had been following one another so persistently for some time; but when his arrest and trial were decreed, he broke out despairingly, and said:

"No! it's no use. I don't want any jail, I don't want any trial; I've had all the hard luck I want, and all the miseries. Hang me now, and let me out! It would all come out, anyway—there couldn't anything save me. He has told it all, just as if he'd been with me and seen it—*I* don't know how he found out; and you'll find the barrel and things, and then I wouldn't have any chance any more. I killed him; and *you'd* have done it too, if he'd treated you like a dog, and you only a boy, and weak and poor, and not a friend to help you."

"And served him damned well right!" broke in Ham Sandwich. "Looky here, boys—"

From the constable: "Order! Order, gentlemen!"

A voice: "Did your uncle know what you was up to?"

"No, he didn't."

"Did he give you the matches, sure enough?"

"Yes, he did; but he didn't know what I wanted them for."

"When you was out on such a business as that, how did you venture to risk having him along—and him a *detective?* How's that?"

The boy hesitated, fumbled with his buttons in an embarrassed way, then said, shyly:

"I know about detectives, on account of having them in the family; and if you don't want them to find out about a thing, it's best to have them around when you do it."

The cyclone of laughter which greeted this naive discharge of wisdom did not modify the poor little waif's embarrassment in any large degree.

Chapter 9

From a letter to Mrs. Stillman, dated merely "Tuesday."

Fetlock Jones was put under lock and key in an unoccupied log cabin, and left there to await his trial. Constable Harris provided him with a couple of days' rations, instructed him to keep a good guard over himself, and promised to look in on him as soon as further supplies should be due.

Next morning a score of us went with Hillyer, out of friendship, and helped him bury his late relative, the unlamented Buckner, and I acted as first assistant pallbearer, Hillyer acting as chief. Just as we had finished our labors a ragged and melancholy stranger, carrying an old handbag, limped by with his head down, and I caught the scent I had chased around the globe! It was the odor of Paradise to my perishing hope!

In a moment I was at his side and had laid a gentle hand upon his shoulder. He slumped to the ground as if a stroke of lightning had withered him in his tracks; and as the boys came running he struggled to his knees and put up his pleading hands to me, and out of his chattering jaws he begged me to persecute him no more, and said:

"You have hunted me around the world, Sherlock Holmes, God is my witness I have never done any man harm!"

A glance at his wild eyes showed us that he was insane. That was my work, mother! The tidings of your death can some day repeat the misery I felt in that moment, but nothing else can ever do it. The boys lifted him up, and gathered about him, and were full of pity of him, and said the gentlest and touchingest things to him, and said cheer up and don't be troubled, he was among friends now, and they would take care of him, and protect him, and hang any man that laid a hand on him. They are just like so many mothers, the rough mining camp boys are, when you wake up the south side of their hearts; yes, and just like so many reckless and unreasoning children when you wake up the opposite of that muscle. They did everything they could think of to comfort him, but nothing succeeded until Wells-Fargo Ferguson, who is a clever strategist, said:

"If it's only Sherlock Holmes that's troubling you, you needn't worry any more."

"Why?" asked the forlorn lunatic, eagerly.

"Because he's dead again."

"Dead! Dead! Oh, don't trifle with a poor wreck like me. *Is* he dead? On honor, now—is he telling me true, boys?"

"True as you're standing there!" said Ham Sandwich, and they all backed up the statement in a body.

"They hung him in San Bernardino last week," added Ferguson, clinching the matter, "whilst he was searching around after you. Mistook him for another man. They're sorry, but they can't help it now."

"They're a-building him a monument," said Ham Sandwich, with the air of a person who had contributed to it, and knew.

"James Walker" drew a deep sigh—evidently a sigh of relief—and said nothing; but his eyes lost something of their wildness, his countenance cleared visibly, and its drawn look relaxed a little. We all went to our cabin, and the boys cooked him the best dinner the camp could furnish the materials for, and while they were about it Hillyer and I outfitted him from hat to shoe-leather with new clothes of ours, and made a comely and presentable old gentleman of him. "Old" is the right word, and a pity, too: old by the droop of him, and the frost upon his hair, and the marks which sorrow and distress have left upon his face; though he is only in his prime in the matter of years. While he ate, we smoked and chatted; and when he was finishing he found his voice at last, and of his own accord broke out with his personal history. I cannot furnish his exact words, but I will come as near it as I can.

THE "WRONG MAN'S" STORY

It happened like this: I was in Denver. I had been there many years; sometimes I remember how many, sometimes I don't—but it isn't any matter. All of a sudden I got a notice to leave, or

I would be exposed for a horrible crime committed long before—years and years before—in the East.

I knew about that crime, but I was not the criminal; it was a cousin of mine of the same name. What should I better do? My head was all disordered by fear, and I didn't know. I was allowed very little time—only one day, I think it was. I would be ruined if I was published, and the people would lynch me, and not believe what I said. It is always the way with lynching: when they find out it is a mistake they too are sorry, but it is late—the same as it was with Mr. Holmes, you see. So I said I would sell out and get money to live on, and run away until it blew over and I could come back with my proofs. Then I escaped in the fight and went a long way off in the mountains somewhere, and lived disguised and had a false name.

I got more and more troubled and worried, and my troubles made me see spirits and hear voices, and I could not think straight and clear on any subject, but got confused and involved and had to give it up, because my head hurt so. It got to be worse and worse; more spirits and more voices. They were about me all the time; at first only in the night, then in the day too. They were always whispering around my bed and plotting against me, and it broke my sleep and kept me ragged out, because I got no good rest.

And then came the worst. One fight the whispers said, "We'll never manage, because we can't *see* him, and so can't point him out to the people."

They sighed; then one said: "We must bring Sherlock Holmes. He can be here in twelve days."

They all agreed, and whispered and jibbered with joy. But my heart broke; for I had read about that man, and knew what it would be to have him upon my track, with his superhuman penetration and tireless energies.

The spirits went away to fetch him, and I got up at once in the middle of the night and fled away, carrying nothing but the handbag that had my money in it—thirty thousand dollars; two-thirds of it are in the bag there yet. It was forty days before that man caught up on my track. I just escaped. From habit he had written his real name on a tavern register, but had scratched it out and written "Dagger Barclay" in the place of it. But fear gives you a watchful eye and keen, and I read the true name through the scratches, and fled like a deer.

He has hunted me all over this world for three years and a

half—the Pacific states, Australasia, India—everywhere you can think of; then back to Mexico and up to California again, giving me hardly any rest; but that name on the registers always saved me, and what is left of me is alive yet. And I am so tired! A cruel time he has given me, yet I give you my honor I have never harmed him nor any man.

That was the end of the story, and it stirred those boys to bloodheat, be sure of it. As for me—each word burnt a hole in me where it struck.

We voted that the old man should bunk with us, and be my guest and Hillyer's. I shall keep my own counsel, naturally; as soon as he is well rested and nourished, I shall take him to Denver and rehabilitate his fortunes.

The boys gave the old fellow the bone-smashing good-fellowship handshake of the mines, and then scattered away to spread the news.

At dawn next morning Wells-Fargo Ferguson and Ham Sandwich called us softly out, and said, privately:

"That news about the way that old stranger has been treated has spread all around, and the camps are up. They are piling in from everywhere, and are going to lynch the P'fessor. Constable Harris is in a dead funk, and has telephoned the sheriff. Come along!"

We started on a run. The others were privileged to feel as they chose, but in my heart's privacy I hoped the sheriff would arrive in time; for I had small desire that Sherlock Holmes should hang for my deeds, as you can easily believe. I had heard a good deal about the sheriff, but for reassurance's sake I asked:

"Can he stop a mob?"

"Can *he* stop a mob! Can Jack *Fairfax* stop a mob! Well, I should smile! Ex-desperado—nineteen scalps on his string. Can *he!* Oh, I *say!*"

As we tore up the gulch, distant cries and shouts and yells rose faintly on the still air, and grew steadily in strength as we raced along. Roar after roar burst out, stronger and stronger, nearer and nearer; and at last, when we closed up upon the multitude massed in the open area in front of the tavern, the crash of sound was deafening. Some brutal roughs from Daly's gorge had Holmes in their grip, and he was the calmest man there; a contemptuous smile played about his lips, and if any fear of death was in his British heart, his iron personality was master of it and no sign of it was allowed to appear.

"Come to a vote, men!" This from one of the Daly gang, Shadbelly Higgins. "Quick! is it hang, or shoot?"

"Neither!" shouted one of his comrades. "He'd be alive again in a week; burning's the only permanency for *him.*"

The gangs from all the outlying camps burst out in a thunder-crash of approval, and went struggling and surging toward the prisoner, and dosed around him, shouting, "Fire! fire's the ticket!" They dragged him to the horse-post, backed him against it, chained him to it, and piled wood and pine cones around him waist-deep. Still the strong face did not blench, and still the scornful smile played about the thin lips.

"A match! fetch a match!"

Shadbelly struck it, shaded it with his hand, stooped, and held it under a pine cone. A deep silence fell upon the mob. The cone caught, a tiny flame flickered about it a moment or two. I seemed to catch the sound of distant hoofs—it grew more distinct—still more and more distinct, more and more definite, but the absorbed crowd did not appear to notice it. The match went out. The man struck another, stooped, and again the flame rose; this time it took hold and began to spread—here and there men turned away their faces. The executioner stood with the charred match in his fingers, watching his work. The hoofbeats turned a projecting crag, and now they came thundering down upon us. Almost the next moment there was a shout:

"The sheriff!"

And straightway he came tearing into the midst, stood his horse almost on his hind feet, and said:

"Fall back, you guttersnipes!"

He was obeyed. By all but their leader. He stood his ground, and his hand went to his revolver. The sheriff covered him promptly, and said:

"Drop your hand, you parlor desperado. Kick the fire away. Now unchain the stranger."

The parlor desperado obeyed. Then the sheriff made a speech; sitting his horse at martial ease, and not warming his words with any touch of fire, but delivering them in a measured and deliberate way, and in a tone which harmonized with their character and made them impressively disrespectful.

"You're a nice lot—now ain't you? Just about eligible to travel with this bilk here—Shadbelly Higgins—this loudmouthed sneak that shoots people in the back and calls himself a desperado. If there's anything I do particularly despise, it's a lynching mob; I've never seen one that had a man in it. It has to tally up a hundred against one before it can pump up pluck enough to tackle a sick tailor. It's made up of cowards, and so is the community that breeds it; and ninety-nine times out of a hundred the sheriff's another one." He paused—apparently to turn that last idea over in his mind and taste the juice of it—then he went on: "The sheriff that lets a mob take a prisoner away from him is the lowest-down coward there is. By the statistics there was a hundred and eighty-two of them drawing sneak pay in America last year. By the way it's going, pretty soon there'll be a new disease in the doctor-books—*sheriff complaint.*" That idea pleased him—any one could see it. "People will say, 'Sheriff sick again?' 'Yes; got the same old thing.' And next there'll be a new title. People won't say, 'He's running for sheriff of Rapaho County,' for instance; they'll say, 'He's running for Coward of Rapaho.' Lord, the idea of a grown-up person being afraid of a lynch mob!"

He turned an eye on the captive, and said, "Stranger, who are you, and what have you been doing?"

"My name is Sherlock Holmes, and I have not been doing anything."

It was wonderful, the impression which the sound of that name made on the sheriff, notwithstanding he must have come posted. He spoke up with feeling, and said it was a blot on the country that a man whose marvelous exploits had filled the world with their fame and their ingenuity, and whose histories of them had won every reader's heart by the brilliancy and charm of their literary setting, should be visited under the stars and Stripes by an outrage like this. He apologized in the name of the whole nation, and made Holmes a most handsome bow, and told Constable Harris to see him to his quarters, and hold himself personally responsible if he was molested again. Then he turned to the mob and said:

"Hunt your holes, you scum!" which they did; then he said: "Follow me, Shadbelly; I'll take care of your case myself. No—keep your pop-gun; whenever I see the day that I'll be afraid to have you behind me with that thing, it'll be time for me to join last year's hundred and eighty-two;" and he rode off in a walk, Shadbelly following.

When we were on our way back to our cabin, toward breakfast-time, we ran upon the news that Fetlock Jones had escaped from his lock-up in the night and is gone! Nobody is sorry. Let his uncle track him out if he likes; it is in his line; the camp is not interested.

Chapter X

Ten days later.

"James Walker" is all right in body now, and his mind shows improvement too. I start with him for Denver tomorrow morning.

Next night. Brief note, mailed at a way-station.

As we were starting, this morning, Hillyer whispered to me: "Keep this news from Walker until you think it safe and not likely to disturb his mind and check his improvement: the ancient crime he spoke of was really committed—and by his cousin, as he said. *We buried the real criminal* the other day—the unhappiest man that has lived in a century—Flint Buckner. His real name was Jacob Fuller? There, mother, by help of me, an unwitting mourner, your husband and my father is in his grave. Let him rest.

The Five Boons of Life

I

In the morning of life came the good fairy with her basket and said:

"Here are gifts. Take one, leave the others. And be wary choose wisely; oh, choose wisely! for only one of them is valuable."

The gifts were five: Fame, Love, Riches, Pleasure, Death. The youth said eagerly:

"There is no need to consider"; and he chose Pleasure.

He went out into the world and sought out the pleasures that youth delights in. But each in its turn was short-lived and disappointing, vain and empty; and each, departing, mocked him. In the end he said: "These years I have wasted. If I could but choose again, I would choose wisely."

II

The fairy appeared, and said:

"Four of the gifts remain. Choose once more; and oh, remember—time is flying, and only one of them is precious."

The man considered long, then chose Love; and did not mark the tears that rose in the fairy's eyes.

After many, many years the man sat by a coffin, in an empty home. And he communed with himself, saying: "One by one they have gone away and left me; and now she lies here, the dearest and the last. Desolation after desolation has swept over me; for each hour of happiness the treacherous trader, Love, has sold me I have paid a thousand hours of grief. Out of my heart of hearts I curse him."

III

"Choose again." It was the fairy speaking. "The years have taught you wisdom—surely it must be so. Three gifts remain. Only one of them has any worth—remember it, and choose warily."

The man reflected long, then chose Fame; and the fairy, sighing, went her way.

Years went by and she came again, and stood behind the man where he sat solitary in the fading day, thinking. And she knew his thought:

"My name filled the world, and its praises were on every tongue, and it seemed well with me for a little while. How little a while it was! Then came envy; then detraction; then calumny; then hate; then persecution. Then derision, which is the beginning of the end. And last of all came pity, which is the funeral of fame. Oh, the bitterness and misery of renown! target for mud in its prime, for contempt and compassion in its decay."

IV

"Choose yet again." It was the fairy's voice. "Two gifts remain. And do not despair. In the beginning there was but one that was precious, and it is still here."

"Wealth—which is power! How blind I was!" said the man. "Now, at last, life will be worth the living. I will spend, squander, dazzle. These mockers and despisers will crawl in the dirt before me, and I will feed my hungry heart with their envy. I will have all luxuries, all joys, all enchantments of the spirit, all contentments of the body that man holds dear. I will buy, buy, buy! deference, respect, esteem, worship—every pinchbeck grace of life the market of a trivial world can furnish forth. I have lost much time, and chosen badly heretofore, but let that pass; I was ignorant then, and could but take for best what seemed so."

Three short years went by, and a day came when the man sat shivering in a mean garret; and he was gaunt and wan and hollow-eyed, and clothed in rags; and he was gnawing a dry crust and mumbling:

"Curse all the world's gifts, for mockeries and gilded lies! And miscalled, every one. They are not gifts, but merely lendings. Pleasure, Love, Fame, Riches: they are but temporary disguises for lasting realities—Pain, Grief, Shame, Poverty. The fairy said true; in all her store there was but one gift which was precious, only one that was not valueless. How poor and cheap and mean I know those others now to be, compared with that inestimable one, that dear and sweet and kindly one, that steeps in dreamless and enduring sleep the pains that persecute the body, and the shames and griefs that eat the mind and heart. Bring it! I am weary. I would rest."

V

The fairy came, bringing again four of the gifts, but Death was wanting. She said:

"I gave it to a mother's pet, a little child. It was ignorant, but trusted me, asking me to choose for it. You did not ask me to choose."

"Oh, miserable me! What is there left for me?"

"What not even you have deserved: the wanton insult of Old Age."

Was It Heaven? Or Hell?

I

"You told a *lie?*"

"You confess it—you actually confess it—you told a lie!"

II

The family consisted of four persons: Margaret Lester, widow, aged thirty-six; Helen Lester, her daughter, aged sixteen; Mrs. Lester's maiden aunts, Hannah and Hester Gray, twins, aged sixty-seven. Waking and sleeping, the three women spent their days and nights in adoring the young girl; in watching the movements of her sweet spirit in the mirror of her face; in refreshing their souls with the vision of her bloom and beauty; in listening to the music of her voice; in gratefully recognizing how rich and fair for them was the world with this presence in it; in shuddering to think how desolate it would be with this light gone out of it.

By nature—and inside—the aged aunts were utterly dear and lovable and good, but in the matter of morals and conduct their training had been so uncompromisingly strict that it had made them exteriorly austere, not to say stern. Their influence was effective in the house; so effective that the mother and the daughter conformed to its moral and religious requirements cheerfully, contentedly, happily, unquestioningly. To do this was become second nature to them. And so in this peaceful heaven there were no clashings, no irritations, no fault-findings, no heart-burnings.

In it a lie had no place. In it a lie was unthinkable. In it speech was restricted to absolute truth, iron-bound truth, implacable and uncompromising truth, let the resulting consequences be what they might. At last, one day, under stress of circumstances, the darling of the house sullied her lips with a lie—and confessed it, with tears and self-upbraidings. There are not any words that can paint the consternation of the aunts. It was as if the sky had crumpled up and collapsed and the earth had tumbled to ruin with a crash. They sat side by side, white and stern, gazing speechless upon the culprit, who was on her knees before them with her face buried first in one lap and then the other, moaning and sobbing, and appealing for sympathy and forgiveness and getting no response, humbly kissing the hand of the one, then of the other, only to see it withdrawn as suffering defilement by those soiled lips.

Twice, at intervals, Aunt Hester said, in frozen amazement,

"You told a *lie?*"

Twice, at intervals, Aunt Hannah followed with the muttered and amazed ejaculation,

"You confess it—you actually confess it—you told a lie!"

It was all they could say. The situation was new, unheard-of, incredible; they could not understand it, they did not know how to take hold of it, it approximately paralyzed speech.

At length it was decided that the erring child must be taken to her mother, who was ill, and who ought to know what had happened. Helen begged, besought, implored that she might be spared this further disgrace, and that her mother might be spared the grief and pain of it; but this could not be: duty required this sacrifice, duty takes precedence of all things, nothing can absolve one from a duty, with a duty no compromise is possible.

Helen still begged, and said the sin was her own, her mother had had no hand in it—why must she be made to suffer for it?

But the aunts were obdurate in their righteousness, and said the law that visited the sins of the parent upon the child was by all right and reason reversible; and therefore it was but just that the innocent mother of a sinning child should suffer her rightful share of the grief and pain and shame which were the allotted wages of the sin.

The three moved toward the sickroom.

At this time the doctor was approaching the house. He was still a good distance away, however. He was a good doctor and a good man, and he had a good heart, but one had to know him a year to get over hating him, two years to learn to endure him, three to learn to like him, and four or five to learn to love him. It was a slow and trying education, but it paid. He was of great stature; he had a leonine head, a leonine face, a rough voice, and an eye which was sometimes a pirate's and sometimes a woman's, according to the mood. He knew nothing about etiquette, and cared nothing about it; in speech, manner, carriage, and conduct he was the reverse of conventional. He was flank, to the limit; he had opinions on all subjects; they were always on tap and ready for delivery, and he cared not a farthing whether his listener liked them or didn't. Whom he loved he loved, and manifested it; whom he didn't love he hated, and published it from the house-tops. In his young days he had been a sailor, and the salt airs of all the seas blew from him yet. He was a sturdy and loyal Christian, and believed he was the best one in the land, and the only one whose Christianity was perfectly sound, healthy, full-charged with common-sense, and had no decayed places in it. People who had an ax to grind, or people who for any reason wanted to get on the soft side of him, called him The Christian—a phrase whose delicate flattery was music to his ears, and whose capital T was such an enchanting and vivid object to him that he could *see* it when it fell out of a person's mouth even in the dark. Many who were fond of him stood on their consciences with both feet and brazenly called him by that large title habitually, because it was a pleasure to them to do anything that would please him; and with eager and cordial malice his extensive and diligently cultivated crop of enemies gilded it, beflowered it, expanded it to "The *Only* Christian." Of these two titles, the latter had the wider currency; the enemy, being greatly in the majority, attended to that. Whatever the doctor believed, he believed with all his heart, and would fight for it whenever he got the chance; and if the intervals between chances grew to be irksomely wide, he would invent ways of shortening them himself. He was severely conscientious, according to his rather independent lights, and whatever he took to be a duty he performed, no matter whether the judgment of the professional moralists agreed with his own or not. At sea, in his young days, he had used profanity freely, but as soon as he was converted he made a rule, which he rigidly stuck to ever afterwards, never to use it except on the rarest occasions, and then only when duty commanded. He had been a hard drinker at sea, but after his conversion he became a firm and outspoken teetotaler, in order to be an example to the young, and from that time forth he seldom drank; never, indeed, except when it seemed to him to be a duty—a condition which sometimes occurred a couple of times a year, but never as many as five times.

Necessarily such a man is impressionable, impulsive, emotional. This one was, and had no gift at hiding his feelings; or if he had it he took no trouble to exercise it. He carried his soul's prevailing weather in his face, and when he entered a room the parasols or the umbrellas went up—figuratively speaking—according to the indications. When the soft light was in his eye it meant approval, and delivered a benediction; when he came with a frown he lowered the temperature ten degrees. He was a well-beloved man in the house of his friends, but sometimes a dreaded one.

He had a deep affection for the Lester household, and its several members returned this feeling with interest. They mourned over his kind of Christianity, and he frankly scoffed at theirs; but both parties went on loving each other just the same.

He was approaching the house—out of the distance; the aunts and the culprit were moving toward the sick-chamber.

III

The three last named stood by the bed; the aunts austere, the transgressor softly sobbing. The mother turned her head on the pillow; her tired eyes flamed up instantly with sympathy and passionate mother-love when they fell upon her child, and she opened the refuge and shelter of her arms.

"Wait!" said Aunt Hannah, and put out her hand and stayed the girl from leaping into them.

"Helen," said the other aunt, impressively, "tell your mother all. Purge your soul; leave nothing unconfessed."

Standing stricken and forlorn before her judges, the young girl mourned her sorrowful tale through to the end, then in a passion of appeal cried out:

"Oh, mother, can't you forgive me? won't you forgive me?—I am so desolate!"

"Forgive you, my darling? Oh, come to my arms!—there, lay your head upon my breast, and be at peace. If you had told a thousand lies—"

There was a sound—a warning—the clearing of a throat. The aunts glanced up, and withered in their clothes—there stood the doctor, his face a thundercloud. Mother and child knew nothing of his presence; they lay locked together, heart to heart, steeped in immeasurable content, dead to all things else. The physician stood many moments glaring and glooming upon the scene before him; studying it, analyzing it, searching out its genesis; then he put up his hand and beckoned to the aunts. They came trembling to him and stood humbly before him and waited. He bent down and whispered:

"Didn't I tell you this patient must be protected from all excitement? What the hell have you been doing? Clear out of the place!"

They obeyed. Half an hour later he appeared in the parlor, serene, cheery, clothed in sunshine, conducting Helen, with his arm about her waist, petting her, and saying gentle and playful things to her; and she also was her sunny and happy self again.

"Now, then," he said, "good-bye, dear. Go to your room, and keep away from your mother, and behave yourself. But wait—put out your tongue. There, that will do—you're as sound as a nut!" He patted her cheek and added, "Run along now; I want to talk to these aunts."

She went from the presence. His face clouded over again at once; and as he sat down he said:

"You two have been doing a lot of damage—and maybe some good. Some good, yes—such as it is. That woman's disease is typhoid! You've brought it to a show-up, I think, with your insanities, and that's a service—such as it is. I hadn't been able to determine what it was before."

With one impulse the old ladies sprang to their feet, quaking with terror.

"Sit down! What are you proposing to do?"

"Do? We must fly to her. We—"

"You'll do nothing of the kind; you've done enough harm for one day. Do you want to squander all your capital of crimes and follies on a single deal? Sit down, I tell you. I have arranged for her to sleep; she needs it; if you disturb her without my orders, I'll brain you—if you've got the materials for it."

They sat down, distressed and indignant, but obedient, under compulsion. He proceeded:

"Now, then, I want this case explained. *They* wanted to explain it to me—as if there hadn't been emotion and excitement enough already. You knew my orders; how did you dare to go in there and get up that riot?"

Hester looked appealingly at Hannah; Hannah returned a beseeching look at Hester—neither wanted to dance to this unsympathetic orchestra. The doctor came to their help. He said,

"Begin, Hester."

Fingering at the fringes of her shawl, and with lowered eyes, Hester said, timidly:

"We should not have disobeyed for any ordinary cause, but this was vital. This was a duty. With a duty one has no choice; one must put all lighter considerations aside and perform it. We were obliged to arraign her before her mother. She had told a lie."

The doctor glowered upon the woman a moment, and seemed to be trying to work up in his mind an understanding of a wholly incomprehensible proposition; then he stormed out:

"She told a lie! *Did* she? God bless my soul! I tell a million a day! And so does every doctor. And so does everybody—including you—for that matter. And *that* was the important thing that authorized you to venture to disobey my orders and imperil that woman's life! Look here, Hester Gray, this is pure lunacy; that girl *couldn't* tell a lie that was intended to injure a person. The thing is impossible—absolutely impossible. You know it yourselves—both of you; you know it perfectly well."

Hannah came to her sister's rescue:

"Hester didn't mean that it was that kind of a lie, and it wasn't. But it was a lie."

"Well, upon my word, I never heard such nonsense! Haven't you got sense enough to discriminate between lies? Don't you know the difference between a lie that helps and a lie that hurts?"

"*All* lies are sinful," said Hannah, setting her lips together like a vise; "all lies are forbidden."

The Only Christian fidgeted impatiently in his chair. He wanted to attack this proposition, but he did not quite know how or where to begin. Finally he made a venture:

"Hester, wouldn't you tell a lie to shield a person from an undeserved injury or shame?"

"No."

"Not even a friend?"

"No."

"Not even your dearest friend?"

"No. I would not."

The doctor struggled in silence awhile with this situation; then he asked,

"Not even to save him from bitter pain and misery and grief?"

"No. Not even to save his life."

Another pause. Then,

"Nor his soul."

There was a hush—a silence which endured a measurable interval—then Hester answered, in a low voice, but with decision,

"Nor his soul."

No one spoke for a while; then the doctor said,

"Is it with you the same, Hannah?"

"Yes," she answered.

"I ask you both—why?"

"Because to tell such a lie, or any lie, is a sin, and could cost us the loss of our own souls—*would*, indeed, if we died without time to repent."

"Strange . . . strange . . . it is past belief." Then he asked, roughly, "Is such a soul as that *worth* saving?" He rose up, mumbling and grumbling, and started for the door, stumping vigorously along. At the threshold he turned and rasped out an admonition: "Reform! Drop this mean and sordid and selfish devotion to the saving of your shabby little souls, and hunt up something to do that's got some dignity to it! Risk your souls! risk them in good causes; then if you lose them, why should you care? Reform!"

The good old gentlewomen sat paralyzed, pulverized, outraged, insulted, and brooded in bitterness and indignation over these blasphemies. They were hurt to the heart, poor old ladies, and said they could never forgive these injuries.

"Reform!"

They kept repeating that word resentfully. "Reform—and learn to tell lies!"

Time slipped along, and in due course a change came over their spirits. They had completed the human being's first duty—which is to think about himself until he has exhausted the subject, then he is in a condition to take up minor interests and think of other people. This changes the complexion of his spirits—generally wholesomely. The minds of the two old ladies reverted to their beloved niece and the fearful disease which had smitten her; instantly they forgot the hurts their self-love had received, and a passionate desire rose in their hearts to go to the help of the sufferer and comfort her with their love, and minister to her, and labor for her the best they could with their weak hands, and joyfully and affectionately wear out their poor old bodies in her dear service if only they might have the privilege.

"And we shall have it!" said Hester, with the tears running down her face. "There are no nurses comparable to us, for there are no others that will stand their watch by that bed till they drop and die, and God knows we would do that."

"Amen," said Hannah, smiling approval and endorsement through the mist of moisture that blurred her glasses. "The doctor knows us, and knows we will not disobey again; and he will call no others. He will not dare!"

"Dare?" said Hester, with temper, and dashing the water from her eyes; "he will dare anything—that Christian devil! But it will do no good for him to try it this time—but, laws! Hannah, after all's said and done, he is gifted and wise and good, and he would not think of such a thing . . . . It is surely time for one of us to go to that room. What is keeping him? Why doesn't he come and say so?"

They caught the sound of his approaching step. He entered, sat down, and began to talk.

"Margaret is a sick woman," he said. "She is still sleeping, but she will wake presently; then one of you must go to her. She will be worse before she is better. Pretty soon a night-and-day watch must be set. How much of it can you two undertake?"

"All of it!" burst from both ladies at once.

The doctor's eyes flashed, and he said, with energy:

"You *do* ring true, you brave old relics! And you shall do all of the nursing you can, for there's none to match you in that divine office in this town; but you can't do all of it, and it would be a crime to let you." It was grand praise, golden praise, coming from such a source, and it took nearly all the resentment out of the aged twins' hearts. "Your Tilly and my old Nancy shall do the rest—good nurses both, white souls with black skins, watchful, loving, tender—just perfect nurses!—and competent liars from the cradle. . . . Look you! keep a little watch on Helen; she is sick, and is going to be sicker."

The ladies looked a little surprised, and not credulous; and Hester said:

"How is that? It isn't an hour since you said she was as sound as a nut."

The doctor answered, tranquilly,

"It was a lie."

The ladies turned upon him indignantly, and Hannah said,

"How can you make an odious confession like that, in so indifferent a tone, when you know how we feel about all forms of—"

"Hush! You are as ignorant as cats, both of you, and you don't know what you are talking about. You are like all the rest of the moral moles: you lie from morning till night, but because you don't do it with your mouths, but only with your lying eyes, your lying inflections, your deceptively misplaced emphasis, and your misleading gestures, you turn up your complacent noses and parade before God and the world as saintly and unsmirched Truth-Speakers, in whose cold-storage souls a lie would freeze to death if it got there! Why will you humbug yourselves with that foolish notion that no lie is a lie except a spoken one? What is the difference between lying with your eyes and lying with your mouth? There is none; and if you would reflect a moment you would see that it is so. There isn't a human being that doesn't tell a gross of lies every day of his life; and you—why, between you, you tell thirty thousand; yet you flare up here in a lurid hypocritical horror because I tell that child a benevolent and sinless lie to protect her from her imagination, which would get to work and warm up her blood to a fever in an hour, if I were disloyal enough to my duty to let it. Which I should probably do if I were interested in saving my soul by such disreputable means.

"Come, let us reason together. Let us examine details. When you two were in the sickroom raising that riot, what would you have done if you had known I was coming?"

"Well, what?"

"You would have slipped out and carried Helen with you—wouldn't you?"

The ladies were silent.

"What would be your object and intention?"

"Well, what?"

"To keep me from finding out your guilt; to beguile me to infer that Margaret's excitement proceeded from some cause not known to you. In a word, to tell me a lie—a silent lie. Moreover, a possibly harmful one."

The twins colored, but did not speak.

"You not only tell myriads of silent lies, but you tell lies with your mouths—you two."

"*That* is not so!"

"It is so. But only harmless ones. You never dream of uttering a harmful one. Do you know that that is a concession—and a confession?"

"How do you mean?"

"It is an unconscious concession that harmless lies are not criminal; it is a confession that you constantly *make* that discrimination. For instance, you declined old Mrs. Foster's invitation last week to meet those odious Higbies at supper—in a polite note in which you expressed regret and said you were very sorry you could not go. It was a lie. It was as unmitigated a lie as was ever uttered. Deny it, Hester—with another lie."

Hester replied with a toss of her head.

"That will not do. Answer. Was it a lie, or wasn't it?"

The color stole into the cheeks of both women, and with a struggle and an effort they got out their confession: "It was a lie."

"Good—the reform is beginning; there is hope for you yet; you will not tell a lie to save your dearest friend's soul, but you will spew out one without a scruple to save yourself the discomfort of telling an unpleasant truth."

He rose. Hester, speaking for both, said, coldly:

"We have lied; we perceive it; it will occur no more. To lie is a sin. We shall never tell another one of any kind whatsoever, even lies of courtesy or benevolence, to save any one a pang or a sorrow decreed for him by God."

"Ah, how soon you will fall! In tact, you have fallen already; for what you have just uttered is a lie. Good-bye. Reform! One of you go to the sickroom now."

IV

Twelve days later.

Mother and child were lingering in the grip of the hideous disease. Of hope for either there was little. The aged sisters looked white and worn, but they would not give up their posts. Their hearts were breaking, poor old things, but their grit was steadfast and indestructible. All the twelve days the mother had pined for the child, and the child for the mother, but both knew that the prayer of these longings could not be granted. When the mother was told—on the first day—that her disease was typhoid, she was frightened, and asked if there was danger that Helen could have contracted it the day before, when she was in the sick-chamber on that confession visit. Hester told her the doctor had poo-poo'd the idea. It troubled Hester to say it, although it was true, for she had not believed the doctor; but when she saw the mother's joy in the news, the pain in her conscience lost something of its force—a result which made her ashamed of the constructive deception which she had practiced though not ashamed enough to make her distinctly and definitely wish she had refrained from it. From that moment the sick woman understood that her daughter must remain away, and she said she would reconcile herself to the separation the best she could, for she would rather suffer death than have her child's health imperiled. That afternoon Helen had to take to her bed, ill. She grew worse during the night. In the morning her mother asked after her:

"Is she well?"

Hester turned cold; she opened her lips, but the words refused to come. The mother lay languidly looking, musing, waiting; suddenly she turned white and gasped out, "Oh, my God! what is it? is she sick?"

Then the poor aunt's tortured heart rose in rebellion, and words came:

"No—be comforted; she is well."

The sick woman put all her happy heart in her gratitude:

"Thank God for those dear words! Kiss me. How I worship you for saying them."

Hester told this incident to Hannah, who received it with a rebuking look, and said, coldly,

"Sister, it was a lie."

Hester's lips trembled piteously; she choked down a sob, and said,

"Oh, Hannah, it was a sin, but I could not help it; I could not endure the flight and the misery that were in her face."

"No matter. It was a lie. God will hold you to account for it."

"Oh, I know it, I know it," cried Hester, wringing her hands, "but even if it were now, I could not help it. I know I should do it again."

"Then take my place with Helen in the morning. I will make the report myself."

Hester clung to her sister, begging and imploring: "Don't, Hannah, oh, don't—you will kill her."

"I will at least speak the truth."

In the morning she had a cruel report to bear to the mother, and she braced herself for the trial. When she returned from her mission, Hester was waiting, pale and trembling, in the hall. She whispered,

"Oh, how did she take it—that poor, desolate mother?" Hannah's eyes were swimming in tears. She said,

"God forgive me, I told her the child was well!"

Hester gathered her to her heart, with a grateful "God bless you, Hannah!" and poured out her thankfulness in an inundation of worshipping praises.

After that, the two knew the limit of their strength, and accepted their fate. They surrendered humbly, and abandoned themselves to the hard requirements of the situation. Daily they told the morning lie, and confessed their sin in prayer; not asking forgiveness, as not being worthy of it, but only wishing to make record that they realized their wickedness and were not desiring to hide it or excuse it.

Daily, as the fair young idol of the house sank lower and lower, the sorrowful old aunts painted her glowing bloom and her fresh young beauty to the wan mother, and winced under the stabs her ecstasies of joy and gratitude gave them.

In the first days, while the child had strength to hold a pencil, she wrote fond little love notes to her mother, in which she concealed her illness; and these the mother read and re-read through happy eyes wet with thankful tears, and kissed them over and over again, and treasured them as precious things under her pillow.

Then came a day when the strength was gone from the hand, and the mind wandered, and the tongue babbled pathetic incoherences. This was a sore dilemma for the poor aunts. There were no love notes for the mother. They did not know what to do. Hester began a carefully studied and plausible explanation, but lost the track of it and grew confused; suspicion began to show in the mother's face, then alarm. Hester saw it, recognized the imminence of the danger, and descended to the emergency, pulling herself resolutely together and plucking victory from the open jaws of defeat. In a placid and convincing voice she said:

"I thought it might distress you to know it, but Helen spent the night at the Sloanes'. There was a little parry there, and although she did not want to go, and you so sick, we persuaded her, she being young and needing the innocent pastimes of youth, and we believing you would approve. Be sure she will write the moment she comes."

"How good you are, and how dear and thoughtful for us both! Approve? Why, I thank you with all my heart. My poor little exile! Tell her I want her to have every pleasure she can—I would not rob her of one. Only let her keep her health, that is all I ask. Don't let that suffer; I could not bear it. How thankful I am that she escaped this infection—and what a narrow risk she ran, Aunt Hester! Think of that lovely face all dulled and burnt with fever. I can't bear the thought of it. Keep her health. Keep her bloom! I can see her now, the dainty creature—with the big blue earnest eyes; and sweet, oh, so sweet and gentle and winning! Is she as beautiful as ever, dear Aunt Hester?"

"Oh, more beautiful and bright and charming than ever she was before, if such a thing can be"—and Hester turned away and fumbled with the medicine bottles, to hide her shame and grief.

V

After a little, both aunts were laboring upon a difficult and baffling work in Helen's chamber. Patiently and earnestly, with their stiff old fingers, they were trying to forge the required note. They made failure after failure, but they improved little by little all the time. The pity of it all, the pathetic humor of it, there was none to see; they themselves were unconscious of it. Often their tears fell upon the notes and spoiled them; sometimes a single misformed word made a note risky which could have been ventured but for that; but at last Hannah produced one whose script was a good enough imitation of Helen's to pass any but a suspicious eye, and bountifully enriched it with the petting phrases and loving nicknames that had been familiar on the child's lips from her nursery days. She carried it to the mother, who took it with avidity, and kissed it, and fondled it, reading its precious words over and over again, and dwelling with deep contentment upon its closing paragraph:

"Mousie darling, if I could only see you, and kiss your eyes, and feel your arms about me! I am so glad my practicing does not disturb you. Get well soon. Everybody is good to me, but I am so lonesome without you, dear mamma."

"The poor child, I know just how she feels. She cannot be quite happy without me; and I—oh, I live in the light of her eyes! Tell her she must practice all she pleases; and, Aunt Hannah—tell her I can't hear the piano this far, nor her dear voice when she sings: God knows I wish I could. No one knows how sweet that voice is to me; and to think—some day it will be silent! What are you crying for?"

"Only because—because—it was just a memory. When I came away she was singing 'Loch Lomond.' The pathos of it! It always moves me so when she sings that."

"And me, too. How heartbreakingly beautiful it is when some youthful sorrow is brooding in her breast and she sings it for the mystic healing it brings. . . . . Aunt Hannah?"

"Dear Margaret?"

"I am very ill. Sometimes it comes over me that I shall never hear that dear voice again."

"Oh, don't—don't, Margaret! I can't bear it!"

Margaret was moved and distressed, and said, gently: "There—there—let me put my arms around you. Don't cry. There—put your cheek to mine. Be comforted. I wish to live. I will live if I can. Ah, what could she do without me! . . . Does she often speak of me?—but I know she does."

"Oh, all the time—all the time!"

"My sweet child! She wrote the note the moment she came home?"

"Yes—the first moment. She would not wait to take off her things."

"I knew it. It is her dear, impulsive, affectionate way. I knew it without asking, but I wanted to hear you say it. The petted wife knows she is loved, but she makes her husband tell her so, every day, just for the joy of hearing it . . . . She used the pen this time. That is better; the pencil marks could rub out, and I should grieve for that. Did you suggest that she use the pen?"

"Y-no—she—it was her own idea."

The mother looked her pleasure, and said:

"I was hoping you would say that. There was never such a dear and thoughtful child! . . . Aunt Hannah?"

"Dear Margaret?"

"Go and tell her I think of her all the time, and worship her. Why—you are crying again. Don't be so worried about me, dear; I think there is nothing to fear, yet."

The grieving messenger carried her message, and piously delivered it to unheeding ears. The girl babbled on unaware; looking up at her with wondering and startled eyes flaming with fever, eyes in which was no light of recognition—

"Are you—no, you are not my mother. I want her—oh, I want her! She was here a minute ago—I did not see her go. Will she come? will she come quickly? will she come now? . . . There are so many houses . . . and they oppress me so . . . and everything whirls and turns and whirls . . . oh, my head, my head!"—and so she wandered on and on, in her pain, flitting from one torturing fancy to another, and tossing her arms about in a weary and ceaseless persecution of unrest.

Poor old Hannah wetted the parched lips and softly stroked the hot brow, murmuring endearing and pitying words, and thanking the Father of all that the mother was happy and did not know.

VI

Daily the child sank lower and steadily lower toward the grave, and daily the sorrowing old watchers carried gilded tidings of her radiant health and loveliness to the happy mother, whose pilgrimage was also now nearing its end. And daily they forged loving and cheery notes in the child's hand, and stood by with remorseful consciences and bleeding hearts, and wept to see the grateful mother devour them and adore them and treasure them away as things beyond price, because of their sweet source, and sacred because their child's hand had touched them.

At last came that kindly friend who brings healing and peace to all. The lights were burning low. In the solemn hush which precedes the dawn vague figures flitted soundless along the dim hall and gathered silent and awed in Helen's chamber, and grouped themselves about her bed, for a warning had gone forth, and they knew. The dying girl lay with closed lids, and unconscious, the drapery upon her breast faintly rising and falling as her wasting life ebbed away. At intervals a sigh or a muffled sob broke upon the stillness. The same haunting thought was in all minds there: the pity of this death, the going out into the great darkness, and the mother not here to help and hearten and bless.

Helen stirred; her hands began to grope wistfully about as if they sought something—she had been blind some hours. The end was come; all knew it. With a great sob Hester gathered her to her breast, crying, "Oh, my child, my darling!" A rapturous light broke in the dying girl's face, for it was mercifully vouchsafed her to mistake those sheltering arms for another's; and she went to her rest murmuring, "Oh, mamma, I am so happy—I so longed for you—now I can die."

Two hours later Hester made her report. The mother asked, "How is it with the child?"

"She is well."

VII

A sheaf of white crêpe and black was hung upon the door of the house, and there it swayed and rustled in the wind and whispered its tidings. At noon the preparation of the dead was finished, and in the coffin lay the fair young form, beautiful, and in the sweet face a great peace. Two mourners sat by it, grieving and worshipping—Hannah and the black woman Tilly. Hester came, and she was trembling, for a great trouble was upon her spirit. She said,

"She asks for a note."

Hannah's face blanched. She had not thought of this; it had seemed that that pathetic service was ended. But she realized now that that could not be. For a little while the two women stood looking into each other's face, with vacant eyes; then Hannah said,

"There is no way out of it—she must have it; she will suspect, else."

"And she would find out."

"Yes. It would break her heart." She looked at the dead face, and her eyes filled. "I will write it," she said.

Hester carried it. The closing line said:

"Darling Mousie, dear sweet mother, we shall soon be together again. Is not that good news? And it is true; they all say it is true."

The mother mourned, saying:

"Poor child, how will she bear it when she knows? I shall never see her again in life. It is hard, so hard. She does not suspect? You guard her from that?"

"She thinks you will soon be well."

"How good you are, and careful, dear Aunt Hester! None goes near her who could carry the infection?"

"It would be a crime."

"But you see her?"

"With a distance between—yes."

"That is so good. Others one could not trust; but you two guardian angels—steel is not so true as you. Others would be unfaithful; and many would deceive, and lie."

Hester's eyes fell, and her poor old lips trembled.

"Let me kiss you for her, Aunt Hester; and when I am gone, and the danger is past, place the kiss upon her dear lips some day, and say her mother sent it, and all her mother's broken heart is in it."

Within the hour Hester, raining tears upon the dead face, performed her pathetic mission.

VIII

Another day dawned, and grew, and spread its sunshine in the earth. Aunt Hannah brought comforting news to the failing mother, and a happy note, which said again, "We have but a little time to wait, darling mother, then we shall be together."

The deep note of a bell came moaning down the wind.

"Aunt Hannah, it is tolling. Some poor soul is at rest. As I shall be soon. You will not let her forget me?"

"Oh, God knows she never will!"

"Do not you hear strange noises, Aunt Hannah? It sounds like the shuffling of many feet."

"We hoped you would not hear it, dear. It is a little company gathering for—for Helen's sake, poor little prisoner. There will be music—and she loves it so. We thought you would not mind."

"Mind? Oh, no, no—oh, give her everything her dear heart can desire. How good you two are to her, and how good to me. God bless you both, always!"

After a listening pause:

"How lovely! It is her organ. Is she playing it herself, do you think?" Faint and rich and inspiring the chords floated to her ears on the still air. "Yes, it is her touch, dear heart; I recognize it. They are singing. Why—it is a hymn! and the sacredest of all, the most touching, the most consoling. . . . It seems to open the gates of paradise to me. . . . If I could die now . . . ."

Faint and far the words rose out of the stillness—

Nearer, my God, to Thee,
Nearer to Thee,
E'en though it be a cross
That raiseth me.

With the closing of the hymn another soul passed to its rest, and they that had been one in life were not sundered in death. The sisters, mourning and rejoicing, said,

"How blessed it was that she never knew."

IX

At midnight they sat together, grieving, and the angel of the Lord appeared in the midst transfigured with a radiance not of earth; and speaking, said:

"For liars a place is appointed. There they burn in the fires of hell from everlasting unto everlasting. Repent!"

The bereaved fell upon their knees before him and clasped their hands and bowed their gray heads, adoring. But their tongues clung to the roof of their mouths, and they were dumb.

"Speak! that I may bear the message to the chancery of heaven and bring again the decree from which there is no appeal."

Then they bowed their heads yet lower, and one said:

"Our sin is great, and we suffer shame; but only perfect and final repentance can make us whole; and we are poor creatures who have learned our human weakness, and we know that if we were in those hard straits again our hearts would fail again, and we should sin as before. The strong could prevail, and so be saved, but we are lost."

They lifted their heads in supplication. The angel was gone. While they marveled and wept he came again; and bending low, he whispered the decree.

X

Was it Heaven? Or Hell?

[illegible] would [illegible]

[illegible]
[illegible]
[illegible] beings
[illegible]

[illegible] and [illegible] The [illegible] and [illegible]

[illegible]

[illegible]

[illegible] a [illegible] of the [illegible]

[illegible]

[illegible] which [illegible]

[illegible] and one [illegible]

[illegible] and [illegible]

[illegible]

A Dog's Tale

I

My father was a St. Bernard, my mother was a collie, but I am a Presbyterian. This is what my mother told me; I do not know these nice distinctions myself. To me they are only fine large words meaning nothing. My mother had a fondness for such; she liked to say them, and see other dogs look surprised and envious, as wondering how she got so much education. But, indeed, it was not real education; it was only show: she got the words by listening in the dining room and drawing room when there was company, and by going with the children to Sunday-school and listening there; and whenever she heard a large word she said it over to herself many times, and so was able to keep it until there was a dogmatic gathering in the neighborhood, then she would get it off, and surprise and distress them all, from pocket-pup to mastiff, which rewarded her for all her trouble. If there was a stranger he was nearly sure to be suspicious, and when he got his breath again he would ask her what it meant. And she always told him. He was never expecting this, but thought he would catch her; so when she told him, he was the one that looked ashamed, whereas he had thought it was going to be she. The others were always waiting for this, and glad of it and proud of her, for they knew what was going to happen, because they had had experience. When she told the meaning of a big word they were all so taken up with admiration that it never occurred to any dog to doubt if it was the right one; and that was natural, because, for one thing, she answered up so promptly that it seemed like a dictionary speaking, and for another thing, where could they find out whether it was right or not? for she was the only cultivated dog there was. By and by, when I was older, she brought home the word Unintellectual, one time, and worked it pretty hard all the week at different gatherings, making much unhappiness and despondency; and it was at this time that I noticed that during that week she was asked for the meaning at eight different assemblages, and flashed out a fresh definition every time, which showed me that she had more presence of mind than culture, though I said nothing, of course. She had one word which she always kept on hand, and ready, like a life preserver, a kind of emergency word to strap on when she was likely to get washed overboard in a sudden way—that was the word Synonymous. When she happened to fetch out a long word which had had its day weeks before and its prepared meanings gone to her dump-pile, if there was a stranger there of course it knocked him groggy for a couple of minutes, then he would come to, and by that time she would be away down the wind on another tack, and not expecting anything; so when he'd hail and ask her to cash in, I (the only dog on the inside of her game) could see her canvas flicker a moment—but only just a moment—then it would belly out taut and full, and she would say, as calm as a summer's day, "It's synonymous with supererogation," or some godless long reptile of a word like that, and go placidly about and skim away on the next tack, perfectly comfortable, you know, and leave that stranger looking profane and embarrassed, and the initiated slatting the floor with their tails in unison and their faces transfigured with a holy joy.

And it was the same with phrases. She would drag home a whole phrase, if it had a grand sound, and play it six nights and two matinees, and explain it a new way every time—which she had to, for all she cared for was the phrase; she wasn't interested in what it meant, and knew those dogs hadn't wit enough to catch her, anyway. Yes, she was a daisy! She got so she wasn't afraid of anything, she had such confidence in the ignorance of those creatures. She even brought anecdotes that she had heard the family and the dinner guests laugh and shout over; and as a rule she got the nub of one chestnut hitched onto another chestnut, where, of course, it didn't fit and hadn't any point; and when she delivered the nub she fell over and rolled on the floor and laughed and barked in the most insane way, while I could see that she was wondering to herself why it didn't seem as funny as it did when she first heard it. But no harm was done; the others rolled and barked too, privately ashamed of themselves for not seeing the point, and never suspecting that the fault was not with them and there wasn't any to see.

You can see by these things that she was of a rather vain and frivolous character; still, she had virtues, and enough to make up, I think. She had a kind heart and gentle ways, and never harbored resentments for injuries done her, but put them easily out of her mind and forgot them; and she taught her children her kindly way, and from her we learned also to be brave and prompt in time of danger, and not to run away, but face the peril that threatened friend or stranger, and help him the best we could without stopping to think what the cost might be to us. And she taught us not by words only, but by example, and that is the best way and the surest and the most lasting. Why, the brave things she did, the splendid things! she was just a soldier; and so modest about it—well, you couldn't help admiring her, and you couldn't help imitating her; not even a King Charles spaniel could remain entirely despicable in her society. So, as you see, there was more to her than her education.

II

When I was well grown, at last, I was sold and taken away, and I never saw her again. She was brokenhearted, and so was I, and we cried; but she comforted me as well as she could, and said we were sent into this world for a wise and good purpose, and must do our duties without repining, take our life as we might find it, live it for the best good of others, and never mind about the results; they were not our affair. She said men who did like this would have a noble and beautiful reward by and by in another world, and although we animals would not go there, to do well and right without reward would give to our brief lives a worthiness and dignity which in itself would be a reward. She had gathered these things from time to time when she had gone to the Sunday school with the children, and had laid them up in her memory more carefully than she had done with those other words and phrases; and she had studied them deeply, for her good and ours. One may see by this that she had a wise and thoughtful head, for all there was so much lightness and vanity in it.

So we said our farewells, and looked our last upon each other through our tears; and the last thing she said—keeping it for the last to make me remember it the better, I think—was, "In memory of me, when there is a time of danger to another do not think of yourself, think of your mother, and do as she would do."

Do you think I could forget that? No.

III

It was such a charming home!—my new one; a fine great house, with pictures, and delicate decorations, and rich furniture, and no gloom anywhere, but all the wilderness of dainty colors lit up with flooding sunshine; and the spacious grounds around it, and the great garden—oh, greensward, and noble trees, and flowers, no end! And I was the same as a member of the family; and they loved me, and petted me, and did not give me a new name, but called me by my old one that was dear to me because my mother had given it me—Aileen Mavourneen. She got it out of a song; and the Grays knew that song, and said it was a beautiful name.

Mrs. Gray was thirty, and so sweet and so lovely, you cannot imagine it; and Sadie was ten, and just like her mother, just a darling slender little copy of her, with auburn tails down her back, and short frocks; and the baby was a year old, and plump and dimpled, and fond of me, and never could get enough of hauling on my tail, and hugging me, and laughing out its innocent happiness; and Mr. Gray was thirty-eight, and tall and slender and handsome, a little bald in front, alert, quick in his movements, businesslike, prompt, decided, unsentimental, and with that kind of trim-chiseled face that just seems to glint and sparkle with frosty intellectuality! He was a renowned scientist. I do not know what the word means, but my mother would know how to use it and get effects. She would know how to depress a rat-terrier with it and make a lapdog look sorry he came. But that is not the best one; the best one was Laboratory. My mother could organize a Trust on that one that would skin the tax-collars off the whole herd. The laboratory was not a book, or a picture, or a place to wash your hands in, as the college president's dog said—no, that is the lavatory; the laboratory is quite different, and is filled with jars, and bottles, and electrics, and wires, and strange machines; and every week other scientists came there and sat in the place, and used the machines, and discussed, and made what they called experiments and discoveries; and often I came, too, and stood around and listened, and tried to learn, for the sake of my mother, and in loving memory of her, although it was a pain to me, as realizing what she was losing out of her life and I gaining nothing at all; for try as I might, I was never able to make anything out of it at all.

Other times I lay on the floor in the mistress's workroom and slept, she gently using me for a footstool, knowing it pleased me, for it was a caress; other times I spent an hour in the nursery, and got well tousled and made happy; other times I watched by the crib there, when the baby was asleep and the nurse out for a few minutes on the baby's affairs; other times I romped and raced through the grounds and the garden with Sadie till we were tired out, then slumbered on the grass in the shade of a tree while she read her book; other times I went visiting among the neighbor dogs—for there were some most pleasant ones not far away, and one very handsome and courteous and graceful one, a curly-haired Irish setter by the name of Robin Adair, who was a Presbyterian like me, and belonged to the Scotch minister.

The servants in our house were all kind to me and were fond of me, and so, as you see, mine was a pleasant life. There could not be a happier dog than I was, nor a gratefuler one. I will say this for myself for it is only the truth: I tried in all ways to do well and right, and honor my mother's memory and her teachings, and earn the happiness that had come to me, as best I could.

By and by came my little puppy, and then my cup was full, my happiness was perfect. It was the dearest little waddling thing, and so smooth and soft and velvety, and had such cunning little awkward paws, and such affectionate eyes, and such a sweet and innocent face; and it made me so proud to see how the children and their mother adored it, and fondled it, and exclaimed over every little wonderful thing it did. It did seem to me that life was just too lovely to—

Then came the winter. One day I was standing a watch in the nursery. That is to say, I was asleep on the bed. The baby was asleep in the crib, which was alongside the bed, on the side next the fireplace. It was the kind of crib that has a lofty tent over it made of a gauzy stuff that you can see through. The nurse was out, and we two sleepers were alone. A spark from the wood fire was shot out, and it lit on the slope of the tent. I suppose a quiet interval followed, then a scream from the baby woke me, and there was that tent flaming up toward the ceiling! Before I could think, I sprang to the floor in my flight, and in a second was half-way to the door; but in the next half-second my mother's farewell was sounding in my ears, and I was back on the bed again. I reached my head through the flames and dragged the baby out by the waistband, and tugged it along, and we fell to the floor together in a cloud of smoke; I snatched a new hold, and dragged the screaming little creature along and out at the door and around the bend of the hall, and was still tugging away, all excited and happy and proud, when the master's voice shouted—

"Begone, you cursed beast? and I jumped to save myself; but he was wonderfully quick, and chased me up, striking furiously at me with his cane, I dodging this way and that, in terror, and at last a strong blow fell upon my left fore leg, which made me shriek and fall, for the moment, helpless; the cane went up for another blow, but never descended, for the nurse's voice rang wildly out, "The nursery's on fire!" and the master rushed away in that direction, and my other bones were saved.

The pain was cruel, but, no matter, I must not lose any time; he might come back at any moment; so I limped on three legs to the other end of the hall, where there was a dark little stairway leading up into a garret where old boxes and such things were kept, as I had heard say, and where people seldom went. I managed to climb up there, then I searched my way through the dark amongst the piles of things, and hid in the secretest place I could find. It was foolish to be afraid there, yet still I was; so afraid that I held in and hardly even whimpered, though it would have been such a comfort to whimper, because that cases the pain, you know. But I could lick my leg, and that did me some good.

For half an hour there was a commotion downstairs, and shoutings, and rushing footsteps, and then there was quiet again. Quiet for some minutes, and that was grateful to my spirit, for then my fears began to go down; and fears are worse than pains—oh, much worse. Then came a sound that froze me! They were calling me—calling me by name—hunting for me!

It was muffled by distance, but that could not take the terror out of it, and it was the most dreadful sound to me that I had ever heard. It went all about, everywhere, down there: along the halls, through all the rooms, in both stories, and in the basement and the cellar; then outside, and further and further away—then back, and all about the house again, and I thought it would never, never stop. But at last it did, hours and hours after the vague twilight of the garret had long ago been blotted out by black darkness.

Then in that blessed stillness my terrors fell little by little away, and I was at peace and slept. It was a good rest I had, but I woke before the twilight had come again. I was feeling fairly comfortable, and I could think out a plan now. I made a very good one; which was, to creep down, all the way down the back stairs, and hide behind the cellar door, and slip out and escape when the ice-man came at dawn, whilst he was inside filling the refrigerator; then I would hide all day, and start on my journey when night came; my journey to—well, anywhere where they would not know me and betray me to the master. I was feeling almost cheerful now; then suddenly I thought, Why, what would life be without my puppy!

That was despair. There was no plan for me; I saw that; I must stay where I was; stay, and wait, and take what might come—it was not my affair; that was what life is—my mother had said it. Then—well, then the calling began again! All my sorrows came back. I said to myself, the master will never forgive. I did not know what I had done to make him so bitter and so unforgiving, yet I judged it was something a dog could not understand, but which was clear to a man and dreadful.

They called and called—days and nights, it seemed to me. So long that the hunger and thirst near drove me mad, and I recognized that I was getting very weak. When you are this way you sleep a great deal, and I did. Once I woke in an awful fright—it seemed to me that the calling was right there in the garret! And so it was: it was Sadie's voice, and she was crying; my name was falling from her lips all broken, poor thing, and I could not believe my ears for the joy of it when I heard her say,

"Come back to us—oh, come back to us, and forgive—it is all so sad without our—"

I broke in with *such* a grateful little yelp, and the next moment Sadie was plunging and stumbling through the darkness and the lumber and shouting for the family to hear, "She's found, she's found!"

The days that followed—well, they were wonderful. The mother and Sadie and the servants—why, they just seemed to worship me. They couldn't seem to make me a bed that was fine enough; and as for food, they couldn't be satisfied with anything but game and delicacies that were out of season; and every day the friends and neighbors flocked in to hear about my heroism—that was the name they called it by, and it means agriculture. I remember my mother pulling it on a kennel once, and explaining it that way, but didn't say what agriculture was, except that it was synonymous with intramural incandescence; and a dozen times a day Mrs. Gray and Sadie would tell the tale to newcomers, and say I risked my life to save the baby's, and both of us had burns to prove it, and then the company would pass me around and pet me and exclaim about me, and you could see the pride in the eyes of Sadie and her mother; and when the people wanted to know what made me limp, they looked ashamed and changed the subject, and sometimes when people hunted them this way and that way with questions about it, it looked to me as if they were going to cry.

And this was not all the glory; no, the master's friends came, a whole twenty of the most distinguished people, and had me in the laboratory, and discussed me as if I was a kind of discovery; and some of them said it was wonderful in a dumb beast, the finest exhibition of instinct they could call to mind; but the master said, with vehemence, "It's far above instinct; it's *reason*, and many a man, privileged to be saved and go with you and me to a better world by right of its possession, has less of it than this poor silly quadruped that's foreordained to perish"; and then he laughed, and said, "Why, look at me—I'm a sarcasm! bless you, with all my grand intelligence, the only thing I inferred was that the dog had gone mad and was destroying the child, whereas but for the beast's intelligence—it's *reason*, I tell you!—the child would have perished?

They disputed and disputed, and I was the very center and subject of it all, and I wished my mother could know that this grand honor had come to me; it would have made her proud.

Then they discussed optics, as they called it, and whether a certain injury to the brain would produce blindness or not, but they could not agree about it, and said they must test it by experiment by and by; and next they discussed plants, and that interested me, because in the summer Sadie and I had planted seeds—l helped her dig the holes, you know—and after days and days a little shrub or a flower came up there, and it was a wonder how that could happen; but it did, and I wished I could talk—I would have told those people about it and shown them how much I knew, and been all alive with the subject; but I didn't care for the optics; it was dull, and when they came back to it again it bored me, and I went to sleep.

Pretty soon it was spring, and sunny and pleasant and lovely, and the sweet mother and the children patted me and the puppy good-bye, and went away on a journey and a visit to their kin, and the master wasn't any company for us, but we played together and had good times, and the servants were kind and friendly, so we got along quite happily and counted the days and waited for the family.

And one day those men came again, and said now for the test, and they took the puppy to the laboratory, and I limped three-leggedly along, too, feeling proud, for any attention shown the puppy was a pleasure to me, of course. They discussed and experimented, and then suddenly the puppy shrieked, and they set him on the floor, and he went staggering around, with his head all bloody, and the master clapped his hands and shouted:

"There, I've won—confess it! He's as blind as a bat?"

And they all said,

"It's so—you've proved your theory, and suffering humanity owes you a great debt from henceforth," and they crowded around him, and wrung his hand cordially and thankfully, and praised him.

But I hardly saw or heard these things, for I ran at once to my little darling, and snuggled close to it where it lay, and licked the blood, and it put its head against mine, whimpering softly, and I knew in my heart it was a comfort to it in its pain and trouble to feel its mother's touch, though it could not see me. Then it drooped down, presently, and its little velvet nose rested upon the floor, and it was still, and did not move any more.

Soon the master stopped discussing a moment, and rang in the footman, and said, "Bury it in the far corner of the garden," and then went on with the discussion, and I trotted after the footman, very happy and grateful, for I knew the puppy was out of its pain now, because it was asleep. We went far down the garden to the furthest end, where the children and the nurse and the puppy and I used to play in the summer in the shade of a great elm, and there the footman dug a hole, and I saw he was going to plant the puppy, and I was glad, because it would grow and come up a fine handsome dog, like Robin Adair, and be a beautiful surprise for the family when they came home; so I tried to help him dig, but my lame leg was no good, being stiff, you know, and you have to have two, or it is no use. When the footman had finished and covered little Robin up, he patted my head, and there were tears in his eyes, and he said, "Poor little doggie, you SAVED *his* child."

I have watched two whole weeks, and he doesn't come This last week a flight has been stealing upon me. I think there is something terrible about this. I do not know what it is, but the fear makes me sick, and I cannot eat, though the servants bring me the best of food; and they pet me so, and even come in the night, and cry, and say, "Poor doggie—do give it up and come home; *don't* break our hearts? and all this terrifies me the more, and makes me sure something has happened. And I am so weak; since yesterday I cannot stand on my feet anymore. And within this hour the servants, looking toward the sun where it was sinking out of sight and the night chill coming on, said things I could not understand, but they carried something cold to my heart.

"Those poor creatures! They do not suspect. They will come home in the morning, and eagerly ask for the little doggie that did the brave deed, and who of us will be strong enough to say the truth to them: 'The humble little friend is gone where go the beasts that perish.'"

The $30,000 Bequest

I

Lakeside was a pleasant little town of five or six thousand inhabitants, and a rather pretty one, too, as towns go in the Far West. It had church accommodations for 35,000, which is the way of the Far West and the South, where everybody is religious, and where each of the Protestant sects is represented and has a plant of its own. Rank was unknown in Lakeside—unconfessed, anyway; everybody knew everybody and his dog, and a sociable friendliness was the prevailing atmosphere.

Saladin Foster was bookkeeper in the principal store, and the only high-salaried man of his profession in Lakeside. He was thirty-five years old, now; he had served that store for fourteen years; he had begun in his marriage-week at four hundred dollars a year, and had climbed steadily up, a hundred dollars a year for four years; from that time forth his wage had remained eight hundred—a handsome figure indeed, and everybody conceded that he was worth it.

His wife, Electra, was a capable helpmeet, although—like himself—a dreamer of dreams and a private dabbler in romance. The first thing she did, after her marriage—child as she was, aged only nineteen—was to buy an acre of ground on the edge of the town, and pay down the cash for twenty-five dollars, all her fortune. Saladin had less, by fifteen. She instituted a vegetable garden there, got it farmed on shares by the nearest neighbor, and made it pay her a hundred percent a year. Out of Saladin's first year's wage she put thirty dollars in the savings bank, sixty out of his second, a hundred out of his third, a hundred and fifty out of his fourth. His wage went to eight hundred a year, then, and meantime two children had arrived and increased the expenses, but she banked two hundred a year from the salary, nevertheless, thenceforth. When she had been married seven years she built and furnished a pretty and comfortable two thousand-dollar house in the midst of her garden-acre, paid half of the money down, and moved her family in. Seven years later she was out of debt and had several hundred dollars out earning its living.

Earning it by the rise in landed estate; for she had long ago bought another acre or two and sold the most of it at a profit to pleasant people who were willing to build, and would be good neighbors and furnish a genial comradeship for herself and her growing family. She had an independent income from safe investments of about a hundred dollars a year; her children were growing in years and grace; and she was a pleased and happy woman. Happy in her husband, happy in her children, and the husband and the children were happy in her. It is at this point that this history begins.

The youngest girl, Clytemnestra—called Clytie for short—was eleven; her sister, Gwendolen—called Gwen for short—was thirteen; nice girls, and comely. The names betray the latent romance-tinge in the parental blood, the parents' names indicate that the tinge was an inheritance. It was an affectionate family, hence all four of its members had pet names. Saladin's was a curious and unsexing one—Sally; and so was Electra's—Aleck. All day long Sally was a good and diligent bookkeeper and salesman; all day long Aleck was a good and faithful mother and housewife, and thoughtful and calculating businesswoman; but in the cozy living room at night they put the plodding world away and lived in another and a fairer, reading romances to each other, dreaming dreams, comrading with kings and princes and stately lords and ladies in the flash and stir and splendor of noble palaces and grim and ancient castles.

II

Now came great news! Stunning news, joyous news, in fact. It came from a neighboring State, where the family's only surviving relative lived. It was Sally's relative—a sort of vague and indefinite uncle or second or third cousin by the name of Tilbury Foster, seventy and a bachelor, reputed well-off and correspondingly sour and crusty. Sally had tried to make up to him once, by letter, in a bygone time, and had not made that mistake again. Tilbury now wrote to Sally, saying he should shortly die, and should leave him thirty thousand dollars, cash; not for love, but because money had given him most of his troubles and exasperations, and he wished to place it where there was good hope that it would continue its malignant work. The bequest would be found in his will, and would be paid over. *Provided*, that Sally should be able to prove to the executors that he had *taken no notice of the gift by spoken word or by letter, had made no inquiries concerning the moribund's progress toward the everlasting tropics, and had not attended the funeral.*

As soon as Aleck had partially recovered from the tremendous emotions created by the letter, she sent to the relative's habitat and subscribed for the local paper.

Man and wife entered into a solemn compact, now, to never mention the great news to any one while the relative lived, lest some ignorant person carry the fact to the deathbed and distort it and make it appear that they were disobediently thankful for the bequest, and just the same as confessing it and publishing it, right in the face of the prohibition.

For the rest of the day Sally made havoc and confusion with his books, and Aleck could not keep her mind on her affairs, nor even take up a flower pot or book or a stick of wood without forgetting what she had intended to do with it. For both were dreaming.

"Thir-ty thousand dollars!"

All day long the music of those inspiring words sang through those people's heads.

From his marriage-day forth, Aleck's grip had been upon the purse, and Sally had seldom known what it was to be privileged to squander a dime on non-necessities.

"Thir-ty thousand dollars!" the song went on and on. A vast sum, an unthinkable sum!

All day long Aleck was absorbed in planning how to invest it, Sally in planning how to spend it.

There was no romance-reading that night. The children took themselves away early, for the parents were silent, distraught, and strangely unentertaining. The good-night kisses might as well have been impressed upon vacancy, for all the response they got; the parents were not aware of the kisses, and the children had been gone an hour before their absence was noticed. Two pencils had been busy during that hour—note-making; in the way of plans. It was Sally who broke the stillness at last. He said, with exultation—

"Ah, it'll be grand, Aleck! Out of the first thousand we'll have a horse and a buggy for summer, and a cutter and a skin lap-robe for winter."

Aleck responded, with decision and composure—

"Out of the *capital?* Nothing of the kind. Not if it was a million!"

Sally was deeply disappointed; the glow went out of his face.

"Oh, Aleck!" he said, reproachfully. "We've always worked so hard and been so scrimped; and now that we are rich, it does seem—"

He did not finish, for he saw her eye soften; his supplication had touched her. She said, with gentle persuasiveness—

"We must not spend the capital, dear, it would not be wise. Out of the income from it—"

"That will answer, that will answer, Aleck! How dear and good you are! There will be a noble income, and if we can spend that—"

"Not *all* of it, dear, not all of it, but you can spend a part of it. That is, a reasonable part. But the whole of the capital—every penny of it—must be put right to work, and kept at it. You see the reasonableness of that, don't you?"

"Why, ye-s. Yes, of course. But we'll have to wait so long. Six months before the first interest falls due."

"Yes—maybe longer."

"Longer, Aleck? Why? Don't they pay half-yearly?"

"*That* kind of an investment—yes; but I sha'n't invest in that way."

"What way then?"

"For big returns."

"Big. That's good. Go on, Aleck. What is it?"

"Coal. The new mines. Cannel. I mean to put in ten thousand. Ground floor. When we organize, we'll get three shares for one."

"By George but it sounds good, Aleck! Then the shares will be worth—how much? And when?"

"About a year. They'll pay ten per cent, half-yearly, and be worth thirty thousand. I know all about it; the advertisement is in the Cincinnati paper here."

"Land, thirty thousand for ten—in a year! Let's jam in the whole capital and pull out ninety! I'll write and subscribe right now—tomorrow it may be too late."

He was flying to the writing desk but Aleck stopped him and put him back in his chair. She said—

"Don't lose your head so. We mustn't subscribe till we've got the money; don't you know that?"

Sally's excitement went down a degree or two, but he was not wholly appeased.

"Why, Aleck, we'll *have* it, you know—and so soon, too. He's probably out of his troubles before this, it's a hundred to nothing he's selecting his brimstone-shovel this very minute. Now, I think—"

Aleck shuddered, and said—

"How *can* you, Sally! Don't talk in that way, it is perfectly scandalous."

"Oh, well, make it a halo, if you like, *I* don't care for his outfit, I was only just talking. Can't you let a person talk?"

"But why should you *want* to talk in that dreadful way? How would you like to have people talk so about *you*, and you not cold yet?"

"Nor likely to be, for *one* while, I reckon, if my last act was giving away money for the sake of doing somebody a harm with it. But never mind about Tilbury, Aleck, let's talk about something worldly. It does seem to me that that mine is the place for the whole thirty. What's the objection?"

"All the eggs in one basket—that's the objection."

"All right, if you say so. What about the other twenty? What do you mean to do with that?"

"There is no hurry; I am going to look around before I do anything with it."

"All right, if your mind's made up," sighed Sally. He was deep in thought, a while, then he said—

"There'll be twenty thousand profit coming from the ten a year from now. We can spend that, can't we, Aleck?"

Aleck shook her head.

"No, dear," she said, "it won't sell high till we've had the first semiannual dividend. You can spend part of that."

"Shucks, only *that*—and a whole year to wait! Confound it, I—"

"Oh, do be patient! It might even be declared in three months—it's quite within the possibilities."

"Oh, jolly! oh, thanks? and Sally jumped up and kissed his wife in gratitude. "It'll be three thousand—three whole thousand! how much of it can we spend, Aleck? Make it liberal—do, dear, that's a good fellow."

Aleck was pleased; so pleased that she yielded to the pressure and conceded a sum which her judgment told her was a foolish extravagance—a thousand dollars. Sally kissed her half a dozen times and even in that way could not express all his joy and thankfulness. This new access of gratitude and affection carried Aleck quite beyond the bounds of prudence, and before she could restrain herself she had made her darling another grant—a couple of thousand out of the fifty or sixty which she meant to clear within a year out of the twenty which still remained of the bequest. The happy tears sprang to Sally's eyes, and he said—

"Oh, I want to hug you? And he did it. Then he got his notes and sat down and began to check off, for first purchase, the luxuries which he should earliest wish to secure. "Horse—buggy—cutter—lap-robe—patent-leathers—dog—plug hat—church pew—stem-winder—new teeth—say, Aleck!"

"Well?"

"Ciphering away, aren't you? That's right. Have you got the twenty thousand invested yet?"

"No, there's no hurry about that; I must look around first, and think."

"But you are ciphering; what's it about?"

"Why, I have to find work for the thirty thousand that comes out of the coal, haven't I?"

"Scott, what a head! I never thought of that. How are you getting along? Where have you arrived?"

"Not very far—two years or three. I've turned it over twice; once in oil and once in wheat."

"Why, Aleck, it's splendid! How does it aggregate?"

"I think—well, to be on the safe side, about a hundred and eighty thousand clear, though it will probably be more."

"My! isn't it wonderful? By gracious, luck has come our way at last, after all the hard sledding. Aleck!"

"Well?"

"I'm going to cash-in a whole three hundred on the missionaries—what real right have we to care for expenses?

"You couldn't do a nobler thing, dear; and it's just like your generous nature, you unselfish boy."

The praise made Sally poignantly happy, but he was fair and just enough to say it was rightfully due to Aleck rather than to himself, since but for her he should never have had the money.

Then they went up to bed, and in their delirium of bliss they forgot and left the candle burning in the parlor. They did not remember until they were undressed; then Sally was for letting it burn; he said they could afford it, if it was a thousand. But Aleck went down and put it out.

A good job, too; for on her way back she hit on a scheme that would turn the hundred and eighty thousand into half a million before it had had time to get cold.

III

The little newspaper which Aleck had subscribed for was a Thursday sheet; it would make the trip of five hundred miles from Tilbury's village and arrive on Saturday. Tilbury's letter had started on Friday, more than a day too late for the benefactor to die and get into that week's issue, but in plenty of time to make connection for the next output. Thus the Fosters had to wait almost a complete week to find out whether anything of a satisfactory nature had happened to him or not. It was a long, long week, and the strain was a heavy one. The pair could hardly have borne it if their minds had not had the relief of wholesome diversion. We have seen that they had that. The woman was piling up fortunes right along, the man was spending them—spending all his wife would give him a chance at, at any rate.

At last the Saturday came, and the *Weekly Sagamore* arrived. Mrs. Eversly Bennett was present. She was the Presbyterian parson's wife, and was working the Fosters for a charity. Talk now died a sudden death—on the Foster side. Mrs. Bennett presently discovered that her hosts were not hearing a word she was saying; so she got up, wondering and indignant, and went away. The moment she was out of the house, Aleck eagerly tore the wrapper from the paper, and her eyes and Sally's swept the columns for the death notices. Disappointment! Tilbury was not anywhere mentioned. Aleck was a Christian from the cradle, and duty and the force of habit required her to go through the motions. She pulled herself together and said, with a pious two-percent trade joyousness:

"Let us be humbly thankful that he has been spared; and—"

"Damn his treacherous hide, I wish—"

"Sally! For shame!"

"I don't care!" retorted the angry man. "It's the way *you* feel, and if you weren't so immorally pious you'd be honest and say so."

Aleck said, with wounded dignity:

"I do not see how you can say such unkind and unjust things. There is no such thing as immoral piety."

Sally felt a pang, but tried to conceal it under a shuffling attempt to save his case by changing the form of it—as if changing the form while retaining the juice could deceive the expert he was trying to placate. He said:

"I didn't mean so bad as that, Aleck; I didn't really mean immoral piety, I only meant—meant—well, conventional piety, you know; er—shop piety; the—the—why, *you* know what I mean, Aleck—the—well, where you put up the plated article and play it for solid, you know, without intending anything improper, but just out of trade habit, ancient policy, petrified custom, loyalty to—to—hang it, I can't find the right words, but *you* know what I mean, Aleck, and that there isn't any harm in it. I'll try again. You see, it's this way. If a person—"

"You have said quite enough," said Aleck, coldly; "let the subject be dropped."

"*I'm* willing," fervently responded Sally, wiping the sweat from his forehead and looking the thankfulness he had no words for. Then, musingly, he apologized to himself. "I certainly held threes—I *know* it—but I drew and didn't fill. That's where I'm so often weak in the game. If I had stood pat—but I didn't. I never do. I don't know enough."

Confessedly defeated, he was properly tame now and subdued. Aleck forgave him with her eyes.

The grand interest, the supreme interest, came instantly to the front again; nothing could keep it in the background many minutes on a stretch. The couple took up the puzzle of the absence of Tilbury's death notice. They discussed it every which way, more or less hopefully, but they had to finish where they began, and concede that the only really sane explanation of the absence of the notice must be—and without doubt was—that Tilbury was not dead. There was something sad about it, something even a little unfair, maybe, but there it was, and had to be put up with. They were agreed as to that. To Sally it seemed a strangely inscrutable dispensation; more inscrutable than usual, he thought; one of the most unnecessarily inscrutable he could call to mind, in fact—and said so, with some feeling; but if he was hoping to draw Aleck he failed; she reserved her opinion, if she had one; she had not the habit of taking injudicious risks in any market, worldly or other.

The pair must wait for next week's paper—Tilbury had evidently postponed. That was their thought and their decision. So they put the subject away, and went about their affairs again, with as good heart as they could.

Now, if they had but known it, they had been wronging Tilbury all the time. Tilbury had kept faith, kept it to the fetter; he was dead, he had died to schedule. He was dead more than four days now and used to it; entirely dead, perfectly dead, as dead as any other new person in the cemetery; dead in abundant time to get into that week's *Sagamore*, too, and only shut out by an accident; an accident which could not happen to a metropolitan journal, but which happens easily to a poor little village rag like the *Sagamore*. On this occasion, just as the editorial page was being locked up, a gratis quart of strawberry water-ice arrived from Hostetter's Ladies' and Gents' Ice-Cream Parlors, and the stickful of rather chilly regret over Tilbury's translation got crowded out to make room for the editor's frantic gratitude.

On its way to the standing-galley Tilbury's notice got pied. Otherwise it would have gone into some future edition, for weekly *Sagamores* do not waste "live" matter, and in their galleys "live" matter is immortal, unless a pi accident intervene. But a thing that gets pied is dead, and for such there is no resurrection; its chance of seeing print is gone, forever and ever. And so, let Tilbury like it or not, let him rave in his grave to his fill, no matter—no mention of his death would ever see the light in the *Weekly Sagamore.*

IV

Five weeks drifted tediously along. The *Sagamore* arrived regularly on the Saturdays, but never once contained a mention of Tilbury Foster. Sally's patience broke down at this point, and he said, resentfully:

"Damn his livers, he's immortal?

Aleck gave him a very severe rebuke, and added, with icy solemnity:

"How would you feel if you were suddenly cut off just after such an awful remark had escaped out of you?"

Without sufficient reflection Sally responded:

"I'd feel I was lucky I hadn't got caught with it *in* me."

Pride had forced him to say something, and as he could not think of any rational thing to say he flung that out. Then he stole a base—as he called it—that is, slipped from the presence, to keep from getting brayed in his wife's discussion-mortar.

Six months came and went. The *Sagamore* was still silent about Tilbury. Meantime Sally had several times thrown out a feeler—that is, a hint that he would like to know. Aleck had ignored the hints. Sally now resolved to brace up and risk a frontal attack. So he squarely proposed to disguise himself and go to Tilbury's village and surreptitiously find out as to the prospects. Aleck put her foot on the dangerous project with energy and decision. She said:

"What can you be thinking of? You do keep my hands full! You have to be watched all the time, like a little child, to keep you from walking into the fire. You'll stay right where you are!"

"Why, Aleck, I could do it and not be found out—I'm certain of it."

"Sally Foster, don't you know you would have to inquire around?"

"Of course, but what of it? Nobody would suspect who I was."

"Oh, listen to the man! Some day you've got to prove to the executors that you never inquired. What then?"

He had forgotten that detail. He didn't reply; there wasn't anything to say. Aleck added:

"Now then, drop that notion out of your mind, and don't ever meddle with it again. Tilbury set that trap for you. Don't you know it's a trap? He is on the watch, and fully expecting you to blunder into it. Well, he is going to be disappointed—at least while I am on deck. Sally!"

"Well?"

"As long as you live, if it's a hundred years, don't you ever make an inquiry. Promise!"

"All right," with a sigh and reluctantly.

Then Aleck softened and said:

"Don't be impatient. We are prospering; we can wait; there is no hurry. Our small dead-certain income increases all the time; and as to futures, I have not made a mistake yet—they are piling up by the thousands and the tens of thousands. There is not another family in the State with such prospects as ours. Already we are beginning to roll in eventual wealth. You know that, don't you?"

"Yes, Aleck, it's certainly so."

"Then be grateful for what God is doing for us, and stop worrying. You do not believe we could have achieved these prodigious results without His special help and guidance, do you?"

Hesitatingly, "N-no, I suppose not." Then, with feeling and admiration, "And yet, when it comes to judiciousness in watering a stock or putting up a hand to skin Wall Street I don't give in that *you* need any outside amateur help, if I do I wish I—"

"Oh, *do* shut up! I know you do not mean any harm or any irreverence, poor boy, but you can't seem to open your mouth without letting out things to make a person shudder. You keep me in constant dread. For you and for all of us. Once I had no fear of the thunder, but now when I hear it I—"

Her voice broke and she began to cry, and could not finish. The sight of this smote Sally to the heart, and he took her in his arms and petted her and comforted her and promised better conduct, and upbraided himself and remorsefully pleaded for forgiveness.

And he was in earnest, and sorry for what he had done and ready for any sacrifice that could make up for it.

And so, in privacy he thought long and deeply over the matter, resolving to do what should seem best. It was easy to *promise* reform; indeed he had already promised it. But would that do any real good, any permanent good? No, it would be but temporary—he knew his weakness, and confessed it to himself with sorrow—he could not keep the promise. Something surer and better must be devised; and he devised it. At cost of precious money which he had long been saving up, shilling by shilling, he put a lightning rod on the house.

At a subsequent time he relapsed.

What miracles habit can do! and how quickly and how easily habits are acquired—both trifling habits and habits which profoundly change us. If by accident we wake at two in the morning a couple of nights in succession, we have need to be uneasy, for another repetition can turn the accident into a habit; and a month's dallying with whiskey—but we all know these commonplace facts.

The castle-building habit, the daydreaming habit—how it grows! what a luxury it becomes; how we fly to its enchantments at every idle moment, how we revel in them, steep our souls in them, intoxicate ourselves with their beguiling fantasies—oh, yes, and how soon and how easily our dream-life and our material life become so intermingled and so fused together that we can't quite tell which is which, any more.

By and by Aleck subscribed for a Chicago daily and for the *Wall Street Pointer*. With an eye single to finance she studied these as diligently all the week as she studied her Bible Sundays. Sally was lost in admiration, to note with what swift and sure strides her genius and judgment developed and expanded, in the forecasting and handling of the securities of both the material and spiritual markets. He was proud of her nerve and daring in exploiting worldly stocks, and just as proud of her conservative caution in working her spiritual deals. He noted that she never lost her head in either case; that with a splendid courage she often went short on worldly futures, but heedfully drew the line there—she was always long on the others. Her policy was quite sane and simple, as she explained it to him: what she put into earthly futures was for speculation, what she put into spiritual futures was for investment; she was willing to go into the one on a margin, and take chances, but in the case of the other, "margin her no margins"—she wanted to cash-in a hundred cents per dollar's-worth, and have the stock transferred on the books.

It took but a very few months to educate Aleck's imagination and Sally's. Each day's training added something to the spread and effectiveness of the two machines. As a consequence, Aleck made imaginary money much taster than at first she had dreamed of making it, and Sally's competency in spending the overflow of it kept pace with the strain put upon it, right along. In the beginning Aleck had given the coal speculation a twelvemonth in which to materialize, and had been loath to grant that this term might possibly be shortened by nine months. But that was the feeble work, the nursery-work, of a financial fancy that had had no teaching, no experience, no practice. These aids soon came, then that nine months vanished, and the imaginary ten-thousand-dollar investment came marching home with three hundred percent profit on its back!

It was a great day for the pair of Fosters. They were speechless for joy. Also speechless for another reason: after much watching of the market, Aleck had lately, with fear and trembling, made her first flyer on a "margin," using the remaining twenty thousand of the bequest in this risk. In her mind's eye she had seen it climb, point by point—always with a chance that the market would break—until at last her anxieties were too great for further endurance—she being new to the margin-business and unhardened, as yet—and she gave her imaginary broker an imaginary order by imaginary telegraph to sell. She said forty thousand dollars profit was enough. The sale was made on the very day that the coal-venture had returned with its rich freight. As I have said, the couple were speechless. They sat dazed and blissful, that night, trying to realize the immense fact, the overwhelming fact, that they were actually worth a hundred thousand dollars in clean imaginary cash. Yet so it was.

It was the last time that ever Aleck was afraid of a margin; at least afraid enough to let it break her sleep and pale her cheek to the extent that this first experience in that line had done.

Indeed it was a memorable night. Gradually the realization that they were rich sank securely home into the souls of the pair, then they began to place the money. If we could have looked out through the eyes of these dreamers, we should have seen their tidy little wooden house disappear, and a two-story brick with a cast-iron fence in front of it take its place; we 'should have seen a three-globed gas-chandelier grow down from the parlor ceiling; we should have seen the homely rag carpet turn to noble Brussels, a dollar and a half a yard; we should have seen the plebeian fireplace vanish away and a recherché big base-burner with isinglass windows take position and spread awe around. And we should have seen other things, too; among them the buggy, the lap-robe, the stovepipe hat, and so on.

From that time forth, although the daughters and the neighbors saw only the same old wooden house there, it was a two-story brick to Aleck and Sally; and not a night went by that Aleck did not worn, about the imaginary gas bills, and get for all comfort Sally's reckless retort, "What of it? we can afford it."

Before the couple went to bed, that first night that they were rich, they had decided that they must celebrate. They must give a party—that was the idea. But how to explain it—to the daughters and the neighbors? They could not expose the fact that they were rich. Sally was willing, even anxious, to do it; but Aleck kept her head and would not allow it. She said that although the money was as good as in, it would be as well to wait until it was actually in. On that policy she took her stand, and would not budge. The great secret must be kept, she said—kept from the daughters and everybody else.

The pair were puzzled. They must celebrate, they were determined to celebrate, but since the secret must be kept, what could they celebrate? No birthdays were due for three months. Tilbury wasn't available, evidently he was going to live forever; what the nation *could* they celebrate? That was Sally's way of putting it; and he was getting impatient, too, and harassed. But at last he hit it—just by sheer inspiration, as it seemed to him—and all their troubles were gone in a moment; they would celebrate the Discovery of America. A splendid idea!

Aleck was almost too proud of Sally for words—she said *she* never would have thought of it. But Sally, although he was bursting with delight in the compliment and with wonder at himself, tried not to let on, and said it wasn't really anything, anybody could have done it. Whereat Aleck, with a prideful toss of her happy head, said—

"Oh, certainly! Anybody could—oh, anybody! Hosannah Dilkins, for instance! Or maybe Adelbert Peanut—oh, *dear*—yes! Well, I'd like to see them try it, that's all. Dear-me-suz, if they could think of the discovery of a forty-acre island it's more than *I* believe they could; and as for a whole continent, why, Sally Foster, you know perfectly well it would strain the livers and lights out of them and *then* they couldn't!"

The dear woman, she knew he had talent; and if affection made her overestimate the size of it a little, surely it was a sweet and gentle crime, and forgivable for its source's sake.

V

The celebration went off well. The friends were all present, both the young and the old. Among the young were Flossie and Gracie Peanut and their brother Adelbert, who was a rising young journeyman tinner, also Hosannah Dilkins, Jr., journeyman plasterer, just out of his apprenticeship. For many months Adelbert and Hosannah had been showing interest in Gwendolen and Clytemnestra Foster, and the parents of the girls had noticed this with private satisfaction. But they suddenly realized now that that feeling had passed. They recognized that the changed financial conditions had raised up a social bar between their daughters and the young mechanics. The daughters could now look higher—and must. Yes, must. They need marry nothing below the grade of lawyer or merchant; poppa and momma would take care of this; there must be no mésalliances.

However, these thinkings and projects of theirs were private, and did not show on the surface, and therefore threw no shadow upon the celebration. What showed upon the surface was a serene and lofty contentment and a dignity of carriage and gravity of deportment which compelled the admiration and likewise the wonder of the company. All noticed it, all commented upon it, but none was able to divine the secret of it. It was a marvel and a mystery. Three several persons remarked, without suspecting what clever shots they were making:

"It's as if they'd come into property."

That was just it, indeed.

Most mothers would have taken hold of the matrimonial matter in the old regulation way; they would have given the girls a talking to, of a solemn sort and untactful—a lecture calculated to defeat its own purpose, by producing tears and secret rebellion; and the said mothers would have further damaged the business by requesting the young mechanics to discontinue their attentions. But this mother was different. She was practical. She said nothing to any of the young people concerned, nor to any one else except Sally. He listened to her and understood; understood and admired. He said:

"I get the idea. Instead of finding fault with the samples on view, thus hurting feelings and obstructing trade without occasion, you merely offer a higher class of goods for the money, and leave nature to take her course. It's wisdom, Aleck, solid wisdom, and sound as a nut. Who's your fish? Have you nominated him yet?"

No, she hadn't. They must look the market over—which they did. To start with, they considered and discussed Bradish, rising young lawyer, and Fulton, rising young dentist. Sally must invite them to dinner. But not right away; there was no hurry, Aleck said. Keep an eye on the pair, and wait; nothing would be lost by going slowly in so important a matter.

It turned out that this was wisdom, too; for inside of three weeks Aleck made a wonderful strike which swelled her imaginary hundred thousand to four hundred thousand of the same quality. She and Sally were in the clouds that evening. For the first time they introduced champagne at dinner. Not real champagne, but plenty real enough for the amount of imagination expended on it. It was Sally that did it, and Aleck weakly submitted. At bottom both were troubled and ashamed, for he was a high-up Son of Temperance, and at funerals wore an apron which no dog could look upon and retain his reason and his opinion; and she was a W.C.T.U., with all that that implies of boiler-iron virtue and unendurable holiness. But there it was: the pride of riches was beginning its disintegrating work. They had lived to prove, once more, a sad truth which had been proven many times before in the world: that whereas principle is a great and noble protection against showy and degrading vanities and vices, poverty is worth six of it. More than four hundred thousand dollars to the good! They took up the matrimonial matter again. Neither the dentist nor the lawyer was mentioned; there was no occasion; they were out of the running. Disqualified. They discussed the son of the pork-packer and the son of the village banker. But finally, as in the previous case, they concluded to wait and think, and go cautiously and sure.

Luck came their way again. Aleck, ever watchful, saw a great and risky chance, and took a daring flyer. A time of trembling, of doubt, of awful uneasiness followed, for nonsuccess meant absolute ruin and nothing short of it. Then came the result, and Aleck, faint with joy, could hardly control her voice when she said:

"The suspense is over, Sally—and we are worth a cold million!"

Sally wept for gratitude, and said:

"Oh, Electra, jewel of women, darling of my heart, we are free at last, we roll in wealth, we need never scrimp again. It's a case for Veuve Cliquot!" and he got out a pint of spruce-beer and made sacrifice, he saying "Damn the expense," and she rebuking him gently with reproachful but humid and happy eyes.

They shelved the pork-packer's son and the banker's son, and sat down to consider the Governor's son and the son of the Congressman.

VI

It were a weariness to follow in detail the leaps and bounds the Foster fictitious finances took from this time forth. It was marvelous, it was dizzying, it was dazzling. Everything Aleck touched turned to fairy gold, and heaped itself glittering toward the firmament. Millions upon millions poured in, and still the mighty stream flowed thundering along, still its vast volume increased. Five millions—ten millions—twenty-thirty—was there never to be an end?

Two years swept by in a splendid delirium, the intoxicated Fosters scarcely noticing the flight of time. They were now worth three hundred million dollars; they were in every board of directors of every prodigious combine in the country; and still, as time drifted along, the millions went on piling up, five at a time, ten at a time, as fast as they could tally them off almost. The three hundred doubled itself—then doubled again—and yet again—and yet once more!

Twenty-four hundred millions!

The business was getting a little confused. It was necessary to take an account of stock, and straighten it out. The Fosters knew it, they felt it, they realized that it was imperative; but they also knew that to do it properly and perfectly the task must be carried to a finish without a break when once it was begun. A ten-hours' job; and where could they find ten leisure hours in a bunch? Sally was selling pins and sugar and calico all day and every day; Aleck was cooking and washing dishes and sweeping and making beds all day and every day, with none to help, for the daughters were being saved up for high society. The Fosters knew there was one way to get the ten hours, and only one. Both were ashamed to name it; each waited for the other to do it. Finally Sally said—

"Somebody's got to give in. It's up to me. Consider that I've named it—never mind pronouncing it out loud."

Aleck colored, but was grateful. Without further remark, they fell. Fell, and broke the Sabbath. For that was their only free ten-hour stretch. It was but another step in the downward path. Others would follow. Vast wealth has temptations which fatally and surely undermine the moral structure of persons not habituated to its possession.

They pulled down the shades and broke the Sabbath. With hard and patient labor they overhauled their holdings, and listed them. And a long-drawn procession of formidable names it was! Starting with the Railway Systems, Steamer Lines, Standard Oil, Ocean Cables, Diluted Telegraph, and all the rest, and winding up with Klondike, De Beers, Tammany Graft, and Shady Privileges in the Post Office Department.

Twenty-four hundred millions, and all safely planted in Good Things, gilt-edged and interest-bearing. Income, $120,000,000 a year. Aleck fetched a long purr of soft delight, and said—

"Is it enough?"

"It is, Aleck."

"What shall we do?"

"Stand pat."

"Retire from business?"

"That's it."

"I am agreed. The good work is finished; we will take a long rest and enjoy the money."

"Good! Aleck?"

"Yes, dear?"

"How much of the income can we spend?"

"The whole of it."

It seemed to her husband that a ton of chains fell from his limbs. He did not say a word; he was happy beyond the power of speech.

After that, they broke the Sabbaths right along, as fast as they turned up. It is the first wrong steps that count. Every Sunday they put in the whole day, after morning service, on inventions—inventions of ways to spend the money. They got to continuing this delicious dissipation until past midnight; and at every séance Aleck lavished millions upon great charities and religious enterprises, and Sally lavished like sums upon matters to which (at first) he gave definite names. Only at first. Later the names gradually lost sharpness of outline, and eventually faded into "sundries," thus becoming entirely—but safely—undescriptive. For Sally was crumbling. The placing of these millions added seriously and most uncomfortably to the family expenses—in tallow candles. For a while Aleck was worried. Then, after a little, she ceased to worry, for the occasion of it was gone. She was pained, she was grieved, she was ashamed; but she said nothing, and so became an accessory. Sally was taking candles; he was robbing the store. It is ever thus. Vast wealth, to the person unaccustomed to it, is a bane; it eats into the flesh and bone of his morals. When the Fosters were poor, they could have been trusted with untold candles. But now they—but let us not dwell upon it. From candles to apples is but a step: Sally got to taking apples; then soap; then maple sugar; then canned goods; then crockery. How easy it is to go from bad to worse, when once we have started upon a downward course!

Meantime, other effects had been milestoning the course of the Fosters' splendid financial march. The fictitious brick dwelling had given place to an imaginary granite one with a checkerboard mansard roof; in time this one disappeared and gave place to a still grander home—and so on and so on. Mansion after mansion, made of air, rose, higher, broader, finer, and each in its turn vanished away; until now, in these latter great days, our dreamers were in fancy housed, in a distant region, in a sumptuous vast palace which looked out from a leafy summit upon a noble prospect of vale and river and receding hills steeped in tinted mists—and all private, all the property of the dreamers; a palace swarming with liveried servants, and populous with guests of fame and power, hailing from all the world's capitals, foreign and domestic.

This palace was far, far away toward the rising sun, immeasurably remote, astronomically remote, in Newport, Rhode Island, Holy Land of High Society, ineffable Domain of the American Aristocracy. As a rule, they spent a part of every Sabbath—after morning service—in this sumptuous home, the rest of it they spent in Europe, or in dawdling around in their private yacht. Six days of sordid and plodding Fact-life at home on the ragged edge of Lakeside and straitened means, the seventh in Fairyland—such had become their program and their habit.

In their sternly restricted Fact-life they remained as of old—plodding, diligent, careful, practical, economical. They stuck loyally to the little Presbyterian Church, and labored faithfully in its interests and stood by its high and tough doctrines with all their mental and spiritual energies. But in their Dream-life they obeyed the invitations of their fancies, whatever they might be, and howsoever the fancies might change. Aleck's fancies were not very capricious, and not frequent, but Sally's scattered a good deal. Aleck, in her dream-life, went over to the Episcopal camp, on account of its large official titles; next she became High-Church on account of the candles and shows; and next she naturally changed to Rome, where there were cardinals and more candles. But these excursions were as nothing to Sally's. His dream-life was a glowing and continuous and persistent excitement, and he kept every part of it fresh and sparkling by frequent changes, the religious part along with the rest. He worked his religions hard, and changed them with his shirt.

The liberal spendings of the Fosters upon their fancies began early in their prosperities, and grew in prodigality step by step with their advancing fortunes. In time they became truly enormous. Aleck built a university or two per Sunday; also a hospital or two; also a Rowton hotel or so; also a batch of churches; now and then a cathedral; and once, with untimely and ill-chosen playfulness, Sally said, "It was a cold day when she didn't ship a cargo of missionaries to persuade unreflecting Chinamen to trade off twenty-four carat Confucianism for counterfeit Christianity."

This rude and unfeeling language hurt Aleck to the heart, and she went from the presence crying. That spectacle went to his own heart, and in his pain and shame he would have given worlds to have those unkind words back. She had uttered no syllable of reproach—and that cut him. Not one suggestion that he look at his own record—and she could have made, oh, so many, and such blistering ones! Her generous silence brought a swift revenge, for it turned his thoughts upon himself, it summoned before him a spectral procession, a moving vision of his life as he had been leading it these past few years of limitless prosperity, and as he sat there reviewing it his cheeks burned and his soul was steeped in humiliation. Look at her life—how fair it was, and tending ever upward; and look at his own—how frivolous, how charged with mean vanities, how selfish, how empty, how ignoble! And its trend—never upward, but downward, ever downward!

He instituted comparisons between her record and his own. He had found fault with her—so he mused—*he!* And what could he say for himself? When she built her first church what was he doing? Gathering other blasé multimillionaires into a Poker Club; defiling his own palace with it; losing hundreds of thousands to it at every sitting, and sillily vain of the admiring notoriety it made for him. When she was building her first university, what was he doing? Polluting himself with a gay and dissipated secret life in the company of other fast bloods, multimillionaires in money and paupers in character. When she was building her first foundling asylum, what was he doing? Alas! When she was projecting her noble Society for the Purifying of the Sex, what was he doing? Ah, what, indeed! When she and the W.C.T.U. and the Woman with the Hatchet, moving with resistless march, were sweeping the fatal bottle from the land, what was he doing? Getting drunk three times a day. When she, builder of a hundred cathedrals, was being gratefully welcomed and blest in papal Rome and decorated with the Golden Rose which she had so honorably earned, what was he doing? Breaking the bank at Monte Carlo.

He stopped. He could go no farther; he could not bear the rest. He rose up, with a great resolution upon his lips: this secret life should be revealed, and confessed; no longer would he live it clandestinely; he would go and tell her All.

And that is what he did. He told her All; and wept upon her bosom; wept, and moaned, and begged for her forgiveness. It was a profound shock, and she staggered under the blow, but he was her own, the core of her heart, the blessing of her eyes, her all in all, she could deny him nothing, and she forgave him. She felt that he could never again be quite to her what he had been before; she knew that he could only repent, and not reform; yet all morally defaced and decayed as he was, was he not her own, her very own, the idol of her deathless worship? She said she was his serf, his slave, and she opened her yearning heart and took him in.

VII

One Sunday afternoon some time after this they were sailing the summer seas in their dream-yacht, and reclining in lazy luxury under the awning of the afterdeck. There was silence, for each was busy with his own thoughts. These seasons of silence had insensibly been growing more and more frequent of late; the old nearness and cordiality were waning. Sally's terrible revelation had done its work; Aleck had tried hard to drive the memory of it out of her mind, but it would not go, and the shame and bitterness of it were poisoning her gracious dream-life. She could see now (on Sundays) that her husband was becoming a bloated and repulsive Thing. She could not close her eyes to this, and in these days she no longer looked at him, Sundays, when she could help it.

But she—was she herself without blemish? Alas, she knew she was not. She was keeping a secret from him, she was acting dishonorably toward him, and many a pang it was costing her. *She was breaking the compact, and concealing it from him.* Under strong temptation she had gone into business again; she had risked their whole fortune in a purchase of all the railway systems and coal and steel companies in the country on a margin, and she was now trembling, every Sabbath hour, lest through some chance word of hers he find it out. In her misery and remorse for this treachery she could not keep her heart from going out to him in pity; she was filled with compunctions to see him lying there, drunk and content, and never suspecting. Never suspecting—trusting her with a perfect and pathetic trust, and she holding over him by a thread a possible calamity of so devastating a—

"*Say*—Aleck?"

The interrupting words brought her suddenly to herself. She was grateful to have that persecuting subject from her thoughts, and she answered, with much of the old-time tenderness in her tone: "Yes, dear."

"Do you know, Aleck, I think we are making a mistake—that is, you are. I mean about the marriage business." He sat up, fat and froggy and benevolent, like a bronze Buddha, and grew earnest. "Consider—it's more than five years. You've continued the same policy from the start: with every rise, always holding on for five points higher. Always when I think we are going to have some weddings, you see a bigger thing ahead, and I undergo another disappointment. *I* think you are too hard to please. Some day we'll get left. First, we turned down the dentist and the lawyer. That was all right—it was sound. Next, we turned down the banker's son and the pork-butchers heir—right again, and sound. Next, we turned down the Congressman's son and the Governor's—right as a trivet, I confess it. Next, the Senator's son and the son of the vice-president of the United States—perfectly right, there's no permanency about those little distinctions. Then you went for the aristocracy; and I thought we had struck oil at last—yes. We would make a plunge at the Four Hundred, and pull in some ancient lineage, venerable, holy, ineffable, mellow with the antiquity of a hundred and fifty years, disinfected of the ancestral odors of salt cod and pelts all of a century ago, and unsmirched by a day's work since; and then! why, then the marriages, of course. But no, along comes a pair of real aristocrats from Europe, and straightway you throw over the half-breeds. It was awfully discouraging, Aleck! Since then, what a procession! You turned down the baronets for a pair of barons; you turned down the barons for a pair of viscounts; the viscounts for a pair of earls; the earls for a pair of marquises; the marquises for a brace of dukes. *Now*, Aleck, cash in!—you've played the limit. You've got a job lot of four dukes under the hammer; of four nationalities; all sound in wind and limb and pedigree, all bankrupt and in debt up to the ears. They come high, but we can afford it. Come, Aleck, don't delay any longer, don't keep up the suspense: take the whole layout, and leave the girls to choose!"

Aleck had been smiling blandly and contentedly all through this arraignment of her marriage-policy; a pleasant light, as of triumph with perhaps a nice surprise peeping out through it, rose in her eyes, and she said, as calmly as she could—

"Sally, what would you say to—*royalty?*"

Prodigious! Poor man, it knocked him silly, and he fell over the garboard-strake and barked his shin on the cat-heads. He was dizzy for a moment, then he gathered himself up and limped over and sat down by his wife and beamed his old-time admiration and affection upon her in floods, out of his bleary eyes.

"By George!" he said, fervently. "Aleck, you *are* great—the greatest woman in the whole earth! I can't ever learn the whole size of you. I can't ever learn the immeasurable deeps of you. Here I've been considering myself qualified to criticize your game. *I!* Why, if I had stopped to think, I'd have known you had a lone hand up your sleeve. Now, dear heart, I'm all red-hot impatience—tell me about it!"

The flattered and happy woman put her lips to his car and whispered a princely name. It made him catch his breath, it lit his face with exultation.

"Land!" he said, "it's a stunning catch! He's got a gambling hell, and a graveyard, and a bishop, and a cathedral—all his very own. And all gilt-edged five-hundred-percent stock, every detail of it; the tidiest little property in Europe. And that graveyard—it's the selectest in the world: none but suicides admitted; *yes*, sir, and the free-list suspended, too, *all* the time. There isn't much land in the principality, but there's enough: eight hundred acres in the graveyard and forty-two outside. It's a *sovereignty*—that's the main thing; *lands* nothing. There's plenty land, Sahara's drugged with it."

Aleck glowed; she was profoundly happy. She said—

"Think of it, Sally—it is a family that has never married outside the Royal and Imperial Houses of Europe: our grandchildren will sit upon thrones!"

"True as you live, Aleck—and bear scepters, too; and ham die them as naturally and nonchalantly as I handle a yardstick. It's a grand catch, Aleck. He's corralled, is he? Can't get away? You didn't take him on a margin?"

"No. Trust me for that. He's not a liability, he's an asset. So is the other one."

"Who is it, Aleck?"

"His Royal Highness Sigismund-Siegfried-Lauenfeld-Dinkelspiel-Schwartzenberg Blutwurst, Hereditary Grand Duke of Katzenyammer."

"No! You can't mean it!"

"It's as true as I'm sitting here, I give you my word," she answered.

His cup was full, and he hugged her to his heart with rapture, saying—

"How wonderful it all seems, and how beautiful! It's one of the oldest and noblest of the three hundred and sixty-four ancient German principalities, and one of the few that was allowed to retain its royal estate when Bismarck got done trimming them. I know that farm, I've been there. It's got a ropewalk and a candle-factory and an army. Standing army. Infantry and cavalry. Three soldiers and a horse. Aleck, it's been a long wait, and full of heart-break and hope deferred, but God knows I am happy now. Happy, and grateful to you, my own, who have done it all. When is it to be?"

"Next Sunday."

"Good. And we'll want to do these weddings up in the very regalest style that's going. It's properly due to the royal quality of the parties of the first part. Now as I understand it, there is only one kind of marriage that is sacred to royalty, exclusive to royalty: it's the morganatic."

"What do they call it that for, Sally?"

"I don't know; but anyway it's royal, and royal only."

"Then we will insist upon it. More—I will compel it. It is morganatic marriage or none."

"That settles it!" said Sally, rubbing his hands with delight. "And it will be the very first in America. Aleck, it will make Newport sick."

Then they fell silent, and drifted away upon their dream-wings to the far regions of the earth to invite all the crowned heads and their families and provide gratis transportation for them.

VIII

During three days the couple walked upon air, with their heads in the clouds. They were but vaguely conscious of their surroundings, they saw all things dimly, as through a veil, they were steeped in dreams, often they did not hear when they were spoken to, they often did not understand when they heard; they answered confusedly or at random; Sally sold molasses by weight, sugar by the yard, and furnished soap when asked for candles, and Aleck put the cat in the wash and fed milk to the soiled linen. Everybody was stunned and amazed, and went about muttering, "What *can* be the matter with the Fosters?"

Three days. Then came events! Things had taken a happy turn, and for forty-eight hours Aleck's imaginary corner had been booming. Up—up—still up! Cost-point was passed. Still up—and up—and up! Five points above cost—then ten—fifteen—twenty! Twenty points cold profit on the vast venture, now, and Aleck's imaginary brokers were shouting frantically by imaginary long-distance, "Sell! sell! for Heaven's sake *sell!*"

She broke the splendid news to Sally, and he, too, said "Sell! sell—oh, don't make a blunder, now, you own the earth!—sell, sell!" But she set her iron will and lashed it amidships, and said she would hold on for five points more if she died for it.

It was a fatal resolve. The very next day came the historic crash, the record crash, the devastating crash, when the bottom fell out of Wall Street, and the whole body of gilt-edged stocks dropped ninety-five points in five hours, and the multimillionaire was seen begging his bread in the Bowery. Aleck sternly held her grip and "put up" as long as she could, but at last there came a call which she was powerless to meet, and her imaginary brokers sold her out. Then, and not till then, the man in her was vanquished, and the woman in her resumed sway. She put her arms about her husband's neck and wept, saying—

"I am to blame, do not forgive me, I cannot bear it. We are paupers! Paupers, and I am so miserable. The weddings will never come off; all that is past; we could not even buy the dentist, now."

A bitter reproach was on Sally's tongue: "I *begged* you to sell, but you—" He did not say it; he had not the heart to add a hurt to that broken and repentant spirit. A nobler thought came to him and he said—

"Bear up, my Aleck, all is not lost! You really never invested a penny of my uncle's bequest, but only its unmaterialized future; what we have lost was only 'the increment harvested from that future by your incomparable financial judgment and sagacity. Cheer up, banish these griefs; we still have the thirty thousand untouched; and with the experience which you have acquired, think what you will be able to do with it in a couple of years! The marriages are not off, they are only postponed."

These were blessed words. Aleck saw how true they were, and their influence was electric; her tears ceased to flow, and her great spirit rose to its full stature again. With flashing eye and grateful heart, and with hand uplifted in pledge and prophecy, she said—

"Now and here I proclaim—"

But she was interrupted by a visitor. It was the editor and proprietor of the *Sagamore.* He had happened into Lakeside to pay a duty-call upon an obscure grandmother of his who was nearing the end of her pilgrimage, and with the idea of combining business with grief he had looked up the Fosters, who had been so absorbed in other things for the past four years that they had neglected to pay up their subscription. Six dollars due. No visitor could have been more welcome. He would know all about Uncle Tilbury and what his chances might be getting to be, cemeterywards. They could of course ask no questions, for that would squelch the bequest, but they could nibble around on the edge of the subject and hope for results. The scheme did not work. The obtuse editor did not know he was being nibbled at; but at last, chance accomplished what art had failed in. In illustration of something under discussion which required the help of metaphor, the editor said—

"Land, it's as tough as Tilbury Foster!—as *we* say."

It was sudden, and it made the Fosters jump. The editor noticed it, and said, apologetically—

"No harm intended, I assure you. It's just a saying; just a joke, you know—nothing in it. Relation of yours?"

Sally crowded his burning eagerness down, and answered with all the indifference he could assume—

"I—well, not that I know of, but we've heard of him." The editor was thankful, and resumed his composure. Sally added, "Is he—is he—well?"

"Is he *well?* Why, bless you he's in Sheol these five years!"

The Fosters were trembling with grief, though it felt like joy. Sally said, non-committally—and tentatively:

"Ah, well, such is life, and none can escape—not even the rich are spared."

The editor laughed.

"If you are including Tilbury," said he, "it don't apply. *He* hadn't a cent; the town had to bury him."

The Fosters sat petrified for two minutes; petrified and cold. Then, white-faced and weak-voiced, Sally asked:

"Is it true? Do you *know* it to be true?"

"Well, I should say! I was one of the executors. He hadn't anything to leave but a wheelbarrow, and he left that to me. It hadn't any wheel, and wasn't any good. Still, it was something, and so, to square up, I scribbled off a sort of a little obituarial send-off for him, but it got crowded out."

The Fosters were not listening—their cup was full, it could contain no more. They sat with bowed heads, dead to all things but the ache at their hearts.

An hour later. Still they sat there, bowed, motionless, silent, the visitor long ago gone, they unaware.

Then they stirred, and lifted their heads wearily and gazed at each other wistfully, dreamily, dazed; then presently began to twaddle to each other in a wandering and childish way. At intervals they lapsed into silences, leaving a sentence unfinished, seemingly either unaware of it or losing their way. Sometimes, when they woke out of these silences, they had a dim and transient consciousness that something had happened to their minds; then with a dumb and yearning solicitude they would softly caress each other's hands in mutual compassion and support, as if they would say: "I am near you, I will not forsake you, we will bear it together; somewhere there is release and forgetfulness, somewhere there is a grave and peace; be patient, it will not be long."

They lived yet two years, in mental night, always brooding, steeped in vague regrets and melancholy dreams, never speaking; then release came to both on the same day.

Toward the end the darkness lifted from Sally's ruined mind for a moment, and he said:

"Vast wealth, acquired by sudden and unwholesome means, is a snare. It did us no good, transient were its feverish pleasures; yet for its sake we threw away our sweet and simple and happy life—let others take warning by us."

He lay silent a while, with closed eyes; then as the chill of death crept upward toward his heart, and consciousness was fading from his brain, he muttered:

"Money had brought him misery, and he took his revenge upon us, who had done him no harm. He had his desire: with base and cunning calculation he left us but thirty thousand, knowing we would try to increase it, and ruin our life and break our hearts. Without added expense he could have left us far above desire of increase, far above the temptation to speculate, and a kinder soul would have done it; but in him was no generous spirit, no pity, no—"

What Is Man?

February, 1905. The studies for these papers were begun twenty-five or twenty-seven years ago. The papers were written seven years ago. I have examined them once or twice per year since and found them satisfactory. I have just examined them again, and am still satisfied that they speak the truth.

Every thought in them has been thought (and accepted as unassailable truth) by millions upon millions of men—and concealed, kept private. Why did they not speak out? Because they dreaded (*and could not bear*) the disapproval of the people around them. Why have not I published? The same reason has restrained me, I think. I can find no other.

I

a. *Man the Machine* b. *Personal Merit*

[The Old Man and the Young Man had been conversing. The Old Man had asserted that the human being is merely a machine, and nothing more. The Young Man objected, and asked him to go into particulars and furnish his reasons for his position.]

OLD MAN. What are the materials of which a steam engine is made?

YOUNG MAN. Iron, steel, brass, white-metal, and so on.

O. M. Where are these found?

Y. M. In the rocks.

O. M. In a pure state?

Y. M. No—in ores.

O. M. Are the metals suddenly deposited in the ores?

Y. M. No—it is the patient work of countless ages.

O. M. You could make the engine out of the rocks themselves?

Y. M. Yes, a brittle one and not valuable.

O. M. You would not require much, of such an engine as that?

Y. M. No—substantially nothing.

O. M. To make a fine and capable engine, how would you proceed?

Y. M. Drive tunnels and shafts into the hills; blast out the iron ore; crush it, smelt it, reduce it to pig iron; put some of it through the Bessemer process and make steel of it. Mine and treat and combine the several metals of which brass is made.

O. M. Then?

Y. M. Out of the perfected result, build the fine engine.

O. M. You would require much, of this one?

Y. M. Oh, indeed yes.

O. M. It could drive lathes, drills, planers, punches, polishers, in a word all the cunning machines of a great factory?

Y. M. It could.

O. M. What could the stone engine do?

Y. M. Drive a sewing machine, possibly—nothing more, perhaps.

O. M. Men would admire the other engine and rapturously praise it?

Y. M. Yes.

O. M. But not the stone one?

Y. M. No.

O. M. The merits of the metal machine would be far above those of the stone one?

Y. M. Of course.

O. M. Personal merits?

Y. M. *Personal* merits? How do you mean?

O. M. It would be personally entitled to the credit of its own performance?

Y. M. The engine? Certainly not.

O. M. Why not?

Y. M. Because its performance is not personal. It is a result of the law of its construction. It is not a *merit* that it does the things which it is set to do—it can't *help* doing them.

O. M. And it is not a personal demerit in the stone machine that it does so little?

Y. M. Certainly not. It does no more and no less than the law of its make permits and compels it to do. There is nothing *personal* about it; it cannot choose. In this process of "working up to the matter" is it your idea to work up to the proposition that a man and a machine are about the same thing, and that there is no personal merit in the performance of either?

O. M. Yes—but do not be offended; I am meaning no offense. What makes the grand difference between the stone engine and the steel one? Shall we call it training, education? Shall we call the stone engine a savage and the steel one a civilized man? The original rock contained the stuff of which the steel one was built—but along with it a lot of sulfur and stone and other obstructing inborn heredities, brought down from the old geologic ages—prejudices, let us call them. Prejudices which nothing within the rock itself had either *power* to remove or any *desire* to remove. Will you take note of that phrase?

Y. M. Yes. I have written it down: "Prejudices which nothing within the rock itself had either power to remove or any desire to remove." Go on.

O. M. Prejudices which must be removed by *outside influences* or not at all. Put that down.

Y. M. Very well "Must be removed by outside influences or not at all." Go on.

O. M. The iron's prejudice against ridding itself of the cumbering rock. To make it more exact, the iron's absolute *indifference* as to whether the rock be removed or not. Then comes the *outside influence* and grinds the rock to powder and sets the ore free. The iron in the ore is still captive. An *outside influence* smelts it free of the clogging ore. The iron is emancipated iron, now, but indifferent to further progress. An *outside influence* beguiles it into the Bessemer furnace and refines it into steel of the first quality. It is educated, now—its training is complete. And it has reached its limit. By no possible process can it be educated into *gold.* Will you set that down?

Y. M. Yes: "Everything has its limit—iron ore cannot be educated into gold."

O. M. There are gold men, and tin men, and copper men, and leaden men, and steel men, and so on—and each has the limitations of his nature, his heredities, his training and his environment. You can build engines out of each of those metals, and they will all perform, but you must not require the weak ones to do equal work with the stronger ones. In each case, to get the best results, you must free the metal from its obstructing prejudicial ores by education—smelting, refining, and so forth.

Y. M. You have arrived at man, now?

O. M. Yes. Man the machine—man, the impersonal engine. Whatsoever a man is, is due to his *make*, and to the *influences* brought to bear upon it by his heredities, his habitat, his associations. He is moved, directed, COMMANDED, by *exterior* influences—*solely.* He *originates* nothing, himself—not even an opinion, not even a thought.

Y. M. Oh, come! Where did I get my opinion that this which you are talking is all foolishness?

O. M. It is a quite natural opinion—indeed an inevitable opinion—but *you* did not create the materials out of which it is formed. They are odds and ends of thoughts, impressions, feelings, gathered unconsciously from a thousand books, a thousand conversations, and from streams of thought and feeling which have flowed down into your heart and brain out of the hearts and brains of ten centuries of ancestors. *Personally* you did not create even the smallest microscopic fragment of the materials out of which your opinion is made; and personally you cannot claim even the slender merit of *putting the borrowed materials together.* That was done *automatically*—by your mental machinery, in strict accordance with the law of that machinery's construction. And you not only did not make that machinery yourself, but you have *not even any command over it.*

Y. M. This is too much. You think I could have formed no opinion but that one?

O. M. Spontaneously? No. And *you did not form that one;* your machinery did it for you—automatically and instantly, without reflection or the need of it.

Y. M. Suppose I had reflected? How then?

O. M. Suppose you try.

Y. M. (*After a quarter of an hour.*) I have reflected.

O. M. You mean you have tried to change your opinion—as an experiment?

Y. M. Yes.

O. M. With success?

Y. M. No. It remains the same; it is impossible to change it.

O. M. I am sorry, but you see, yourself, that your mind is merely a machine, nothing more. You have no command over it, it has no command over itself—it is worked *solely from the outside.* That is the law of its make; it is the law of all machines.

Y. M. Can't I *ever* change one of these automatic opinions?

O. M. No. You can't, yourself, but *exterior influences* can do it.

Y. M. And exterior ones *only?*

O. M. Yes—exterior ones only.

Y. M. That position is untenable—I may say ludicrously untenable.

O. M. What makes you think so?

Y. M. I don't merely think it, I know it. Suppose I resolve to enter upon a course of thought, and study, and reading, with the deliberate purpose of changing that opinion; and suppose I succeed. *That* is not the work of an exterior impulse, the whole of it is mine and personal; for I originated the project.

O. M. Not a shred of it. *It grew out of this talk with me.* But for that it would never have occurred to you. No man ever originates anything. All his thoughts, all his impulses, come *from the outside.*

Y. M. It's an exasperating subject. The *first* man had original thoughts, anyway; there was nobody to draw from.

O. M. It is a mistake. Adam's thoughts came to him from the outside. *You* have a fear of death. You did not invent that—you got it from outside, from talk and teaching. Adam had no fear of death—none in the world.

Y. M. Yes he had.

O. M. When he was created?

Y. M. No.

O. M. When, then?

Y. M. When he was threatened with it.

O. M. Then it came from the *outside.* Adam is quite big enough; let us not try to make a god of him. *None but gods have ever had a thought which did not come from the outside.* Adam probably had a good head, but it was of no sort of use to him until it was filled up *from the outside.* He was not able to invent the triflingest little thing with it. He had not a shadow of a notion of the difference between good and evil—he had to get the idea *from the outside.* Neither he nor Eve was able to originate the idea that it was immodest to go naked: the knowledge came in with the apple *from the outside.* A man's brain is so constructed that *it can originate nothing whatever.* It can only use material obtained outside. It is merely a machine; and it works automatically, not by will power. *It has no command over itself, its owner has no command over it.*

Y. M. Well, never mind Adam; but certainly Shakespeare's creations —

O. M. No, you mean Shakespeare's *imitations.* Shakespeare created nothing. He correctly observed, and he marvelously painted. He exactly portrayed people whom *God* had created, but he created none himself. Let us spare him the slander of charging him with trying. Shakespeare could not create. *He was a machine, and machines do not create.*

Y. M. Where *was* his excellence, then?

O. M. In this. He was not a sewing machine, like you and me, he was a Gobelin loom. The threads and the colors came into him *from the outside;* outside influences, suggestions, *experiences,* (reading, seeing plays, playing plays, borrowing ideas, and so on), framed the patterns in his mind and started up its complex and admirable machinery, and *it automatically* turned out that pictured and gorgeous fabric which still compels the astonishment of the world. If Shakespeare had been born and bred on a barren and unvisited rock in the ocean his mighty intellect would have had no *outside material* to work with, and could have invented none; and *no outside influences,* teachings, moldings, persuasions, inspirations, of a valuable sort, and could have invented none; and so, Shakespeare would have produced nothing. In Turkey he would have produced something—something up to the highest limit of Turkish influences, associations and training. In France he would have produced something better—something up to the highest limit of the French influences and training. In England he rose to the highest limit attainable through the *outside helps afforded by that lands ideals, influences and training.* You and I are but sewing machines. We must turn out what we can; we must do our endeavor, and care nothing at all when the unthinking reproach us for not turning out Gobelins.

Y. M. And so we are mere machines! And machines may not

boast, nor feel proud of their performance, nor claim personal merit for it, nor applause and praise. It is an infamous doctrine.

O. M. It isn't a doctrine, it is merely a fact.

Y. M. I suppose, then, there is no more merit in being brave than in being a coward?

O. M. *Personal* merit? No. A brave man does not create his bravery. He is entitled to no personal credit for possessing it. It is born to him. A baby born with a billion dollars—where is the personal merit in that? A baby born with nothing—where is the personal demerit in that? The one is fawned upon, admired, worshipped, by sycophants, the other is neglected and despised—where is the sense in it?

Y. M. Sometimes a timid man sets himself the task of conquering his cowardice and becoming brave—and succeeds. What do you say to that?

O. M. That it shows the value of *training in right directions over training in wrong ones.* Inestimably valuable is training, influence, education, in right directions—*training one's self-approbation to elevate its ideals.*

Y. M. But as to merit—the personal merit of the victorious coward's project and achievement?

O. M. There isn't any. In the world's view he is a worthier man than he was before, but *he* didn't achieve the change—the merit of it is not his.

Y. M. Whose, then?

O. M. His make, and the influences which wrought upon it from the outside.

Y. M. His make?

O. M. Yes. To start with, he was *not* utterly and completely a coward, or the influences would have had nothing to work upon. He was not afraid of a cow, though perhaps of a bull; not afraid of a woman, but afraid of a man. There was something to build upon. There was a seed. No seed, no plant. Did he make that *seed* himself, or was it born in him? It was no merit of *his* that the seed was there.

Y. M. Well, anyway, the idea of *cultivating* it, the resolution to cultivate it, was meritorious, and he originated that.

O. M. He did nothing of the kind. It came whence all impulses, good or bad, come—from *outside.* If that timid man had lived all his life in a community of human rabbits; had never read of brave deeds; had never heard speech of them; had never heard any one praise them nor express envy of the heroes that had done them, he would have had no more idea of bravery than Adam had of modesty, and it could never by any possibility have occurred to him to *resolve* to become brave. He *could not originate the idea*—it had to come to him from the *outside*. And so, when he heard bravery extolled and cowardice derided, it woke him up. He was ashamed. Perhaps his sweetheart turned up her nose and said "I am told that you are a coward!" It was not *he* that turned over the new leaf—she did it for him. *He* must not strut around in the merit of it—it is not his.

Y. M. But anyway he reared the plant after she watered the seed.

O. M. No. *Outside influences* reared it. At the command—and trembling—he marched out into the field—with other soldiers and in the daytime, not alone and in the dark. He had the *influence of example*, he drew courage from his comrades' courage; he was afraid, and wanted to run, but he did not dare; he was *afraid* to run, with all those soldiers looking on. He was progressing, you see—the moral fear of shame had risen superior to the physical fear of harm. By the end of the campaign experience will have taught him that not *all* who go into battle get hurt—an outside influence which will be helpful to him; and he will also have learned how sweet it is to be praised for courage and be huzza'd at with tear-choked voices as the war-worn regiment marches past the worshipping multitude with the flags flying and the drums beating. After that he will be as securely brave as any veteran in the army—and there will not be a shade nor suggestion of *personal merit* in it anywhere; it will all have come from the *outside*. The Victoria Cross breeds more heroes than—

Y. M. Hang it, where is the sense in his becoming brave if he is to get no credit for it?

O. M. Your question will answer itself presently. It involves an important detail of man's make which we have not yet touched upon.

Y. M. What detail is that?

O. M. The impulse which moves a person to do things—the only impulse that ever moves a person to do a thing.

Y. M. The *only* one! Is there but one?

O. M. That is all. There is only one.

Y. M. Well, certainly that is a strange enough doctrine. What is the sole impulse that ever moves a person to do a thing?

O. M. The impulse to *content his own spirit*—the *necessity* of contenting his own spirit and *winning its approval.*

Y. M. Oh, come, that won't do!

O. M. Why won't it?

Y. M. Because it puts him in the attitude of always looking out for his own comfort and advantage; whereas an unselfish man often does a tiring solely for another person's good when it is a positive disadvantage to himself.

O. M. It is a mistake. The act must do *him* good, FIRST; otherwise he will not do it. He may *think* he is doing it solely for the other person's sake, but it is not so; he is contenting his own spirit *first*—the other person's benefit has to always take *second* place.

Y. M. What a fantastic idea! What becomes of self-sacrifice? Please answer me that.

O. M. What is self-sacrifice?

Y. M. The doing good to another person where no shadow nor suggestion of benefit to one's self can result from it.

2

Man's Sole Impulse—The Securing of His Own Approval

O. M. There have been instances of it—you think?

Y. M. *Instances?* Millions of them!

O. M. You have not jumped to conclusions? You have examined them—critically?

Y. M. They don't need it; the acts themselves reveal the golden impulse back of them.

O. M. For instance?

Y. M. Well, then, for instance. Take the case in the book here. The man lives three miles up town. It is bitter cold, blowing hard, snowing hard, midnight. He is about to enter the horse-car when a gray and ragged old woman, a touching picture of misery, puts out her lean hand and begs for rescue from hunger and death. The man finds that he has but a quarter in his pocket, but he does not hesitate; he gives it to her and trudges home through the storm. There—it is noble, it is beautiful; its grace is marred by no fleck or blemish or suggestion of self-interest.

O. M. What makes you think that?

Y. M. Pray what else could I think? Do you imagine that there is some other way of looking at it?

O. M. Can you put yourself in the man's place and tell me what he felt and what he thought?

Y. M. Easily. The sight of that suffering old face pierced his generous heart with a sharp pain. He could not bear it. He could endure the three-mile walk in the storm, but he could not endure the tortures his conscience would suffer if he turned his back and left that poor old creature to perish. He would not have been able to sleep, for thinking of it.

O. M. What was his state of mind on his way home?

Y. M. It was a state of joy which only the self-sacrificer knows. His heart sang, he was unconscious of the storm.

O. M. He slept well?

Y. M. One cannot doubt it.

O. M. Very well. Now let us add up the details and see how much he got for his twenty-five cents. Let us try to find out the *real* why of his making the investment. In the first place *he* couldn't bear the pain which the suffering old face gave him. So he was thinking of *his* pain—this good man. He must buy a salve for it. If he did not succor the old woman his conscience would torture him all the way home. Thinking of his pain again. He must buy relief from that. If he didn't relieve the old woman *he* would not get any sleep. He must buy some sleep—still thinking of *himself*, you see. Thus, to sum up, he bought himself free of a sharp pain in his heart, he bought himself free of the tortures of a waiting conscience, he bought a whole night's sleep—all for twenty-five cents! This able trader got a hundred dollars' worth of clean profit out of an investment of twenty-five cents. It should make Wall Street ashamed of itself: On his way home his heart was joyful, and it sang—profit on top of profit! The impulse which moved the man to succor the old woman was—*first*—to *content his own spirit;* secondly, to relieve *her* sufferings. Is it your opinion that men's acts proceed from one central and unchanging and inalterable impulse, or from a variety of impulses?

Y. M. From a variety, of course—some high and fine and noble, others not. What is your opinion?

O. M. That there is but one law, one source.

Y. M. That both the noblest impulses and the basest proceed from that one source?

O. M. Yes.

Y. M. Will you put that law into words?

O. M. Yes. This is the law. Keep it in your mind. *From his cradle to his grave a man never does a single thing which has any* FIRST AND FOREMOST *object but one—to secure peace of mind, spiritual comfort, for* HIMSELF.

Y. M. Come! He never does anything for any one else's comfort, spiritual or physical?

O. M. No. *Except on those distinct terms*—that it shall *first* secure *his own* spiritual comfort. Otherwise, he will not do it.

Y. M. It will be easy to expose the falsity of that proposition.

O. M. For instance?

Y. M. Take that noble passion, love of country, patriotism. A man who loves peace and dreads pain, leaves his pleasant home and his weeping family and marches out to manfully expose himself to hunger, cold, wounds and death. Is that seeking spiritual comfort?

O. M. He loves peace and dreads pain?

Y. M. Yes.

O. M. Then perhaps there is something that he loves more than he loves peace—*the approval of his neighbors and the public.* And perhaps there is something which he dreads more than he dreads pain—the *disapproval* of his neighbors and the public. If he is sensitive to shame he will go to the field—not because his spirit will be *entirely* comfortable there, but because it will be more comfortable there than it would be if he remained at home. He will always do the thing which will bring him the *most* mental comfort—for that is *the sole law of his life.* He leaves the weeping family behind; he is sorry to make them uncomfortable, but not sorry enough to sacrifice his *own* comfort to secure theirs.

Y. M. Do you really believe that mere public opinion could force a timid and peaceful man to—

O. M. Go to the wars? Yes—public opinion can force some men to do *anything.*

Y. M. *Anything?*

O. M. Yes—anything.

Y. M. I don't believe that. Can it force a right-principled man to do a wrong thing?

O. M. Yes.

Y. M. Can it force a kind man to do a cruel thing?

O. M. Yes.

Y. M. Give an instance.

O. M. Alexander Hamilton was a conspicuously high-principled man. He regarded dueling as wrong, and as opposed to the teachings of religion—but in deference to *public opinion* he fought a duel. He deeply loved his family, but to buy public approval he treacherously deserted them and threw his life away, ungenerously leaving them to lifelong sorrow in order that he might stand well with a foolish world. In the then condition of the public standards of honor he could not have been comfortable with the stigma upon him of having refused to fight. The teachings of religion, his devotion to his family, his kindness of heart, his high principles, all went for nothing when they stood in the way of his spiritual comfort. A man will do *anything,* no matter what it is, *to secure his spiritual comfort;* and he can neither be forced nor persuaded to any act which has not that goal for its object. Hamilton's act was compelled by the inborn necessity of contenting his own spirit; in this it was like all the other acts of his life, and like all the acts of all men's lives. Do you see where the kernel of the matter lies? A man cannot be comfortable without *his own* approval. He will secure the largest share possible of that, at all costs, all sacrifices.

Y. M. A minute ago you said Hamilton fought the duel to get the *public* approval.

O. M. I did. By refusing to fight the duel he could have secured his family's approval and a large share of his own; but the public approval was more valuable in his eyes than all other approvals put together—in the earth or above it; to secure that would furnish him the *most* comfort of mind, the most self-approval; so he sacrificed all other values to get it.

Y. M. Some noble souls have refused to fight duels, and have manfully braved the public contempt.

O. M. They acted *according to their make.* They valued their principles and the approval of their families *above* the public approval. They took the thing they valued *most* and let the rest go. They took what would give them the *largest* share of *personal contentment and approval*—a man *always* does. Public opinion cannot force that kind of men to go to the wars. When they go, it is for other reasons. Other spirit-contenting reasons.

Y. M. Always spirit-contenting reasons?

O. M. There are no others.

Y. M. When a man sacrifices his life in trying to save a little child from a burning building, what do you call that?

O. M. When he does it, it is the law of *his* make. *He* can't bear to see the child in that peril, (a man of a different make *could*), and so he tries to save the child, and loses his life. But he has got what he was after—*his own approval.*

Y. M. What do you call Love, Hate, Charity, Revenge, Humanity, Magnanimity, Forgiveness?

O. M. Different results of the one Master Impulse: the necessity of scouring one's self-approval. They wear diverse clothes and are subject to diverse moods, but in whatsoever ways they masquerade they are the *same person* all the time. To change the figure, the *compulsion* that moves a man—and there is but the one—is the necessity of securing the contentment of his own spirit. When it stops, the man is dead.

Y. M. This is foolishness. Love—

O. M. Why, love is that impulse, that law, in its most uncompromising form. It will squander life and everything else on its object. Not *primarily* for the object's sake, but for its *own.* When its object is happy *it* is happy—and that is what it is unconsciously after.

Y. M. You do not even except the lofty and gracious passion of mother-love?

O. M. No, *it* is the absolute slave of that law. The mother will go naked to clothe her child; she will starve that it may have food; suffer torture to save it from pain; die that it may live. She takes a living *pleasure* in making these sacrifices. *She does it for that reward*—that self-approval, that contentment, that peace, that comfort. *She would do it for your child* IF SHE COULD GET THE SAME PAY.

Y. M. This is an infernal philosophy of yours.

O. M. It isn't a philosophy, it is a fact.

Y. M. Of course you must admit that there are some acts which—

O. M. No. There is *no* act, large or small, fine or mean, which springs from any motive but the one—the necessity of appeasing and contenting one's own spirit.

Y. M. The world's philanthropists.

O. M. I honor them, I uncover my head to them—from habit and training; but *they*, could not know comfort or happiness or self-approval if they did not work and spend for the unfortunate. It makes *them* happy to see others happy; and so with money and labor they buy what they are after *happiness, self-approval.* Why don't misers do the same thing? Because they can get a thousand-fold more happiness by *not* doing it. There is no other reason. They follow the law of their make.

Y. M. What do you say of duty, for duty's sake?

O. M. That *it does not exist.* Duties are not performed for duty's *sake*, but because their *neglect* would make the man *uncomfortable.* A man performs but *one* duty—the duty of contenting his spirit, the duty of making himself agreeable to himself. If he can most satisfyingly perform this sole and only duty, by *helping* his neighbor, he will do it; if he can most satisfyingly perform it by *swindling* his neighbor, he will do that. But always he looks out for Number One—*first;* the effects upon others are a *secondary* matter. Men pretend to self-sacrifices, but this is a thing which, in the ordinary value of the phrase, *does not exist and has not existed.* A man often honestly *thinks* he is sacrificing himself merely and solely for some one else, but he is deceived: his bottom impulse is to content a requirement of his nature and training, and thus acquire peace for his soul.

Y. M. Apparently, then, all men, both good and bad ones, devote their lives to contenting their consciences?

O. M. Yes. That is a good enough name for it: Conscience—that independent Sovereign, that insolent absolute Monarch inside of a man who is the man's Master. There are all kinds of consciences, because there are all kinds of men. You satisfy an assassin's conscience in one way, a philanthropist's in another, a miser's in another, a burglar's in still another. As a *guide* or *incentive* to any authoritatively prescribed line of morals or conduct, (leaving *training* out of the account), a man's conscience is totally valueless. I knew a kindhearted Kentuckian whose self-approval was lacking—whose conscience was troubling him, to phrase it with exactness—*because* he had neglected to kill a certain man—a man whom he had never seen. The stranger had killed this man's friend in a fight, this man's Kentucky training made it his duty to kill the stranger for it. He neglected this duty—kept dodging it, shirking it, putting it off, and his unrelenting conscience kept persecuting him for this conduct. At last, to get ease of mind, comfort, self-approval, he hunted up the stranger and took his life. It was an immense act of *self-sacrifice*, (as per the usual definition), for he did not want to do it, and he never would have done it if he could have bought a contented spirit and an unworried mind at smaller cost. But we are so made that we will pay *anything* for that contentment—even another man's life.

Y. M. You spoke a moment ago of *trained* consciences. You mean that we are not *born* with consciences competent to guide us aright?

O. M. If we were, children and savages would know right from wrong, and not have to be taught it.

Y. M. But consciences can be *trained?*

O. M. Yes.

Y. M. Of course by parents, teachers, the pulpit, and books.

O. M. Yes—they do their share; they do what they can.

Y. M. And the rest is done by—

O. M. Oh, a million unnoticed influences—for good or bad; influences which work without rest during every waking moment of a man's life, from cradle to grave.

Y. M. You have tabulated these?

O. M. Many of them—yes.

Y. M. Will you read me the result?

O. M. Another time, yes. It would take an hour.

Y. M. A conscience can be trained to shun evil and prefer good?

O. M. Yes.

Y. M. But will prefer it for spirit-contenting reasons only?

O. M. It *can't* be trained to do a thing for any *other* reason. The thing is impossible.

Y. M. There *must* be a genuinely and utterly self-sacrificing act recorded in human history somewhere.

O. M. You are young. You have many years before you. Search one out.

Y. M. It does seem to me that when a man sees a fellow-being struggling in the water and jumps in at the risk of his life to save him—

O. M. Wait. Describe the *man.* Describe the *fellow-being.* State if there is an *audience* present; or if they are *alone.*

Y. M. What have these things to do with the splendid act?

O. M. Very much. Shall we suppose, as a beginning, that the two are alone, in a solitary place, at midnight?

Y. M. If you choose.

O. M. And that the fellow-being is the man's daughter?

Y. M. Well, n-no—make it some one else.

O. M. A filthy, drunken ruffian, then?

Y. M. I see. Circumstances alter cases. I suppose that if there was no audience to observe the act, the man wouldn't perform it.

O. M. But there is here and there a man who *would.* People, for instance, like the man who lost his life trying to save the child from the fire; and like the man who gave the needy old woman his 25 cents and walked home in the storm—there are here and there men like that who would do it. And why? Because they couldn't *bear* to see a fellow-being struggling in the water and not jump in and help. It would give *them* pain. They would save the fellow-being on that account. *They wouldn't do it otherwise.* They strictly obey the law which I have been insisting upon. You must remember and always distinguish the people who *can't bear* things from the people who *can.* It will throw light upon a number of apparently "self sacrificing" cases.

Y. M. Oh, dear, it's all so disgusting.

O. M. Yes. And so true.

Y. M. Come—take the good boy who does things which he doesn't want to do, in order to gratify his mother.

O. M. He does seven-tenths of the act because it gratifies *him* to gratify his mother. Throw the bulk of advantage the other way and the good boy would not do the act. He *must* obey the iron law. None can escape it.

Y. M. Well, take the case of a bad boy who—

O. M. You needn't mention it, it is a waste of time. It is no matter about the bad boy's act. Whatever it was, he had a spirit-contenting reason for it. Otherwise you have been misinformed, and he didn't do it.

Y. M. It is very exasperating. A while ago you said that a man's conscience is not a born judge of morals and conduct, but has to be taught and trained. Now I think a conscience can get drowsy and lazy, but I don't think it can go wrong; and if you wake it up—

A LITTLE STORY

O. M. I will tell you a little story:

Once upon a time an Infidel was a guest in the house of a Christian widow whose little boy was ill and near to death. The Infidel often watched by the bedside and entertained the boy with talk, and he used these opportunities to satisfy a strong longing of his nature—that desire which is in us all to better other people's condition by having them think as we think. He was successful. But the dying boy, in his last moments, reproached him and said—

"I believed, and was happy in it; you have taken my belief away, and my comfort Now I have nothing left, and I die miserable; for the things which you have told me do not take the place of that which I have lost."

And the mother, also, reproached the Infidel, and said—

"My child is forever lost, and my heart is broken. How could you do this crud thing? We had done you no harm, but only kindness; we made our house your home, you were welcome to all we had, and this is our reward."

The heart of the Infidel was filled with remorse for what he had done, and he said—

"It was wrong —I see it now; but I was only trying to do him good. In my view he was in error; it seemed my duty to teach him the truth."

Then the mother said—

"I had taught him, all his little life, what I believed to be the truth, and in his believing faith both of us were happy. Now he is dead—and lost; and I am miserable. Our faith came down to us through centuries of believing ancestors; what right had you, or any one, to disturb it? Where was your honor, where was your shame?"

Y. M. He was a miscreant, and deserved death!

O. M. He thought so himself, and said so.

Y. M. Ah—you see, *his conscience was awakened!*

O. M. Yes—his Self-Disapproval was. It *pained* him to see the mother suffer. He was sorry he had done a thing which brought him pain. It did not occur to him to think of the mother when he was misteaching the boy, for he was absorbed in providing *pleasure* for himself, then. Providing it by satisfying what he believed to be a call of duty.

Y. M. Call it what you please, it is to me a case of *awakened conscience.* That awakened conscience could never get itself into that species of trouble again. A cure like that is a *permanent* cure.

O. M. Pardon—I had not finished the story. We are creatures of *outside influences*—we originate *nothing* within. Whenever we take a new line of thought and drift into a new line of belief and action, the impulse is *always* suggested from the *outside.* Remorse so preyed upon the Infidel that it dissolved his harshness toward the boy's religion and made him come to regard it with tolerance, next with kindness, and presently with tenderness, for the boy's sake and the mother's. Finally he found himself examining it. From that moment his progress in his new trend was steady and rapid. He became a believing Christian. And now his remorse for having robbed the dying boy of his faith and his salvation was bitterer than ever. It gave him no rest, no peace. He *must* have rest and peace—it is the law of our nature. There seemed but one way to get it; he must devote himself to saving imperiled souls. He became a missionary. He landed in a pagan country ill and helpless. A native widow took him into her humble home and nursed him back to convalescence. Then her young boy was taken hopelessly ill, and the grateful missionary helped her tend him. Here was his first opportunity to repair a part of the wrong done to the other boy by doing a precious service for this one by undermining his foolish faith in his false gods. He was successful. But the dying boy in his last moments reproached him, and said—

"I believed, and was happy in it; you have taken my belief away, and my comfort. Now I have nothing left, and I die miserable; for the things which you have told me do not take the place of that which I have lost."

And the mother, also, reproached the missionary, and said —

"My child is forever lost, and my heart is broken. How could you do this cruel thing? We had done you no harm, but only kindness; we made our house your home, you were welcome to all we had, and this is our reward."

The heart of the missionary was filled with remorse for what he had done, and he said—

"It was wrong —I see it now; but I was only trying to do him good. In my view he was in error; it seemed my duty to teach him the truth."

Then the mother said—

"I had taught him, all his little life, what I believed to be the truth, and in his believing faith both of us we, happy. Now he is dead—and lost; and I am miserable. Our faith came down to us through centuries of believing ancestors; what right had you, or any one, to disturb it? Where was your honor, where was your shame?"

The missionary's anguish of remorse and sense of treachery were as bitter and persecuting and unappeasable, now, as they had been in the former case. The story is finished. What is your comment?

Y. M. The man's conscience was a fool! It was morbid. It didn't know right from wrong.

O. M. I am not sorry to hear you say that. If you grant that one man's conscience doesn't know right from wrong, it is an admission that there are others like it. This single admission pulls down the whole doctrine of infallibility of judgment in consciences. Meantime there is one thing which I ask you to notice.

Y. M. What is that?

O. M. That in both cases the man's *act* gave him no spiritual discomfort, and that he was quite satisfied with it and got pleasure out of it. But afterward when it resulted in *pain* to *him*, he was sorry. Sorry it had inflicted pain upon the others, *but for no reason under the sun except that their pain gave* HIM *pain.* Our consciences take no notice of pain inflicted upon others until it reaches a point where it gives pain to *us.* In *all* cases without exception we are absolutely indifferent to another person's pain until his sufferings make us uncomfortable. Many an infidel would not have been troubled by that Christian mother's distress. Don't you believe that?

Y. M. Yes. You might almost say it of the *average* infidel, I think.

O. M. And many a missionary, sternly fortified by his sense of duty, would not have been troubled by the pagan mother's distress—Jesuit missionaries in Canada in the early French times, for instance; see episodes quoted by Parkman.

Y. M. Well, let us adjourn. Where have we arrived?

O. M. At this. That we (mankind), have ticketed ourselves with a number of qualities to which we have given misleading names. Love, Hate, Charity, Compassion, Avarice, Benevolence, and so on. I mean, we attach *misleading* meanings to the names. They are all forms of self-contentment, self-gratification, but the names so disguise them that they distract our attention from the fact. Also, we have smuggled a word into the dictionary which ought not to be there at all—self-sacrifice. It describes a thing which does not exist. But worst of all, we ignore and never mention the Sole Impulse which dictates and compels a man's every act: the imperious necessity of securing his own approval, in every emergency and at all costs. To it we owe all that we are. It is our breath, our heart, our blood. It is our only spur, our whip, our goad, our only impelling power; we have no other. Without it we should be mere inert images, corpses; no one would do anything, there would be no progress, the world would stand still. We ought to stand reverently uncovered when the name of that stupendous power is uttered.

Y. M. I am not convinced.

O. M. You will be, when you think.

3

Instances in Point

O. M. Have you given thought to the Gospel of Self-Approval since we talked?

Y. M. I have.

O. M. It was I that moved you to it. That is to say, an *outside influence* moved you to it—not one that originated in your own head. Will you try to keep that in mind and not forget it?

Y. M. Yes. Why?

O. M. Because by and by, in one of our talks, I wish to further impress upon you that neither you, nor I, nor any man ever originates a thought in his own head. *The utterer of a thought always utters a secondhand one.*

Y. M. Oh, now—

O. M. Wait. Reserve your remark till we get to that part of our discussion—tomorrow or next day, say. Now, then, you have been considering the proposition that no act is ever born of any but a self-contenting impulse—(primarily). You have sought. What have you found?

Y. M. I have not been very fortunate. I have examined many fine and apparently self-sacrificing deeds in romances and biographies, but—

O. M. Under searching analysis the ostensible self-sacrifice disappeared? It naturally would.

Y. M. But here in this novel is one which seems to promise. In the Adirondack woods is a wage earner and lay preacher in the lumber camps who is of noble character and deeply religious. An earnest and practical laborer in the New York slums comes up there on vacation—he is leader of a section of the University Settlement. Holme, the lumberman, is fired with a desire to throw away his excellent worldly prospects and go down and save souls on the East Side. He counts it happiness to make this sacrifice for the glory of God and for the cause of Christ. He resigns his place, makes the sacrifice cheerfully, and goes to the East Side and preaches Christ and Him crucified every day and every night to little groups of half-civilized foreign paupers who scoff at him. But he rejoices in the scoffings, since he is suffering them in the great cause of Christ. You have so filled my mind with suspicions that I was constantly expecting to find a hidden questionable impulse back of all this, but I am thankful to say I have failed. This man saw his duty, and for *duty's sake* he sacrificed self and assumed the burden it imposed.

O. M. Is that as far as you have read?

Y. M. Yes.

O. M. Let us read further, presently. Meantime, in sacrificing himself—*not* for the glory of God, *primarily*, as *he* imagined, but *first* to content that exacting and inflexible master within him—*did he sacrifice anybody else?*

Y. M. How do you mean?

O. M. He relinquished a lucrative post and got mere food and lodging in place of it. Had he dependents?

Y. M. Well—yes.

O. M. In what way and to what extent did his self-sacrifice affect *them?*

Y. M. He was the support of a superannuated father. He had a young sister with a remarkable voice—he was giving her a musical education, so that her longing to be self-supporting might be gratified. He was furnishing the money to put a young brother through a polytechnic school and satisfy his desire to become a civil engineer.

O. M. The old father's comforts were now curtailed?

Y. M. Quite seriously. Yes.

O. M. The sister's music lessons had to stop?

Y. M. Yes.

O. M. The young brother's education—well an extinguishing blight fell upon that happy dream, and he had to go to sawing wood to support the old father, or something like that?

Y. M. It is about what happened. Yes.

O. M. What a handsome job of self-sacrificing he did do! It seems to me that he sacrificed everybody *except* himself. Haven't I told you that no man *ever* sacrifices himself; that there is no instance of it upon record anywhere; and that when a man's Interior Monarch requires a thing of its slave for either its *momentary* or its *permanent* contentment, that thing must and will be furnished and that command obeyed, no matter who may stand in the way and suffer disaster by it? That man *ruined his family* to please and content his Interior Monarch —

Y. M. And help Christ's cause.

O. M. Yes—*secondly*. Not firstly. *He* thought it was firstly.

Y. M. Very well, have it so, if you will. But it could be that he argued that if he saved a hundred souls in New York—

O. M. The sacrifice of the *family* would be justified by that great profit upon the—the—what shall we call it?

Y. M. Investment?

O. M. Hardly. How would *speculation* do? how would *gamble* do? Not a solitary soul-capture was sure. He played for a possible thirty-three hundred per cent profit. It was *gambling*—with his family for "chips." However, let us see how the game came out. Maybe we can get on the track of the secret original impulse, the *real* impulse, that moved him to so nobly self-sacrifice his family in the Savior's cause under the superstition that he was sacrificing himself. I will read a chapter or so . . . . Here we have it! it was bound to expose itself sooner or later. He preached to the East-Side rabble a season, then went back to his old dull and obscure life in the lumber camps "*hurt to the heart, his pride humbled.*" Why? Were not his efforts acceptable to the Savior, for Whom alone they were made? Dear me, that detail is *lost sight of*, is not even referred to, the fact that it started out as a motive is entirely forgotten! Then what is the trouble? The authoress quite innocently and unconsciously gives the whole business away. The trouble was this: this man merely *preached* to the poor; that is not the University Settlement's way; it deals in larger and better things than that, and it did not enthuse over that crude Salvation Army eloquence. It was courteous to Holme—but cool. It did not pet him, did not take him to its bosom. "*Perished were all his dreams of distinction, the praise and grateful approval of—*" Of whom? The Savior? No; the Savior is not mentioned. Of whom, then? Of "his *fellow-workers.*" Why did he want that? Because the Master inside of him wanted it, and would not be content without it. That emphasized sentence quoted above, reveals the secret we have been seeking, the original impulse, the *real* impulse, which moved the obscure and unappreciated Adirondack lumberman to sacrifice his family and go on that crusade to the East Side —which said original impulse was this, to wit: without knowing it *he went there to show a neglectful world the large talent that was in him, and rise to distinction.* As I have warned you before, *no* act springs from any but the one law, the one motive. But I pray you, do not accept this law upon my say-so, but diligently examine for yourself. Whenever you read of a self-sacrificing act or hear of one, or of a duty done for *duty's sake*, take it to pieces and look for the *real* motive. It is always there.

Y. M. I do it every day. I cannot help it, now that I have gotten started upon the degrading and exasperating quest. For it is hatefully interesting!—in fact, fascinating is the word. As soon as I come across a golden deed in a book I have to stop and take it apart and examine it, I cannot help myself.

O. M. Have you ever found one that defeated the rule?

Y. M. No—at least, not yet. But take the case of servant-tipping in Europe. You pay the *hotel* for service; you owe the servants *nothing*, yet you pay them, besides. Doesn't that defeat it?

O. M. In what way?

Y. M. You are not *obliged* to do it, therefore its source is compassion for their ill-paid condition, and—

O. M. Has that custom ever vexed you, annoyed you, irritated you?

Y. M. Well—yes.

O. M. Still you succumbed to it?

Y. M. Of course.

O. M. Why of course?

Y. M. Well, custom is law, in a way, and laws must be submitted to—Everybody recognizes it as a *duty.*

O. M. Then you pay the irritating tax for *duty's* sake?

Y. M. I suppose it amounts to that.

O. M. Then the impulse which moves you to submit to the tax is not *all* compassion, charity, benevolence?

Y. M. Well—perhaps not.

O. M. Is *any* of it?

Y. M. I—perhaps I was too hasty in locating its source.

O. M. Perhaps so. In case you ignored the custom would you get prompt and effective service from the servants?

Y. M. Oh, hear yourself talk! Those European servants? Why, you wouldn't get any at all, to speak of.

O. M. Couldn't *that* work as an impulse to move you to pay the tax?

Y. M. I am not denying it.

O. M. Apparently, then, it is a case of for-duty's-sake with a little self-interest added?

Y. M. Yes, it has the look of it. But here is a point: we pay that tax knowing it to be unjust and an extortion; yet we go away with a pain at the heart if we think we have been stingy with the poor fellows; and we heartily wish we were back again, so that we could do the right thing, and *more* than the right thing, the *generous* thing. I think it will be difficult for you to find any thought of self in that impulse.

O. M. I wonder why you should think so. When you find service charged in the *hotel* bill does it annoy you?

Y. M. No.

O. M. Do you ever complain of the amount of it?

Y. M. No, it would not occur to me.

O. M. The *expense*, then, is not the annoying detail. It is a fixed charge, and you pay it cheerfully, you pay it without a murmur. When you came to pay the servants, how would you like it if each of the men and maids had a fixed charge?

Y. M. Like it? I should rejoice!

O. M. Even if the fixed tax were a shade *more* than you had been in the habit of paying in the form of tips?

Y. M. Indeed, yes!

O. M. Very well, then. As I understand it, it isn't really compassion nor yet duty that moves you to pay the tax, and it isn't the *amount* of the tax that annoys you. Yet *something* annoys you. What is it?

Y. M. Well, the trouble is, you never know *what* to pay, the tax varies so, all over Europe.

O. M. So you have to guess?

Y. M. There is no other way. So you go on thinking and thinking, and calculating and guessing, and consulting with other people and getting their views; and it spoils your sleep, nights, and makes you distraught in the daytime, and while you are pretending to look at the sights you are only guessing and guessing and guessing all the time, and being worried and miserable.

O. M. And all about a debt which you don't owe and don't have to pay unless you want to! Strange. What is the purpose of the guessing?

Y. M. To guess out what is right to give them, and not be unfair to any of them.

O. M. It has a quite noble look—taking so much pains and using up so much valuable time in order to be just and fair to a poor servant to whom you owe nothing, but who needs money and is ill paid.

Y. M. I think, myself, that if there is any ungracious motive back of it it will be hard to find.

O. M. How do you know when you have not paid a servant fairly?

Y. M. Why, he is silent; does not thank you. Sometimes he gives you a look that makes you ashamed. You are too proud to rectify your mistake there, with people looking, but afterward you keep on wishing and wishing you *had* done it. My, the shame and the pain of it! Sometimes you see, by the signs, that you have hit it *just right*, and you go away mightily satisfied. Sometimes the man is so effusively thankful that you know you have given him a good deal *more* than was necessary.

O. M. *Necessary?* Necessary for what?

Y. M. To content him.

O. M. How do you feel *then?*

Y. M. Repentant.

O. M. It is my belief that you have *not* been concerning yourself in guessing out his just dues, but only in ciphering out what would *content* him. And I think you had a self-deluding reason for that.

Y. M. What was it?

O. M. If you fell short of what he was expecting and wanting, you would get a look which would *shame you before folk.* That would give you *pain.* You—for you are only working for yourself, not *him.* If you gave him too much you would be *ashamed of yourself* for it, and that would give you pain—another case of thinking of yourself, protecting *yourself*, saving *yourself from discomfort.* You never think of the servant once—except to guess out how to secure *his approval.* If you get that, you get your *own* approval, and that is the sole and only thing you are after. The Master inside of you is then satisfied, contented, comfortable; there was *no other* thing at stake, as a matter of first interest, anywhere in the transaction.

FURTHER INSTANCES

Y. M. Well, to think of it: self-sacrifice for others, the grandest thing in man, ruled out! nonexistent!

O. M. Are you accusing me of saying that?

Y. M. Why, certainly.

O. M. I haven't said it.

Y. M. What did you say, then?

O. M. That no man has ever sacrificed himself in the common meaning of that phrase—which is, self-sacrifice for another *alone*. Men make daily sacrifices for others, but it is for their own sake *first*. The act must content their own spirit *first*. The other beneficiaries come second.

Y. M. And the same with duty for duty's sake?

O. M. Yes. No man performs a duty for mere duty's sake; the act must content his spirit *first*. He must feel better for *doing* the duty than he would for shirking it. Otherwise he will not do it.

Y. M. Take the case of the *Berkeley Castle*.

O. M. It was a noble duty, greatly performed. Take it to pieces and examine it, if you like.

Y. M. A British troop-ship crowded with soldiers and their wives and children. She struck a rock and began to sink. There was room in the boats for the women and children only. The colonel lined-up his regiment on the deck and said "it is our duty to die, that they may be saved." There was no murmur, no protest. The boats carried away the women and children. When the death-moment was come, the colonel and his officers took their several posts, the men stood at shoulder-arms, and so, as on dress parade, with their flag flying and the drums beating, they went down, a sacrifice to duty, for duty's sake. Can you view it as other than that?

O. M. It was something as fine as that, as exalted as that. Could you have remained in those ranks and gone down to your death in that unflinching way?

Y. M. Could I? No, I could not.

O. M. Think. Imagine yourself there, with that watery doom creeping higher and higher around you.

Y. M. I can imagine it. I feel all the horror of it. I could not have endured it, I could not have remained in my place. I know it.

O. M. Why?

Y. M. There is no why about it: I know myself, and I know I couldn't *do* it.

O. M. But it would be your *duty* to do it.

Y. M. Yes, I know—but I couldn't.

O. M. It was more than a thousand men, yet not one of them flinched. Some of them must have been born with your temperament; if they could do that great duty for duty's sake, why not you? Don't you know that you could go out and gather together a thousand clerks and mechanics and put them on that deck and ask them to die for duty's sake, and not two dozen of them would stay in the ranks to the end?

Y. M. Yes, I know that.

O. M. But you *train* them, and put them through a campaign or two; then they would be soldiers; soldiers, with a soldier's pride, a soldier's self-respect, a *soldier's* ideals. They would have to content a soldier's spirit then, not a clerk's, not a mechanic's. They could not content that spirit by shirking a soldier's duty, could they?

Y. M. I suppose not.

O. M. Then they would do the duty not for the *duty's* sake, but for their *own* sake—primarily. The *duty* was *just the same*, and just as imperative, when they were clerks, mechanics, raw recruits, but they wouldn't perform it for that. As clerks and mechanics they had other ideals, another spirit to satisfy, and they satisfied it. They *had* to; it is the law. *Training* is potent. Training toward higher, and higher, and ever higher ideals is worth any man's thought and labor and diligence.

Y. M. Consider the man who stands by his duty and goes to the stake rather than be recreant to it.

O. M. It is his make and his training. He has to content the spirit that is in him, though it cost him his life. Another man, just as sincerely religious, but of different temperament, will fail of that duty, though recognizing it as a duty, and grieving to be unequal to it; but he must content the spirit that is in him—he cannot help it. He could not perform that duty for duty's *sake*, for that would not content his spirit, and the contenting of his spirit must be looked to *first*. It takes precedence of all other duties.

Y. M. Take the case of a clergyman of stainless private morals who votes for a thief for public office, on his own party's ticket, and against an honest man on the other ticket.

O. M. He has to content his spirit. He has no public morals; he has no private ones, where his party's prosperity is at stake. He will always be true to his make and training.

4

Training

Y. M. You keep using that word—training. By it do you particularly mean—

O. M. Study, instruction, lectures, sermons? That is a part of it—but not a large part. I mean *all* the outside influences. There are a million of them. From the cradle to the grave, during all his waking hours, the human being is under training. In the very first rank of his trainers stands *association.* It is his human environment which influences his mind and his feelings, furnishes him his ideals, and sets him on his road and keeps him in it. If he leaves that road he will find himself shunned by the people whom he most loves and esteems, and whose approval he most values. He is a chameleon; by a law of his nature he takes the color of his place of resort. The influences about him create his preferences, his aversions, his politics, his tastes, his morals, his religion. He creates none of these things for himself: He *thinks* he does, but that is because he has not examined into the matter. You have seen Presbyterians?

Y. M. Many.

O. M. How did they happen to be Presbyterians and not Congregationalists? And why were the Congregationalists not Baptists, and the Baptists Roman Catholics, and the Roman Catholics Buddhists, and the Buddhists Quakers, and the Quakers Episcopalians, and the Episcopalians Millerites, and the Millerites Hindus, and the Hindus Atheists, and the Atheists Spiritualists, and the Spiritualists Agnostics, and the Agnostics Methodists, and the Methodists Confucians, and the Confucians Unitarians, and the Unitarians Mohammedans, and the Mohammedans Salvation Warriors, and the Salvation Warriors Zoroastrians, and the Zoroastrians Christian Scientists, and the Christian Scientists Mormons—and so on?

Y. M. You may answer your question yourself.

O. M. That list of sects is not a record of *studies*, searchings, seekings after light; it mainly (and sarcastically) indicates what *association* can do. If you know a man's nationality you can come within a split hair of guessing the complexion of his religion: English—Protestant; American—ditto; Spaniard, Frenchman, Irishman, Italian, South American, Austrian—Roman Catholic; Russian—Greek Catholic; Turk—Mohammedan; and so on. And when you know the man's religious complexion, you know what sort of religious books he reads when he wants some more light, and what sort of books he avoids, lest by accident he get more light than he wants. In America if you know which party-collar a voter wears, you know what his associations are, and how he came by his politics, and which breed of newspaper he reads to get light, and which breed he diligently avoids, and which breed of mass meetings he attends in order to broaden his political knowledge, and which breed of mass meetings he doesn't attend, except to refute its doctrines with brickbats. We are always hearing of people who are around *seeking after Truth*. I have never seen a (permanent) specimen. I think he has never lived. But I have seen several entirely sincere people who *thought* they were (permanent) Seekers after Truth. They sought diligently, persistently, carefully, cautiously, profoundly, with perfect honesty and a nicely adjusted judgment—until they believed that without doubt or question they had found the Truth. *That was the end of the search.* The man spent the rest of his life hunting up shingles wherewith to protect his Truth from the weather. If he was seeking after political Truth he found it in one or another of the hundred political gospels which govern men in the earth; if he was seeking after the Only True Religion he found it in one or another of the three thousand that are on the market. In any case, when he found his Truth *he sought no further*; but from that day forth, with his soldering iron in one hand and his bludgeon in the other he tinkered its leaks and reasoned with objectors. There have been innumerable Temporary, Seekers after Truth—have you ever heard of a Permanent one? In the very nature of man such a person is impossible. However, to drop back to the text—training: all training is one form or another of *outside influence*, and *association* is the largest part of it. A man is never anything but what his outside influences have made him. They train him downwards or they train him upwards—but they *train* him; they are at work upon him all the time.

Y. M. Then if he happen by the accidents of life to be evilly placed there is no help for him, according to your notions—he must train downwards.

O. M. No help for him? No help for this chameleon? It is a mistake. It is in his chameleonship that his greatest good fortune lies. He has only to change his habitat—his *associations*. But the impulse to do it must come from the *outside*—he cannot originate it himself, with that purpose in view. Sometimes a very small and accidental thing can furnish him the initiatory impulse and start him on a new road, with a new ideal. The chance remark of a sweetheart, "I hear that you are a coward" may water a seed that shall sprout and bloom and flourish, and end in producing a surprising fruitage in the fields of war. The history of man is full of such accidents. The accident of a broken leg brought a profane and ribald soldier under religious influences and furnished him a new ideal. From that accident sprang the Order of the Jesuits, and it has been shaking thrones, changing policies, and doing other tremendous work for two hundred years—and will go on. The chance reading of a book, or of a paragraph in a newspaper can start a man on a new track and make him renounce his old associations and seek new ones that are *in sympathy with his new ideal;* and the result, for that man, can be an entire change of his way of life.

Y. M. Are you hinting at a scheme of procedure?

O. M. Not a new one—an old one. Old as mankind.

Y. M. What is it?

O. M. Merely the laying of traps for people. Traps baited *with Initiatory Impulses toward high ideals*. It is what the tract distributor does. It is what the missionary does. It is what governments ought to do.

Y. M. Don't they?

O. M. In one way they do, in another way they don't. They separate the small-pox patients from the healthy people, but in dealing with crime they put the healthy into the pest-house along with the sick. That is to say, they put the beginners in with the confirmed criminals. This would be well if man were naturally inclined to good, but he isn't, and so *association* makes the beginners worse than they were when they went into captivity. It is putting a very severe punishment upon the comparatively innocent. However, all governments are hard on the innocent at times. They hang a man—which is a trifling punishment; this breaks the hearts of his family—which is a heavy one. They comfortably jail and feed a wife-beater, and leave his innocent wife and children to starve.

Y. M. Do you believe in the doctrine that man is equipped with an intuitive perception of good and evil?

O. M. Adam hadn't it.

Y. M. But has man acquired it since?

O. M. No. I think he has no intuitions of any kind. He gets *all* his ideas, all his impressions, all his opinions, from the outside. I keep repeating this, in the hope that I may so impress it upon you that you will be interested to observe and examine for yourself and see whether it is true or false.

Y. M. Where did you get your own aggravating notions?

O. M. From the *outside*. I did not invent them. They are gathered from a thousand unknown sources. Mainly *unconsciously* gathered.

Y. M. Don't you believe that God could make an inherently honest man?

O. M. Yes, I know He could. I also know that He never did make one.

Y. M. A wiser observer than you has recorded the fact that "an honest man's the noblest work of God."

O. M. He didn't record a fact, he recorded a falsity. It is windy, and sounds well, but it is not true. God makes a man with honest and dishonest *possibilities* in him, and stops there. The man's *associations* develop the possibilities—the one set or the other. The result is accordingly an honest man or a dishonest one.

Y. M. And the honest one is not entitled to—

O. M. Praise? No. How often must I tell you that? He is not the architect of his honesty.

Y. M. Now then, I will ask you to tell me where there is any sense in training people to lead virtuous lives. What is gained by it?

O. M. The man himself gets large advantages out of it, and that is the main thing—to *him*. He is not a peril to his neighbors, he is not a damage to them—and so *they* get an advantage out of his virtues. That is the main thing to *them.* To train men to lead virtuous lives is an inestimably important thing. It can make this life comparatively comfortable to the parties concerned; the *neglect* of this training can make this life a constant peril and distress to the parties concerned.

Y. M. You have said that training is everything; that training is the man *himself,* for it makes him what he is.

O. M. I said training and *another* thing. Let that other thing pass, for the moment. What were you going to say?

Y. M. We have an old servant. She has been with us twenty-two years. Her service used to be faultless, but now she has become very forgetful. We are all fond of her; we all recognize that she cannot help the infirmity, which age has brought her; the rest of the family do not scold her for her remissnesses, but at times I do—I can't seem to control myself. Don't I try? I do try. Now, then, when I was ready to dress, this morning, no clean clothes had been put out. I lost my temper; I lose it easiest and quickest in the early morning. I rang; and immediately began to warn myself not to show temper, and to be careful and speak gently. I safeguarded myself most carefully. I even chose the very words I would use: "You've forgotten the clean clothes, Jane." When she appeared in the door I opened my mouth to say that phrase—and out of it, moved by an instant surge of passion which I was not expecting and hadn't time to put under control, came the hot rebuke, "You've forgotten them again!" You say a man always does the thing which will best please his Interior Master. Whence came the impulse to make careful preparation to save the girl the humiliation of a rebuke? Did that come from the Master, who is always primarily concerned about *himself?*

O. M. Unquestionably. There is no other source for any impulse. *Secondarily* you made preparation to save the girl, but *primarily* its object was to save yourself, by contenting the Master.

Y. M. How do you mean?

O. M. Has any member of the family ever implored you to watch your temper and not fly out at the girl?

Y. M. Yes. My mother.

O. M. You love her?

Y. M. Oh, more than that!

O. M. You would always do anything in your power to please her?

Y. M. It is a delight to me to do anything to please her!

O. M. Why? *You would do it for pay, solely—profit.* What profit would you expect and certainly receive, from the investment?

Y. M. Personally? None. To please *her* is enough.

O. M. It appears, then, that your object, primarily, *wasn't* to save the girl a humiliation, but to *please your mother.* It also appears that to please your mother gives *you* a strong pleasure. Is not that the profit which you get out of the investment? Isn't that the *real* profit and *first* profit?

Y. M. Oh, well? Go on.

O. M. In *all* transactions, the Interior Master looks to it that *you get the first profit.* Otherwise there is no transaction.

Y. M. Well, then, if I was so anxious to get that profit and was so intent upon it, why did I throw it away by losing my temper?

O. M. In order to get *another* profit which suddenly superseded it in value.

Y. M. Where was it?

O. M. Ambushed behind your born temperament, and waiting for a chance. Your native warm temper jumped suddenly to the front, and *for the moment* its influence was more powerful than your mother's, and abolished it. In that instant you were eager to flash out a hot rebuke and enjoy it. You did enjoy it, didn't you?

Y. M. For—for a quarter of a second. Yes—I did.

O. M. Very well, it is as I have said: the thing which will give you the most pleasure, the *most* satisfaction, in any moment or *fraction* of a moment, is the thing you will always do. You must content the Master's *latest* whim, whatever it may be.

Y. M. But when the tears came into the old so, want's eyes I could have cut my hand off for what I had done.

O. M. Right. You had humiliated *yourself*, you see; you had given yourself *pain.* Nothing is of *first* importance to a man except results which damage him or profit him—all the rest is *secondary.* Your Master was displeased with you, although you had obeyed him. He required a prompt *repentance;* you obeyed again; you *had* to—there is never any escape from his commands. He is a hard master, and fickle; he changes his mind in the fraction of a second, but you must be ready to obey, and you will obey, *always*. If he requires repentance, to content him, you will always furnish it. He must be nursed, petted, coddled, and kept contented, let the terms be what they may.

Y. M. Training! Oh, what is the use of it? Didn't I, and didn't my mother try to train me up to where I would no longer fly out at that girl?

O. M. Have you never managed to keep back a scolding?

Y. M. Oh, certainly—many times.

O. M. More times this year than last?

Y. M. Yes, a good many more.

O. M. More times last year than the year before?

Y. M. Yes.

O. M. There is a large improvement, then, in the two years?

Y. M. Yes, undoubtedly.

O. M. Then your question is answered. You see there *is* use in training. Keep on. Keep faithfully on. You are doing well.

Y. M. Will my reform reach perfection?

O. M. It will. Up to *your* limit.

Y. M. My limit? What do you mean by that?

O. M. You remember you said that I said training was *everything*. I corrected you, and said "training and *another* thing." That other thing is *temperament*—that is, the disposition you were born with. *You can't eradicate your disposition nor any rag of it*— you can only put a pressure on it and keep it down and quiet. You have a warm temper?

Y. M. Yes.

O. M. You will never get rid of it; but by watching it you can keep it down nearly all the time. *Its presence is your limit.* Your reform will never quite reach perfection, for your temper will beat you now and then, but you will come near enough. You have made valuable progress and can make more. There is use in training. Immense use. Presently you will reach a new stage of development, then your progress will be easier; will proceed on a simpler basis, anyway.

Y. M. Explain.

O. M. You keep back your scoldings now, to please yourself by pleasing your *mother*; presently the mere triumphing over your temper will delight your vanity, and confer a more delicious pleasure and satisfaction upon you than even the approbation of your *mother* confers upon you now. You will then labor for yourself directly and at *first hand*, not by the roundabout way through your mother. It simplifies the matter, and it also strengthens the impulse.

Y. M. Ah, dear! But I shan't ever reach the point where I will spare the girl for *her* sake *primarily*, not mine?

O. M. Why—yes. In heaven.

Y. M. (*After a reflective pause.*) Temperament. Well, I see one must allow for temperament. It is a large factor, sure enough. My mother is thoughtful, and not hot-tempered. When I was dressed I went to her room; she was not there, I called, she answered from the bathroom. I heard the water running. I inquired. She answered, without temper, that Jane had forgotten her bath, and she was preparing it herself: I offered to ring, but she said, "No, don't do that; it would only distress her to be confronted with her lapse, and would be a rebuke; she doesn't deserve that—she is not to blame for the tricks her memory serves her." I say—has my mother an Interior Master?—and where was he?

O. M. He was there. There, and looking out for his own peace and pleasure and contentment. The girl's distress would have pained *your mother.* Otherwise the girl would have been rung up, distress and all. I know women who would have gotten a No. 1 *pleasure* out of ringing Jane up—and so they would infallibly have pushed the button and obeyed the law of their make and training, which are the servants of their Interior Masters. It is quite likely that a part of your mother's forbearance came from training. The *good* kind of training—whose best and highest function is to see to it that every time it confers a satisfaction upon its pupil a benefit shall 'fall at second hand upon others.

Y. M. If you were going to condense into an admonition your plan for the general betterment of the race's condition, how would you word it?

ADMONITION

O. M. Diligently train your ideals *upward* and *still upward* toward a summit where you will find your chiefest pleasure in conduct which, while contenting you, will be sure to confer benefits upon your neighbor and the community.

Y. M. Is that a new gospel?

O. M. No.

Y. M. It has been taught better?

O. M. For ten thousand years.

Y. M. By whom?

O. M. All the great religions—all the great gospels.

Y. M. Then there is nothing new about it.

O. M. Oh, yes there is. It is candidly stated, this time. That has not been done before.

Y. M. How do you mean?

O. M. Haven't I put *you* FIRST, and your neighbor and the community *afterward?*

Y. M. Well, yes, that is a difference, it is true.

O. M. The difference between straight speaking and crooked; the difference between frankness and shuffling.

Y. M. Explain.

O. M. The others offer you a hundred bribes to be good, thus conceding that the Master inside of you must be conciliated and contented first, and that you will do nothing at *first hand* but for his sake; then they turn square around and require you to do good for *others'* sake *chiefly;* and to do your duty for duty's *sake,* chiefly; and to do *unselfish* things; and to do acts of *self-sacrifice.* Thus at the outset we all stand upon the same ground—recognition of the supreme and absolute Monarch that resides in man, and we all grovel before him and appeal to him; then those others dodge and shuffle, and face around and unfrankly and inconsistently and illogically change the form of their appeal and direct its persuasions to man's *second-place* powers and to powers which have *no existence* in him, thus advancing them to *first* place; whereas in my Admonition I stick logically and consistently to the original position: I place the Interior Master's requirements *first,* and keep them there.

Y. M. If we grant, for the sake of argument, that your scheme and the other schemes aim at and produce the same result—*right living*—has yours an advantage over the others?

O. M. One, yes—a large one. It has no concealments, no deceptions. When a man leads a right and valuable life under it he is not deceived as to the *real* chief motive which impels him to it—in those other cases he is.

Y. M. Is that an advantage? Is it an advantage to live a lofty life for a mean reason? In the other cases he lives the lofty life under the *impression* that he is living it for a lofty reason. Is not that an advantage?

O. M. Perhaps so. The same advantage he might get out of thinking himself a duke, and living a duke's life, and parading in ducal fuss and feathers, when he wasn't a duke at all, and could find it out if he would only examine the herald's records.

Y. M. But anyway, he is obliged to do a duke's part; he puts his hand in his pocket and does his benevolences on as big a scale as he can stand, and that benefits the community.

O. M. He could do that without being a duke.

Y. M. But would he?

O. M. Don't you see where you are arriving?

Y. M. Where?

O. M. At the standpoint of the other schemes: That it is good morals to let an ignorant duke do showy benevolences for pride's sake, a pretty low motive, and go on doing them unwarned, lest if he were made acquainted with the actual motive which prompted them he might shut up his purse and cease to be good?

Y. M. But isn't it best to leave him in ignorance, as long as he *thinks* he is doing good for others' sake?

O. M. Perhaps so. It is the position of the other schemes. They think humbug is good enough morals when the dividend on it is good deeds and handsome conduct.

Y. M. It is my opinion that under your scheme of a man's doing a good deed for his *own* sake first-off, instead of first for the *good deed's* sake, no man would ever do one.

O. M. Have you committed a benevolence lately?

Y. M. Yes. This morning.

O. M. Give the particulars.

Y. M. The cabin of the old negro woman who nursed me when I was a child and who saved my life once at risk of her own, was burned last night, and she came mourning this morning, and pleading for money to build another one.

O. M. You furnished it?

Y. M. Certainly.

O. M. You were glad you had the money?

Y. M. Money? I hadn't it. I sold my horse.

O. M. You were glad you had the horse?

Y. M. Of course I was; for if I hadn't had the horse I should have been incapable, and my *mother* would have captured the chance to set old Sally up.

O. M. You were cordially glad you were not caught out and incapable?

Y. M. Oh, I just was!

O. M. Now then—

Y. M. Stop where you are! I know your whole catalogue of questions, and I could answer everyone of them without your wasting the time to ask them; but I will summarize the whole thing in a single remark: I did the charity knowing it was because the act would give *me* a splendid pleasure, and because old Sally's moving gratitude and delight would give *me* another one; and because the reflection that she would be happy now and out of her trouble would fill *me* full of happiness. I did the whole thing with my eyes open and recognizing and realizing that I was looking out for my share of the profits *first.* Now then, I have confessed. Go on.

O. M. I haven't anything to offer; you have covered the whole ground. Could you have been any *more* strongly moved to help Sally out of her trouble—could you have done the deed any more eagerly—if you had been under the delusion that you were doing it for *her* sake and profit only?

Y. M. No! Nothing in the world could have made the impulse which moved me more powerful, more masterful, more thoroughly irresistible. I played the limit!

O. M. Very well. You begin to suspect—and I claim to *know*—that when a man is a shade *more strongly moved* to do *one* of two things or of two dozen things than he is to do any one of the others, he will infallibly do that *one* thing, be it good or be it evil; and if it be good, not all the beguilements of all the casuistries can increase the strength of the impulse by a single shade or add a shade to the comfort and contentment he will get out of the act.

Y. M. Then you believe that such tendency toward doing good as is in men's hearts would not be diminished by the removal of the delusion that good deeds are done primarily for the sake of No. 2 instead of for the sake of No. 1?

O. M. That is what I fully believe.

Y. M. Doesn't it somehow seem to take from the dignity of the deed?

O. M. If there is dignity, in falsity, it does. It removes that.

Y. M. What is left for the moralist to do?

O. M. Teach unreservedly what he already teaches with one side of his mouth and takes back with the other: Do right *for your own sake*, and be happy in knowing that your *neighbor* will certainly share in the benefits resulting.

Y. M. Repeat your Admonition.

O. M. *Diligently train your ideals upward and still upward toward a summit where you will find your chiefest pleasure in conduct which, while contenting you, will be sure to confer benefits upon your neighbor and the community.*

Y. M. One's *every* act proceeds from exterior influences, you think?

O. M. Yes.

Y. M. If I conclude to rob a person, I am not the *originator* of the idea, but it came in from the *outside?* I see him handling money—for instance—and *that* moves me to the crime?

O. M. That, by itself? O, certainly not. It is merely the *latest* outside influence of a procession of preparatory influences stretching back over a period of years. No *single* outside influence can make a man do a thing which is at war with his training. The most it can do is to start his mind on a new track and open it to the reception of *new* influences—as in the case of Ignatius Loyola. In time these influences can train him to a point where it will be consonant with his new character to yield to the *final* influence and do that thing. I will put the case in a form which will make my theory clear to you, I think. Here are two ingots of virgin gold. They shall represent a couple of characters which have been refined and perfected in the virtues by years of diligent right training. Suppose you wanted to break down these strong and well compacted characters—what influence would you bring to bear upon the ingots?

Y. M. Work it out yourself. Proceed.

O. M. Suppose I turn upon one of them a steam-jet during a long succession of hours. Will there be a result?

Y. M. None that I know of.

O. M. Why?

Y. M. A steam-jet cannot break down such a substance.

O. M. Very well. The steam is an *outside influence*, but it is ineffective, because the gold *takes no interest in it.* The ingot remains as it was. Suppose we add to the steam some quicksilver in a vaporized condition, and turn the jet upon the other ingot. Will there be an instantaneous result?

Y. M. No.

O. M. The *quicksilver* is an outside influence which gold (by its peculiar nature—say *temperament, disposition*), *cannot be indifferent to.* It stirs the interest of the gold, although we do not perceive it; but a *single* application of the influence works no damage. Let us continue the application in a steady stream, and call each minute a year. By the end of ten or twenty minutes—ten or twenty years—the little ingot is sodden with quicksilver, rotten with quicksilver, its virtues are gone, its character is degraded. At last it is ready to yield to a temptation which it would have taken no notice of, ten or twenty years ago. We will apply that temptation in the form of a pressure with my finger. You note the result?

Y. M. Yes; the ingot has crumbled to sand. I understand, now. It is not the *single* outside influence that does the work, but only the *last* one of a long and disintegrating accumulation of them. I see, now, how my *single* impulse to rob the man is not the one that makes me do it, but only the *last* one of a preparatory series. You might illustrate it with a parable.

A PARABLE

O. M. I will. There was once a pair of New England boys—twins. They were alike in good dispositions, feckless morals, and personal appearance. They were the models of the Sunday school. At fifteen George had an opportunity to go as cabin boy in a whale-ship, and sailed away for the Pacific. Henry remained at home in the village. At eighteen George was a sailor before the mast, and Henry was teacher of the advanced Bible class. At twenty-two George, through fighting-habits and drinking-habits acquired at sea and in the sailor boarding houses of the European and Oriental ports, was a common rough in Hong Kong, and out of a job; and Henry was superintendent of the Sunday school. At twenty-six George was a wanderer, a tramp, and Henry was pastor of the village church. Then George came home, and was Henry's guest. One evening a man passed by and turned down the lane, and Henry said, with a pathetic smile, "Without intending me a discomfort, that man is always keeping me reminded of my pinching poverty for he carries heaps of money about him, and goes by here every evening of his life." That *outside influence*—that remark—was enough for George, but *it* was not the one that made him ambush the man and rob him, it merely represented the eleven years' accumulation of such influences, and gave birth to the act for which their long gestation had made preparation. It had never entered the head of Henry to rob the man—his ingot had been subjected to clean steam only; but George's had been subjected to vaporized quicksilver.

5

More About the Machine

NOTE.—When Mrs. W. asks how can a millionaire give a single dollar to colleges and museums while one human being is destitute of bread; she has answered her question herself. Her feeling for the poor shows that she has a standard of benevolence; therefore she has conceded the millionaire's privilege of having a standard; since she evidently requires him to adopt her standard she is by that act requiring herself to adopt his. The human being always looks down when he is examining another person's standard, he never finds one that he has to examine by looking up.

THE MAN-MACHINE AGAIN

Y. M. You really think man is a mere machine?

O. M. I do.

Y. M. And that his mind works automatically and is independent of his control—carries on thought on its own hook?

O. M. Yes. It is diligently at work, unceasingly at work, during every waking moment. Have you never tossed about all night, imploring, beseeching, commanding your mind to stop work and let you go to sleep?—you who perhaps imagine that your mind is your servant and must obey your orders, think what you tell it to think, and stop when you tell it to stop. When it chooses to work, there is no way to keep it still for an instant. The brightest man would not be able to supply it with subjects if he had to hunt them up. If it needed the man's help it would wait for him to give it work when he wakes in the morning.

Y. M. Maybe it does.

O. M. No, it begins right away, before the man gets wide enough awake to give it a suggestion. He may go to sleep saying, "The moment I wake I will think upon such and such a subject," but he will fail. His mind will be too quick for him; by the time he has become nearly enough awake to be half conscious, he will find that it is already at work on another subject. Make the experiment and see.

Y. M. At any rate he can make it stick to a subject if he wants to.

O. M. Not if it finds another that suits it better. As a rule it will listen to neither a dull speaker nor a bright one. It refuses all persuasion. The dull speaker wearies it and sends it far away in idle dreams; the bright speaker throws out stimulating ideas which it goes chasing after and is at once unconscious of him and his talk. You cannot keep your mind from wandering, if it wants to; it is master, not you.

AFTER AN INTERVAL OF DAYS

O. M. Now, dreams—but we will examine that later. Meantime, did you try commanding your mind to wait for orders from you, and not do any thinking on its own hook?

Y. M. Yes, I commanded it to stand ready to take orders when I should wake in the morning.

O. M. Did it obey?

Y. M. No. It went to thinking about something of its own initiation, without waiting for me. Also—as you suggested—at night I appointed a theme for it to begin on in the morning, and commanded it to begin on that one and no other.

O. M. Did it obey?

Y. M. No.

O. M. How many times did you try the experiment?

Y. M. Ten.

O. M. How many successes did you score?

Y. M. Not one.

O. M. It is as I have said: the mind is independent of the man. He has no control over it, it does as it pleases. It will take up a subject in spite of him; it will stick to it in spite of him; it will throw it aside in spite of him. It is entirely independent of him.

Y. M. Go on. Illustrate.

O. M. Do you know chess?

Y. M. I learned it a week ago.

O. M. Did your mind go on playing the game all night that first night?

Y. M. Don't mention it!

O. M. It was eagerly, unsatisfiably interested; it rioted in the combinations; you implored it to drop the game and let you get some sleep?

Y. M. Yes. It wouldn't listen; it played right along. It wore me out and I got up haggard and wretched in the morning.

O. M. At some time or other you have been captivated by a ridiculous rhyme-jingle?

Y. M. Indeed, yes!

"I saw Esau kissing Kate,
And she saw I saw Esau;
I saw Esau, he saw Kate,
And she saw—"

And so on. My mind went mad with joy over it. It repeated it all day and all night for a week in spite of all I could do to stop it, and it seemed to me that I must surely go crazy.

O. M. And the new popular song?

Y. M. Oh, yes! "In the Swee-eet By and By;" etc. Yes, the new popular song with the taking melody sings thro' one's head day and night, asleep and awake, till one is a wreck. There is no getting the mind to let it alone.

O. M. Yes, asleep as well as awake. The mind is quite independent. It is master. You have nothing to do with it. It is so apart from you that it can conduct its affairs, sing its songs, play its chess, weave its complex and ingeniously-constructed dreams, while you sleep. It has no use for your help, no use for your guidance, and never uses either, whether you be asleep or awake. You have imagined that you could originate a thought in your mind, and you have sincerely believed you could do it.

Y. M. Yes, I have had that idea.

O. M. Yet you can't originate a dream-thought for it to work out, and get it accepted?

Y. M. No.

O. M. And you can't dictate its procedure after it has originated a dream-thought for itself?

Y. M. No. No one can do it. Do you think the waking mind and the dream-mind are the same machine?

O. M. There is argument for it. We have wild and fantastic day-thoughts? Things that are dream-like?

Y. M. Yes—like Mr. Wells's man who invented a drug that made him invisible; and like the Arabian tales of the Thousand Nights.

O. M. And there are dreams that are rational, simple, consistent and unfantastic?

Y. M. Yes. I have dreams that are like that. Dreams which are just like real life; dreams in which there are several persons with distinctly differentiated characters—inventions of my mind and yet strangers to me: a vulgar person; a refined one; a wise person; a fool; a cruel person; a kind and compassionate one; a quarrelsome person; a peacemaker; old persons and young; beautiful girls and homely ones. They talk in character, each preserves his own characteristics. There are vivid fights, vivid and biting insults, vivid love-passages; there are tragedies and comedies, there are griefs that go to one's heart, there are sayings and doings that make you laugh: indeed the whole thing is exactly like real life.

O. M. Your dreaming mind originates the scheme, consistently and artistically develops it, and carries the little drama creditably through—all without help or suggestion from you?

Y. M. Yes.

O. M. It is argument that it could do the like awake without help or suggestion from you—and I think it does. It is argument that it is the same old mind in both cases, and never needs your help. I think the mind is purely a machine, a thoroughly independent machine, an automatic machine. Have you tried the other experiment which I suggested to you?

Y. M. Which one?

O. M. The one which was to determine how much influence you have over your mind—if any.

Y. M. Yes, and got more or less entertainment out of it. I did as you ordered: I placed two texts before my eyes—one a dull one and barren of interest, the other one full of interest, inflamed with it, white-hot with it. I commanded my mind to busy itself solely with the dull one.

O. M. Did it obey?

Y. M. Well, no, it didn't. It busied itself with the other one.

O. M. Did you try hard to make it obey?

Y. M. Yes, I did my honest best.

O. M. What was the text which it refused to be interested in or think about?

Y. M. It was this question: If A owes B a dollar and a half, and B owes C two and three-quarters, and C owes A thirty-five cents, and D and A together owe E and B three-sixteenths of—of—I don't remember the rest, now, but anyway it was wholly uninteresting, and I could not force my mind to stick to it even half a minute at a time; it kept flying off to the other text.

O. M. What was the other text?

Y. M. It is no matter about that.

O. M. But what was it?

Y. M. A photograph.

O. M. Your own?

Y. M. No. It was hers.

O. M. You really made an honest good test. Did you make a second trial?

Y. M. Yes. I commanded my mind to interest itself in the

morning paper's report of the pork market, and at the same time I reminded it of an experience of mine of sixteen years ago. It refused to consider the pork, and gave its whole blazing interest to that ancient incident.

O. M. What was the incident?

Y. M. An armed desperado slapped my face in the presence of twenty spectators. It makes me wild and murderous every time I think of it.

O. M. Good tests, both; very good tests. Did you try my other suggestion?

Y. M. The one which was to prove to me that if I would leave my mind to its own devices it would find things to think about without any of my help, and thus convince me that it was a machine, an automatic machine, set in motion by exterior influences, and as independent of me as it could be if it were in some one else's skull? Is that the one?

O. M. Yes.

Y. M. I tried it. I was shaving. I had slept well, and my mind was very lively, even gay and frisky. It was reveling in a fantastic and joyful episode of my remote boyhood which had suddenly flashed up in my memory—moved to this by the spectacle of a yellow cat picking its way carefully along the top of the garden wall. The color of this cat brought the bygone cat before me, and I saw her walking along a side-step of the pulpit; saw her walk onto a large sheet of sticky flypaper and get all her feet involved; saw her struggle and fall down, helpless and dissatisfied; saw her go on struggling, on her back and getting more and more dissatisfied, more and more urgent, more and more unreconciled, more and more mutely profane; saw the silent congregation quivering like jelly, and the tears running down their faces. I saw it all. The sight of the tears whisked my mind to a far distant and a sadder scene—in Tierra del Fuego—and with Darwin's eves I saw a naked great savage hurl his little boy against the rocks for a trifling fault; saw the poor mother gather up her dying child and hug it to her breast and weep, uttering no word. Did my mind stop to mourn with that nude black sister of mine? No—it was far away from that scene in an instant, and was busying itself with an ever-recurring and disagreeable dream of mine. In this dream I always find myself, stripped to my shirt, cringing and dodging about in the midst of a great drawing room throng of finely dressed ladies and gentlemen, and wondering how I got there. And so on and so on, picture after picture, incident after incident, a drifting panorama of ever-changing, ever-dissolving views manufactured by my mind without any help from me—why, it would take me two hours to merely name the multitude of things my mind tallied off and photographed in fifteen minutes, let alone describe them to you.

O. M. A man's mind, left free, has no use for his help. But there is one way whereby he can get its help when he desires it.

Y. M. What is that way?

O. M. When your mind is racing along from subject to subject and strikes an inspiring one, open your mouth and begin to talk upon that matter—or take your pen and use that. It will interest your mind and concentrate it, and it will pursue the subject with satisfaction. It will take full charge, and furnish the words itself.

Y. M. But don't I tell it what to say?

O. M. There are certainly occasions when you haven't time. The words leap out before you know what is coming.

Y. M. For instance?

O. M. Well, take a "flash of wit"—repartee. Flash is the right word. It is out instantly. There is no time to arrange the words. There is no thinking, no reflecting. Where there is a wit-mechanism it is automatic in its action, and needs no help. Where the wit-mechanism is lacking, no amount of study and reflection can manufacture the product.

Y. M. You really think a man originates nothing, creates nothing.

THE THINKING-PROCESS

O. M. I do. Men perceive, and their brain-machines automatically combine the things perceived. That is all.

Y. M. The steam-engine?

O. M. It takes fifty men a hundred years to invent it. One meaning of invent is discover. I use the word in that sense. Little by little they discover and apply the multitude of details that go to make the perfect engine. Watt noticed that confined steam was strong enough to lift the lid of the teapot. He didn't create the idea, he merely discovered the fact; the cat had noticed it a hundred times. From the teapot he evolved the cylinder—from the displaced lid he evolved the piston rod. To attach something to the piston-rod to be moved by it, was a simple matter—crank and wheel. And so there was a working engine.* One by one, improvements were discovered by men who used their eyes, not their creative powers—for they hadn't any—and now, after a hundred years the patient contributions of fifty or a hundred observers stand compacted in the wonderful machine which drives the ocean liner.

Y. M. A Shakespearean play?

O. M. The process is the same. The first actor was a savage. He reproduced in his theatrical war-dances, scalp-dances, and so on, incidents which he had seen in real life. A more advanced civilization produced more incidents, more episodes; the actor and the storyteller borrowed them. And so the drama grew, little by little, stage by stage. The elaborate Shakespearean play was the final outcome. It is made up of the facts of life, not creations. It took centuries to develop the Greek drama. It borrowed from preceding ages; it lent to the ages that came after. Men observe and combine, that is all. So does a rat.

Y. M. How?

O. M. He observes a smell, he infers a cheese, he seeks and finds. The astronomer observes this and that; adds his this and that to the this-and-thats of a hundred predecessors, infers an invisible planet, seeks it and finds it. The rat gets into a trap; gets out with trouble; infers that cheese in traps lacks value, and meddles with that trap no more. The astronomer is very proud of his achievement; the rat is proud of his. Yet both are machines, they have done machine-work, they have originated nothing, they have no right to be vain, the whole credit belongs to their Maker. They are entitled to no honors, no praises, no monuments when they die, no remembrance. One is a complex and elaborate machine, the other a simple and limited machine, but they are alike in principle, function and process, and neither of them works otherwise than automatically, and neither of them may

*The Marquess of Worcester had done all of this more than a century earlier.

righteously claim a personal superiority, or a *personal* dignity above the other.

Y. M. In earned personal dignity, then, and in personal merit for what he does, it follows of necessity that he is on the same level as a rat?

O. M. His brother the rat; yes, that is how it seems to me. Neither of them being entitled to any personal merit for what he does, it follows of necessity that neither of them has a right to arrogate to himself (personally-created) superiorities over his brother.

Y. M. Are you determined to go on believing in these insanities? Would you go on believing in them in the face of able arguments backed by collated facts and instances?

O. M. I have been a humble, earnest and sincere Truth Seeker.

Y. M. Very well?

O. M. The humble, earnest and sincere Truth Seeker is always convertible by such means.

Y. M. I am thankful to God to hear you say this, for now I know that your conversion—

O. M. Wait. You misunderstand. I said I have *been* a Truth Seeker.

Y. M. Well?

O. M. I am not that now. Have you forgotten? I told you that there are none but temporary Truth Seekers; that a permanent one is a human impossibility; that as soon as the Seeker finds what he is thoroughly convinced is the Truth, he seeks no further, but gives the rest of his days to hunting for junk to patch it and caulk it and prop it with, and make it weatherproof and keep it from caving in on him. Hence the Presbyterian remains a Presbyterian, the Mohammedan a Mohammedan, the Spiritualist a Spiritualist, the Democrat a Democrat, the Republican a Republican, the Monarchist a Monarchist; and if a humble, earnest and sincere Seeker after Truth should find it in the proposition that the moon is made of green cheese nothing could ever budge him from that position; for he is nothing but an automatic machine, and must obey the laws of his construction.

Y. M. And so—

O. M. Having found the Truth; perceiving that beyond question Man has but one moving impulse—the contenting of his own spirit—and is merely a Machine and entitled to no personal merit for anything he does, it is not humanly possible for me to seek further. The rest of my days will be spent in patching and painting and puttying and caulking my priceless possession, and in looking the other way when an imploring argument or a damaging fact approaches.

6

Instinct and Thought

Y. M. It is odious. Those drunken theories of yours, advanced a while ago—concerning the rat and all that—strip Man bare of all his dignities, grandeurs, sublimities.

O. M. He hasn't any to strip—they are shams, stolen clothes. He claims credits which belong solely to his Maker.

Y. M. But you have no right to put him on a level with the rat.

O. M. I don't—morally. That would not be fair to the rat. The rat is well above him, there.

Y. M. Are you joking?

O. M. No, I am not.

Y. M. Then what do you mean?

O. M. That comes under the head of the Moral Sense. It is a large question. Let us finish with what we are about now, before we take it up.

Y. M. Very well. You have seemed to concede that you place Man and the rat on *a* level. What is it? The intellectual?

O. M. In form—not in degree.

Y. M. Explain.

O. M. I think that the rat's mind and the man's mind are the same machine, but of unequal capacities—like yours and Edison's; like the African pigmy's and Homer's; like the Bushman's and Bismarck's.

Y. M. How are you going to make that out, when the lower animals have no mental quality but instinct, while man possesses reason?

O. M. What is instinct?

Y. M. It is a merely unthinking and mechanical exercise of

inherited habit.

O. M. What originated the habit?

Y. M. The first animal started it, its descendants have inherited it.

O. M. How did the first one come to start it?

Y. M. I don't know; but it didn't *think* it out.

O. M. How do you know it didn't?

Y. M. Well—I have a right to suppose it didn't, anyway.

O. M. I don't believe you have. What is thought?

Y. M. I know what you call it: the mechanical and automatic putting together of impressions received from the outside, and drawing an inference from them.

O. M. Very good. Now my idea of the meaningless term "instinct" is, that it is merely *petrified thought;* thought solidified and made inanimate by habit; thought which was once alive and awake, but is become unconscious—walks in its sleep, so to speak.

Y. M. Illustrate it.

O. M. Take a herd of cows, feeding in a pasture. Their heads are all turned in one direction. They do that instinctively; they gain nothing by it, they have no reason for it, they don't know why they do it. It is an inherited habit which was originally thought—that is to say, observation of an exterior fact, and a valuable inference drawn from that observation and confirmed by experience. The original wild ox noticed that with the wind in his favor he could smell his enemy in time to escape; then he inferred that it was worth while to keep his nose to the wind. That is the process which man calls reasoning. Man's thought-machine works just like the other animals', but it is a better one and more Edisonian. Man, in the ox's place, would go further, reason wider: he would face a part of the herd the other way and protect both front and rear.

Y. M. Did you say the term instinct is meaningless?

O. M. I think it is a bastard word. I think it confuses us; for as a rule it applies itself to habits and impulses which had a far-off origin in thought, and now and then breaks the rule and applies itself to habits which can hardly claim a thought origin.

Y. M. Give an instance.

O. M. Well, in putting on trousers a man always inserts the same old leg first—never the other one. There is no advantage in that, and no sense in it. All men do it, yet no man ever thought it out and adopted it of set purpose, I imagine. But it is a habit which is transmitted, no doubt, and will continue to be transmitted.

Y. M. Can you prove that the habit exists?

O. M. You can prove it, if you doubt. If you will take a man to a clothing store and watch him try on a dozen pairs of trousers, you will see.

Y. M. The cow-illustration is not—

O. M. Sufficient to show that a dumb animal's mental machine is just the same as a man's and its reasoning-processes the same? I will illustrate further. If you should hand Mr. Edison a box which you caused to fly open by some concealed device, he would infer a spring, and would hunt for it and find it. Now an uncle of mine had an old horse who used to get into the closed lot where the corn-crib was and dishonestly take the corn. I got the punishment myself, as it was supposed that I heedlessly failed to insert the wooden pin which kept the gate closed. These persistent punishments fatigued me; they also caused me to infer the existence of a culprit, somewhere; so I hid myself and watched the gate. Presently the horse came and pulled out the pin with his teeth and went in. Nobody taught him that; he had observed—then thought it out for himself. His process did not differ from Edison's; he put this and that together and drew an inference—and the peg, too; but I made him sweat for it.

Y. M. It has something of the seeming of thought about it. Still, it is not very elaborate. Enlarge.

O. M. Suppose that Edison has been enjoying some one's hospitalities. He comes again, by and by, and the house is vacant. He infers that his host has moved. A while afterward, in another town, he sees the man enter a house; he infers that that is the new home, and follows to inquire. Here, now, is the experience of a gull, as related by a naturalist. The scene is a Scotch fishing village where the gulls were kindly treated. This particular gull visited a cottage; was fed; came next day and was fed again; came into the house, next time, and ate with the family; kept on doing this almost daily, thereafter. But once the gull was away on a journey for a few days, and when it returned the house was vacant. Its friends had removed to a village three miles distant. Several months later it saw the head of the family on the street there, followed him home, entered the house without excuse or apology, and became a daily guest again. Gulls do not rank high, mentally, but this one had memory and the reasoning faculty, you see, and applied them Edisonially.

Y. M. Yet it was not an Edison and couldn't be developed into one.

O. M. Perhaps not; could you?

Y. M. That is neither here nor there. Go on.

O. M. If Edison were in trouble and a stranger helped him out of it and next day he got into the same difficulty again, he would infer the wise thing to do in case he knew the stranger's address. Here is a case of a bird and a stranger as related by a naturalist. An English gentleman saw a bird flying around about his dog's head, down in the grounds, and uttering cries of distress. He went there to see about it. The dog had a young bird in his mouth—unhurt. The gentleman rescued it and put it on a bush and brought the dog away. Early the next morning the mother-bird came for the gentleman, who was sitting on his verandah, and by its maneuvers persuaded him to follow it to a distant part of the grounds—flying a little way in front of him and waiting for him to catch up, and so on; and keeping to the winding path, too, instead of flying the near way across lots. The distance covered was four hundred yards. The same dog was the culprit; he had the young bird again, and once more he had to give it up. Now the mother-bird had reasoned it all out: since the stranger had helped her once, she inferred that he would do it again; she knew where to find him, and she went upon her errand with confidence. Her mental processes were what Edison's would have been. She put this and that together—and that is all that thought *is*—and out of them built her logical arrangement of inferences. Edison couldn't have done it any better himself.

Y. M. Do you believe that many of the dumb animals can think?

O. M. Yes—the elephant, the monkey, the horse, the dog, the parrot, the macaw, the mocking-bird, and many others. The elephant whose mate fell into a pit, and who dumped dirt and rubbish into the pit till the bottom was raised high enough to enable the captive to step out, was equipped with the reasoning quality. I conceive that all animals that can learn things through teaching and drilling have to know how to observe, and put this and that together and draw an inference—the process of thinking. Could you teach an idiot the manual of arms, and to advance, retreat, and go through complex field maneuvers at the word of command?

Y. M. Not if he were a thorough idiot.

O. M. Well, canary birds can learn all that; dogs and elephants learn all sorts of wonderful things. They must surely be able to notice, and to put things together, and say to themselves, "I get the idea, now: when I do so and so, as per order, I am praised and fed; when I do differently, I am punished." Fleas can be taught nearly anything that a Congressman can.

Y. M. Granting, then, that dumb creatures are able to think upon a low plane, is there any that can think upon a high one? Is there one that is well up toward man?

O. M. Yes. As a thinker and planner the ant is the equal of any savage race of men; as a self-educated specialist in several arts she is the superior of any savage race of men; and in one or two high mental qualities she is above the reach of any man, savage or civilized.

Y. M. O, come! you are abolishing the intellectual frontier which separates man and beast.

O. M. I beg your pardon. One cannot abolish what does not exist.

Y. M. You are not in earnest, I hope. You cannot mean to seriously say there is no such frontier.

O. M. I do say it seriously. The instances of the horse, the gull, the mother-bird and the elephant show that those creatures put their this's and that's together just as Edison would have done it and drew the same inferences that he would have drawn. Their mental machinery was just like his, also its manner of working. Their equipment was as inferior to his, in elaboration, as a Waterbury is inferior to the Strasburg clock, but that is the only difference—there is no frontier.

Y. M. It looks exasperatingly true; and is distinctly offensive. It elevates the dumb beast to—to—

O. M. Let us drop that lying phrase, and call them the Unrevealed Creatures; so far as we can know, there is no such thing as a dumb beast.

Y. M. On what grounds do you make that assertion?

O. M. On quite simple ones. "Dumb" beast suggests an animal that has no thought-machinery, no understanding, no speech, no way of communicating what is in its mind. We know that a hen *has* speech. We cannot understand everything she says, but we easily learn two or three of her phrases. We know when she is saying "I've laid an egg"; we know when she is saying to the chicks, "Run here, dears, I've found a worm"; we know what she is saying when she voices a warning: "Quick! hurry! gather yourselves under mamma, there's a hawk coming? We understand the cat when she stretches herself out, purring with affection and contentment and lifts up a soft voice and says "Come, kitties, supper's ready"; we understand her when she goes mourning about and says "Where can they be?—they are lost—won't you help me hunt for them?" and we understand the disreputable Tom when he challenges at midnight from his shed: "You come over here, you product of immoral commerce, and I'll make your fur fly!" We understand a few of a dog's phrases, and we learn to understand a few of the remarks and gestures of any bird or other animal that we domesticate and observe. The clearness and exactness of the few of the hen's speeches which we understand is argument that she can communicate to her kind a hundred things which we cannot comprehend—in a word, that she can converse. And this argument is also applicable in the case of others of the great army of the Unrevealed. It is just like man's vanity and impertinence to call an animal dumb because it is dumb to his dull perceptions. Now as to the ant—

Y. M. Yes, go back to the ant, the creature that—as you seem to think—sweeps away the last vestige of an intellectual frontier between man and the Unrevealed.

O. M. That is what she surely does. In all his history the aboriginal Australian never thought out a house for himself and built it. The ant is an amazing architect. She is a wee little creature, but she builds a strong and enduring house eight feet high—a house which is as large in proportion to her size as is the largest capitol or cathedral in the world compared to man's size. No savage race has produced architects who could approach the ant in genius or culture. No civilized race has produced architects who could plan a house better for the uses proposed than can hers. Her house contains a throne room; nurseries for her young; granaries; apartments for her soldiers, her workers, etc.; and they and the multifarious halls and corridors which communicate with them are arranged and distributed with an educated and experienced eye for convenience and adaptability.

Y. M. That could all be mere instinct.

O. M. It would elevate the savage much above what he is, if he had it. But let us look further before we decide. The ant has soldiers—battalions, regiments, armies; and they have their appointed captains and generals, who lead them to battle.

Y. M. That could be instinct, too.

O. M. We will look still further. The ant has a system of government; it is well planned, elaborate, and is well carried on.

Y. M. Instinct again.

O. M. She has crowds of slaves, and is a hard and unjust employer of forced labor.

Y. M. Instinct.

O. M. She has cows, and milks them.

Y. M. Instinct, of course.

O. M. In Texas she lays out a farm twelve feet square, plants it, weeds it, cultivates it, gathers the crop and stores it away.

Y. M. Instinct, all the same.

O. M. The ant discriminates between friend and stranger. Sir John Lubbock took ants from two different nests, made them drunk with whisky and laid them, unconscious, by one of the nests, near some water. Ants from this nest came and examined and discussed these disgraced creatures, then carried their friends home and threw the strangers overboard. Sir John repeated the experiment a number of times. For a while the sober ants did as they had done at first—carried their friends home and threw the strangers overboard. But finally they lost patience, seeing that their reformatory efforts went for nothing, and threw both friends and strangers overboard. Come—is this instinct, or is it thoughtful and intelligent discussion of a thing new—absolutely new—to their experience; with a verdict arrived at, sentence passed, and judgment executed? Is it instinct?—thought petrified by ages of habit—or isn't it brand new thought, inspired by the new occasion, the new circumstances?

Y. M. I have to concede it. It was not a result of habit; it has all the look of reflection, thought, putting this and that together, as you phrase it. I believe it was thought.

O. M. I will give you another instance of thought. Franklin had a cup of sugar on a table in his room. The ants got at it. He tried several preventives; the ants rose superior to them. Finally he contrived one which shut off access; probably set the table's legs in pans of water, or drew a circle of tar around the cup, I don't remember. At any rate he watched to see what they would do. They tried various schemes, failures, every one. The ants were badly puzzled. Finally they held a consultation, discussed the problem, arrived at a decision—and this time they beat that great philosopher. They formed in procession, crossed the floor, climbed the wall, marched across the ceiling to a point just over the cup, then one by one they let go and fell down into it! Was that instinct-thought petrified by ages of inherited habit?

Y. M. No, I don't believe it was. I believe it was a newly-reasoned scheme to meet a new emergency.

O. M. Very well. You have conceded the reasoning power in two instances. I come now to a mental detail wherein the ant is a long way the superior of any human being. Sir John Lubbock proved by many experiments that an ant knows a stranger-ant of her own species in a moment, even when the stranger is disguised—with paint. Also, he proved that an ant knows every individual in her hive of 500,000 souls. Also, that after a year's absence of one of the 500,000 she will straightway recognize the returned absentee and grace the recognition with an affectionate welcome. How were these recognitions made? Not by color, for painted ants were recognized. Not by smell for ants that had been dipped in chloroform were recognized. Not by speech and not by antennae signs nor contacts, for the drunken and motionless ants were recognized and the friend discriminated from the stranger. The ants were all of the one species, therefore the friends had to be recognized by form and feature—friends who formed part of a hive of 500,000! Has any man a memory for form and feature approaching that?

Y. M. Certainly not.

o. m. Franklin's ants and Lubbock's ants show fine capacities for putting this and that together in new and untried emergencies and deducing smart conclusions from the combinations—a man's mental process exactly. With memory to help, man preserves his observations and reasonings, reflects upon them, adds to them, recombines, and so proceeds, stage by stage, to far results—from the tea kettle to the ocean greyhound's complex engine; from personal labor to slave labor; from wigwam to palace; from the capricious chase to agriculture and stored food; from nomadic life to stable government and concentrated authority from incoherent hordes to massed armies. The ant has observation, the reasoning faculty, and the preserving adjunct of a prodigious memory; she has duplicated man's development and the essential features of his civilization, and you call it all instinct!

y. m. Perhaps I lacked the reasoning faculty myself

o. m. Well, don't tell anybody, and don't do it again.

y. m. We have come a good way. As a result—as I understand it—I am required to concede that there is absolutely no intellectual frontier separating Man and the Unrevealed Creatures?

o. m. That is what you are required to concede. There is no such frontier—there is no way to get around that. Man has a finer and more capable machine in him than those others, but it is the same machine and works in the same way. And neither he nor those others can command the machine— it is strictly automatic, independent of control, works when it pleases, and when it doesn't please, can't be forced.

y. m. Then man and the other animals are all alike, as to mental machinery, and there isn't any difference of any stupendous magnitude between them, except in quality, not in kind.

o. m. That is about the state of it—intellectually. There are pronounced limitations on both sides. We can't learn to understand much of their language, but the dog, the elephant, etc., learn to understand a very great deal of ours. To that extent they are our superiors. On the other hand they can't learn reading, writing, etc., nor any of our fine and high things, and there we have a large advantage over them.

y. m. Very well, let them have what they've got, and welcome;

there is still a wall, and a lofty one. They haven't the Moral Sense; we have it, and it lifts us immeasurably above them.

O. M. What makes you think that?

Y. M. Now look here—let us call a halt. I have stood the other infamies and insanities and that is enough; I am not going to have man and the other animals put on the same level morally.

O. M. I wasn't going to hoist man up to that.

Y. M. This is too much! I think it is not right to jest about such things.

O. M. I am not jesting, I am merely reflecting a plain and simple truth—and without uncharitableness. The fact that man knows right from wrong proves his *intellectual* superiority to the other creatures; but the fact that he can *do* wrong proves his *moral* inferiority to any creature that *cannot.* It is my belief that this position is not assailable.

FREE WILL

Y. M. What is your opinion regarding Free Will?

O. M. That there is no such thing. Did the man possess it who gave the old woman his last shilling and trudged home in the storm?

Y. M. He had the choice between succoring the old woman and leaving her to suffer. Isn't it so?

O. M. Yes, there was a choice to be made, between bodily comfort on the one hand and the comfort of the spirit on the other. The body made a strong appeal, of course—the body would be quite sure to do that; the spirit made a counter appeal. A choice had to be made between the two appeals, and was made. Who or what determined that choice?

Y. M. Any one but you would say that the man determined it, and that in doing it he exercised Free Will.

O. M. We are constantly assured that every man is endowed with Free Will, and that he can and must exercise it where he is offered a choice between good conduct and less-good conduct. Yet we clearly saw that in that man's case he really had no Free Will: his temperament, his training, and the daily influences which had molded him and made him what he was, *compelled* him to rescue the old woman and thus save *himself*—save himself from spiritual pain, from unendurable wretchedness. He did not make the choice, it was made *for* him by forces which he could not control. Free Will has always existed in *words*, but it stops there, I think—stops short of *fact.* I would not use those words—Free Will—but others.

Y. M. What others?

O. M. Free Choice.

Y. M. What is the difference?

O. M. The one implies untrammeled power to *act* as you please, the other implies nothing beyond a mere *mental process:* the critical ability to determine which of two things is nearest right and just.

Y. M. Make the difference clear, please.

O. M. The mind can freely *select, choose, point out*, the right and just one—its function stops there. It can go no further in the matter. It has no authority to say that the right one shall be acted upon and the wrong one discarded. That authority is in other hands.

Y. M. The man's?

O. M. In the machine which stands for him. In his born disposition and the character which has been built around it by training and environment.

Y. M. It will act upon the right one of the two?

O. M. It will do as it pleases in the matter. George Washington's machine would act upon the right one; Pizarro's mind would know which was the right one and which the wrong, but the Master inside of Pizarro would act upon the wrong one.

Y. M. Then as I understand it a bad man's mental machinery calmly and judicially points out which of two things is right and just—

O. M. Yes, and his *moral* machinery will freely act upon the one or the other, according to its make, and be quite indifferent to the *mind's* feelings concerning the matter—that is, *would* be, if the mind had any feelings; which it hasn't. It is merely a thermometer: it registers the heat and the cold, and cares not a farthing about either.

Y. M. Then we must not claim that if a man *knows* which of two things is right he is absolutely *bound* to do that thing?

O. M. His temperament and training will decide what he shall do, and he will do it; he cannot help himself, he has no authority over the matter. Wasn't it right for David to go out and slay Goliath?

Y. M. Yes.

O. M. Then it would have been equally *right* for any one else to do it?

Y. M. Certainly.

O. M. Then it would have been *right* for a born coward to attempt it?

Y. M. It would—yes.

O. M. You know that no born coward ever would have attempted it, don't you?

Y. M. Yes.

O. M. You know that a born coward's make and temperament would be an absolute and insurmountable bar to his ever essaying such a thing, don't you?

Y. M. Yes, I know it.

O. M. He clearly perceives that it would be *right* to try it?

Y. M. Yes.

O. M. His mind has Free Choice in determining that it would be *right* to try it?

Y. M. Yes.

O. M. Then if by reason of his inborn cowardice he simply can *not* essay it, what becomes of his Free Will? where is his Free Will? why claim that he has Free Will when the plain facts show that he hasn't? why contend that because he and David *see* the right alike, both must *act* alike? why impose the same laws upon goat and lion?

Y. M. There is really no such thing as Free Will?

O. M. It is what I think. There is *Will.* But it has nothing to do with *intellectual perceptions of right and wrong*, and is not under their command. David's temperament and training had Will, and it was a compulsory force; David had to obey its decrees, he had no choice. The coward's temperament and training possess Will, and *it* is compulsory; it commands him to avoid danger, and he obeys, he has no choice. But neither the Davids nor the cowards possess Free Will—will that may do the right or do the wrong, as their *mental* verdict shall decide.

NOT TWO VALUES, BUT ONLY ONE

Y. M. There is one thing which bothers me: I can't tell where you draw the line between *material* covetousness and *spiritual* covetousness.

O. M. I don't draw any.

Y. M. How do you mean?

O. M. There is no such thing as *material* covetousness. All covetousness is spiritual.

Y. M. *All* longings, desires, ambitions *spiritual*, never material?

O. M. Yes. The Master in you requires that in *all* cases you shall content his *spirit*—that alone. He never requires anything else, he never interests himself in any other matter.

Y. M. Ah, come! When he covets somebody's money—isn't that rather distinctly material and gross?

O. M. No. The money is merely a symbol—it represents in visible and concrete form a *spiritual desire*. Any so-called material thing that you want is merely a symbol; you want it not for *itself*, but because it will content your spirit for the moment.

Y. M. Please particularize.

O. M. Very well. Maybe the thing longed for is a new hat. You get it and your vanity is pleased, your spirit contented. Suppose your friends deride the hat, make fun of it: at once it loses its value; you are ashamed of it, you put it out of your sight, you never want to see it again.

Y. M. I think I see. Go on.

O. M. It is the same hat, isn't it? It is in no way altered. But it wasn't the *hat* you wanted, but only what it stood for—a something to please and content your *spirit*. When it failed of that, the whole of its value was gone. There are no *material* values, there are only spiritual ones. You will hunt in vain for a material value that is *actual*, *real*—there is no such thing. The only value it possesses, for even a moment, is the spiritual value back of it: remove that and it is at once worthless—like the hat.

Y. M. Can you extend that to money?

O. M. Yes. It is merely a symbol, it has no *material* value; you think you desire it for its own sake, but it is not so. You desire it for the spiritual content it will bring; if it fail of that, you discover that its value is gone. There is that pathetic tale of the man who labored like a slave, unresting, unsatisfied, until he had accumulated a fortune, and was happy over it, jubilant about it; then in a single week a pestilence swept away all whom he held dear and left him desolate. His money's value was gone. He realized that his joy in it came not from the money itself, but from the spiritual contentment he got out of his family's enjoyment of the pleasures and delights it lavished upon them. Money has no *material* value; if you remove its spiritual value nothing is left but dross. It is so with all things, little or big, majestic or trivial—there are no exceptions. Crowns, scepters, pennies, paste jewels, village notoriety, world-wide fame—they are all the same, they have no material value: while they content the spirit they are precious, when this fails they are worthless.

A DIFFICULT QUESTION

Y. M. You keep me confused and perplexed all the time by your elusive terminology. Sometimes you divide a man up into two or three separate personalities, each with authorities, jurisdictions and responsibilities of its own, and when he is in that condition I can't grasp him. Now when *I* speak of a man, he is *the whole thing in one*, and easy to hold and contemplate.

O. M. That is pleasant and convenient, if true. When you speak of "my body," who is the "my?"

Y. M. It is the "me."

O. M. The body is a property, then, and the Me owns it. Who is the Me?

Y. M. The Me is *the whole thing;* it is a common property; an undivided ownership, vested in the whole entity.

O. M. If the Me admires a rainbow, is it the whole Me that admires it, including the hair, hands, heels and all?

Y. M. Certainly not. It is my *mind* that admires it.

O. M. So *you* divide the Me yourself. Everybody does; everybody must. What, then, definitely, is the Me?

Y. M. I think it must consist of just those two parts—the body and the mind.

O. M. You think so? If you say "I believe the world is round," who is the "I" that is speaking?

Y. M. The mind.

O. M. If you say "I grieve for the loss of my father," who is the "I?"

Y. M. The mind.

O. M. Is the mind exercising an intellectual function when it examines and accepts the evidence that the world is round?

Y. M. Yes.

O. M. Is it exercising an intellectual function when it grieves for the loss of your father?

Y. M. No. That is not cerebration, brain-work, it is a matter of *feeling.*

O. M. Then its source is not in your mind, but in your *moral* territory?

Y. M. I have to grant it.

O. M. Is your mind a part of your *physical* equipment?

Y. M. No. It is independent of it; it is spiritual.

O. M. Being spiritual, it cannot be affected by physical influences?

Y. M. No

O. M. Does the mind remain sober when the body is drunk?

Y. M. Well—no.

O. M. There *is* a physical effect present, then?

Y. M. It looks like it.

O. M. A cracked skull has resulted in a crazy mind. Why should that happen if the mind is spiritual, and *independent* of physical influences?

Y. M. Well—I don't know.

O. M. When you have a pain in your foot, how do you know it?

Y. M. I feel it.

O. M. But you do not feel it until a nerve reports the hurt to the brain. Yet the brain is the seat of the mind, is it not?

Y. M. I think so.

O. M. But isn't spiritual enough to learn what is happening in the outskirts without the help of the *physical* messenger? You perceive that the question of who or what the Me is, is not a simple one at all. You say "I admire the rainbow," and "I believe the world is round? and in these cases we find that the Me is not all speaking, but only the *mental* part. You say 'q grieve," and again the Me is not all speaking, but only the *moral* part. You say the mind is wholly spiritual; then you say "I have a pain" and find that this time the Me is mental *and* spiritual combined. We all use the "I" in this indeterminate fashion, there is no help for it. We imagine a Master and King over what you call The Whole Thing, and we speak of him as "L" but when we try to define him we find we cannot do it. The intellect and the feelings can act quite *independently* of each other; we recognize that, and we look around for a Ruler who is master over both, and can serve as a *definite and indisputable* "I," and enable us to know what we mean and who or what we are talking about when we use that pronoun, but we have to give it up and confess that we cannot find him. To me, Man is a machine, made up of many mechanisms; the moral and mental ones acting automatically in accordance with the impulses of an interior Master who is built out of born-temperament and an accumulation of multitudinous outside influences and trainings; a machine whose *one* function is to secure the spiritual contentment of the Master, be his desires good or be they evil; a machine whose Will is absolute and must be obeyed, and always *is* obeyed.

Y. M. Maybe the Me is the Soul?

O. M. Maybe it is. What is the Soul?

Y. M. I don't know.

O. M. Neither does any one else.

THE MASTER-PASSION

Y. M. What is the Master?—or, in common speech, the Conscience? Explain it.

O. M. It is that mysterious autocrat, lodged in a man, which compels the man to content its desires. It may be called the Master Passion—the hunger for Self-Approval.

Y. M. Where is its scat?

O. M. In man's moral constitution.

Y. M. Are its commands for the man's good?

O. M. It is indifferent to the man's good; it never concerns itself about anything but the satisfying of its own desires. It can be *trained* to prefer things which will be for the man's good, but it will prefer them only because they will content it better than other things would.

Y. M. Then even when it is trained to high ideals it is still looking out for its own contentment, and not for the man's good?

O. M. True. Trained or untrained it cares nothing for the man's good, and never concerns itself about it.

Y. M. It seems to be an *immoral* force seated in the man's moral constitution?

O. M. It is a *colorless* force seated in the man's moral constitution. Let us call it an instinct—a blind, unreasoning instinct, which cannot and does not distinguish between good morals and bad ones, and cares nothing for results to the man provided its own contentment be secured; and it will *always* secure that.

Y. M. It seeks money, and it probably considers that that is an advantage for the man?

O. M. It is not always seeking money, it is not always seeking power, nor office, nor any other *material* advantage. In *all* cases it seeks a *spiritual* contentment, let the *means* be what they may. Its desires are determined by the man's temperament—and it is lord over that. Temperament, Conscience, Susceptibility, Spiritual Appetite, are in fact the same thing. Have you ever heard of a person who cared nothing for money?

Y. M. Yes. A scholar who would not leave his garret and his books to take a place in a business house at a large salary.

O. M. He had to satisfy his master—that is to say, his temperament, his Spiritual Appetite—and it preferred the books to money. Are there other cases?

Y. M. Yes, the hermit.

O. M. It is a good instance. The hermit endures solitude, hunger, cold, and manifold perils, to content his autocrat, who prefers these things, and prayer and contemplation, to money or to any show or luxury that money can buy. Are there others?

Y. M. Yes. The artist, the poet, the scientist.

O. M. Their autocrat prefers the deep pleasures of these occupations, either well paid or ill paid, to any others in the market, at any price. You *realize* that the Master Passion—the contentment of the spirit—concerns itself with many things besides so-called material advantage, material prosperity, cash, and all that?

Y. M. I think I must concede it.

O. M. I believe you must. There are perhaps as many Temperaments that would refuse the burdens and vexations and distinctions of public office as there are that hunger after them. The one set of Temperaments seek the contentment of the spirit, and that alone; and this is exactly the case with the other set. Neither set seeks anything *but* the contentment of the spirit. If the one is sordid, both are sordid; and equally so, since the end in view is precisely the same in both cases. And in both cases Temperament decides the preference—and Temperament is *born,* not made.

CONCLUSION

O. M. You have been taking a holiday?

Y. M. Yes; a mountain-tramp covering a week. Are you ready to talk?

O. M. Quite ready. What shall we begin with?

Y. M. Well, lying abed resting-up, two days and nights, I have thought over all these talks, and passed them carefully in review. With this result: that . . . . that . . . . are you intending to publish your notions about Man some day?

O. M. Now and then, in these past twenty years, the Master inside of me has half-intended to order me to set them to paper and publish them. Do I have to tell you why the order has remained unissued, or can you explain so simple a thing without my help?

Y. M. By your doctrine, it is simplicity itself: outside influences moved your interior Master to give the order; stronger outside influences deterred him. Without the outside influences, neither of these impulses could ever have been born, since a person's brain is incapable of originating an idea within itself.

O. M. Correct. Go on.

Y. M. The matter of publishing or withholding is still in your Master's hands. If, some day, an outside influence shall determine him to publish, he will give the order, and it will be obeyed.

O. M. That is correct. Well?

Y. M. Upon reflection I have arrived at the conviction that

the publication of your doctrines would be harmful. Do you pardon me?

O. M. Pardon *you?* You have done nothing. You are an instrument—a speaking-trumpet. Speaking-trumpets are not responsible for what is said through them. Outside influences—in the form of lifelong teachings, trainings, notions, prejudices, and other second-hand importations—have persuaded the Master within you that the publication of these doctrines would be harmful. Very well, this is quite natural, and was to be expected; in fact was inevitable. Go on; for the sake of ease and convenience, stick to habit: speak in the first person, and tell me what your Master thinks about it.

Y. M. Well, to begin: it is a desolating doctrine; it is not inspiring, enthusing, uplifting. It takes the glory out of man, it takes the pride out of him, it takes the heroism out of him, it denies him all personal credit, all applause; it not only degrades him to a machine, but allows him no control over the machine; makes a mere coffee-mill of him, and neither permits him to supply the coffee nor turn the crank; his sole and piteously humble function being to grind coarse or fine, according to his make, outside impulses doing all the rest.

O. M. It is correctly stated. Tell me—what do men admire most in each other?

Y. M. Intellect, courage, majesty of build, beauty of countenance, charity, benevolence, magnanimity, kindliness, heroism, and—and—

O. M. I would not go any further. These are *elementals.* Virtue, fortitude, holiness, truthfulness, loyalty, high ideals—these, and all the related qualities that are named in the dictionary, are *made out of the elementals*, by blendings, combinations, and shadings of the elementals, just as one makes green by blending blue and yellow, and makes several shades and tints of red by modifying the elemental red. There are seven elemental colors, they are all in the rainbow; out of them we manufacture and name fifty shades of them. You have named the elementals of the human rainbow, and also one *blend*—heroism, which is made out of courage and magnanimity. Very well, then; which of these elements does the possessor of it manufacture for himself? Is it intellect?

Y. M. No.

O. M. Why?

Y. M. He is born with it.

O. M. Is it courage?

Y. M. No. He is born with it.

O. M. Is it majesty of build, beauty of countenance?

Y. M. No. They are birthrights.

O. M. Take those others—the elemental moral qualities—charity, benevolence, magnanimity, kindliness; fruitful seeds, out of which spring, through cultivation by outside influences, all the manifold blends and combinations of virtues named in the dictionaries: does man manufacture any one of those seeds, or are they all born in him?

Y. M. Born in him.

O. M. Who manufactures them, then?

Y. M. God.

O. M. Where does the credit of it belong?

Y. M. To God.

O. M. And the glory of which you spoke, and the applause?

Y. M. To God.

O. M. Then it is *you* who degrade man. You make him claim glory, praise, flattery, for every valuable thing he possesses—*borrowed* finery, the whole of it; no rag of it earned by himself, not a detail of it produced by his own labor. *You* make man a humbug; have I done worse by him?

Y. M. You have made a machine of him.

O. M. Who devised that cunning and beautiful mechanism, a man's hand?

Y. M. God.

O. M. Who devised the law by which it automatically hammers out of a piano an elaborate piece of music, without error, while the man is thinking about something else, or talking to a friend?

Y. M. God.

O. M. Who devised the blood? Who devised the wonderful machinery which automatically drives its renewing and refreshing streams through the body, day and night, without assistance or advice from the man? Who devised the man's mind, whose machinery works automatically, interests itself in what it pleases, regardless of his will or desire, labors all night when it likes, deaf to his appeals for mercy? God devised all these things. I have not made man a machine, God made him a machine. I am merely calling attention to the fact, nothing more. Is it wrong to call attention to a fact? Is it a crime?

Y. M. I think it is wrong to *expose* a fact when harm can come of it.

O. M. Go on.

Y. M. Look at the matter as it stands now. Man has been taught that he is the supreme marvel of the Creation; he believes it; in all the ages he has never doubted it, whether he was a naked savage, or clothed in purple and fine linen, and civilized. This has made his heart buoyant, his life cheery. His pride in himself, his sincere admiration of himself, his joy in what he supposed were his own and unassisted achievements, and his exultation over the praise and applause which they evoked—these have exalted him, enthused him, ambitioned him to higher and higher flights; in a word, made his life worth the living. But by your scheme, all this is abolished: he is degraded to a machine, he is a nobody, his noble prides wither to mere vanities; let him strive as he may, he can never be any better than his humblest and stupidest neighbor; he would never be cheerful again, his life would not be worth the living.

O. M. You really think that?

Y. M. I certainly do.

O. M. Have you ever seen me uncheerful, unhappy?

Y. M. No.

O. M. Well, *I* believe these things. Why have they not made me unhappy?

Y. M. Oh, well—temperament, of course! You never let *that* escape from your scheme.

O. M. That is correct. If a man is born with an unhappy temperament, nothing can make him happy; if he is born with a happy temperament, nothing can make him unhappy.

Y. M. What—not even a degrading and heart-chilling system of beliefs?

O. M. Beliefs? Mere beliefs? Mere convictions? They are powerless. They strive in vain against inborn temperament.

Y. M. I can't believe that, and I don't.

O. M. Now you are speaking hastily. It shows that you have not studiously examined the facts. Of all your intimates, which one is the happiest? Isn't it Burgess?

Y. M. Easily.

O. M. And which one is the unhappiest? Henry Adams?

Y. M. Without a question!

O. M. I know them well. They are extremes, abnormals; their temperaments are as opposite as the poles. Their life-histories are about alike—but look at the results! Their ages are about the same—around about fifty. Burgess has always been buoyant, hopeful, happy; Adams has always been cheerless, hopeless, despondent. As young fellows, both tried country journalism—and failed. Burgess didn't seem to mind it; Adams couldn't smile, he could only mourn and groan over what had happened, and torture himself with vain regrets for not having done so-and-so instead of so-and-so—*then* he would have succeeded. They tried the law—and failed. Burgess remained happy—because he couldn't help it, Adams was wretched—because he couldn't help it. From that day to this, those two men have gone on trying things and failing: Burgess has come out happy and cheerful every time, Adams the reverse. Now we do absolutely know that these men's inborn temperaments have remained unchanged through all the vicissitudes of their material affairs. Let us see how it is with their immaterialities. Both have been zealous democrats; both have been zealous republicans; both have been zealous mug-wumps. Burgess has always found happiness and Adams unhappiness, in these several political beliefs and in their migrations out of them. Both of these men have been Presbyterians, Universalists, Methodists, Catholics,—then Presbyterians again, then Methodists again. Burgess has always found rest in these excursions, and Adams unrest; they are trying Christian Science, now, with the customary result, the inevitable result. No political or religious belief can make Burgess unhappy or the other man happy. I assure you it is purely a matter of temperament. Beliefs are *acquirements*, temperaments are *born;* beliefs are subject to change, nothing whatever can change temperament.

Y. M. You have instanced extreme temperaments.

O. M. Yes. The half dozen others are modifications of the extremes. But the law is the same. Where the temperament is two-thirds happy, or two-thirds unhappy, no political or religious beliefs can change the proportions. The vast majority of temperaments are pretty equally balanced; the intensities are absent, and this enables a nation to learn to accommodate itself to its political and religious circumstances and like them, be satisfied with them, at last prefer them. Nations do not *think*, they only *feel.* They get their feelings at secondhand—through their temperaments, not their brains. A nation can be brought—by force of circumstances, not argument—to reconcile itself to *any kind of government or religion that can be devised;* in time it will fit itself to the required conditions; later, it will prefer them; and will fiercely fight for them. As instances, you have all history: the Greeks, the Romans, the Persians, the Egyptians, the Russians, the Germans, the French, the English, the Spaniards, the Americans, the South Americans, the Japanese, the Chinese, the Hindus, the Turks—a thousand wild and tame religions, every kind of government that can be thought of from tiger to house-cat, each nation *knowing* it has the only true religion and the only sane system of government, each despising all the others, each an ass and not suspecting it, each proud of its fancied supremacy, each perfectly sure it is the pet of God, each with doubting confidence summoning Him to take command in time of war, each surprised when He goes over to the enemy, but by habit able to excuse it and resume compliments—in a word, the whole human race content, always content, persistently content, indestructibly content, happy, thankful, proud, *no matter what its religion is, nor whether its master be tiger or house-cat.* Am I stating facts? You know I am. Is the human race cheerful? You know it is. Considering what it can stand, and be happy, you do me too much honor when you think that *I* can place before it a system of plain cold facts that can take the cheerfulness out of it. Nothing can do that. Everything has been tried. Without success. I beg you not to be troubled.

can change the proportions ... [illegible]

[illegible] without the alternatives [illegible] [illegible] to [illegible] recommend [illegible] [illegible] and [illegible] ... and like [illegible] [illegible] ...

[illegible]

... and [illegible]

... the English, the Spaniards, the [illegible] ... the Japanese, the [illegible]

[illegible]

... you think that I can [illegible] ... [illegible]

... hath... What [illegible] ... troubled [illegible]

Hunting the Deceitful Turkey

When I was a boy my uncle and his big boys hunted with the rifle, the youngest boy Fred and I with a shotgun—a small single-barreled shotgun which was properly suited to our size and strength; it was not much heavier than a broom. We carried it turn about, half an hour at a time. I was not able to hit anything with it, but I liked to try. Fred and I hunted leathered small game, the others hunted deer, squirrels, wild turkeys, and such things. My uncle and the big boys were good shots. They killed hawks and wild geese and such like on the wing; and they didn't wound or kill squirrels, they *stunned* them. When the dogs treed a squirrel, the squirrel would scamper aloft and run out on a limb and flatten himself along it, hoping to make himself invisible in that way—and not quite succeeding. You could see his wee little ears sticking up. You couldn't see his nose, but you knew where it was. Then the hunter, despising a "rest" for his rifle, stood up and took offhand aim at the limb and sent a bullet into it immediately under the squirrel's nose, and down tumbled the animal, unwounded but unconscious; the dogs gave him a shake and he was dead. Sometimes when the distance was great and the wind not accurately allowed for, the bullet would hit the squirrel's head; the dogs could do as they pleased with that one—the hunter's pride was hurt, and he wouldn't allow it to go into the gamebag.

In the first faint gray of the dawn the stately wild turkeys would be stalking around in great flocks, and ready to be sociable and answer invitations to come and converse with other excursionists of their kind. The hunter concealed himself and imitated the turkey-call by sucking the air through the legbone of a turkey which had previously answered a call like that and lived only just long enough to regret it. There is nothing that furnishes a perfect turkey-call except that bone. Another of Nature's treacheries, you see. She is full of them; half the time she doesn't know which she likes best—to betray her child or protect it. In the case of the turkey she is badly mixed: she gives it a bone to be used in getting it into trouble, and she also furnishes it with a trick for getting itself out of the trouble again. When a mamma-turkey answers an invitation and finds she has made a mistake in accepting it, she does as the mamma-partridge does—remembers a previous engagement and goes limping and scrambling away, pretending to be very lame; and at the same time she is saying to her not-visible children, "Lie low, keep still, don't expose yourselves; I shall be back as soon as I have beguiled this shabby swindler out of the country."

When a person is ignorant and confiding, this immoral device can have tiresome results. I followed an ostensibly lame turkey over a considerable part of the United States one morning, because I believed in her and could not think she would deceive a mere boy, and one who was trusting her and considering her honest. I had the single-barreled shotgun, but my idea was to catch her alive. I often got within rushing distance of her, and then made my rush; but always, just as I made my final plunge and put my hand down where her back had been, it wasn't there; it was only two or three inches from there and I brushed the tail-feathers as I landed on my stomach—a very close call, but still not quite close enough; that is, not close enough for success, but just close enough to convince me that I could do it next time. She always waited for me, a little piece away, and let on to be resting and greatly fatigued; which was a lie, but I believed it, for I still thought her honest long after I ought to have begun to doubt her, suspecting that this was no way for a high-minded bird to be acting. I followed, and followed, and followed, making my periodical rushes, and getting up and brushing the dust off, and resuming the voyage with patient confidence; indeed, with a confidence which grew, for I could see by the change of climate and vegetation that we were getting up into the high latitudes, and as she always looked a little tireder and a little more discouraged after each rush, I judged that I was safe to win, in the end, the competition being purely a matter of staying power and the advantage lying with me from the start because she was lame.

Along in the afternoon I began to feel fatigued myself. Neither of us had had any rest since we first started on the excursion, which was upwards of ten hours before, though latterly we had paused awhile after rushes, I letting on to be thinking about something else; but neither of us sincere, and both of us warning for the other to call game but in no real hurry about it, for indeed those little evanescent snatches of rest were very grateful to the feelings of us both; it would naturally be so, skirmishing along like that ever since dawn and not a bite in the mean time; at least for me, though sometimes as she lay on her side fanning herself with a wing and praying for strength to get out of this difficulty a grasshopper happened along whose time had come, and that was well for her, and fortunate, but I had nothing—nothing the whole day.

More than once, after I was very tired, I gave up taking her alive, and was going to shoot her, but I never did it, although it was my right, for I did not believe I could hit her; and besides, she always stopped and posed, when I raised the gun, and this made me suspicious that she knew about me and my marksmanship, and so I did not care to expose myself to remarks.

I did not get her, at all. When she got tired of the game at last, she rose from almost under my hand and flew aloft with the rush and whir of a shell and lit on the highest limb of a great tree and sat down and crossed her legs and smiled down at me, and seemed gratified to see me so astonished.

I was ashamed, and also lost; and it was while wandering the woods hunting for myself that I found a deserted log cabin and had one of the best meals there that in my life-days I have eaten. The weed-grown garden was full of ripe tomatoes, and I ate them ravenously, though I had never liked them before. Not more than two or three times since have I tasted anything that was so delicious as those tomatoes. I surfeited myself with them, and did not taste another one until I was in middle life. I can eat them now, but I do not like the look of them. I suppose we have all experienced a surfeit at one time or another. Once, in stress of circumstances, I ate part of a barrel of sardines, there being nothing else at hand, but since then I have always been able to get along without sardines.

Extract from Captain Stormfield's Visit to Heaven

TAKEN FROM HIS OWN MS.
BY MARK TWAIN

Well, when I had been dead about thirty years, I begun to get a little anxious. Mind you, I had been whizzing through space all that time, like a comet. *Like* a comet! Why, Peters, I laid over the lot of them! Of course there warn't any of them going my way, as a steady thing, you know, because they travel in a long circle like the loop of a lasso, whereas I was pointed as straight as a dart for the Hereafter; but I happened on one every now and then that was going my way for an hour or so, and then we had a bit of a brush together. But it was generally pretty, one-sided, because I sailed by them the same as if they were standing still. An ordinary comet don't make more than about 200,000 miles a minute. Of course when I came across one of that sort—like Encke's and Halley's comets, for instance—it warn't anything but just a flash and a vanish, you see. You couldn't rightly call it a race. It was as if the comet was a gravel-train and I was a telegraph dispatch. But after I got outside of our astronomical system, I used to flush a comet occasionally that was something *like.* We haven't got any such comets—ours don't begin. One night I was swinging along at a good round gait, everything taut and trim, and the wind in my favor—I judged I was going about a million miles a minute—it might have been more, it couldn't have been less—when I flushed a most uncommonly big one about three points off my starboard bow. By his stern lights I judged he was bearing about northeast-and-by-north-half east. Well, it was so near my course that I wouldn't throw away the chance; so I fell off a point, steadied my helm, and went for him. You should have heard me whiz, and seen the electric fur fly! In about a minute and a half I was fringed out with an electrical nimbus that flamed around for miles and miles and lit up all space like broad day. The comet was burning blue in the distance, like a sickly torch, when I first sighted him, but he begun to grow bigger and bigger as I crept up on him. I slipped up on him so fast that when I had gone about 150,000,000 miles I was close enough to be swallowed up in the phosphorescent glory of his wake, and I couldn't see anything for the glare. Thinks I, it won't do to run into him, so I shunted to one side and tore along. By and by I closed up abreast of his tail. Do you know what it was like? It was like a gnat closing up on the continent of America. I forged along. By and by I had sailed along his coast for a little upwards of a hundred and fifty million miles, and then I could see by the shape of him that I hadn't even got up to his waistband yet. Why, Peters, *we* don't know anything about comets, down here. If you want to see comets that are comets, you've got to go outside of our solar system—where there's room for them, you understand. My friend, I've seen comets out there that couldn't even lay down inside the *orbits* of our noblest comets without their tails hanging over.

Well, I boomed along another hundred and fifty million miles, and got up abreast his shoulder; as you may say. I was feeling pretty fine, I tell you; but just then I noticed the officer of the deck come to the side and hoist his glass in my direction. Straight off I heard him sing out—

"Below there, ahoy! Shake her up, shake her up! Heave on a hundred million billion tons of brimstone!"

"Ay—ay, sir!"

"Pipe the starboard watch! All hands on deck!"

"Ay—ay, sir!"

"Send two hundred thousand million men aloft to shake out royals and skyscrapers!"

"Ay—ay, sir!"

"Hand the stuns'ls! Hang out every rag you've got! Clothe her from stem to rudder-post!"

"Ay—ay, sir!"

In about a second I begun to see I'd woke up a pretty ugly customer, Peters. In less than ten seconds that comet was just a blazing cloud of red-hot canvas. It was piled up into the heavens clean out of sight—the old thing seemed to swell out and occupy all space; the sulfur smoke from the furnaces—oh, well, nobody can describe the way it rolled and tumbled up into the skies, and nobody can half describe the way it smelt. Neither can anybody begin to describe the wax, that monstrous craft begun to crash along. And such another powwow—thousands of bo's'n's whistles screaming at once, and a crew like the populations of a hundred thousand worlds like ours all swearing at once. Well, I never heard the like of it before.

We roared and thundered along side by side, both doing our level best, because I'd never struck a comet before that could lay over me, and so I was bound to beat this one or break something. I judged I had some reputation in space, and I calculated to keep it. I noticed I wasn't gaining as fast, now, as I was before, but still I was gaining. There was a power of excitement on board the comet. Upwards of a hundred billion passengers swarmed up from below and rushed to the side and begun to bet on the race. Of course this careened her and damaged her speed. My, but wasn't the mate mad! He jumped at that crowd, with his trumpet in his hand, and sung out—

"Amidships! amidships, you——!* or I'll brain the last idiot of you!"

Well, sir, I gained and gained, little by little, till at last I went skimming sweetly by the magnificent old conflagration's nose. By this time the captain of the comet had been rousted out, and he stood there in the red glare for'ard, by the mate, in his shirt-sleeves and slippers, his hair all rats' nests and one suspender hanging, and how sick those two men did look! I just simply couldn't help putting my thumb to my nose as I glided away, and singing out—

"Ta-ta! ta-ta! Any word to send to your family?"

Peters, it was a mistake. Yes, sir, I've often regretted that—it was a mistake. You see, the captain had given up the race, but that remark was too tedious for him—he couldn't stand it. He turned to the mate, and says he—

"Have we got brimstone enough of our own to make the trip?"

"Yes, sir."

"Sure?"

"Yes, sir—more than enough."

---

*The captain could not remember what this word was. He said it was in a foreign tongue.

"How much have we got in cargo for Satan?"

"Eighteen hundred thousand billion quintillions of kazarks."

"Very well, then, let his boarders freeze till the next comet comes. Lighten ship! Lively, now, lively, men! Heave the whole cargo overboard!"

Peters, look me in the eye and be calm. I found out, over there, that a kazark is exactly the bulk of *a hundred and sixty-nine worlds like ours!* They hove all that load overboard. When it fell it wiped out a considerable raft of stars just as clean as if they'd been candles and somebody blow'd them out. As for the race, that was at an end. The minute she was lightened the comet swung along by me the same as if I was anchored. The captain stood on the stern, by the after-davits, and put his thumb to his nose and sung out—

"Ta-ta! ta-ta! Maybe *you've* got some message to send your friends in the Everlasting Tropics!"

Then he hove up his other suspender and started for'ard, and inside of three-quarters of an hour his craft was only a pale torch again in the distance. Yes, it was a mistake, Peters—that remark of mine. I don't reckon I'll ever get over being sorry about it. I'd 'a' beat the bully of the firmament if I'd kept my mouth shut.

But I've wandered a little off the track of my tale; I'll get back on my course again. Now you see what kind of speed I was making. So, as I said, when I had been tearing along this way about thirty years I begun to get uneasy. Oh, it was pleasant enough, with a good deal to find out, but then it was kind of lonesome, you know. Besides, I wanted to get somewhere. I hadn't shipped with the idea of cruising forever. First off, I liked the delay, because I judged I was going to fetch up in pretty warm quarters when I got through; but towards the last I begun to feel that I'd rather go to—well, most any place, so as to finish up the uncertainty.

Well, one night—it was always night, except when I was rushing by some star that was occupying the whole universe with its fire and its glare—light enough then, of course, but I necessarily left it behind in a minute or two and plunged into a solid week of darkness again. The stars ain't so close together as they look to be. Where was I? Oh yes; one night I was sailing along, when I discovered a tremendous long row of blinking lights away on the horizon ahead. As I approached, they begun to tower and swell and look like mighty furnaces. Says I to myself—

"By George, I've arrived at last—and at the wrong place, just as I expected!"

Then I fainted. I don't know how long I was insensible, but it must have been a good while, for when I came to, the darkness was all gone and there was the loveliest sunshine and the balmiest, fragrantest air in its place. And there was such a marvelous world spread out before me—such a glowing, beautiful, bewitching country. The things I took for furnaces were gates, miles high, made all of flashing jewels, and they pierced a wall of solid gold that you couldn't see the top of, nor yet the end of, in either direction. I was pointed straight for one of these gates, and a-coming like a house afire. Now I noticed that the skies were black with millions of people, pointed for those gates. What a roar they made, rushing through the air! The ground was as thick as ants with people, too—billions of them, I judge.

I lit. I drifted up to a gate with a swarm of people, and when it was my turn the head clerk says, in a business-like way—

"Well quick! Where are you from?"

"San Francisco," says I.

"San Fran—*what?*" says he.

"San Francisco."

He scratched his head and looked puzzled, then he says—"Is it a planet?"

By George, Peters, think of it! "*Planet?*" says I; "it's a city. And moreover, it's one of the biggest, and finest and—"

"There, there!" says he, "no time here for conversation. We don't deal in cities, here. Where are you from in a general way?"

"Oh," I says, "I beg pardon. Put me down for California."

I had him *again*, Peters! He puzzled a second, then he says, sharp and irritable—

"I don't know any such planet—is it a constellation?"

"Oh, my goodness!" says I. "Constellation, says you? No—it's a State."

"Man, we don't deal in States here. *Will* you tell me where you are from *in general—at large*, don't you understand?"

"Oh, now I get your idea," I says. "I'm from America—the United States of America."

Peters, do you know I had him *again?* If I hadn't I'm a clam! His face was as blank as a target after a militia shooting match. He turned to an under-clerk and says—

"Where is America? *What* is America?"

The under-clerk answered up prompt and says—

"There ain't any such orb."

"*Orb?*" says I. "Why, what are you talking about, young man? It ain't an orb; it's a country; it's a continent. Columbus discovered it; I reckon likely you've heard of him, anyway. America—why, sir, America—"

"Silence!" says the head clerk. "Once for all, where—are—you—*from?*"

"Well," says I, "I don't know anything more to say—unless I lump things, and just say I'm from the world."

"Ah," says he, brightening up, "now that's something like! *What* world?"

Peters, he had *me*, that time. I looked at him, puzzled, he looked at me, worried. Then he burst our "Come, come, what world?"

Says I, "Why, *the* world, of course."

"*The* world!" he says. "H'm! there's billions of them! . . . Next!"

That meant for me to stand aside. I done so, and a sky-blue man with seven heads and only one leg hopped into my place. I took a walk. It just occurred to me, then, that all the myriads I had seen swarming to that gate, up to this time, were just like that creature. I tried to run across somebody I was acquainted with, but they were out of acquaintances of mine just then. So I thought the thing all over and finally sidled back there pretty meek and feeling rather stumped, as you may say.

"Well?" said the head clerk.

"Well, sir," I says, pretty humble, "I don't seem to make out which world it is I'm from. But you may know it from this—it's the one the Savior saved."

He bent his head at the Name. Then he says, gently—

"The worlds He has saved are like to the gates of heaven in number—none can count them. What astronomical system is your world in?—perhaps that may assist."

"It's the one that has the sun in it—and the moon—and Mars"—he shook his head at each name—hadn't ever heard of them, you see—"and Neptune—and Uranus—and Jupiter—"

"Hold on!" says he, "hold on a minute. Jupiter . . . Jupiter . . . . Seems to me we had a man from there eight or nine hundred years ago—but people from that system very seldom enter by this gate." All of a sudden he begun to look me so straight in the eye that I thought he was going to bore through me. Then he says, very deliberate, "Did you come *straight here* from your system?"

"Yes, sir," I says—but I blushed the least little bit in the world when I said it.

He looked at me very stern, and says—

"That is not true; and this is not the place for prevarication. You wandered from your course. How did that happen?"

Says I, blushing again—

"I'm sorry, and I take back what I said, and confess. I raced a little with a comet one day—only just the least little bit—only the tiniest lit—"

"So—so," says he—and without any sugar in his voice to speak of.

I went on, and says—

"But I only fell off just a bare point, and I went right back on my course again the minute the race was over."

"No matter—that divergence has made all this trouble. It has brought you to a gate that is billions of leagues from the right one. If you had gone to your own gate they would have known all about your world at once and there would have been no delay. But we will try to accommodate you." He turned to an under-clerk and says—

"What system is Jupiter in?"

"I don't remember, sir, but I think there is such a planet in one of the little new systems away out in one of the thinly worlded corners of the universe. I will see."

He got a balloon and sailed up and up and up, in front of a map that was as big as Rhode Island. He went on up till he was out of sight, and by and by he came down and got something to eat and went up again. To cut a long story short, he kept on doing this for a day or two, and finally he came down and said he thought he had found that solar system, but it might be flyspecks. So he got a microscope and went back. It turned out better than he feared. He had rousted out our system, sure enough. He got me to describe our planet and its distance from our sun, and then he says to his chief—

"Oh, I know the one he means, now, sir. It is on the map. It is called the Wart."

Says I to myself, "Young man, it wouldn't be wholesome for you to go down *there* and call it the Wart."

Well, they let me in, then, and told me I was safe forever and wouldn't have any more trouble.

Then they turned from me and went on with their work, the same as if they considered my case all complete and shipshape. I was a good deal surprised at this, but I was diffident about speaking up and reminding them. I did so hate to do it, you know; it seemed a pity, to bother them, they had so much on their hands. Twice I thought I would give up and let the thing go; so twice I started to leave, but immediately I thought what a figure I should cut stepping out amongst the redeemed in such a rig, and that made me hang back and come to anchor again. People got to eyeing me—clerks, you know wondering why I didn't get under weigh. I couldn't stand this long—it was too uncomfortable. So at last I plucked up courage and tipped the head clerk a signal. He says—

"What, you here yet? What's wanting?"

Says I, in a low voice and very confidential, making a trumpet with my hands at his ear—

"I beg pardon, and you mustn't mind my reminding you, and seeming to meddle, but hain't you forgot something?" He studied a second, and says—

"Forgot something? . . . No, not that I know of."

"Think," says I.

He thought. Then he says—

"No, I can't seem to have forgot anything. What is it?"

"Look at me," says I, "look me all over."

He done it.

"Well?" says he.

"Well," says I, "you don't notice anything? If I branched out amongst the elect looking like this, wouldn't I attract considerable attention?—wouldn't I be a little conspicuous?"

"Well," he says, "I don't see anything the matter. What do you lack?"

"Lack! Why, I lack my harp, and my wreath, and my halo, and my hymn-book, and my palm branch—I lack everything that a body naturally requires up here, my friend."

Puzzled? Peters, he was the worst puzzled man you ever saw. Finally he says—

"Well, you seem to be a curiosity every way a body takes you. I never heard of these things before."

I looked at that man a while in solid astonishment; then I says—

"Now, I hope you won't take it as an offense, for I don't mean any, but really, for a man that has been in the Kingdom as long as I reckon you have, you do seem to know powerful little about its customs."

"Its customs!" says he. "Heaven is a large place, good friend. Large empires have many and diverse customs. Even small dominions have, as you doubtless know by what you have seen of the matter on a small scale in the Wart. How can you imagine I could ever learn the varied customs of the countless kingdoms of heaven? It makes my head ache to think of it. I know the customs that prevail in those portions inhabited by peoples that are appointed to enter by my own gate—and hark ye, that is quite enough knowledge for one individual to try to pack into his head in the thirty-seven millions of years I have devoted night and day to that study. But the idea of learning the customs of the whole appalling expanse of heaven—O man, how insanely you talk! Now I don't doubt that this odd costume you talk about is the fashion in that district of heaven you belong to, but you won't be conspicuous in this section without it."

I felt all right, if that was the case, so I bade him good day and left. All day I walked toward the far end of a prodigious hall of the office, hoping to come out into heaven any moment, but it was a mistake. That hall was built on the general heavenly plan—it naturally couldn't be small. At last I got so tired I couldn't go any further; so I sat down to rest, and begun to tackle the queerest sort of strangers and ask for information; but I didn't get any; they couldn't understand my language, and I could not understand theirs. I got dreadfully lonesome. I was so downhearted and homesick I wished a hundred times I never had died. I turned back, of course. About noon next day, I got back at last and was on hand at the booking-office once more. Says I to the head clerk—

"I begin to see that a man's got to be in his own heaven to be happy."

"Perfectly correct," says he. "Did you imagine the same heaven would suit all sorts of men?"

"Well, I had that idea—but I see the foolishness of it. Which way am I to go to get to my district?"

He called the under-clerk that had examined the map, and he gave me general directions. I thanked him and started; but he says—

"Wait a minute; it is millions of leagues from here. Go outside and stand on that red wishing-carpet; shut your eyes, hold your breath, and wish yourself there."

"I'm much obliged," says I; "why didn't you dart me through when I first arrived?"

"We have a good deal to think of here; it was your place to think of it and ask for it. Good-bye, we probably sha'nt see you in this region for a thousand centuries or so."

"In that case, *o revoor*," says I.

I hopped on to the carpet and held my breath and shut my eyes and wished I was in the booking-office of my own section. The very next instant a voice I knew sung out in a business kind of a way—

"A harp and a hymn-book, pair of wings and a halo, size 13, for Cap'n Eli Stormfield, of San Francisco!—make him out a clean bill of health, and let him in."

I opened my eyes. Sure enough, it was a Pi Ute Injun I used to know in Tulare County; mighty good fellow—I remembered being at his funeral, which consisted of him being burnt and the other Injuns gauming their faces with his ashes and howling like wildcats. He was powerful glad to see me, and you may make up your mind I was just as glad to see him, and feel that I was in the right kind of a heaven at last.

Just as far as your eye could reach, there was swarms of clerks, running and bustling around, tricking out thousands of Yanks, and Mexicans and English and A-rabs, and all sorts of people in their new outfits; and when they gave me my kit and I put on my halo and took a look in the glass, I could have jumped over a house for joy, I was so happy. "Now *this* is something like!" says I. "Now," says I, "I'm all right—show me a cloud."

Inside of fifteen minutes I was a mile on my way toward the cloud-banks and about a million people along with me. Most of us tried to fly, but some got crippled and nobody made a success of it. So we concluded to walk, for the present, till we had had some wing practice.

We begun to meet swarms of folks who were coming back. Some had harps and nothing else; some had hymn-books and nothing else; some had nothing at all; all of them looked meek and uncomfortable; one young fellow hadn't anything left but his halo, and he was carrying that in his hand; all of a sudden he offered it to me and says—

"Will you hold it for me a minute?"

Then he disappeared in the crowd. I went on. A woman asked me to hold her palm branch, and then *she* disappeared. A girl got me to hold her harp for her, and by George, *she* disappeared; and so on and so on, till I was about loaded down to the guards. Then comes a smiling old gentleman and asked me hold *his* things. I swabbed off the perspiration and says, pretty tart—

"I'll have to get you to excuse me, my friend—*I* ain't no hat rack."

About this time I begun to run across piles of those traps, lying in the road. I just quietly dumped my extra cargo along with them. I looked around, and, Peters, that whole nation that was following me were loaded down the same as I'd been. The return crowd had got them to hold their things a minute, you see. They all dumped their loads, too, and we went on.

When I found myself perched on a cloud, with a million other people, I never felt so good in my life. Says I, "Now this is according to the promises; I've been having my doubts, but now I *am* in heaven, sure enough." I gave my palm branch a wave or two, for luck, and then I tautened up my harp-strings and struck in. Well, Peters, you can't imagine anything like the row we made. It was grand to listen to, and made a body thrill all over, but there was considerable many tunes going at once, and that was a drawback to the harmony, you understand; and then there was a lot of Injun tribes, and they kept up such another war-whooping that they kind of took the tuck out of the music. By and by I quit performing, and judged I'd take a rest. There was quite a nice mild old gentleman sitting next to me, and I noticed he didn't take a hand; I encouraged him, but he said he was naturally bashful, and was afraid to try before so many people. By and by the old gentleman said he never could seem to enjoy music somehow. The fact was, I was beginning to feel the same way; but I didn't say anything. Him and I had a considerable long silence, then, but of course it warn't noticeable in that place. After about sixteen or seventeen hours, during which I played and sung a little, now and then—always the same tune, because I didn't know any other—I laid down my harp and begun to fan myself with my palm branch. Then we both got to sighing pretty regular. Finally, says he—

"Don't you know any tune but the one you've been pegging at all day?"

"Not another blessed one," says I.

"Don't you reckon you could learn another one?" says he.

"Never," says I; "I've tried to, but I couldn't manage it."

"It's a long time to hang to the one—eternity, you know."

"Don't break my heart," says I; "I'm getting low-spirited enough already."

After another long silence, says he—

"Are you glad to be here?"

Says I, "Old man, I'll be frank with you. This *ain't* just as near my idea of bliss as I thought it was going to be, when I used to go to church."

Says he, "What do you say to knocking off and calling it half a day?"

"That's me," says I. "I never wanted to go off watch so bad in my life."

So we started. Millions were coming to the cloud-bank all the time, happy and hosannahing; millions were leaving it all the time, looking mighty quiet, I tell you. We laid for the newcomers, and pretty soon I'd got them to hold all my things a minute, and then I was a tree man again and most outrageously happy. Just then I ran across old Sam Bartlett, who had been dead a long time, and stopped to have a talk with him. Says I—

"Now tell me—is this to go on forever? Ain't there anything else for a change?"

Says he—

"I'll set you right on that point very quick. People take the figurative language of the Bible and the allegories for literal, and the first thing they ask for when they get here is a halo and a harp, and so on. Nothing that's harmless and reasonable is refused a body here, if he asks it in the right spirit. So they are outfitted with these things without a word. They go and sing and play just about one day, and that's the last you'll ever see them in the choir. They don't need anybody to tell them that that sort of thing wouldn't make a heaven—at least not a heaven that a sane man could stand a week and remain sane. That cloud-bank is placed where the noise can't disturb the old inhabitants, and so there ain't any harm in letting everybody get up there and cure himself as soon as he comes.

"Now you just remember this—heaven is as blissful and lovely as it can be; but it's just the busiest place you ever heard of. There ain't any idle people here after the first day. Singing hymns and waving palm branches through all eternity is pretty when you hear about it in the pulpit, but it's as poor a way to put in valuable time as a body could contrive. It would just make a heaven of warbling ignoramuses, don't you see? Eternal Rest sounds comforting in the pulpit, too. Well, you try it once, and see how heavy time will hang on your hands. Why, Stormfield, a man like you, that had been active and stirring all his life, would go mad in six months in a heaven where he hadn't anything to do. Heaven is the very last place to come to *rest* in—and don't you be afraid to bet on that!"

Says I—

"Sam, I'm as glad to hear it as I thought I'd be sorry. I'm glad I come, now."

Says he—

"Cap'n, ain't you pretty physically tired?"

Says I—

"Sam, it ain't any name for it! I'm dog-tired."

"Just so—just so. You've earned a good sleep, and you'll get it. You've earned a good appetite, and you'll enjoy your dinner. It's the same here it is on earth—you've got to earn a thing, square and honest, before you enjoy it. You can't enjoy first and earn afterwards. But there's this difference, here: you can choose your own occupation, and all the powers of heaven will be put forth to help you make a success of it, if you do your level best. The shoemaker on earth that had the soul of a poet in him won't have to make shoes here."

"Now that's all reasonable and right," says I. "Plenty of work, and the kind you hanker after; no more pain, no more suffering—"

"Oh, hold on; there's plenty of pain here—but it don't kill. There's plenty of suffering here, but it don't last. You see, happiness ain't a *thing in itself*—it's only a *contrast* with something that ain't pleasant. That's all it is. There ain't a thing you can mention that is happiness in its own self—it's only so by contrast with the other thing. And so, as soon as the novelty is over and the force of the contrast dulled, it ain't happiness any longer, and you have to get something fresh. Well, there's plenty of pain and suffering in heaven—consequently there's plenty of contrasts, and just no end of happiness."

Says I, "It's the sensiblest heaven I've heard of yet, Sam, though it's about as different from the one I was brought up on as a live princess is different from her own wax figger."

Along in the first months I knocked around about the Kingdom, making friends and looking at the country, and finally settled down in a pretty likely region, to have a rest before taking another start. I went on making acquaintances and gathering up information. I had a good deal of talk with an old baldheaded angel by the name of Sandy McWilliams. He was from somewhere in New Jersey. I went about with him, considerable. We used to lay around, warm afternoons, in the shade of a rock, on some meadow-ground that was pretty high and out of the marshy slush of his cranberry-farm, and there we used to talk about all kinds of things, and smoke pipes. One day, says I—

"About how old might you be, Sandy?"

"Seventy-two."

"I judged so. How long you been in heaven?"

"Twenty-seven years, come Christmas."

"How old was you when you come up?"

"Why, seventy-two, of course."

"You can't mean it?"

"Why can't I mean it?"

"Because, if you was seventy-two then, you are naturally ninety-nine now."

"No, but I ain't. I stay the same age I was when I come."

"Well," says I, "come to think, there's something just there that I want to ask about. Down below, I always had an idea that in heaven we would all be young, and bright, and spry."

"Well, you *can* be young if you want to. You've only got wish."

"Well, then, why didn't you wish?"

"I did. They all do. You'll try it, some day, like enough; but you'll get tired of the change pretty soon."

"Why?"

"Well, I'll tell you. Now you've always been a sailor; did you ever try some other business?"

"Yes, I tried keeping grocery, once, up in the mines; but I couldn't stand it; it was too dull—no stir, no storm, no life about it; it was like being part dead and part alive, both at the same time. I wanted to be one thing or t'other. I shut up shop pretty quick and went to sea."

"That's it. Grocery people like it, but you couldn't. You see you wasn't used to it. Well, I wasn't used to being young, and I couldn't seem to take any interest in it. I was strong, and handsome, and had curly hair—yes, and wings, too!—gay wings like a butterfly. I went to picnics and dances and parties with the fellows, and tried to carry on and talk nonsense with the girls, but it wasn't any use; I couldn't take to it—fact is, it was an awful bore. What I wanted was early to bed and early to rise, and something to *do;* and when my work was done, I wanted to sit quiet, and smoke and think—not tear around with a parcel of giddy young kids. You can't think what I suffered whilst I was young."

"How long was you young?"

"Only two weeks. That was plenty for me. Laws, I was so lonesome! You see, I was full of the knowledge and experience of seventy-two years; the deepest subject those young folks could strike was only *a-b-c* to me. And to hear them argue—Oh, my! It would have been funny, if it hadn't been so pitiful. Well, I was so hungry for the ways and the sober talk I was used to, that I tried to ring in with the old people, but they wouldn't have it. They considered me a conceited young upstart, and gave me the cold shoulder. Two weeks was a plenty for me. I was glad to get back my bald head again, and my pipe, and my old drowsy reflections in the shade of a rock or a tree."

"Well," says I, "do you mean to say you're going to stand still at seventy-two, forever?"

"I don't know, and I ain't particular. But I ain't going to drop back to twenty-five any more—I know that, mighty well. I know a sight more than I did twenty-seven years ago, and I enjoy learning, all the time, but I don't seem to get any older. That is, bodily—my mind gets older, and stronger, and better seasoned, and more satisfactory."

Says I, "If a man comes here at ninety, don't he ever set himself back?"

"Of course he does. He sets himself back to fourteen; tries it a couple of hours, and feels like a fool; sets himself forward to twenty; it ain't much improvement; tries thirty, fifty, eighty, and finally ninety—finds he is more at home and comfortable at the same old figure he is used to than any other way. Or, if his mind begun to fail him on earth at eighty, that's where he finally sticks up here. He sticks at the place where his mind was last at its best, for there's where his enjoyment is best, and his ways most set and established."

"Does a chap of twenty-five stay always twenty-five, and look it?"

"If he is a fool, yes. But if he is bright, and ambitious and industrious, the knowledge he gains and the experiences he has, change his ways and thoughts and likings, and make him find his best pleasure in the company of people above that age; so he allows his body to take on the look of as many added years as he needs to make him comfortable and proper in that sort of society; he lets his body go on taking the look of age, according as he progresses, and by and by he will be bald and wrinkled outside, and wise and deep within."

"Babies the same?"

"Babies the same. Laws, what asses we used to be, on earth, about these things! We said we'd be always young in heaven. We didn't say *how* young—we didn't think of that, perhaps—that is, we didn't all think alike, anyway. When I was a boy of seven, I suppose I thought we'd all be twelve, in heaven; when I was twelve, I suppose I thought we'd all be eighteen or twenty in heaven; when I was forty, I begun to go back; I remember I hoped we'd all be about *thirty* years old in heaven. Neither a man nor a boy ever thinks the age he *has* is exactly the best one—he puts the *right* age a few years older or a few years younger than he is. Then he makes that ideal age the general age of the heavenly people. And he expects everybody *to stick* at that age—stand stock-still—and expects them to enjoy it!—Now just think of the idea of standing still in heaven! Think of a heaven made up entirely of hoop-rolling, marble-playing cubs of seven years!—or of awkward, diffident, sentimental immaturities of nineteen!—or of vigorous people of thirty, healthy-minded, brimming with ambition, but chained hand and foot to that one age and its limitations like so many helpless galley-slaves! Think of the dull sameness of a society made up of people all of one age and one set of looks, habits, tastes and feelings. Think how superior to it earth would be, with its variety of types and faces and ages, and the enlivening attrition of the myriad interests that come into pleasant collision in such a variegated society."

"Look here," says I, "do you know what you're doing?"

"Well, what am I doing?"

"You are making heaven pretty comfortable in one way, but you are playing the mischief with it in another."

"How you talk! Would heaven be heaven if you couldn't slander folks?"

"Come to think, I don't believe it would—for some people—but I hadn't thought of it before."

"For 'some people'? There you hit it. The trouble on earth is, that they leave out the *some-people* class—they try to fix up a heaven for only one kind of people. It won't work. There's all kinds here—and God cares for all kinds. He makes all happy; if He can't do it in one way. He does it in another. He doesn't leave anybody out in the cold."

II

I had been having considerable trouble with my wings. The day after I helped the choir I made a dash or two with them, but was not lucky. First off, I flew thirty yards, and then fouled an Irishman and brought him down—brought us both down, in fact. Next, I had a collision with a Bishop—and bowled him down, of course. We had some sharp words, and I felt pretty cheap, to come banging into a grave old person like that, with a million strangers looking on and smiling to themselves.

I saw I hadn't got the hang of the steering, and so couldn't rightly tell where I was going to bring up when I started. I went afoot the rest of the day, and let my wings hang. Early next morning I went to a private place to have some practice. I got up on a pretty high rock, and got a good start, and went swooping down, aiming for a bush a little over three hundred yards off; but I couldn't seem to calculate for the wind, which was about two points abaft my beam. I could see I was going considerable to looard of the bush, so I worked my starboard wing slow and went ahead strong on the port one, but it wouldn't answer; I could see I was going to broach to, so I slowed down on both, and lit. I went back to the rock and took another chance at it. I aimed two or three points to starboard of the bush—yes, more than that—enough so as to make it nearly a headwind. I done well enough, but made pretty poor time. I could see, plain enough, that on a headwind, wings was a mistake. I could see that a body could sail pretty close to the wind, but he couldn't go in the wind's eye. I could see that if I wanted to go a-visiting any distance from home, and the wind was ahead, I might have to wait days, maybe, for a change; and I could see, too, that these things could not be any use at all in a gale; if you tried to run before the wind, you would make a mess of it, for there isn't any way to shorten sail—like reefing, you know—you have to take it *all* in—shut your feathers down flat to your sides. That would *land* you, of course. You could lay to, with your head to the wind—that is the best you could do, and right hard work you'd find it, too. If you tried any other game, you would founder, sure.

I judge it was about a couple of weeks or so after this that I dropped old Sandy McWilliams a note one day—it was a Tuesday—and asked him to come over and take his manna and quails with me next day; and the first thing he did when he stepped in was to twinkle his eye in a sly way, and say—

"Well, Cap, what you done with your wings?"

I saw in a minute that there was some sarcasm done up in that rag somewheres, but I never let on. I only says—

"Gone to the wash."

"Yes," he says, in a dry sort of way, "they mostly go to the wash—about this time—I've often noticed it. Fresh angels are powerful neat. When do you look for 'em back?"

"Day after tomorrow," says I.

He winked at me, and smiled.

Says I—

"Sandy, out with it. Come—no secrets among friends. I notice you don't ever wear wings—and plenty others don't. I've been making an ass of myself—is that it?"

"That is about the size of it. But it is no harm. We all do it at first. It's perfectly natural. You see, on earth we jump to such foolish conclusions as to things up here. In the pictures we always saw the angels with wings on—and that was all right; but we jumped to the conclusion that that was their way of getting around—and that was all wrong. The wings ain't anything but a uniform, that's all. When they are in the field—so to speak—they always wear them; you never see an angel going with a message anywhere without his wings, any more than you would see a military officer presiding at a court martial without his uniform, or a postman delivering letters, or a policeman walking his beat, in plain clothes. But they ain't to *fly* with! The wings are for show, not for use. Old experienced angels are like officers of the regular army—they dress plain, when they are off duty. New angels are like the militia—never shed the uniform—always fluttering and floundering around in their wings, butting people down, flapping here, and there, and everywhere, always imagining they are attracting the admiring eye—well, they just think they are the very most important people in heaven. And when you see one of them come sailing around with one wing tipped up and t'other down, you can make up your mind he is saying to himself: 'I wish Mary Ann in Arkansaw could see me now. I reckon she'd wish she hadn't shook me.' No, they're just for show, that's all—only just for show."

"I judge you've got it about right, Sandy," says I.

"Why, look at it yourself," says he. "*You* ain't built for wings—no man is. You know what a grist of years it took you to come here from the earth—and yet you were booming along faster than any cannonball could go. Suppose you had to fly that distance with your wings—wouldn't eternity have been over before you got here? Certainly. Well, angels have to go to the earth every day—millions of them—to appear in visions to dying children and good people, you know—it's the heft of their business. They appear with their wings, of course, because they are on official service, and because the dying persons wouldn't know they were angels if they hadn't wings—but do you reckon they fly with them? It stands to reason they don't. The wings would wear out before they got half-way; even the pin-feathers would be gone; the wing flames would be as bare as kite sticks before the paper is pasted on. The distances in heaven are billions of times greater; angels have to go all over heaven every day; could they do it with their wings alone? No, indeed; they wear the wings for style, but they travel any distance in an instant by wishing. The wishing-carpet of the Arabian Nights was a sensible idea—but our earthly idea of angels flying these awful distances with their clumsy wings was foolish.

"Our young saints, of both sexes, wear wings all the time—blazing red ones, and blue and green, and gold, and variegated, and rainbowed, and ring-streaked-and-striped ones—and nobody finds fault. It is suitable to their time of life. The things are beautiful and they set the young people off. They are the most striking and lovely part of their outfit—a halo don't *begin*."

"Well," says I, "I've tucked mine away in the cupboard, and I allow to let them lay there till there's mud."

"Yes—or a reception."

"What's that?"

"Well, you can see one tonight if you want to. There's a barkeeper from Jersey City, going to be received."

"Go on—tell me about it."

"This barkeeper got converted at a Moody and Sankey meeting, in New York, and started home on the ferry-boat, and there was a collision and he got drowned. He is of a class that think all heaven goes wild with joy when a particularly hard lot like him is saved; they think all heaven turns out hosannahing to welcome them; they think there isn't anything talked about in the realms of the blest but their case, for that day. This barkeeper thinks there hasn't been such another stir here in years, as his coming is going to raise.—And I've always noticed this peculiarity about a dead barkeeper—he not only expects all hands to turn out when he arrives, but he expects to be received with a torchlight procession."

"I reckon he is disappointed, then."

"No, he isn't. No man is allowed to be disappointed here. Whatever he wants, when he comes—that is, any reasonable and unsacrilegious thing—he can have. There's always a millions or billions of young folks around who don't want any better entertainment than to fill up their lungs and swarm out with their torches and have a high time over a barkeeper. It tickles the barkeeper till he can't rest, it makes a charming lark for the young folks, it don't do anybody any harm, it don't cost a rap, and it keeps up the place's reputation for making all comers happy and content."

"Very good. I'll be on hand and see them land the barkeeper."

"It is manners to go in full dress. You want to wear your wings, you know, and your other things."

"Which ones?"

"Halo, and harp, and palm branch, and all that."

"Well," says I, "I reckon I ought to be ashamed of myself, but the fact is I left them laying around that day I resigned from the choir. I haven't got a rag to wear but this robe and the wings."

"That's all right. You'll find they've been raked up and saved for you. Send for them."

"I'll do it, Sandy. But what was it you was saying about unsacrilegious things, which people expect to get, and will be disappointed about?"

"Oh, there are a lot of such things that people expect and don't get. For instance, there's a Brooklyn preacher by the name of Talmage, who is laying up a considerable disappointment for himself. He says, every now and then in his sermons, that the first thing he does when he gets to heaven, will be to fling his arms around Abraham, Isaac and Jacob, and kiss them and weep on them. There's millions of people down there on earth that are promising themselves the same thing. As many as sixty thousand people arrive here every single day, that want to run straight to Abraham, Isaac and Jacob, and hug them and weep on them. Now mind you, sixty thousand a day is a pretty heavy contract for those old people. If they were a mind to allow it, they wouldn't ever have anything to do, year in and year out, but stand up and be hugged and wept on thirty-two hours in the twenty-four. They would be tired out and as wet as muskrats all the time. What would heaven be, to *them?* It would be a mighty good place to get out of—you know that, yourself. Those are kind and gentle old Jews, but they ain't any fonder of kissing the emotional highlights of Brooklyn than you be. You mark my words, Mr. T.'s endearments are going to be declined, with thanks. There are limits to the privileges of the elect, even in heaven. Why, if Adam was to show himself to every newcomer that wants to call and gaze at him and strike him for his autograph, he would never have time to do anything else but just that. Talmage has said he is going to give Adam some of his attentions, as well as A., I. and J. But he will have to change his mind about that."

"Do you think Talmage will really come here?"

"Why, certainly, he will; but don't you be alarmed; he will run with his own kind, and there's plenty of them. That is the main charm of heaven—there's all kinds here—which wouldn't be the case if you let the preachers tell it. Anybody can find the sort he prefers, here, and he just lets the others alone, and they let him alone. When the Deity builds a heaven, it is built right, and on a liberal plan."

Sandy sent home for his things, and I sent for mine, and about nine in the evening we begun to dress. Sandy says—

"This is going to be a grand time for you, Stormy. Like as not some of the patriarchs will turn out."

"No, but will they?"

"Like as not. Of course they are pretty exclusive. They hardly ever show themselves to the common public, I believe they never turn out except for an eleventh-hour convert. They wouldn't do it then, only earthly tradition makes a grand show pretty necessary on that kind of an occasion."

"Do they all turn out, Sandy?"

"Who?—all the patriarchs? Oh, no—hardly ever more than a couple. You will be here fifty thousand years—maybe more—before you get a glimpse of all the patriarchs and prophets. Since I have been here, Job has been to the front once, and once Ham and Jeremiah both at the same time. But the finest thing that has happened in my day was a year or so ago; that was Charles Peace's reception—him they called 'the Bannercross Murderer'—an Englishman. There were four patriarchs and two prophets on the Grand Stand that time—there hasn't been anything like it since Captain Kidd came; Abel was there—the first time in twelve hundred years. A report got around that Adam was coming; well, of course Abel was enough to bring a crowd, all by himself, but there is nobody that can draw like Adam. It was a false report, but it got around, anyway, as I say, and it will be a long day before I see the like of it again. The reception was in the English department, of course, which is eight hundred and eleven million miles from the New Jersey line. I went, along with a good many of my neighbors, and it was a sight to see, I can tell you. Flocks came from all the departments. I saw Esquimaux there, and Tartars, negroes, Chinamen—people from everywhere. You see a mixture like that in the Grand Choir, the first day you land here, but you hardly ever see it again. There were billions of people; when they were singing or hosannahing, the noise was wonderful; arid even when their tongues were still the drumming of the wings was nearly enough to burst your head, for all the sky was as thick as if it was snowing angels. Although Adam was not there, it was a great time anyway, because we had three Archangels on the Grand Stand—it is a seldom thing that even one comes out."

"What did they look like, Sandy?"

"Well, they had shining faces, and shining robes, and wonderful rainbow wings, and they stood eighteen feet high, and wore swords, and held their heads up in a noble way, and looked like soldiers."

"Did they have halos?"

"No—anyway, not the hoop kind. The archangels and the upper-class patriarchs wear a finer thing than that. It is a round, solid, splendid glory of gold, that is blinding to look at. You have often seen a patriarch in a picture, on earth, with that thing on—you remember it?—he looks as if he had his head in a brass platter. That don't give you the right idea of it at all—it is much more shining and beautiful."

"Did you talk with those archangels and patriarchs, Sandy?"

"Who—*I?* Why, what can you be thinking about, Stormy? I ain't worthy to speak to such as they."

"Is Talmage?"

"Of course not. You have got the same mixed-up idea about these things that everybody has down there. I had it once, but I got over it. Down there they talk of the heavenly King—and that is right—but then they go right on speaking as if this was a Republic and everybody was on a dead level with everybody else, and privileged to fling his arms around anybody he comes across, and be hail-fellow-well-met with all the elect, from the highest down. How tangled up and absurd that is! How are you going to have a republic under a king? How are you going to have a republic at all, where the head of the government is absolute, holds his place forever, and has no parliament, no council to meddle or make in his affairs, nobody voted for, nobody elected, nobody in the whole universe with a voice in the government, nobody asked to take a hand in its matters, and nobody *allowed* to do it? Fine republic, ain't it?"

"Well, yes—it *is* a little different from the idea I had—but I thought I might go around and get acquainted with the grandees, anyway—not exactly splice the main-brace with them, you know, but shake hands and pass the time of day."

"Could Tom, Dick and Harry call on the Cabinet of Russia and do that?—on Prince Gottschakoff, for instance?"

"I reckon not, Sandy."

"Well, this is Russia—only more so. There's not the shadow of a republic about it anywhere. There are ranks, here. There are viceroys, princes, governors, sub-governors, sub-sub-governors, and a hundred orders of nobility, grading along down from grand-ducal archangels, stage by stage, till the general level is struck, where there ain't any titles. Do you know what a prince of the blood is, on earth?"

"No."

"Well, a prince of the blood don't belong to the royal family exactly, and he don't belong to the mere nobility of the kingdom; he is lower than the one, and higher than t'other. That's about the position of the patriarchs and prophets here. There's some mighty high nobility here—people that you and I ain't worthy to polish sandals for—and *they* ain't worthy to polish sandals for the patriarchs and prophets. That gives you a kind of an idea of their rank, don't it? You begin to see how high up they are, don't you? Just to get a two-minute glimpse of one of them is a thing for a body to remember and tell about for a thousand years. Why, Captain, just think of this: if Abraham was to set his foot down here by this door, there would be a railing set up around that foot-track right away, and a shelter put over it, and people would flock here from all over heaven, for hundreds and hundreds of years, to look at it. Abraham is one of the parties that Mr. Talmage, of Brooklyn, is going to embrace, and kiss, and weep on, when he comes. He wants to lay in a good stock of tears, you know, or five to one he will go dry before he gets a chance to do it."

"Sandy," says I, "I had an idea that *I* was going to be equals with everybody here, too, but I will let that drop. It don't matter, and I am plenty happy enough anyway."

"Captain, you are happier than you would be, the other way. These old patriarchs and prophets have got ages the start of you; they know more in two minutes than you know in a year. Did you ever try to have a sociable improving-time discussing winds, and currents and variations of compass with an undertaker?"

"I get your idea, Sandy. He couldn't interest me. He would be an ignoramus in such things—he would bore me, and I would bore him."

"You have got it. You would bore the patriarchs when you talked, and when they talked they would shoot over your head. By and by you would say, 'Good morning, your Eminence, I will call again'—but you wouldn't. Did you ever ask the slush-boy to come up in the cabin and take dinner with you?"

"I get your drift again, Sandy. I wouldn't be used to such grand people as the patriarchs and prophets, and I would be sheepish and tongue-tied in their company, and mighty glad to get out of it. Sandy, which is the highest rank, patriarch or prophet?"

"Oh, the prophets hold over the patriarchs. The newest prophet, even, is of a sight more consequence than the oldest patriarch. Yes, sir, Adam himself has to walk behind Shakespeare."

"Was Shakespeare a prophet?"

"Of course he was; and so was Homer, and heaps more. But Shakespeare and the rest have to walk behind a common tailor from Tennessee, by the name of Billings; and behind a horse-doctor named Sakka, from Afghanistan. Jeremiah, and Billings and Buddha walk together, side by side, right behind a crowd from planets not in our astronomy; next come a dozen or two from Jupiter and other worlds; next come Daniel, and Sakka and Confucius; next a lot from systems outside of ours; next come Ezekiel, and Mahomet, Zoroaster, and a knife-grinder from ancient Egypt; then there is a long string, and after them, away down toward the bottom, come Shakespeare and Homer, and a shoemaker named Marais, from the back settlements of France."

"Have they really rung in Mahomet and all those other heathens?"

"Yes—they all had their message, and they all get their reward. The man who don't get his reward on earth, needn't bother—he will get it here, sure."

"But why did they throw off on Shakespeare, that way, and put him away down there below those shoemakers and horse-doctors and knife-grinders—a lot of people nobody ever heard of?"

"That is the heavenly justice of it—they warn't rewarded according to their deserts, on earth, but here they get their rightful rank. That tailor Billings, from Tennessee, wrote poetry that Homer and Shakespeare couldn't begin to come up to; but nobody would print it, nobody read it but his neighbors, an ignorant lot, and they laughed at it. Whenever the village had a drunken frolic and a dance, they would drag him in and crown him with cabbage leaves, and pretend to bow down to him; and one night when he was sick and nearly starved to death, they had him out and crowned him, and then they rode him on a rail about the village, and everybody followed along, beating tin pans and yelling. Well, he died before morning. He wasn't ever expecting to go to heaven, much less that there was going to be any fuss made over him, so I reckon he was a good deal surprised when the reception broke on him."

"Was you there, Sandy?"

"Bless you, no?

"Why? Didn't you know it was going to come off?"

"Well, I judge I did. It was the talk of these realms—not for a day, like this barkeeper business, but for twenty years before the man died."

"Why the mischief didn't you go, then?"

"Now how you talk! The like of me go meddling around at the reception of a prophet? A mudsill like me trying to push in and help receive an awful grandee like Edward J. Billings? Why, I should have been laughed at for a billion miles around. I shouldn't ever heard the last of it."

"Well, who did go, then?"

"Mighty few people that you and I will ever get a chance to see, Captain. Not a solitary commoner ever has the luck to see a reception of a prophet, I can tell you. All the nobility, and all the patriarchs and prophets—every last one of them—and all the archangels, and all the princes and governors and viceroys, were there—and *no* small fry—not a single one. And mind you, I'm not talking about only the grandees from *our* world, but the princes and patriarchs and so on from *all* the worlds that shine in our sky, and from billions more that belong in systems upon systems away outside of the one our sun is in. There were some prophets and patriarchs there that ours ain't a circumstance to, for rank and illustriousness and all that. Some were from Jupiter and other worlds in our own system, but the most celebrated were three poets, Saa, Bo and Soof, from great planets in three different and very remote systems. These three names are common and familiar in every nook and corner of heaven, clear from one end of it to the other—fully as well known as the eighty Supreme Archangels, in fact—whereas our Moses, and Adam, and the rest, have not been heard of outside of our world's little corner of heaven, except by a few very learned men scattered here and there—and they always spell their names wrong, and get the performances of one mixed up with the doings of another, and they almost always locate them simply *in our solar system*, and think that is enough without going into little details such as naming the particular world they are from. It is like a learned Hindu showing off how much he knows by saying

Longfellow lives in the United States—as if he lived all over the United States, and as if the country was so small you couldn't throw a brick there without hitting him. Between you and me, it does gravel me, the cool way people from those monster worlds outside our system snub our little world, and even our system. Of course we think a good deal of Jupiter, because our world is only a potato to it, for size; but then there are worlds in other systems that Jupiter isn't even a mustard-seed to—like the planet Goobra, for instance, which you couldn't squeeze inside the orbit of Halley's comet without straining the rivets. Tourists from Goobra (I mean parties that lived and died there—natives) come here, now and then, and inquire about our world, and when they find out it is so little that a streak of lightning can flash clear around it in the eighth of a second, they have to lean up against something to laugh. Then they screw a glass into their eye and go to examining *us*, as if we were a curious kind of foreign bug, or something of that sort. One of them asked me how long our day was; and when I told him it was twelve hours long, as a general thing, he asked me if people where I was from considered it worth while to get up and wash for such a day as that. That is the way with those Goobra people—they can't seem to let a chance go by to throw it in your face that their day is three hundred and twenty-two of our years long. This young snob was just of age—he was six or seven thousand of his days old—say two million of our years—and he had all the puppy airs that belong to that time of life—that turning-point when a person has got over being a boy and yet ain't quite a man exactly. If it had been anywhere else but in heaven, I would have given him a piece of my mind. Well, anyway, Billings had the grandest reception that has been seen in thousands of centuries, and I think it will have a good effect. His name will be carried pretty far, and it will make our system talked about, and maybe our world, too, and raise us in the respect of the general public of heaven. Why, look here—Shakespeare walked backwards before that tailor from Tennessee, and scattered flowers for him to walk on, and Homer stood behind his chair and waited on him at the banquet. Of course that didn't go for much *there*, amongst all those big foreigners from other systems, as they hadn't heard of Shakespeare or Homer either, but it would amount to considerable down there on our little earth if they could know about it. I wish there was something *in* that miserable spiritualism, so we could send them word. That Tennessee village would set up a monument to Billings, then, and his autograph would outsell Satan's. Well, they had grand times at that reception—a small-fry noble from Hoboken told me all about it—Sir Richard Duffer, Baronet."

"What, Sandy a nobleman from Hoboken? How is that?"

"Easy enough. Duffer kept a sausage-shop and never saved a cent in his life because he used to give all his spare meat to the poor, in a quiet way. Not tramps—no, the other sort—the sort that will starve before they will beg—honest square people out of work. Dick used to watch hungry-looking men and women and children, and track them home, and find out all about them from the neighbors, and then feed them and find them work. As nobody ever *saw* him give anything to anybody, he had the reputation of being mean; he died with it, too, and everybody said it was a good riddance; but the minute he landed here, they made him a baronet, and the very first words Dick the sausage-maker of Hoboken heard when he stepped upon the heavenly shore were, 'Welcome, Sir Richard Duffer!' It surprised him some, because he thought he had reasons to believe he was pointed for a warmer climate than this one."

All of a sudden the whole region fairly rocked under the crash of eleven hundred and one thunder blasts, all let off at once, and Sandy says—

"There, that's for the barkeep."

I jumped up and says—

"Then let's be moving along, Sandy; we don't want to miss any of this thing, you know."

"Keep your seat," he says; "he is only just telegraphed, that is all."

"How?"

"That blast only means that he has been sighted from the signal-station. He is off Sandy Hook. The committees will go down to meet him, now, and escort him in. There will be ceremonies and delays; they won't be coming up the Bay for a considerable time, yet. It is several billion miles away, anyway."

"*I* could have been a barkeeper and a hard lot just as well as not," says I, remembering the lonesome way I arrived, and how there wasn't any committee nor anything.

"I notice some regret in your voice," says Sandy, "and it is natural enough; but let bygones be bygones; you went according to your lights, and it is too late now to mend the thing."

"No, let it slide, Sandy, I don't mind. But you've got a Sandy Hook *here*, too, have you?"

"We've got everything here, just as it is below. All the States and Territories of the Union, and all the kingdoms of the earth and the islands of the sea are laid out here just as they are on the globe—all the same shape they are down there, and all graded to the relative size, only each State and realm and island is a good many billion times bigger here than it is below. There goes another blast."

"What is that one for?"

"That is only another fort answering the first one. They each fire eleven hundred and one thunder blasts at a single dash—it is the usual salute for an eleventh-hour guest; a hundred for each hour and an extra one for the guest's sex; if it was a woman we would know it by their leaving off the extra gun."

"How do we know there's eleven hundred and one, Sandy, when they all go off at once?—and yet we certainly do know."

"Our intellects are a good deal sharpened up, here, in some ways, and that is one of them. Numbers and sizes and distances are so great, here, that we have to be made so we can *feel* them—our old ways of counting and measuring and ciphering wouldn't ever give us an idea of them, but would only confuse us and oppress us and make our heads ache."

After some more talk about this, I says: "Sandy, I notice that I hardly ever see a white angel; where I run across one white angel, I strike as many as a hundred million copper-colored ones—people that can't speak English. How is that?"

"Well, you will find it the same in any State or Territory of the American corner of heaven you choose to go to. I have shot along, a whole week on a stretch, and gone millions and millions of miles, through perfect swarms of angels, without ever seeing a single white one, or hearing a word I could understand. You see, America was occupied a billion years and more, by Injuns and

Aztecs, and that sort of folks, before a white man ever set his foot in it. During the first three hundred years after Columbus's discovery, there wasn't ever more than one good lecture audience of white people, all put together, in America—I mean the whole thing, British Possessions and all; in the beginning of our century there were only 6,000,000 or 7,000,000—say seven; 12,000,000 or 14,000,000 in 1825; say 23,000,000 in 1850; 40,000,000 in 1875. Our death-rate has always been 20 in 1000 per annum. Well, 140,000 died the first year of the century; 280,000 the twenty-fifth year; 500,000 the fiftieth year; about a million the seventy-fifth year. Now I am going to be liberal about this thing, and consider that fifty million whites have died in America from the beginning up to today—make it sixty, if you want to; make it a hundred million—it's no difference about a few millions one way or t'other. Well, now, you can see, yourself, that when you come to spread a little dab of people like that over these hundreds of billions of miles of American territory here in heaven, it is like scattering a ten-cent box of homeopathic pills over the Great Sahara and expecting to find them again. You can't expect us to amount to anything in heaven, and we *don't*—now that is the simple fact, and we have got to do the best we can with it. The learned men from other planets and other systems come here and hang around a while, when they are touring around the Kingdom, and then go back to their own section of heaven and write a book of travels, and they give America about five lines in it. And what do they say about us? They say this wilderness is populated with a scattering few hundred thousand billions of red angels, with now and then a curiously complected *diseased* one. You see, they think we whites and the occasional nigger are Injuns that have been bleached out or blackened by some leprous disease or other—for some peculiarly rascally *sin*, mind you. It is a mighty sour pill for us all, my friend—even the modestest of us, let alone the other kind, that think they are going to be received like a long-lost government bond, and hug Abraham into the bargain. I haven't asked you any of the particulars, Captain, but I judge it goes without saying—if my experience is worth anything—that there wasn't much of a hooraw made over you when you arrived—now was there?"

"Don't mention it, Sandy," says I, coloring up a little; "I wouldn't have had the family see it for any amount you are a mind to name. Change the subject, Sandy, change the subject."

"Well, do you think of settling in the California department of bliss?"

"I don't know. I wasn't calculating on doing anything really definite in that direction till the family come. I thought I would just look around, meantime, in a quiet way, and make up my mind. Besides, I know a good many dead people, and I was calculating to hunt them up and swap a little gossip with them about friends, and old times, and one thing or another, and ask them how they like it here, as far as they have got. I reckon my wife will want to camp in the California range, though, because most all her departed will be there, and she likes to be with folks she knows."

"Don't you let her. You see what the Jersey district of heaven is, for whites; well, the Californian district is a thousand times worse. It swarms with a mean kind of leather-headed mud-colored angels—and your nearest white neighbor is likely to be a million miles away. *What a man mostly misses, in heaven, is company*—company of his own sort and color and language. I have come near settling in the European part of heaven once or twice on that account."

"Well, why didn't you, Sandy?"

"Oh, various reasons. For one thing, although you *see* plenty of whites there, you can't understand any of them, hardly, and so you go about as hungry for talk as you do here. I like to look at a Russian or a German or an Italian—I even like to look at a Frenchman if I ever have the luck to catch him engaged in anything that ain't indelicate—but *looking* don't cure the hunger—what you want is talk."

"Well, there's England, Sandy—the English district of heaven."

"Yes, but it is not so very much better than this end of the heavenly domain. As long as you run across Englishmen born this side of three hundred years ago, you are all right; but the minute you get back of Elizabeth's time the language begins to fog up, and the further back you go the foggier it gets. I had some talk with a Mr. Spenser and a man by the name of Chaucer—old-time poets—but it was no use, I couldn't quite understand them, and they couldn't quite understand me. I have had letters from them since, but it is such broken English I can't make it out. Back of those men's time the English are just simply foreigners, nothing more, nothing less; they talk Danish, German, Norman French, and sometimes a mixture of all three; back of *them*, they talk Latin, and ancient British, Irish, and Gaelic; and then back of these come billions and billions of pure savages that talk a gibberish that Satan himself couldn't understand. The fact is, where you strike one man in the English settlements that you can understand, you wade through awful swarms that talk something you can't make head nor tail of. You see, every country on earth has been overlaid so often, in the course of a billion years, with different kinds of people and different sorts of languages, that this sort of mongrel business was bound to be the result in heaven."

"Sandy," says I, "did you see a good many of the great people history tells about?"

"Yes—plenty. I saw kings and all sorts of distinguished people."

"Do the kings rank just as they did below?"

"No; a body can't bring his rank up here with him. Divine right is a good-enough earthly romance, but it don't go, here. Kings drop down to the general level as soon as they reach the realms of grace. I knew Charles the Second very well—one of the most popular comedians in the English section—draws first rate. There are better, of course—people that were never heard of on earth—but Charles is making a very good reputation indeed, and is considered a rising man. Richard the Lion-hearted is in the prize-ring, and coming into considerable favor. Henry the Eighth is a tragedian, and the scenes where he kills people are done to the very life. Henry the Sixth keeps a religious-book stand."

"Did you ever see Napoleon, Sandy?"

"Often—sometimes in the Corsican range, sometimes in the French. He always hunts up a conspicuous place, and goes frowning around with his arms folded and his field-glass under his arm, looking as grand, gloomy and peculiar as his reputation calls for, and very much bothered because he don't stand as high, here, for a soldier, as he expected to."

"Why, who stands higher?"

"Oh, a *lot* of people *we* never heard of before—the shoemaker and horse-doctor and knife-grinder kind, you know—clodhoppers from goodness knows where, that never handled a sword or fired a shot in their lives—but the soldiership was in them, though they never had a chance to show it. But here they take their right place, and Caesar and Napoleon and Alexander have to take a back seat. The greatest military genius our world ever produced was a bricklayer from somewhere back of Boston—died during the Revolution—by the name of Absalom Jones. Wherever he goes, crowds flock to see him. You see, everybody knows that if he had had a chance he would have shown the world some generalship that would have made all generalship before look like child's play and 'prentice work. But he never got a chance; he tried heaps of times to enlist as a private, but he had lost both thumbs and a couple of front teeth, and the recruiting surgeon wouldn't pass him. However, as I say, everybody knows, now, what he would have been, and so they flock by the million to get a glimpse of him whenever they hear he is going to be anywhere. Caesar, and Hannibal, and Alexander, and Napoleon are all on his staff, and ever so many more great generals; but the public hardly care to look at *them* when *he* is around. Boom! There goes another salute. The barkeeper's off quarantine now."

Sandy and I put on our things. Then we made a wish, and in a second we were at the reception-place. We stood on the edge of the ocean of space, and looked out over the dimness, but couldn't make out anything. Close by us was the Grand Stand—tier on tier of dim thrones rising up toward the zenith. From each side of it spread away the tiers of seats for the general public. They spread away for leagues and leagues—you couldn't see the ends. They were empty and still, and hadn't a cheerful look, but looked dreary, like a theater before anybody comes—gas turned down. Sandy says—

"We'll sit down here and wait. We'll see the head of the procession come in sight away off yonder pretty soon, now."

Says I—

"It's pretty lonesome, Sandy; I reckon there's a hitch somewheres. Nobody but just you and me—it ain't much of a display for the barkeeper."

"Don't you fret, it's all right. There'll be one more gunfire—then you'll see."

In a little while we noticed a sort of a lightish flush, away off on the horizon.

"Head of the torchlight procession," says Sandy.

It spread, and got lighter and brighter; soon it had a strong glare like a locomotive headlight; it kept on getting brighter and brighter till it was like the sun peeping above the horizon-line at sea—the big red rays shot high up into the sky.

"Keep your eyes on the Grand Stand and the miles of seats—sharp!" says Sandy, "and listen for the gunfire."

Just then it burst out, "Boom-boom-boom!" like a million thunderstorms in one, and made the whole heavens rock. Then there was a sudden and awful glare of light all about us, and in that very instant every one of the millions of seats was occupied, and as far as you could see, in both directions, was just a solid pack of people, and the place was all splendidly lit up! It was enough to take a body's breath away. Sandy says—

"That is the way we do it here. No time fooled away; nobody straggling in after the curtain's up. Wishing is quicker work than traveling. A quarter of a second ago these folks were millions of miles from here. When they heard the last signal, all they had to do was to wish, and here they are."

The prodigious choir struck up—

We long to hear thy voice,
To see thee face to face.

It was noble music, but the uneducated chipped in and spoilt it, just as the congregations used to do on earth.

The head of the procession began to pass, now, and it was a wonderful sight. It swept along, thick and solid, five hundred thousand angels abreast, and every angel carrying a torch and singing—the whirring thunder of the wings made a body's head ache. You could follow the line of the procession back, and slanting upward into the sky, far away in a glittering snaky rope, till it was only a faint streak in the distance. The rush went on and on, for a long time, and at last, sure enough, along comes the barkeeper, and then everybody rose, and a cheer went up that made the heavens shake, I tell you! He was all smiles, and had his halo tilted over one ear in a cocky way, and was the most satisfied-looking saint I ever saw. While he marched up the steps of the Grand Stand, the choir struck up—

> The whole wide heaven groans,
> And waits to hear that voice.

There were four gorgeous tents standing side by side in the place of honor, on a broad railed platform in the center of the Grand Stand, with a shining guard of honor round about them. The tents had been shut up all this time. As the barkeeper climbed along up, bowing and smiling to everybody, and at last got to the platform, these tents were jerked up aloft all of a sudden, and we saw four noble thrones of gold, all caked with jewels, and in the two middle ones sat old white-whiskered men, and in the two others a couple of the most glorious and gaudy giants, with platter halos and beautiful armor. All the millions went down on their knees, and stared, and looked glad, and burst out into a joyful kind of murmurs. They said—

"Two archangels!—that is splendid. Who can the others be?"

The archangels gave the barkeeper a stiff little military bow; the two old men rose; one of them said, "Moses and Esau welcome thee!" and then all the four vanished, and the thrones were empty.

The barkeeper looked a little disappointed, for he was calculating to hug those old people, I judge; but it was the gladdest and proudest multitude you ever saw—because they had seen Moses and Esau. Everybody was saying, "Did you see them?—I did—Esau's side face was to me, but I saw Moses full in the face, just as plain as I see you this minute!"

The procession took up the barkeeper and moved on with him again, and the crowd broke up and scattered. As we went along home, Sandy said it was a great success, and the barkeeper would have a right to be proud of it forever. And he said *we* were in luck, too; said we might attend receptions for forty thousand years to come, and not have a chance to see a brace of such grand moguls as Moses and Esau. We found afterwards that we had come near seeing another patriarch, and likewise a genuine prophet besides, but at the last moment they sent regrets. Sandy said there would be a monument put up there, where Moses and Esau had stood, with the date and circumstances, and all about the whole business, and travelers would come for thousands of years and gawk at it, and climb over it, and scribble their names on it.

THE END

A Fable

Once upon a time an artist who had painted a small and very beautiful picture placed it so that he could see it in the mirror. He said, "This doubles the distance and softens it, and it is twice as lovely as it was before."

The animals out in the woods heard of this through the house-cat, who was greatly admired by them because he was so learned, and so refined and civilized, and so polite and highbred, and could tell them so much which they didn't know before, and were not certain about afterward. They were much excited about this new piece of gossip, and they asked questions, so as to get at a full understanding of it. They asked what a picture was, and the cat explained.

"It is a flat thing," he said; "wonderfully flat, marvelously flat, enchantingly flat and elegant. And, oh, so beautiful?

That excited them almost to a frenzy, and they said they would give the world to see it. Then the bear asked:

"What is it that makes it so beautiful?"

"It is the looks of it," said the cat.

This filled them with admiration and uncertainty, and they were more excited than ever. Then the cow asked:

"What is a mirror?"

"It is a hole in the wall," said the cat. "You look in it, and there you see the picture, and it is so dainty and charming and ethereal and inspiring in its unimaginable beauty that your head turns round and round, and you almost swoon with ecstasy."

The ass had not said anything as yet; he now began to throw doubts. He said there had never been anything as beautiful as this before, and probably wasn't now. He said that when it took a whole basketful of sesquipedalian adjectives to whoop up a thing of beauty, it was time for suspicion.

It was easy to see that these doubts were having an effect upon the animals, so the cat went off offended. The subject was dropped for a couple of days, but in the mean time curiosity was taking a fresh start, and there was a revival of interest perceptible. Then the animals assailed the ass for spoiling what could possibly have been a pleasure to them, on a mere suspicion that the picture was not beautiful, without any evidence that such was the case. The ass was not troubled; he was calm, and said there was one way to find out who was in the right, himself or the cat: he would go and look in that hole, and come back and tell what he found there. The animals felt relieved and grateful, and asked him to go at once—which he did.

But he did not know where he ought to stand; and so, through error, he stood between the picture and the mirror. The result was that the picture had no chance, and didn't show up. He returned home and said:

"The cat lied. There was nothing in that hole but an ass. There wasn't a sign of a flat thing visible. It was a handsome ass, and friendly, but just an ass, and nothing more."

The elephant asked:

"Did you see it good and clear? Were you close to it?"

"I saw it good and clear, O Hathi, King of Beasts. I was so close that I touched noses with it."

"This is very strange," said the elephant; "the cat was always truthful before—as far as we could make out. Let another witness try. Go, Baloo, look in the hole, and come and report."

So the bear went. When he came back, he said:

"Both the cat and the ass have lied; there was nothing in the hole but a bear."

Great was the surprise and puzzlement of the animals. Each was now anxious to make the test himself and get at the straight truth. The elephant sent them one at a time.

First, the cow. She found nothing in the hole but a cow.

The tiger found nothing in it but a tiger.

The lion found nothing in it but a lion.

The leopard found nothing in it but a leopard.

The camel found a camel, and nothing more.

Then Hathi was wroth, and said he would have the truth, if he had to go and fetch it himself. When he returned, he abused his whole subjectry for liars, and was in an unappeasable fury with the moral and mental blindness of the cat. He said that anybody but a nearsighted fool could see that there was nothing in the hole but an elephant.

Moral, by the Cat

You can find in a text whatever you bring, if you will stand between it and the mirror of your imagination. You may not see your ears, but they will be there.

The Mysterious Stranger

Chapter 1

It was in 1590—winter. Austria was far away from the world, and asleep; it was still the Middle Ages in Austria and promised to remain so forever. Some even set it away back centuries upon centuries and said that by the mental and spiritual clock it was still the Age of Belief in Austria. But they meant it as a compliment, not a slur, and it was so taken and we were all proud of it. I remember it well, although I was only a boy; and I remember, too, the pleasure it gave me.

Yes, Austria was far from the world, and asleep, and our village was in the middle of that sleep, being in the middle of Austria. It drowsed in peace in the deep privacy of a hilly and woodsy solitude where news from the world hardly ever came to disturb its dreams, and was infinitely content. At its front flowed the tranquil river, its surface painted with cloud-forms and the reflections of drifting arks and stone-boats; behind it rose the woody steeps to the base of the lofty precipice; from the top of the precipice frowned a vast castle, its long stretch of towers and bastions mailed in vines; beyond the river, a league to the left, was a tumbled expanse of forest-clothed hills cloven by winding gorges where the sun never penetrated; and to the right a precipice overlooked the river, and between it and the hills just spoken of lay a far-reaching plain dotted with little homesteads nested among orchards and shade trees.

The whole region for leagues around was the hereditary property of a prince, whose servants kept the castle always in perfect condition for occupancy, but neither he nor his family came there oftener than once in five years. When they came it was as if the lord of the world had arrived and had brought all the glories of its kingdoms along, and when they went they left a calm behind which was like the deep sleep which follows an orgy.

Eseldorf was a paradise for us boys. We were not overmuch pestered with schooling. Mainly we were trained to be good Christians, to revere the Virgin, the Church, and the saints above everything. Beyond these matters we were not required to know much; and, in fact, not allowed to. Knowledge was not good for the common people and could make them discontented with the lot which God had appointed for them, and God would not endure discontentment with His plans. We had two priests. One of them, Father Adolf, was a very zealous and strenuous priest, much considered.

There may have been better priests in some ways than Father Adolf, but there was never one in our commune who was held in more solemn and awful respect. This was because he had absolutely no fear of the Devil. He was the only Christian I have ever known of whom that could be truly said. People stood in deep dread of him on that account, for they thought that there must be something supernatural about him, else he could not be so bold and so confident. All men speak in bitter disapproval of the Devil but they do it reverently, not flippantly, but Father Adolf's way was very different; he called him by every name he could lay his tongue to and it made everyone shudder that heard him; and often he would even speak of him scornfully and scoffingly; then the people crossed themselves and went quickly out of his presence, fearing that something fearful might happen.

Father Adolf had actually met Satan face to face more than once, and defied him. This was known to be so. Father Adolf said it himself. He never made any secret of it, but spoke it right out. And that he was speaking true there was proof in at least one instance, for on that occasion he quarreled with the enemy and intrepidly threw his bottle at him, and there, upon the wall of his study, was the ruddy splotch where it struck and broke.

But it was Father Peter, the other priest, that we all loved best and were sorriest for. Some people charged him with talking around in conversation that God was all goodness and would find a way to save all his poor human children. It was a horrible thing to say but there was never any absolute proof that Father Peter said it, and it was out of character for him to say it too, for he was always good and gentle and truthful. He wasn't charged with saying it in the pulpit, where all the congregation could hear and testify, but only outside, in talk, and it is easy for enemies to manufacture *that.* Father Peter had an enemy and a very powerful one, the astrologer who lived in a tumbled old tower up the valley and put in his nights studying the stars. Every one knew he could foretell wars and famines, though that was not so hard, for there was always a war and generally a famine somewhere. But he could also read any man's life through the stars in a big book he had, and find lost property, and every one in the village except Father Peter stood in awe of him. Even Father Adolf, who had defied the Devil, had a wholesome respect for the astrologer when he came through our village wearing his tall, pointed hat and his long, flowing robe with stars on it, carrying his big book and a staff which was known to have magic power. The bishop himself sometimes listened to the astrologer, it was said, for besides studying the stars and prophesying the astrologer made a great show of piety, which would impress the bishop of course.

But Father Peter took no stock in the astrologer. He denounced him openly as a charlatan—a fraud with no valuable knowledge of any kind or powers beyond those of an ordinary and rather inferior human being, which naturally made the astrologer hate Father Peter and wish to ruin him. It was the astrologer, as we all believed, who originated the story about Father Peter's shocking remark and carried it to the bishop. It was said that Father Peter had made the remark to his niece, Marget, though Marget denied it and implored the bishop to believe her and spare her old uncle from poverty and disgrace. But the bishop wouldn't listen. He suspended Father Peter indefinitely, though he wouldn't go so far as to excommunicate him on the evidence of only one witness, and now Father Peter had been out a couple of years and our other priest, Father Adolf, had his flock.

Those had been hard years for the old priest and Marget. They had been favorites but of course that changed when they came under the shadow of the bishop's frown. Many of their friends fell away entirely, and the rest became cool and distant. Marget was a lovely girl of eighteen when the trouble came and she had the best head in the village, and the most in it. She taught the harp and earned all her clothes and pocket money by her own industry. But her scholars fell off one by one now, she was forgotten when there were dances and parties among the youth of the village, the young fellows stopped coming to the house, all except Wilhelm Meidling—and he could have been spared; she and her uncle were sad and forlorn in their neglect and disgrace, and the sunshine was gone out of their lives. Matters went worse and worse, all through the two years. Clothes were wearing out, bread was harder and harder to get. And now, at last, the very end was come. Solomon Isaacs had lent all the money he was willing to put on the house and gave notice that tomorrow he would foreclose.

Chapter 2

Three of us boys were always together and had been so from the cradle, being fond of one another from the beginning, and this affection deepened as the years went on—Nikolaus Bauman, son of the principal judge of the local court, Seppi Wohlmeyer, son of the keeper of the principal inn, the "Golden Stag," which had a nice garden with shade trees reaching down to the riverside, and pleasure boats for hire, and I was the third—Theodor Fischer, son of the church organist, who was also leader of the village musicians, teacher of the violin, composer, tax-collector of the commune, sexton, and in other ways a useful citizen and respected by all. We knew the hills and the woods as well as the birds knew them, for we were always roaming them when we had leisure—at least, when we were not swimming or boating or fishing, or playing on the ice or sliding downhill.

And we had the run of the castle park and very few had that. It was because we were pets of the oldest servingman in the castle, Felix Brandt, and often we went there nights, to hear him talk about old times and strange things and to smoke with him (he taught us that) and to drink coffee, for he had served in the wars and was at the siege of Vienna; and there, when the Turks were defeated and driven away, among the captured things were bags of coffee, and the Turkish prisoners explained the character of it and how to make a pleasant drink out of it, and now he always kept coffee by him, to drink himself and also to astonish the ignorant with. When it stormed he kept us all night; and while it thundered and lightened outside he told us about ghosts and horrors of every kind, and of battles and murders and mutilations and such things, and made it pleasant and cozy inside; and he told these things from his own experience largely. He had seen many ghosts in his time, and witches and enchanters, and once he was lost in a fierce storm at midnight in the mountains, and by the glare of the lightning had seen the Wild Huntsman rage on the blast with his specter dogs chasing after him through the driving cloud-rack. Also he had seen an incubus once, and several times he had seen the great bat that sucks the blood from the necks of people while they are asleep, fanning them softly with its wings and so keeping them drowsy till they die.

He encouraged us not to fear supernatural things, such as ghosts, and said they did no harm but only wandered about because they were lonely and distressed and wanted kindly notice and compassion, and in time we learned not to be afraid, and even went down with him in the night to the haunted chamber in the dungeons of the castle. The ghost appeared only once, and it went by very dim to the sight and floated noiseless through the air and then disappeared, and we scarcely trembled, he had taught us so well. He said it came up sometimes in the night and woke him by passing its clammy hand over his face but it did him no hurt, it only wanted sympathy and notice. But the strangest thing was that he had seen angels—actual angels out of heaven—and had talked with them. They had no wings, and wore clothes, and talked and looked and acted just like any natural person, and you would never know them for angels except for the wonderful things they did which a mortal could not do, and the way they suddenly disappeared while you were talking with them, which was also a thing which no mortal could do. And he said they were pleasant and cheerful, not gloomy and melancholy, like ghosts.

It was after that kind of a talk one May night that we got up next morning and had a good breakfast with him and then went down and crossed the bridge and went away up into the hills on the left to a woody hilltop which was a favorite place of ours, and there we stretched out on the grass in the shade to rest and smoke and talk over these strange things, for they were in our minds yet and impressing us. But we couldn't smoke, because we had been heedless and left our flint and steel behind.

Soon there came a youth strolling toward us through the trees, and he sat down and began to talk in a friendly way, just as if he knew us. But we did not answer him, for he was a stranger and we were not used to strangers and were shy of them. He had new and good clothes on, and was handsome and had a winning face and a pleasant voice, and was easy and graceful and unembarrassed, not slouchy and awkward and diffident, like other boys. We wanted to be friendly with him but didn't know how to begin. Then I thought of the pipe and wondered if it would be taken as kindly meant if I offered it to him. But I remembered that we had no fire, so I was sorry and disappointed. But he looked up bright and pleased, and said:

"Fire? Oh, that is easy; I will furnish it."

I was so astonished I couldn't speak, for I had not said anything. He took the pipe and blew his breath on it, and the tobacco glowed red and spirals of blue smoke rose up. We jumped up and were going to run, for that was natural; and we did run a few steps, although he was yearningly pleading for us to stay and giving us his word that he would not do us any harm, but only wanted to be friends with us and have company. So we stopped and stood, and wanted to go back, being full of curiosity and wonder, but afraid to venture. He went on coaxing in his soft, persuasive way, and when we saw that the pipe did not blow up and nothing happened, our confidence returned by little and little, and presently our curiosity got to be stronger than our fear, and we ventured back—but slowly and ready to fly at any alarm.

He was bent on putting us at ease and he had the right art; one could not remain doubtful and timorous where a person was so earnest and simple and gentle and talked so alluringly as he did; no, he won us over, and it was not long before we were content and comfortable and chatty, and glad we had found this new friend. When the feeling of constraint was all gone we asked him how he had learned to do that strange thing, and he said he hadn't learned it at all; it came natural to him—like other things—other curious things.

"What ones?"

"Oh, a number; I don't know how many."

"Will you let us see you do them?"

"Do—please!" the others said.

"You won't run away again?"

"No—indeed we won't. Please do. Won't you?"

"Yes, with pleasure; but you mustn't forget your promise, you know."

We said we wouldn't, and he went to a puddle and came back with water in a cup which he had made out of a leaf, and blew upon it and threw it out, and it was a lump of ice the shape of the cup. We were astonished and charmed but not afraid any more; we were very glad to be there and asked him to go on and do some more things. And he did. He said he would give us any kind of fruit we liked, whether it was in season or not. We all spoke at once:

"Orange!"

"Apple!"

"Grapes!"

"They are in your pockets," he said, and it was true. And they were of the best, too, and we ate them and wished we had more, though none of us said so.

"You will find them where those came from," he said, "and everything else your appetites call for; and you need not name the thing you wish; as long as I am with you, you have only to wish and find."

And he said true. There was never anything so wonderful and so interesting. Bread, cakes, sweets, nuts—whatever one wanted, it was there. He ate nothing himself, but sat and chatted and did one curious thing after another to amuse us. He made a tiny toy squirrel out of clay, and it ran up a tree and sat on a limb overhead and barked down at us. Then he made a dog that was not much larger than a mouse, and it treed the squirrel and danced about the tree, excited and barking, and was as alive as any dog could be. It frightened the squirrel from tree to tree and followed it up until both were out of sight in the forest. He made birds out of clay and set them free, and they flew away, singing.

At last I made bold to ask him to tell us who he was.

"An angel," he said, quite simply, and set another bird free and clapped his hands and made it fly away.

A kind of awe fell upon us when we heard him say that and we were afraid again, but he said we need not be troubled, there was no occasion for us to be afraid of an angel, and he liked us, anyway. He went on chatting as simply and unaffectedly as ever, and while he talked he made a crowd of little men and women the size of your finger, and they went diligently to work and cleared and leveled off a space a couple of yards square in the grass and began to build a cunning little castle in it, the women mixing the mortar and carrying it up the scaffoldings in pails on their heads, just as our workwomen have always done, and the men laying the courses of masonry—five hundred of these toy people swarming briskly about and working diligently and wiping the sweat off their faces as natural as life. In the absorbing interest of watching those five hundred little people make the castle grow step by step and course by course, and take shape and symmetry, that feeling and awe soon passed away and we were quite comfortable and at home again. We asked if we might make some people and he said yes, and told Seppi to make some cannon for the walls, and told Nikolaus to make some halberdiers with breastplates and greaves and helmets, and I was to make some cavalry, with horses, and in allotting these tasks he called us by our names but did not say how he knew them. Then Seppi asked him what his own name was, and he said, tranquilly, "Satan," and held out a chip and caught a little woman on it who was falling from the scaffolding and put her back where she belonged, and said, "She is an idiot to step backward like that and not notice what she is about."

It caught us suddenly, that name did, and our work dropped out of our hands and broke to pieces—a cannon, a halberdier, and a horse. Satan laughed, and asked what was the matter. I said, "Nothing, only it seemed a strange name for an angel." He asked why.

"Because it's—it's—well, it's his name, you know."

"Yes—he is my uncle."

He said it placidly but it took our breath for a moment and made our hearts beat. He did not seem to notice that, but mended our halberdiers and things with a touch, handing them to us finished, and said, "Don't you remember?—he was an angel himself, once."

"Yes—it's true," said Seppi, "I didn't think of that."

"Before the Fall he was blameless."

"Yes," said Nikolaus, "he was without sin."

"It is a good family—ours," said Satan; "there is not a better. He is the only member of it that has ever sinned."

I should not be able to make any one understand how exciting it all was. You know that kind of quiver that trembles around through you when you are seeing something so strange and enchanting and wonderful that it is just a fearful joy to be alive and look at it, and you know how you gaze, and your lips turn dry and your breath comes short, but you wouldn't be anywhere but there, not for the world. I was bursting to ask one question—I had it on my tongue's end and could hardly hold it back—but I was ashamed to ask it; it might be a rudeness. Satan set an ox down that he had been making and smiled up at me and said:

"It wouldn't be a rudeness and I should forgive it if it was. Have I seen him? Millions of times. From the time that I was a little child a thousand years old I was his second favorite among the nursery angels of our blood and lineage—to use a human phrase—yes, from that time until the Fall, eight thousand years, measured as you count time."

"Eight—thousand!"

"Yes." He turned to Seppi and went on as if answering something that was in Seppi's mind, "Why, naturally I look like a boy, for that is what I am. With us what you call time is a spacious thing; it takes a long stretch of it to grow an angel to full age." There was a question in my mind, and he turned to me and answered it, "I am sixteen thousand years old—counting as you count." Then he turned to Nikolaus and said: "No, the Fall did not affect me nor the rest of the relationship. It was only he that I was named for who ate of the fruit of the tree and then beguiled the man and the woman with it. We others are still ignorant of sin; we are not able to commit it; we are without blemish, and shall abide in that estate always. We—" Two of the little workmen were quarreling, and in buzzing little bumblebee voices they were cursing and swearing at each other; now came blows and blood; then they locked themselves together in a life-and-death struggle. Satan reached out his hand and crushed the life out of them with his fingers, threw them away, wiped the red from his fingers on his handkerchief, and went on talking where he had left off: "We cannot do wrong; neither have we any disposition to do it, for we do not know what it is."

It seemed a strange speech, in the circumstances, but we barely noticed that, we were so shocked and grieved at the wanton murder he had committed—for murder it was, that was its true name and it was without palliation or excuse, for the men had not wronged him in any way. It made us miserable, for we loved him, and had thought him so noble and so beautiful and gracious and had honestly believed he was an angel, and to have him do this cruel thing—ah, it lowered him so, and we had had such pride in him. He went right on talking just as if nothing had happened, telling about his travels and the interesting things he had seen in the big worlds of our solar systems and of other solar systems far away in the remotenesses of space, and about the customs of the immortals that inhabit them, somehow fascinating us, enchanting us, charming us in spite of the pitiful scene that was now under our eyes, for the wives of the little dead men had found the crushed and shapeless bodies and were crying over them and sobbing and lamenting, and a priest was kneeling there with his hands crossed upon his breast, praying; and crowds and crowds of pitying friends were massed about them, reverently uncovered, with their bare heads bowed and many with the tears running down—a scene which Satan paid no attention to until the small noise of the weeping and praying began to annoy them, then he reached out and took the heavy board seat out of our swing and brought it down and mashed all those people into the earth just as if they had been flies, and went on talking just the same.

An angel, and kill a priest! An angel who did not know how to do wrong and yet destroys in cold blood hundreds of helpless poor men and women who had never done him any harm! It made us sick to see that awful deed and to think that none of those poor creatures was prepared except the priest, for none of them had ever heard a mass or seen a church. And we were witnesses, we had seen these murders done and it was our duty to tell, and let the law take its course.

But he went on talking right along, and worked his enchantments upon us again with that fatal music of his voice. He made us forget everything; we could only listen to him and love him and be his slaves, to do with us as he would. He made us drunk with the joy of being with him and of looking into the heaven of his eyes, and of feeling the ecstasy that thrilled along our veins from the touch of his hand.

Chapter 3

The Stranger had seen everything, he had been everywhere, he knew everything, and he forgot nothing. What another must study, he learned at a glance; there were no difficulties for him. And he made things live before you when he told about them. He saw the world made; he saw Adam created; he saw Samson surge against the pillars and bring the temple down in ruins about him; he saw Caesar's death; he told of the daily life in heaven; he had seen the damned writhing in the red waves of hell; and he made us see all these things, and it was as if we were on the spot and looking at them with our own eyes. And we felt them too, but there was no sign that they were anything to him beyond mere entertainments. Those visions of hell, those poor babes and women and girls and lads and men shrieking and supplicating in anguish—why, we could hardly bear it, but he was as bland about it as if it had been so many imitation rats in an artificial fire.

And always when he was talking about men and women here on the earth and their doings—even their grandest and sublimest—we were secretly ashamed, for his manner showed that to him they and their doings were of paltry poor consequence; often you would think he was talking about flies, if you didn't know. Once he even said in so many words that our people down here were quite interesting to him, notwithstanding they were so dull and ignorant and trivial and conceited, and so diseased and rickety and such a shabby, poor, worthless lot all around. He said it in a quite matter-of-course way and without bitterness, just as a person might talk about bricks or manure or any other thing that was of no consequence and hadn't feelings. I could see he meant no offense but in my thoughts I set it down as not very good manners.

"Manners!" he said. "Why, it is merely the truth, and truth is good manners; manners are a fiction. The castle is done. Do you like it?"

Any one would have been obliged to like it. It was lovely to look at, it was so shapely and fine and so cunningly perfect in all its particulars, even to the little flags waving from the turrets. Satan said we must put the artillery in place now and station the halberdiers and display the cavalry. Our men and horses were a spectacle to see, they were so little like what they were intended for; for, of course, we had no art in making such things. Satan said they were the worst he had seen, and when he touched them and made them alive, it was just ridiculous the way they acted, on account of their legs not being of uniform lengths. They reeled and sprawled around as if they were drunk and endangered everybody's lives around them, and finally fell over and lay helpless and kicking. It made us all laugh, though it was a shameful thing to see. The guns were charged with dirt, to fire a salute, but they were so crooked and so badly made that they all burst when they went off, and killed some of the gunners and crippled the others. Satan said we would have a storm now, and an earthquake if we liked, but we must stand off a piece, out of danger. We wanted to call the people away, too, but he said never mind them; they were of no consequence and we could make more, some time or other, if we needed them.

A small storm-cloud began to settle down black over the castle and the miniature lightning and thunder began to play, and the ground to quiver, and the wind to pipe and wheeze, and the rain to fall, and all the people flocked into the castle for shelter. The cloud settled down blacker and blacker and one could see the castle only dimly through it; the lightning blazed out flash upon flash and pierced the castle and set it on fire, and the flames shone out red and fierce through the cloud, and the people came flying out, shrieking, but Satan brushed them back, paying no attention to our begging and crying and imploring; and in the midst of the howling of the wind and volleying of the thunder the magazine blew up, the earthquake rent the ground wide, and the castle's wreck and ruin tumbled into the chasm, which swallowed it from sight, and closed upon it, with all that innocent life, not one of the five hundred poor creatures escaping. Our hearts were broken; we could not keep from crying.

"Don't cry," Satan said; "they were of no value."

"But they are gone to hell!"

"Oh, it is no matter; we can make plenty more."

It was of no use to try to move him; evidently he was wholly without feeling and could not understand. He was full of bubbling spirits and as gay as if this were a wedding instead of a fiendish massacre. And he was bent on making us feel as he did, and of course his magic accomplished his desire. It was no trouble to him; he did whatever he pleased with us. In a little while we were dancing on that grave and he was playing to us on a strange, sweet instrument which he took out of his pocket; and the music—but there is no music like that, unless perhaps in heaven, and that was where he brought it from, he said. It made one mad, for pleasure; and we could not take our eyes from him, and the looks that went out of our eyes came from our hearts and their dumb speech was worship. He brought the dance from heaven, too, and the bliss of paradise was in it.

Presently he said he must go away on an errand. But we could not bear the thought of it and clung to him, and pleaded with him to stay; and that pleased him and he said so, and said he would not go yet but would wait a little while and we would sit down and talk a few minutes longer; and he told us Satan was only his real name and he was to be known by it to us alone, but he had chosen another one to be called by in the presence of others; just a common one, such as people have—Philip Traum.

It sounded so odd and mean for such a being! But it was his decision and we said nothing; his decision was sufficient.

We had seen wonders this day; and my thoughts began to run on the pleasure it would be to tell them when I got home, but he noticed those thoughts and said:

"No, all these matters are a secret among us four. I do not mind your trying to tell them, if you like, but I will protect your tongues and nothing of the secret will escape from them."

It was a disappointment but it couldn't be helped, and it cost us a sigh or two. We talked pleasantly along and he was always reading our thoughts and responding to them, and it seemed to me that this was the most wonderful of all the things he did, but he interrupted my musings and said:

"No, it would be wonderful for you but it is not wonderful for me. I am not limited like you. I am not subject to human conditions. I can measure and understand your human weaknesses, for I have studied them, but I have none of them. My flesh is not real, although it would seem firm to your touch; my clothes are not real; I am a spirit. Father Peter is coming." We looked around, but did not see any one. "He is not in sight yet, but you will see him presently."

"Do you know him, Satan?"

"No."

"Won't you talk with him when he comes? He is not ignorant and dull like us, and he would so like to talk with you. Will you?"

"Another time, yes, but not now. I must go on my errand after a little. There he is now; you can see him. Sit still, and don't say anything."

We looked up and saw Father Peter approaching through the chestnuts. We three were sitting together in the grass, and Satan sat in front of us in the path. Father Peter came slowly along with his head down, thinking, and stopped within a couple of yards of us and took off his hat and got out his silk handkerchief, and stood there mopping his face and looking as if he were going to speak to us, but he didn't. Presently he muttered, "I can't think what brought me here; it seems as if I were in my study a minute ago—but I suppose I have been dreaming along for an hour and have come all this stretch without noticing; for I am not myself in these troubled days." Then he went mumbling along to himself and walked straight through Satan, just as if nothing were there. It made us catch our breath to see it. We had the impulse to cry out, the way you nearly always do when a startling thing happens, but something mysteriously restrained us and we remained quiet, only breathing fast. Then the trees hid Father Peter after a little, and Satan said:

"It is as I told you—I am only a spirit."

"Yes, one perceives it now," said Nikolaus, "but we are not spirits. It is plain he did not see you, but were we invisible, too? He looked at us, but he didn't seem to see us."

"No, none of us was invisible to him, for I wished it so."

It seemed almost too good to be true, that we were actually seeing these romantic and wonderful things, and that it was not a dream. And there he sat, looking just like anybody—so natural and simple and charming, and chatting along again the same as ever, and—well, words cannot make you understand what we felt. It was an ecstasy; and an ecstasy is a thing that will not go into words; it feels like music, and one cannot tell about music so that another person can get the feeling of it. He was back in the old ages once more now, and making them live before us. He had seen so much, so much! It was just a wonder to look at him and try to think how it must seem to have such experience behind one.

But it made you seem sorrowfully trivial, and the creature of a day, and such a short and paltry day, too. And he didn't say anything to raise up your drooping pride—no, not a word. He always spoke of men in the same old indifferent way—just as one speaks of bricks and manure piles and such things; you could see that they were of no consequence to him, one way or the other. He didn't mean to hurt us, you could see that; just as we don't mean to insult a brick when we disparage it; a brick's emotions are nothing to us; it never occurs to us to think whether it has any or not.

Once when he was bunching the most illustrious kings and conquerors and poets and prophets and pirates and beggars together—just a brick-pile—I was shamed into putting in a word for man, and asked him why he made so much difference between men and himself. He had to struggle with that a moment; he didn't seem to understand how I could ask such a strange question. Then he said:

"The difference between man and me? The difference between a mortal and an immortal? between a cloud and a spirit?" He picked up a wood-louse that was creeping along a piece of bark: "What is the difference between Caesar and this?"

I said, "One cannot compare things which by their nature and by the interval between them are not comparable."

"You have answered your own question," he said. "I will expand it. Man is made of dirt—I saw him made. I am not made of dirt. Man is a museum of diseases, a home of impurities; he comes today and is gone tomorrow; he begins as dirt and departs as stench; I am of the aristocracy of the Imperishables. And man has the *Moral Sense*. You understand? He has the *Moral Sense*. That would seem to be difference enough between us, all by itself."

He stopped there, as if that settled the matter. I was sorry, for at that time I had but a dim idea of what the Moral Sense was. I merely knew that we were proud of having it, and when he talked like that about it, it wounded me and I felt as a girl feels who thinks her dearest finery is being admired and then overhears strangers making fun of it. For a while we were all silent and I, for one, was depressed. Then Satan began to chat again, and soon he was sparkling along in such a cheerful and vivacious vein that my spirits rose once more. He told some very cunning things that put us in a gale of laughter; and when he was telling about the time that Samson tied the torches to the foxes' tails and set them loose in the Philistines' corn, and Samson sitting on the fence slapping his thighs and laughing, with the tears running down his cheeks, and lost his balance and fell off the fence, the memory of that picture got him to laughing, too, and we did have a most lovely and jolly time. By and by he said:

"I am going on my errand now."

"Don't!" we all said. "Don't go; stay with us. You won't come back."

"Yes, I will; I give you my word."

"When? Tonight? Say when."

"It won't be long. You will see."

"We like you."

"And I you. And as a proof of it I will show you something fine to see. Usually when I go I merely vanish, but now I will dissolve myself and let you see me do it."

He stood up and it was quickly finished. He thinned away and thinned away until he was a soap-bubble, except that he kept his shape. You could see the bushes through him as clearly as you see things through a soap-bubble, and all over him played and flashed the delicate iridescent colors of the bubble, and along with them was that thing shaped like a window sash which you always see on the globe of the bubble. You have seen a bubble strike the carpet and lightly bound along two or three times before it bursts. He did that. He sprang—touched the grass—bounded—floated along—touched again—and so on, and presently exploded—puff! and in his place was vacancy.

It was a strange and beautiful thing to see. We did not say anything but sat wondering and dreaming and blinking, and finally Seppi roused up and said, mournfully sighing:

"I suppose none of it has happened."

Nikolaus sighed and said about the same.

I was miserable to hear them say it, for it was the same cold fear that was in my own mind. Then we saw poor old Father Peter wandering along back, with his head bent down, searching the ground. When he was pretty close to us he looked up and saw us, and said, "How long have you been here, boys?"

"A little while, Father."

"Then it is since I came by, and maybe you can help me. Did you come up by the path?"

"Yes, Father."

"That is good. I came the same way. I have lost my wallet. There wasn't much in it, but a very little is much to me, for it was all I had. I suppose you haven't seen anything of it?"

"No, Father, but we will help you hunt."

"It is what I was going to ask you. Why here it is. We hadn't noticed it; yet there it lay, right where Satan stood when he began to melt—if he did melt and it wasn't a delusion. Father Peter picked it up and looked very much surprised.

"It is mine," he said, "but not the contents. This is fat, mine was flat; mine was light, this is heavy." He opened it; it was stuffed as full as it could hold with gold coins. He let us gaze our fill; and of course we did gaze, for we had never seen so much money at one time before. All our mouths came open to say "Satan did it!" but nothing came out. There it was, you see—we couldn't tell what Satan didn't want told; he had said so himself.

"Boys, did you do this?"

It made us laugh. And it made him laugh, too, as soon as he thought what a foolish question it was.

"Who has been here?"

Our mouths came open to answer but stood so for a moment, because we couldn't say "Nobody," for it wouldn't be true, and the right word didn't seem to come; then I thought of the right one, and said it:

"Not a human being."

"That is so," said the others, and let their mouths go shut.

"It is not so," said Father Peter, and looked at us very severely. "I came by here a while ago and there was no one here, but that is nothing; some one has been here since. I don't mean to say that the person didn't pass here before you came, and I don't mean to say that you saw him, but some one did pass, that I know. On your honor—you saw no one?"

"Not a human being."

"That is sufficient; I know you are telling me the truth."

He began to count the money on the path, we on our knees eagerly helping to stack it in little piles.

"It's eleven hundred ducats odd!" he said. "Oh dear! if it were only mine—and I need it so!" and his voice broke and his lips quivered.

"It is yours, sir!" we all cried out at once, "every heller!"

"No—it isn't mine. Only four ducats are mine; the rest . . . !" He fell to dreaming, poor old soul, and caressing some of the coins in his hands, and forgot where he was, sitting there on his heels with his old gray head bare; it was pitiful to see. "No," he said, waking up, "it isn't mine. I can't account for it. I think some enemy . . . it must he trap."

Nikolaus said: "Father Peter, with the exception the astrologer you haven't a real enemy in the Village—nor Marget, either. And not even a half-enemy that's rich enough to chance eleven hundred ducats to do you a mean turn. I'll ask you if that's so or not?"

He couldn't get around that argument and it cheered him up. "But it isn't mine, you see—it isn't mine, in any case."

He said it in a wistful way, like a person that wouldn't be sorry, but glad, if anybody would contradict him.

"It is yours, Father Peter, and we are witness to it. Aren't we, boys?"

"Yes, we are—and we'll stand by it, too."

"Bless your hearts, you do almost persuade me; you do, indeed. If I had only a hundred-odd ducats of it! The house is mortgaged for it, and we've no home for our heads if we don't pay tomorrow. And that four ducats is all we've got in the—"

"It's yours, every bit of it, and you've got to take it—we are bail that it's all right. Aren't we, Theodor? Aren't we, Seppi?"

We two said yes, and Nikolaus stuffed the money back into the shabby old wallet and made the owner take it. So he said he would use two hundred of it, for his house was good enough security for that, and would put the rest at interest till the rightful owner came for it, and on our side we must sign a paper showing how he got the money—a paper to show to the villagers as proof that he had not got out of his troubles dishonestly.

Chapter 4

It made immense talk next day, when Father Peter paid Solomon Isaacs in gold and left the rest of the money with him at interest. Also, there was a pleasant change; many people called at the house to congratulate him and a number of cool old friends became kind and friendly again, and to top all, Marget was invited to a party.

And there was no mystery; Father Peter told the whole circumstance just as it happened and said he could not account for it, only it was the plain hand Providence, so far as he could see.

One or two shook their heads and said privately it looked more like the hand of Satan; and really that seemed a surprisingly good guess for ignorant people like that. Some came slyly buzzing around and tried to coax us boys to come out and "tell the truth," and promised they wouldn't ever tell but only wanted to know their own satisfaction, because the whole thing was so curious. They even wanted to buy the secret and pay money for it, and if we could have invented something that would answer—but we couldn't, we hadn't the ingenuity, so we had to let the chance go by, and it was a pity.

We carried that secret around without any trouble, but the other one, the big one, the splendid one, burned the very vitals of us, it was so hot to get out and we so hot to let it out and astonish people with it. But we had to keep it in; in fact, it kept itself in. Satan said it would, and it did. We went off every day and got to ourselves in the woods so that we could talk about Satan, and really that was the only subject we thought of or cared anything about, and day and night we watched for him and hoped he would come, and we got more and more impatient all the time. We hadn't any interest in the other boys any more and wouldn't take part in their games and enterprises. They seemed so tame, after Satan, and their doings so trifling and commonplace after his adventures in antiquity and the constellations, and his miracles and meltings and explosions and all that.

During the first day we were in a state of anxiety on account of one thing, and we kept going to Father Peter's house on one pretext or another to keep track of it. That was the gold coin; we were afraid it would crumble and turn to dust, like fairy money. If it did—But it didn't. At the end of the day no complaint had been made about it, so after that we were satisfied that it was real gold and dropped the anxiety out of our minds.

There was a question which we wanted to ask Father Peter, and finally we went there the second evening, a little diffidently, after drawing straws, and I asked it as casually as I could, though it did not sound as casual as I wanted, because I didn't know how:

"What is the Moral Sense, sir?"

He looked down, surprised, over his great spectacles, and said, "Why, it is the faculty which enables us to distinguish good from evil."

It threw some light but not a glare, and I was a little disappointed, also to some degree embarrassed. He was waiting for me to go on, so, in default of anything else to say, I asked, "Is it valuable?"

"Valuable? Heavens! lad, it is the one thing that lifts man above the beasts that perish and makes him heir to immortality!"

This did not remind me of anything further to say, so I got out, with the other boys, and we went away with that indefinite sense you have often had of being filled but not farted. They wanted me to explain but I was tired.

We passed out through the parlor, and there was Marget at the spinner teaching Marie Lueger. So one of the deserting pupils was back, and an influential one too; the others would follow. Marget jumped up and ran and thanked us again with tears in her eyes—this was the third time—for saving her and her uncle from being turned into the street, and we told her again we hadn't done it; but that was her way, she never could be grateful enough for anything a person did for her so we let her have her say. And as we passed through the garden, there was Wilhelm Meidling sitting there waiting, for it was getting toward the edge of the evening, and he would be asking Marget to take a walk along the river with him when she was done with the lesson. He was a young lawyer and succeeding fairly well and working his way along, little by little. He was very fond of Marget and she of him. He had not deserted along with the others but had stood his ground all through. His faithfulness was not lost on Marget and her uncle. He hadn't so very much talent but he was handsome and good, and these are a kind of talents themselves and help along. He asked us how the lesson was getting along and we told him it was about done. And maybe it was so; we didn't know anything about it but we judged it would please him, and it did, and didn't cost us anything.

Chapter 5

On the fourth day comes the astrologer from his crumbling old tower up the valley, where he had heard the news, I reckon. He had a private talk with us, and we told him what we could, for we were mightily in dread of him. He sat there studying and studying awhile to himself; then he asked:

"How many ducats did you say?"

"Eleven hundred and seven, sir."

Then he said, as if he were talking to himself: "It is ver-y singular. Yes . . . very strange. A curious coincidence." Then he began to ask questions, and went over the whole ground from the beginning, we answering. By and by he said: "Eleven hundred and six ducats. It is a large sum."

"Seven," said Seppi, correcting him.

"Oh, seven, was it? Of course a ducat more or less isn't of consequence, but you said eleven hundred and six before."

It would not have been safe for us to say he was mistaken but we knew he was. Nikolaus said, "We ask pardon for the mistake, but we meant to say seven."

"Oh, it is no matter, lad; it was merely that I noticed the discrepancy. It is several days, and you cannot be expected to remember precisely. One is apt to be inexact when there is no particular circumstance to impress the count upon the memory."

"But there was one, sir," said Seppi, eagerly.

"What was it, my son?" asked the astrologer, indifferently.

"First, we all counted the piles of coin, each in turn, and all made it the same—eleven hundred and six. But I had slipped one out for fun, when the count began, and now I slipped it back and said, 'I think there is a mistake—there are eleven hundred and seven; let us count again.' We did, and of course I was right. They were astonished; then I told how it came about."

The astrologer asked us if this was so, and we said it was.

"That settles it," he said. "I know the thief now. Lads, the money was stolen."

Then he went away, leaving us very much troubled, and wondering what he could mean. In about an hour we found out, for by that time it was all over the village that Father Peter had been arrested for stealing a great sum of money from the astrologer. Everybody's tongue was loose and going. Many said it was not in Father Peter's character and must be a mistake, but the others shook their heads and said misery and want could drive a suffering man to almost anything. About one detail there were no differences; all agreed that Father Peter's account of how the money came into his hands was just about unbelievable—it had such an impossible look. They said it might have come into the astrologer's hands in some such way, but into Father Peter's, never! Our characters began to suffer now. We were Father Peter's only witnesses; how much did he probably pay us to back up his fantastic tale? People talked that kind of talk to us pretty freely and frankly, and were full of scoffings when we begged them to believe really we had told only the truth. Our parents were harder on us than any one else. Our fathers said we were disgracing our families, and they commanded us to purge ourselves of our lie, and there was no limit to their anger when we continued to say we had spoken true. Our mothers cried over us and begged us to give back our bribe and get back our honest names and save our families from shame, and come out and honorably confess. And at last we were so worried and harassed that we tried to tell the whole thing, Satan and all—but no, it wouldn't come out. We were hoping and longing all the time that Satan would come and help us out of our trouble, but there was no sign of him.

Within an hour after the astrologer's talk with us, Father Peter was in prison and the money sealed up and in the hands of the officers of the law. The money was in a bag, and Solomon Isaacs said he had not touched it since he had counted it; his oath was taken that it was the same money, and that the amount was eleven hundred and seven ducats. Father Peter claimed trial by the ecclesiastical court, but our other priest, Father Adolf, said an ecclesiastical court hadn't jurisdiction over a suspended priest. The bishop upheld him. That settled it; the case would go to trial in the civil court. The court would not sit for some time to come. Wilhelm Meidling would be Father Peter's lawyer and do the best he could, of course, but he told us privately that a weak case on his side and all the power and prejudice on the other made the outlook bad.

So Marget's new happiness died a quick death. No friends came to condole with her and none were expected; an unsigned note withdrew her invitation to the party. There would be no scholars to take lessons. How could she support herself? She could remain in the house, for the mortgage was paid off, though the government and not poor Solomon Isaacs had the mortgage money in its grip for the present. Old Ursula, who was took, chambermaid, housekeeper, laundress, and everything else for Father Peter and had been Marget's nurse in earlier years, said God would provide. But she said that from habit, for she was a good Christian. She meant to help in the providing, to make sure, if she could find a way.

We boys wanted to go and see Marget and show friendliness for her, but our parents were afraid of offending the community and wouldn't let us. The astrologer was going around inflaming everybody against Father Peter, and saying he was an abandoned thief and had stolen eleven hundred and seven gold ducats from him. He said he knew he was a thief from that fact, for it was exactly the sum he had lost and which Father Peter pretended he had "found."

In the afternoon of the fourth day after the catastrophe old Ursula appeared at our house and asked for some washing to do, and begged my mother to keep this secret, to save Marget's pride, who would stop this project if she found it out, yet Marget had not enough to eat and was growing weak. Ursula was growing weak herself and showed it, and she ate of the food that was offered her like a starving person but could not be persuaded to carry any home, for Marget would not eat charity food. She took some clothes down to the stream to wash them, but we saw from the window that handling the bat was too much for her strength; so she was called back and a trifle of money offered her, which she was afraid to take lest Marget should suspect; then she took it, saying she would explain that she found it in the road. To keep it from being a lie and damning her soul, she got me to drop it while she watched; then she went along by there and found it and exclaimed with surprise and joy, and picked it up and went her way. Like the rest of the village, she could tell everyday lies fast enough and without taking any precautions against fire and brimstone on their account, but this was a new kind of lie and it had a dangerous look because she hadn't had any practice in it. After a week's practice it wouldn't have given her any trouble. It is the way we are made.

I was in trouble, for how would Marget live? Ursula could not find a coin in the road every day—perhaps not even a second one. And I was ashamed too, for not having been near Marget, and she so in need of friends; but that was my parents' fault, not mine, and I couldn't help it.

I was walking along the path, feeling very downhearted, when a most cheery and tingling freshening-up sensation went rippling through me and I was too glad for any words, for I knew by that sign that Satan was by. I had noticed it before. Next moment he was alongside of me and I was telling him all my trouble and what had been happening to Marget and her uncle. While we were talking we turned a curve and saw old Ursula resting in the shade of a tree, and she had a lean stray kitten in her lap and was petting it. I asked her where she got it and she said it came out of the woods and followed her, and she said it probably hadn't any mother or any friends and she was going to take it home and take care of it. Satan said:

"I understand you are very poor. Why do you want to add another mouth to feed? Why don't you give it to some rich person?"

Ursula bridled at this and said: "Perhaps you would like to have it. You must be rich, with your fine clothes and quality airs." Then she sniffed and said: "Give it to the rich—the idea! The rich don't care for anybody but themselves; it's only the poor that have feeling for the poor, and help them. The poor and God. God will provide for this kitten."

"What makes you think so?"

Ursula's eyes snapped with anger. "Because I know it!" she said. "Not a sparrow falls to the ground without His seeing it."

"But it falls, just the same. What good is seeing it fall?"

Old Ursula's jaws worked but she could not get any word out for the moment, she was so horrified. When she got her tongue she stormed out, "Go about your business, you puppy, or I will take a stick to you!"

I could not speak, I was so seared. I knew that with his notions about the human race Satan would consider it a matter of no consequence to strike her dead, there being "plenty more," but my tongue stood still, I could give her no warning. But nothing happened; Satan remained tranquil—tranquil and indifferent. I suppose he could not be insulted by Ursula any more than the king could be insulted by a tumble-bug. The old woman jumped to her feet when she made her remark, and did it as briskly as a young girl. It had been many years since she had done the like of that. That was Satan's influence; he was a fresh breeze to the weak and the sick, wherever he came. His presence affected even the lean kitten, and it skipped to the ground and began to chase a leaf. This surprised Ursula and she stood looking at the creature and nodding her head wonderingly, her anger quite forgotten.

"What's come over it?" she said. "Awhile ago it could hardly walk."

"You have not seen a kitten of that breed before," said Satan.

Ursula was not proposing to be friendly with the mocking stranger, and she gave him an ungentle look and retorted: "Who asked you to come here and pester me, I'd like to know? And what do you know about what I've seen and what I haven't seen?"

"You haven't seen a kitten with the hair-spines on its tongue pointing to the front, have you?"

"No—nor you, either."

"Well, examine this one and see."

Ursula was become pretty spry but the kitten was spryer and she could not catch it, and had to give it up. Then Satan said:

"Give it a name, and maybe it will come."

Ursula tried several names but the kitten was not interested.

"Call it Agnes. Try that."

The creature answered to the name and came. Ursula examined its tongue. "Upon my word, it's true!" she said. "I have not seen this kind of a cat before. Is it yours?"

"No."

"Then how did you know its name so pat?"

"Because all cats of that breed are named Agnes; they will not answer to any other."

Ursula was impressed. "It is the most wonderful thing!" Then a shadow of trouble came into her face, for her superstitions were aroused and she reluctantly put the creature down, saying: "I suppose I must let it go; I am not afraid—no, not exactly that, though the priest—well, I've heard people—indeed, many people . . . . And, besides, it is quite well now and can take care of itself." She sighed, and turned to go, murmuring: "It is such a pretty one too, and would be such company—and the house is so sad and lonesome these troubled days . . . . Miss Marget so mournful and just a shadow, and the old master shut up in jail."

"It seems a pity not to keep it," said Satan.

Ursula turned quickly—just as if she were hoping some one would encourage her.

"Why?" she asked, wistfully.

"Because this breed brings luck."

"Does it? Is it true? Young man, do you know it to be true? How does it bring luck?"

"Well, it brings money, anyway."

Ursula looked disappointed. "Money? A cat bring money? The idea! You could never sell it here; people do not buy cats here; one can't even give them away." She turned to go.

"I don't mean sell it. I mean have an income from it. This kind is called the Lucky Cat. Its owner finds four silver groschen in his pocket every morning."

I saw the indignation rising in the old woman's face. She was insulted. This boy was making fun of her. That was her thought. She thrust her hands into her pockets and straightened up to give him a piece of her mind. Her temper was all up, and hot. Her mouth came open and let out three words of a bitter sentence, . . . then it fell silent, and the anger in her face turned to surprise or wonder or fear, or something, and she slowly brought out her hands from her pockets and opened them and held them so. In one was my piece of money, in the other lay four silver groschen. She gazed a little while, perhaps to see if the groschen would vanish away; then she said, fervently:

"It's true—it's true—and I'm ashamed and beg forgiveness, O

dear master and benefactor!" And she ran to Satan and kissed his hand, over and over again, according to the Austrian custom.

In her heart she probably believed it was a witch-cat and an agent of the Devil; but no matter, it was all the more certain to be able to keep its contract and furnish a daily good living for the family, for in matters of finance even the piousest of our peasants would have more confidence in an arrangement with the Devil than with an archangel. Ursula started homeward with Agnes in her arms, and I said I wished I had her privilege of seeing Marget.

Then I caught my breath, for we were there. There in the parlor, and Marget standing looking at us, astonished. She was feeble and pale, but I knew that those conditions would not last in Satan's atmosphere, and it turned out so. I introduced Satan—that is, Philip Traum —and we sat down and talked. There was no constraint. We were simple folk in our village, and when a stranger was a pleasant person we were soon friends. Marget wondered how we got in without her hearing us. Traum said the door was open and we walked in and waited until she should turn around and greet us. This was not true; no door was open; we entered through the walls or the roof or down the chimney, or somehow; but no matter, what Satan wished a person to believe, the person was sure to believe, and so Marget was quite satisfied with that explanation. And then the main part of her mind was on Traum, anyway; she couldn't keep her eyes off him, he was so beautiful. That gratified me, and made me proud. I hoped he would show off some, but he didn't. He seemed only interested in being friendly and telling lies. He said he was an orphan. That made Marget pity him. The water came into her eyes. He said he had never known his mamma, she passed away while he was a young thing, and said his papa was in shattered health and had no property to speak of—in fact, none of any earthly value—but he had an uncle in business down in the tropics and he was very well off and had a monopoly, and it was from this uncle that he drew his support. The very mention of a kind uncle was enough to remind Marget of her own, and her eyes filled again. She said she hoped their two uncles would meet, some day. It made me shudder. Philip said he hoped too; and that made me shudder again.

"Maybe they will," said Marget. "Does your uncle travel much?"

"Oh yes, he goes all about; he has business everywhere."

And so they went on chatting, and poor Marget forgot her sorrow for one little while, anyway. It was probably the only really bright and cheery hour she had known lately. I saw she liked Philip, and I knew she would. And when he told her he was studying for the ministry I could see that she liked him better than ever. And then, when he promised to get her admitted to the jail so that she could see her uncle, that was the capstone. He said he would give the guards a little present, and she must always go in the evening after dark and say nothing "but just show this paper and pass in, and show it again when you come out"—and he scribbled some queer marks on the paper and gave it to her, and she was ever so thankful, and right away was in a fever for the sun to go down; for in that old, cruel time prisoners were not allowed to see their friends, and sometimes they spent years in the jails without ever seeing a friendly face. I judged that the marks on the paper were an enchantment and that the guards would not know what they were doing, nor have any memory of it afterward; and that was indeed the way of it. Ursula put her head in at the door now and said:

"Supper's ready, miss." Then she saw us and looked frightened, and motioned me to come to her, which I did, and she asked if we had told about the cat. I said no, and she was relieved and said please don't, for if Miss Marget knew, she would think it was an unholy cat and would send for a priest and have its gifts all purified out of it, and then there wouldn't be any more dividends. So I said we wouldn't tell and she was satisfied. Then I was beginning to say good-bye to Marget, but Satan interrupted and said, ever so politely—well, I don't remember just the words, but anyway he as good as invited himself to supper, and me, too. Of course Marget was miserably embarrassed, for she had no reason to suppose there would be half enough for a sick bird. Ursula heard him, and she came straight into the room, not a bit pleased. At first she was astonished to see Marget looking so fresh and rosy, and said so; then she spoke up in her native tongue, which was Bohemian, and said—as I learned afterward—"Send him away, Miss Marget; there's not victuals enough."

Before Marget could speak, Satan had the word, and was talking back to Ursula in her own language—which was a surprise to her, and for her mistress, too. He said, "Didn't I see you down the road awhile ago?"

"Yes, sir."

"Ah, that pleases me; I see you remember me." He stepped to her and whispered: "I told you it is a Lucky Cat. Don't be troubled; it will provide."

That sponged the slate of Ursula's feelings clean of its anxieties and a deep, financial joy shone in her eyes. The cat's value was augmenting. It was getting full time for Marget to take some sort of notice of Satan's invitation, and she did it in the best way, the honest way that was natural to her. She said she had little to offer but that we were welcome if we would share it with her.

We had supper in the kitchen and Ursula waited at table. A small fish was in the frying pan, crisp and brown and tempting, and one could see that Marget was not expecting such respectable food as this. Ursula brought it and Marget divided it between Satan and me, declining to take any of it herself, and was beginning to say she did not care for fish today, but she did not finish the remark. It was because she noticed that another fish had appeared in the pan. She looked surprised, but did not say anything. She probably meant to inquire of Ursula about this later. There were other surprises: flesh and game and wines and fruits—things which had been strangers in that house lately; but Marget made no exclamations and now even looked unsurprised, which was Satan's influence of course. Satan talked right along and was entertaining, and made the time pass pleasantly and cheerfully, and although he told a good many lies, it was no harm in him, for he was only an angel and did not know any better. They do not know right from wrong; I knew this, because I remembered what he had said about it. He got on the good side of Ursula. He praised her to Marget confidentially, but speaking just loud enough for Ursula to hear. He said she was a fine woman and he hoped some day to bring her and his uncle together. Very soon Ursula was mincing and simpering around in a ridiculous girlie way, and smoothing out her gown and prinking at herself like a foolish old hen, and all the time pretending she was not hearing what Satan was saying. I was ashamed, for it showed us to be what Satan considered us, a silly race and trivial. Satan said his uncle entertained a great deal, and to have a clever woman presiding over the festivities would double the attractions of the place.

"But your uncle is a gentleman, isn't he?" asked Marget.

"Yes," said Satan indifferently; "some even call him a Prince, out of compliment, but he is not bigoted; to him personal merit is everything, rank nothing."

My hand was hanging down by my chair; Agnes came along and licked it; by this act a secret was revealed. I started to say, "It is all a mistake; this is just a common, ordinary cat; the hair-needles on her tongue point inward, not outward." But the words did not come, because they couldn't. Satan smiled upon me and I understood.

When it was dark Marget took food and wine and fruit in a basket and hurried away to the jail, and Satan and I walked toward my home. I was thinking to myself that I should like to see what the inside of the jail was like; Satan overheard the thought and the next moment we were in the jail. We were in the torture chamber, Satan said. The rack was there, and the other instruments, and there was a smoky lantern or two hanging on the walls and helping to make the place look dim and dreadful. There were people there—and executioners—but as they took no notice of us, it meant that we were invisible. A young man lay bound, and Satan said he was suspected of being a heretic, and the executioners were about to inquire into it. They asked the man to confess to the charge, and he said he could not, for it was not true. Then they drove splinter after splinter under his nails and he shrieked with the pain. Satan was not disturbed but I could not endure it, and had to be whisked out of there. I was faint and sick but the fresh air revived me and we walked toward my home. I said it was a brutal thing.

"No, it was a human thing. You should not insult the brutes by such a misuse of that word; they have not deserved it," and he went on talking like that. "It is like your paltry race—always lying, always claiming virtues which it hasn't got, always denying them to the higher animals, which alone possess them. No brute ever does a cruel thing—that is the monopoly of those with the Moral Sense. When a brute inflicts pain he does it innocently; it is not wrong; for him there is no such thing as wrong. And he does not inflict pain for the pleasure of inflicting it—only man does that. Inspired by that mongrel Moral Sense of his! A sense whose function is to distinguish between right and wrong, with liberty to choose which of them he will do. Now what advantage can he get out of that? He is always choosing, and in nine cases out of ten he prefers the wrong. There shouldn't be any wrong; and without the Moral Sense there couldn't be any. And yet he is such an unreasoning creature that he is not able to perceive that the Moral Sense degrades him to the bottom layer of animated beings and is a shameful possession. Are you feeling better? Let me show you something."

Chapter 6

In a moment we were in a French village. We walked through a great factory of some sort, where men and women and little children were toiling in heat and dirt and a fog of dust; and they were clothed in rags and drooped at their work, for they were worn and half starved, and weak and drowsy. Satan said:

"It is some more Moral Sense. The proprietors are rich and very holy, but the wage they pay to these poor brothers and sisters of theirs is only enough to keep them from dropping dead with hunger. The work-hours are fourteen per day, winter and summer—from six in the morning till eight at night—little children and all. And they walk to and from the pigsties which they inhabit, four miles each way, through mud and slush, rain, snow, sleet, and storm, daily, year in and year out. They get four hours of sleep. They kennel together, three families in a room, in unimaginable filth and stench; and disease comes, and they die off like flies. Have they committed a crime, these mangy things? No. What have they done, that they are punished so? Nothing at all, except getting themselves born into your foolish race. You have seen how they treat a misdoer there in the jail; now you see how they treat the innocent and the worthy. Is your race logical? Are these ill-smelling innocents better off than that heretic? Indeed, no; his punishment is trivial compared with theirs. They broke him on the wheel and smashed him to rags and pulp after we left, and he is dead now and free of your precious race, but these poor slaves here—why, they have been dying for years and some of them will not escape from life for years to come. It is the Moral Sense which teaches the factory proprietors the difference between right and wrong—you perceive the result. They think themselves better than dogs. Ah, you are such an illogical, unreasoning race! And paltry—oh, unspeakably!"

Then he dropped all seriousness and just overstrained himself making fun of us and deriding our pride in our warlike deeds, our great heroes, our imperishable fames, our mighty kings, our ancient aristocracies, our venerable history—and laughed and laughed till it was enough to make a person sick to hear him; and finally he sobered a little and said, "But, after all, it is not all ridiculous; there is a sort of pathos about it when one remembers how few are your days, how childish your pomps, and what shadows you are!"

Presently all things vanished suddenly from my sight and I knew what it meant. The next moment we were walking along in our village, and down toward the river I saw the twinkling lights of the Golden Stag. Then in the dark I heard a joyful cry:

"He's come again!"

It was Seppi Wohlmeyer. He had felt his blood leap and his spirits rise in a way that could mean only one thing and he knew Satan was near, although it was too dark to see him. He came to us and we walked along together, and Seppi poured out his gladness like water. It was as if he were a lover and had found his sweetheart who had been lost. Seppi was a smart and animated boy, and had enthusiasm and expression, and was a contrast to Nikolaus and me. He was full of the last new mystery, now—the disappearance of Hans Oppert, the village loafer. People were beginning to be curious about it, he said. He did not say anxious—curious was the right word, and strong enough. No one had seen Hans for a couple of days.

"Not since he did that brutal thing, you know," he said.

"What brutal thing?" It was Satan that asked.

"Well, he is always clubbing his dog, which is a good dog and his only friend, and is faithful and loves him, and does no one any harm; and two days ago he was at it again, just for nothing—just for pleasure—and the dog was howling and begging, and Theodor and I begged too, but he threatened us and struck the dog again with all his might and knocked one of his eyes out, and he said to us, 'There, I hope you are satisfied now; that's what you have got for him by your damned meddling—and he laughed, the heartless brute." Seppi's voice trembled with pity and anger. I guessed what Satan would say, and he said it.

"There is that misused word again—that shabby slander. Brutes do not act like that, but only men."

"Well, it was inhuman, anyway."

"No, it wasn't, Seppi; it was human—quite distinctly human. It is not pleasant to hear you libel the higher animals by attributing to them dispositions which they are free from and which are found nowhere but in the human heart. None of the higher animals is tainted with the disease called the Moral Sense. Purify your language, Seppi; drop those lying phrases out of it."

He spoke pretty sternly—for him—and I was sorry I hadn't warned Seppi to be more particular about the word he used. I knew how he was feeling. He would not want to offend Satan; he would rather offend all his kin. There was an uncomfortable silence but relief soon came, for that poor dog came along now, with his eye hanging down, and went straight to Satan and began to moan and mutter brokenly, and Satan began to answer in the same way, and it was plain that they were talking together in the dog language. We all sat down in the grass in the moonlight, for the clouds were breaking away now, and Satan took the dog's head in his lap and put the eye back in its place, and the dog was comfortable and he wagged his tail and licked Satan's hand, and looked thankful and said the same; I knew he was saying it, though I did not understand the words. Then the two talked together a bit, and Satan said:

"He says his master was drunk."

"Yes, he was," said we.

"And an hour later he fell over the precipice there beyond the Cliff Pasture."

"We know the place; it is three miles from here."

"And the dog has been often to the village, begging people to go there, but he was only driven away and not listened to."

We remembered it, but hadn't understood what he wanted.

"He only wanted help for the man who had misused him, and he thought only of that and has had no food nor sought any. He has watched by his master two nights. What do you think of your race? Is heaven reserved for it and this dog ruled out, as your teachers tell you? Can your race add anything to this dog's stock of morals and magnanimities?" He spoke to the creature, who jumped up, eager and happy, and apparently ready for orders and impatient to execute them. "Get some men; go with the dog—he will show you that carrion; and take a priest along to arrange about insurance, for death is near."

With the last word he vanished, to our sorrow and disappointment. We got the men and Father Adolf, and we saw the man die. Nobody cared but the dog; he mourned and grieved and licked the dead face, and could not be comforted. We buried him where he was and without a coffin, for he had no money and no friend but the dog. If we had been an hour earlier the priest would have been in time to send that poor creature to heaven, but now he was gone down into the awful fires, to burn forever. It seemed such a pity that in a world where so many people have difficulty to put in their time, one little hour could not have been spared for this poor creature who needed it so much, and to whom it would have made the difference between eternal joy and eternal pain. It gave an appalling idea of the value of an hour, and I thought I could never waste one again without remorse and terror. Seppi was depressed and grieved, and said it must be so much better to be a dog and not run such awful risks. We took this one home with us and kept him for our own. Seppi had a very good thought as we were walking along, and it cheered us up and made us feel much better. He said the dog had forgiven the man that had wronged him so, and maybe God would accept that absolution.

There was a very dull week now, for Satan did not come, nothing much was going on, and we boys could not venture to go and see Marget, because the nights were moonlit and our parents might find us out if we tried. But we came across Ursula a couple of times taking a walk in the meadows beyond the river to air the cat, and we learned from her that things were going well. She had natty new clothes on and bore a prosperous look. The four groschen a day were arriving without a break, but were not being spent for food and wine and such things—the cat attended to all that.

Marget was enduring her forsakenness and isolation fairly well, all things considered, and was cheerful, by help of Wilhelm Meidling. She spent an hour or two every night in the jail with her uncle and had fattened him up with the cat's contributions. But she was curious to know more about Philip Traum, and hoped I would bring him again. Ursula was curious about him herself and asked a good many questions about his uncle. It made the boys laugh, for I had told them the nonsense Satan had been stuffing her with. She got no satisfaction out of us, our tongues being fled.

Ursula gave us a small item of information: money being plenty now, she had taken on a servant to help about the house and run errands. She tried to tell it in a commonplace, matter-of-course way, but she was so set up by it and so vain of it that her pride in it leaked out pretty plainly. It was beautiful to see her veiled delight in this grandeur, poor old thing, but when we heard the name of the servant we wondered if she had been altogether wise; for although we were young, and often thoughtless, we had fairly good perception on some matters. This boy was Gottfried Narr, a dull, good creature, with no harm in him and nothing against him personally; still, he was under a cloud, and properly so, for it had not been six months since a social blight had mildewed the family—his grandmother had been burned as a witch. When that kind of a malady is in the blood it does not always come out with just one burning. Just now was not a good time for Ursula and Marget to be having dealings with a member of such a family, for the witch-terror had risen higher during the past year than it had ever reached in the memory of the oldest villagers. The mere mention of a witch was almost enough to frighten us out of our wits. This was natural enough, because of late years there were more kinds of witches than there used to be; in old times it had been only old women but of late years they were of all ages —even children of eight and nine; it was getting so that anybody might turn out to be a familiar of the Devil—age and sex hadn't anything to do with it. In our little region we had tried to extirpate the witches but the more of them we burned the more of the breed rose up in their places.

Once, in a school for girls only ten miles away the teachers found that the back of one of the girls was all red and inflamed, and they were greatly frightened, believing it to be the Devil's marks. The girl was scared and begged them not to denounce her, and said it was only fleas; but of course it would not do to let the matter rest there. All the girls were examined and eleven out of the fifty were badly marked, the rest less so. A commission was appointed but the eleven only cried for their mothers and would not confess. Then they were shut up, each by herself, in the dark and put on black bread and water for ten days and nights; and by that time they were haggard and wild, and their eyes were dry and they did not cry any more, but only sat and mumbled and would not take the food. Then one of them confessed and said they had often ridden through the air on broomsticks to the witches' Sabbath, and in a bleak place high up in the mountains had danced and drunk and caroused with several hundred other witches and the Evil One, and all had conducted themselves in a scandalous way and had reviled the priests and blasphemed God. That is what she said—not in narrative form, for she was not able to remember any of the details without having them called to her mind one after the other; but the commission did that, for they knew just what questions to ask, they being all written down for the use of witch-commissioners two centuries before. They asked, "Did you do so and so?" and she always said yes and looked weary and tired, and took no interest in it. And so when the other ten heard that this one confessed, they confessed too, and answered yes to the questions. Then they were burned at the stake all together, which was just and right; and everybody went from all the countryside to see it. I went, too; but when I saw that one of them was a bonny, sweet girl I used to play with and looked so pitiful there chained to the stake, and her mother crying over her and devouring her with kisses and clinging around her neck, and saying, "Oh, my God! oh, my God!" it was too dreadful, and I went away.

It was bitter cold weather when Gottfried's grandmother was burned. It was charged that she had cured bad headaches by kneading the person's head and neck with her fingers, as she said, but really by the Devil's help, as everybody knew. They were going to examine her but she stopped them and confessed straight off that her power was from the Devil. So they appointed to burn her next morning, early, in our market square. The officer who was to prepare the fire was there first, and prepared it. She was there next—brought by the constables, who left her and went to fetch another witch. Her family did not come with her. They might be reviled, maybe stoned, if the people were excited. I came and gave her an apple. She was squatting at the fire, warming herself and waiting;

and her old lips and hands were blue with the cold. A stranger came next. He was a traveler, passing through; and he spoke to her gently and, seeing nobody but me there to hear, said he was sorry for her. And he asked if what she confessed was true and she said no. He looked surprised and still more sorry then, and asked her:

"Then why did you confess?"

"I am old and very poor," she said, "and I work for my living. There was no way but to confess. If I hadn't they might have set me free. That would ruin me, for no one would forget that I had been suspected of being a witch, and so I would get no more work and wherever I went they would set the dogs on me. In a little while I would starve. The fire is best; it is soon over. You have been good to me, you two, and I thank you."

She snuggled closer to the fire and put out her hands to warm them, the snowflakes descending soft and still on her old gray head and making it white and whiter. The crowd was gathering now and an egg came flying and struck her in the eye, and broke and ran down her face. There was a laugh at that.

I told Satan all about the eleven girls and the old woman, once, but it did not affect him. He only said it was the human race, and what the human race did was of no consequence. And he said he had seen it made, and it was not made of clay; it was made of mud—part of it was, anyway. I knew what he meant by that—the Moral Sense. He saw the thought in my head and it tickled him and made him laugh. Then he called a bullock out of a pasture and petted it and talked with it, and said:

"There—he wouldn't drive children mad with hunger and flight and loneliness, and then burn them for confessing to things invented for them which had never happened. And neither would he break the hearts of innocent, poor old women and make them afraid to trust themselves among their own race, and he would not insult them in their death-agony. For he is not besmirched with the Moral Sense, but is as the angels are, and knows no wrong, and never does it."

Lovely as he was, Satan could be cruelly offensive when he chose, and he always chose when the human race was brought to his attention. He always turned up his nose at it and never had a kind word for it.

Well, as I was saying, we boys doubted if it was a good time for Ursula to be hiring a member of the Narr family. We were right. When the people found it out they were naturally indignant. And, moreover, since Marget and Ursula hadn't enough to eat themselves, where was the money coming from to feed another mouth? That is what they wanted to know, and in order to find out they stopped avoiding Gottfried and began to seek his society and have sociable conversations with him. He was pleased—not thinking any harm and not seeing the trap—and so he talked innocently along, and was no discreeter than a cow.

"Money!" he said; "they've got plenty of it. They pay me two groschen a week, besides my keep. And they live on the fat of the land, I can tell you; the prince himself can't beat their table."

This astonishing statement was conveyed by the astrologer to Father Adolf on a Sunday morning when he was returning from mass. He was deeply moved, and said:

"This must be looked into."

He said there must be witchcraft at the bottom of it, and told the villagers to resume relations with Marget and Ursula in a private and unostentatious way and keep both eyes open. They were told to keep their own counsel and not rouse the suspicions of the household. The villagers were at first a bit reluctant to enter such a dreadful place, but the priest said they would be under his protection while there and no harm could come to them, particularly if they carried a trifle of holy water along and kept their beads and crosses handy. This satisfied them and made them willing to go; envy and malice made the baser sort even eager to go.

And so poor Marget began to have company again, and was as pleased as a cat. She was like most anybody else—just human and happy in her prosperities and not averse from showing them off a little, and she was humanly grateful to have the warm shoulder turned to her and be smiled upon by her friends and the village again; for of all the hard things to bear, to be cut by your neighbors and left in contemptuous solitude is maybe the hardest.

The bars were down and we could all go there now and we did—our parents and all—day after day. The cat began to strain herself. She provided the top of everything for those companies, and in abundance—among them many a dish and many a wine which they had not tasted before and which they had not even heard of except at secondhand from the prince's servants. And the tableware was much above ordinary, too.

Marget was troubled at times and pursued Ursula with questions to an uncomfortable degree, but Ursula stood her ground and stuck to it that it was Providence and said no word about the cat. Marget knew that nothing was impossible to Providence but she could not help having doubts that this effort was from there, though she was afraid to say so, lest disaster come of it. Witchcraft occurred to her but she put the thought aside, for this was before Gottfried joined the household and she knew Ursula was pious and a bitter hater of witches. By the time Gottfried arrived Providence was established, unshakably entrenched, and getting all the gratitude. The cat made no murmur but went on composedly improving in style and prodigality by experience.

In any community, big or little, there is always a fair proportion of people who are not malicious or unkind by nature and who never do unkind things except when they are overmastered by fear, or when their self-interest is greatly in danger, or some such matter as that. Eseldorf had its proportion of such people, and ordinarily their good and gentle influence was felt, but these were not ordinary times—on account of the witch-dread —and so we did not seem to have any gentle and compassionate hearts left, to speak of. Every person was frightened at the unaccountable state of things at Marget's house, not doubting that witchcraft was at the bottom of it, and fright frenzied their reason. Naturally there were some who pitied Marget and Ursula for the danger that was gathering about them but naturally they did not say so; it would not have been safe. So the others had it all their own way and there was none to advise the ignorant girl and the foolish woman and warn them to modify their doings. We boys wanted to warn them but we backed down when it came to the pinch, being afraid. We found that we were not manly enough nor brave enough to do a generous action when there was a chance that it could get us into trouble. Neither of us confessed this poor spirit to the others but did as other people would have done—dropped the subject and talked about something else. And I knew we all felt mean, eating and drinking Marget's fine things along with those companies of spies and petting her and complimenting her with the rest, and seeing with self-reproach how foolishly happy she was and never saying a word to put her on her guard. And, indeed, she was happy and as proud as a princess, and so grateful to have friends again. And all the time these people were watching with all their eyes and reporting all they saw to Father Adolf.

But he couldn't make head or tail of the situation. There must be an enchanter somewhere on the premises but who was it? Marget was not seen to do any jugglery, nor was Ursula, nor yet Gottfried, and still the wines and dainties never ran short, and a guest could not call for a thing and not get it. To produce these effects was usual enough with witches and enchanters—that part of it was not new, but to do it without any incantations or even any rumblings or earthquakes or lightnings or apparitions—that was new, novel, wholly irregular. There was nothing in the books like this. Enchanted things were always unreal. Gold turned to dirt in an unenchanted atmosphere, food withered away and vanished. But this test failed in the present case. The spies brought samples: Father Adolf prayed over them, exorcised them, but it did no good; they remained sound and real, they yielded to natural decay only and took the usual time to do it.

Father Adolf was not merely puzzled, he was also exasperated; for these evidences very nearly convinced him—privately—that there was no witchcraft in the matter. It did not wholly convince him, for this could be a new kind of witchcraft. There was a way to find out as to this: if this prodigal abundance of provender was not brought in from the outside, but produced on the premises, there was witchcraft, sure.

Chapter 7

Marget announced a party and invited forty people; the date for it was seven days away. This was a fine opportunity. Marget's house stood by itself, and it could be easily watched. All the week it was watched night and day. Marget's household went out and in as usual but they carried nothing in their hands, and neither they nor others brought anything to the house. This was ascertained. Evidently rations for forty people were not being fetched. If they were furnished any sustenance it would have to be made on the premises. It was true that Marget went out with a basket every evening, but the spies ascertained that she always brought it back empty.

The guests arrived at noon and filled the place. Father Adolf followed; also, after a little, the astrologer, without invitation. The spies had informed him that neither at the back nor the front had any parcels been brought in. He entered and found the eating and drinking going on finely, and everything progressing in a lively and festive way. He glanced around and perceived that many of the cooked delicacies and all of the native and foreign fruits were of a perishable character, and he also recognized that these were fresh and perfect. No apparitions, no incantations, no thunder. That settled it. This was witchcraft. And not only that but of a new kind, a kind never dreamed of before. It was a prodigious power, an illustrious power; he resolved to discover its secret. The announcement of it would resound throughout the world, penetrate to the remotest lands, paralyze all the nations with amazement—and carry his name with it, and make him renowned forever. It was a wonderful piece of luck, a splendid piece of luck; the glory of it made him dizzy.

All the house made room for him; Marget politely seated him; Ursula ordered Gottfried to bring a special table for him. Then she decked it and furnished it, and asked for his orders.

"Bring me what you will," he said.

The two servants brought supplies from the pantry, together with white wine and red—a bottle of each. The astrologer, who very likely had never seen such delicacies before, poured out a beaker of red wine, drank it off, poured another, then began to eat with a grand appetite.

I was not expecting Satan, for it was more than a week since I had seen or heard of him but now he came in—I knew it by the feel, though people were in the way and I could not see him. I heard him apologizing for intruding, and he was going away but Marget urged him to stay, and he thanked her and stayed. She brought him along, introducing him to the girls and to Meidling and to some of the elders, and there was quite a rustle of whispers: "It's the young stranger we hear so much about and can't get sight of, he is away so much." "Dear, dear, but he is beautiful—what is his name?" "Philip Traum." "Ah, it fits him!" (You see, "Traum" is German for "Dream.") "What does he do?" "Studying for the ministry, they say." "His face is his fortune—he'll be a cardinal some day." "Where is his home?" "Away down somewhere in the tropics, they say—has a rich uncle down there." And so on. He made his way at once; everybody was anxious to know him and talk with him. Everybody noticed how cool and fresh it was all of a sudden, and wondered at it, for they could see that the sun was beating down the same as before outside, and the sky was clear of clouds, but no one guessed the reason, of course.

The astrologer had drunk his second beaker; he poured out a third. He set the bottle down, and by accident overturned it. He seized it before much was spilled, and held it up to the light, saying, "What a pity—it is royal wine." Then his face lighted with joy or triumph, or something, and he said, "quick! Bring a bowl."

It was brought—a four-quart one. He took up that two-pint bottle and began to pour; went on pouring, the red liquor gurgling and gushing into the white bowl and rising higher and higher up its sides, everybody staring and holding their breath—and presently the bowl was full to the brim.

"Look at the bottle," he said, holding it up, "it is full yet!" I glanced at Satan, and in that moment he vanished. Then Father

Adolf rose up, flushed and excited, crossed himself, and began to thunder in his great voice, "This house is bewitched and accursed!" People began to cry and shriek and crowd toward the door. "I summon this detected household to—"

His words were cut off short. His face became red, then purple, but he could not utter another sound. Then I saw Satan, a transparent film, melt into the astrologer's body; then the astrologer put up his hand, and apparently in his own voice said, "Wait—remain where you are." All stopped where they stood. "Bring a funnel!" Ursula brought it, trembling and scared, and he stuck it in the bottle and took up the great bowl and began to pour the wine back, the people gazing and dazed with astonishment, for they knew the bottle was already full before he began. He emptied the whole of the bowl into the bottle, then smiled out over the room, chuckled, and said, indifferently, "It is nothing—anybody can do it! With my powers I can even do much more."

A frightened cry burst out everywhere. "Oh, my God, he is possessed!" and there was a tumultuous rush for the door which swiftly emptied the house of all who did not belong in it except us boys and Meidling. We boys knew the secret, and would have told it if we could, but we couldn't. We were very thankful to Satan for furnishing that good help at the needful time.

Marget was pale and crying; Meidling looked kind of petrified; Ursula the same; but Gottfried was the worst—he couldn't stand, he was so weak and seared. For he was of a witch family, you know, and it would be bad for him to be suspected. Agnes came loafing in, looking pious and unaware, and wanted to rub up against Ursula and be petted, but Ursula was afraid of her and shrank away from her, but pretending she was not meaning any incivility, for she knew very well it wouldn't answer to have strained relations with that kind of a cat. But we boys took Agnes and petted her, for Satan would not have befriended her if he had not had a good opinion of her, and that was endorsement enough for us. He seemed to trust anything that hadn't the Moral Sense.

Outside, the guests, panic-stricken, scattered in every direction and fled in a pitiable state of terror; and such a tumult as they made with their running and sobbing and shrieking and shouting that soon all the village came flocking from their houses to see what had happened, and they thronged the street and shouldered and jostled one another in excitement and fright; and then Father Adolf appeared, and they fell apart in two walls like the cloven Red Sea, and presently down this lane the astrologer came striding and mumbling, and where he passed the lanes surged back in packed masses and fell silent with awe, and their eyes stared and their breasts heaved and several women fainted; and when he was gone by the crowd swarmed together and followed him at a distance, talking excitedly and asking questions and finding out the facts. Finding out the facts and passing them on to others, with improvements—improvements which soon enlarged the bowl of wine to a barrel, and made the one bottle hold it all and yet remain empty to the last.

When the astrologer reached the market square he went straight to a juggler, fantastically dressed, who was keeping three brass balls in the air, and took them from him and faced around upon the approaching crowd and said: "This poor clown is ignorant of his art. Come forward and see an expert perform."

So saying, he tossed the balls up one after another and set them whirling in a slender bright oval in the air, and added another, then another and another, and soon—no one seeing whence he got them—adding, adding, adding, the oval lengthening all the time, his hands moving so swiftly that they were just a web or a blur and not distinguishable as hands; and such as counted said there were now a hundred balls in the air. The spinning great oval reached up twenty feet in the air and was a shining and glinting and wonderful sight. Then he folded his arms and told the balls to go on spinning without his help—and they did it. After a couple of minutes he said, "There, that will do," and the oval broke and came crashing down, and the balls scattered abroad and rolled every whither. And wherever one of them came the people fell back in dread and no one would touch it. It made him laugh, and he scoffed at the people and called them cowards and old women. Then he turned and saw the tightrope, and said foolish people were daily wasting their money to see a clumsy and ignorant varlet degrade that beautiful art; now they should see the work of a master. With that he made a spring into the air and lit firm on his feet on the rope. Then he hopped the whole length of it back and forth on one foot, with his hands clasped over his eyes; and next he began to throw somersaults, both backward and forward, and threw twenty-seven.

The people murmured, for the astrologer was old and always before had been halting of movement and at times even lame, but he was nimble enough now and went on with his antics in the liveliest manner. Finally he sprang lightly down and walked away and passed up the road and around the corner and disappeared. Then that great, pale, silent, solid crowd drew a deep breath and looked into one another's faces as if they said: "Was it real? Did you see it, or was it only I—and I was dreaming?" Then they broke into a low murmur of talking, and fell apart in couples and moved toward their homes, still talking in that awed way, with faces close together and laying a hand on an arm and making other such gestures as people make when they have been deeply impressed by something.

We boys followed behind our fathers and listened, catching all we could of what they said, and when they sat down in our house and continued their talk they still had us for company. They were in a sad mood, for it was certain, they said, that disaster for the village must follow this awful visitation of witches and devils. Then my father remembered that Father Adolf had been struck dumb at the moment of his denunciation.

"They have not ventured to lay their hands upon an anointed servant of God before," he said; "and how they could have dared it this time I cannot make out, for he wore his crucifix. Isn't it so?"

"Yes," said the others, "we saw it."

"It is serious, friends, it is very serious. Always before, we had a protection. It has failed."

The others shook, as with a sort of chill, and muttered those words over—"It has failed." "God has forsaken us."

"It is true," said Seppi Wohlmeyer's father; "there is nowhere to look for help."

"The people will realize this," said Nikolaus's father, the judge, "and despair will take away their courage and their energies. We have indeed fallen upon evil times."

He sighed, and Wohlmeyer said in a troubled voice, "The report of it all will go about the country, and our village will be shunned as being under the displeasure of God. The Golden Stag will know hard times."

"True, neighbor," said my father, "all of us will suffer—all in repute, many in estate. And, good God!—"

"What is it!"

"That can come—to finish us!"

"Name it—um Gottes Willen!"

"The Interdict!"

It smote like a thunderclap and they were like to swoon with the terror of it. Then the dread of this calamity roused their energies, and they stopped brooding and began to consider ways to avert it. They discussed this, that, and the other way, and talked till the afternoon was far spent, then confessed that at present they could arrive at no decision. So they parted sorrowfully, with oppressed hearts which were filled with bodings.

While they were saying their parting words I slipped out and set my course for Marget's house to see what was happening there. I met many people, but none of them greeted me. It ought to have been surprising but it was not, for they were so distraught with fear and dread that they were not in their right minds, I think; they were white and haggard and walked like persons in a dream, their eyes open but seeing nothing, their lips moving but uttering nothing, and worriedly clasping and unclasping their hands without knowing it.

At Marget's it was like a funeral. She and Wilhelm sat together on the sofa, but said nothing, and not even holding hands. Both were steeped in gloom and Marget's eyes were red from the crying she had been doing. She said:

"I have been begging him to go and come no more, and so save himself alive. I cannot bear to be his murderer. This house is bewitched and no inmate will escape the fire. But he will not go, and he will be lost with the rest."

Wilhelm said he would not go, if there was danger for her, his place was by her and there he would remain. Then she began to cry again and it was all so mournful that I wished I had stayed away. There was a knock, now, and Satan came in, fresh and cheery and beautiful, and brought that winy atmosphere of his and changed the whole thing. He never said a word about what had been happening nor about the awful fears which were freezing the blood in the hearts of the community, but began to talk and rattle on about all manner of gay and pleasant things: and next about music—an artful stroke which cleared away the remnant of Marget's depression and brought her spirits and her interests broad awake. She had not heard any one talk so well and so knowingly on that subject before, and she was so uplifted by it and so charmed that what she was feeling lit up her face and came out in her words, and Wilhelm noticed it and did not look as pleased as he ought to have done. And next Satan branched off into poetry and recited some and did it well, and Marget was charmed again; and again Wilhelm was not as pleased as he ought to have been, and this time Marget noticed it and was remorseful.

I fell asleep to pleasant music that night—the patter of rain upon the panes and the dull growling of distant thunder. Away in the night Satan came and roused me and said: "Come with me. Where shall we go?"

"Anywhere—so it is with you."

Then there was a fierce glare of sunlight, and he said, "This is China."

That was a grand surprise and made me sort of drunk with vanity and gladness to think I had come so far—so much, much farther than anybody else in our village, including Bartel Sperling who had such a great opinion of his travels. We buzzed around over that empire for more than half an hour and saw the whole of it. It was wonderful, the spectacles we saw; and some were beautiful, others too horrible to think. For instance—However, I may go into that by and by and also why Satan chose China for this excursion instead of another place; it would interrupt my tale to do it now. Finally we stopped flitting and lit.

We sat upon a mountain commanding a vast landscape of mountain range and gorge and valley and plain and river, with cities and villages slumbering in the sunlight and a glimpse of blue sea on the farther verge. It was a tranquil and dreamy picture, beautiful to the eye and restful to the spirit. If we could only make a change like that whenever we wanted to, the world would be easier to live in than it is, for change of scene shifts the mind's burdens to the other shoulder and banishes old, shopworn wearinesses from mind and body both.

We talked together, and I had the idea of trying to reform Satan and persuade him to lead a better life. I told him about all those things he had been doing, and begged him to be more considerate and stop making people unhappy. I said I knew he did not mean any harm but that he ought to stop and consider the possible consequences of a thing before launching it in that impulsive and random way of his, then he would not make so much trouble. He was not hurt by this plain speech; he only looked amused and surprised, and said:

"What? I do random things? Indeed, I never do. I stop and consider possible consequences? Where is the need? I know what the consequences are going to be—always."

"Oh, Satan, then how could you do these things?"

"Well, I will tell you, and you must understand if you can. You belong to a singular race. Every man is a suffering-machine and a happiness-machine combined. The two functions work together harmoniously, with a fine and delicate precision, on the give-and-take principle. For every happiness turned out in the one department the other stands ready to modify it with a sorrow or a pain—maybe a dozen. In most cases the man's life is about equally divided between happiness and unhappiness. When this is not the case the unhappiness predominates—always, never the other. Sometimes a man's make and disposition are such that his misery-machine is able to do nearly all the business. Such a man goes through life almost ignorant of what happiness is. Everything he touches, everything he does, brings a misfortune upon him. You have seen such people? To that kind of a person life is not an advantage, is it? It is only a disaster. Sometimes for an hour's happiness a man's machinery makes him pay years of misery. Don't you know that? It happens every now and then. I will give you a case or two presently. Now the people of your village are nothing to me—you know that, don't you?"

I did not like to speak out too flatly, so I said I had suspected it.

"Well, it is true that they are nothing to me. It is not possible that they should be. The difference between them and me is abysmal, immeasurable. They have no intellect."

"No intellect?"

"Nothing that resembles it. At a future time I will examine what man calls his mind and give you the details of that chaos, then you will see and understand. Men have nothing in common with me—there is no point of contact; they have foolish little feelings and foolish little vanities and impertinences and ambitions; their foolish little life is but a laugh, a sigh, and extinction; and they have no sense. Only the Moral Sense. I will show you what I mean. Here is a red spider, not so big as a pin's head. Can you imagine an elephant being interested in him—caring whether he is happy or isn't, or whether he is wealthy or poor, or whether his sweetheart returns his love or not, or whether his mother is sick or well, or whether he is looked up to in society or not, or whether his enemies will smite him or his friends desert him, or whether his hopes will suffer blight or his political ambitions fail, or whether he shall die in the bosom of his family or neglected and despised in a foreign land? These things can never be important to the elephant, they are nothing to him, he cannot shrink his sympathies to the microscopic size of them. Man is to me as the red spider is to the elephant. The elephant has nothing against the spider—he cannot get down to that remote level; I have nothing against man. The elephant is indifferent; I am indifferent. The elephant would not take the trouble to do the spider an ill turn; if he took the notion he might do him a good turn, if it came in his way and cost nothing. I have done men good service but no ill turns.

"The elephant lives a century, the red spider a day; in power, intellect, and dignity the one creature is separated from the other by a distance which is simply astronomical. Yet in these, as in all qualities, man is immeasurably further below me than is the wee spider below the elephant.

"Man's mind clumsily and tediously and laboriously patches little trivialities together and gets a result—such as it is. My mind creates! Do you get the force of that? Creates anything it desires—and in a moment. Creates without material. Creates fluids, solids, colors—anything, everything—out of the airy nothing which is called Thought. A man imagines a silk thread, imagines a machine to make it, imagines a picture, then by weeks of labor embroiders it on canvas with the thread. I think the whole thing, and in a moment it is before you—created.

"I think a poem, music, the record of a game of chess—anything—and it is there. This is the immortal mind—nothing is beyond its reach. Nothing can obstruct my vision; the rocks are transparent to me and darkness is daylight. I do not need to open a book, I take the whole of its contents into my mind at a single glance, through the cover; and in a million years I could not forget a single word of it, or its place in the volume. Nothing goes on in the skull of man, bird, fish, insect, or other creature which can be hidden from me. I pierce the learned man's brain with a single glance, and the treasures which cost him threescore years to accumulate are mine; he can forget and he does forget, but I retain.

"Now, then, I perceive by your thoughts that you are understanding me fairly well. Let us proceed. Circumstances might so fall out that the elephant could like the spider—supposing he can see it—but he could not love it. His love is for his own kind—for his equals. An angel's love is sublime, adorable, divine, beyond the imagination of man—infinitely beyond it! But it is limited to his own august order. If it fell upon one of your race for only an instant, it would consume its object to ashes. No, we cannot love men but we can be harmlessly indifferent to them; we can also like them, sometimes. I like you and the boys, I like Father Peter, and for your sakes I am doing all these things for the villagers."

He saw that I was thinking a sarcasm and he explained his position.

"I have wrought well for the villagers, though it does not look like it on the surface. Your race never know good fortune from ill. They are always mistaking the one for the other. It is because they cannot see into the future. What I am doing for the villagers will bear good fruit some day, in some cases to themselves, in others to unborn generations of men. No one will ever know that I was the cause but it will be none the less true, for all that. Among you boys you have a game: you stand a row of bricks on end a few inches apart, you push a brick, it knocks its neighbor over, the neighbor knocks over the next brick—and so on till all the row is prostrate. That is human life. A child's first act knocks over the initial brick and the rest will follow inexorably. If you could see into the future as I can, you would see everything that was going to happen to that creature, for nothing can change the order of its life after the first event has determined it. That is, nothing will change it, because each act unfailingly begets an act, that act begets another, and so on to the end, and the seer can look forward down the line and see just when each act is to have birth, from cradle to grave."

"Does God order the career?"

"Foreordain it? No. The man's circumstances and environment order it. His first act determines the second and all that follow after. But suppose, for argument's sake, that the man should skip one of these acts, an apparently trifling one, for instance; suppose that it had been appointed that on a certain day, at a certain hour and minute and second and fraction of a second he should go to the well, and he didn't go. That man's career would change utterly from that moment; thence to the grave it would be wholly different from the career which his first act as a child had arranged for him. Indeed, it might be that if he had gone to the well he would have ended his career on a throne, and that omitting to do it would set him upon a career that would lead to beggary and a pauper's grave. For instance: if at any time—say in boyhood—Columbus had skipped the triflingest little link in the chain of acts projected and made inevitable by his first childish act, it would have changed his whole subsequent life, and he would have become a priest and died obscure in an Italian village, and America would not have been discovered for two centuries afterward. I know this. To skip any one of the billion acts in Columbus's chain would have wholly changed his life. I have examined his billion of possible careers and in only one of them occurs the discovery of America. You people do not suspect that all of your acts are of one size and importance, but it is true; to snatch at an appointed fly is as big with fate for you as in any other appointed act—"

"As the conquering of a continent, for instance?"

"Yes. Now, then, no man ever does drop a link—the thing has never happened! Even when he is trying to make up his mind as to whether he will do a thing or not, that itself is a link, an act, and has its proper place in his chain; and when he finally decides an act, that also was the thing which he was absolutely certain to do. You see now that a man will never drop a link in his chain. He cannot. If he made up his mind to try, that project would itself be an unavoidable link—a thought bound to occur to him at that precise moment, and made certain by the first act of his babyhood."

It seemed so dismal!

"He is a prisoner for life," I said sorrowfully, "and cannot get free."

"No, of himself he cannot get away from the consequences of his first childish act. But I can free him."

I looked up wistfully.

"I have changed the careers of a number of your villagers."

I tried to thank him but found it difficult, and let it drop.

"I shall make some other changes. You know that little Lisa Brandt?"

"Oh yes, everybody does. My mother says she is so sweet and so lovely that she is not like any other child. She says she will be the pride of the village when she grows up, and its idol too, just as she is now."

"I shall change her future."

"Make it better?" I asked.

"Yes. And I will change the future of Nikolaus."

I was glad this time, and said, "I don't need to ask about his case; you will be sure to do generously by him."

"It is my intention."

Straight off I was building that great future of Nicky's in my imagination, and had already made a renowned general of him and hofmeister at the court, when I noticed that Satan was waiting for me to get ready to listen again. I was ashamed of having exposed my cheap imaginings to him and was expecting some sarcasms, but it did not happen. He proceeded with his subject:

"Nicky's appointed life is sixty-two years."

"That's grand!" I said.

"Lisa's, thirty-six. But, as I told you, I shall change their lives and those ages. Two minutes and a quarter from now Nikolaus will wake out of his sleep and find the rain blowing in. It was appointed that he should turn over and go to sleep again. But I have appointed that he shall get up and close the window first. That trifle will change his career entirely. He will rise in the morning two minutes later than the chain of his life had appointed him to rise.

By consequence, thenceforth nothing will ever happen to him in accordance with the details of the old chain." He took out his watch and sat looking at it a few moments, then said: "Nikolaus has risen to close the window. His life is changed, his new career has begun. There will be consequences."

It made me feel creepy; it was uncanny.

"But for this change certain things would happen twelve days from now. For instance, Nikolaus would save Lisa from drowning. He would arrive on the scene at exactly the right moment—four minutes past ten, the long-ago appointed instant of time—and the water would be shoal, the achievement easy and certain. But he will arrive some seconds too late, now; Lisa will have struggled into deeper water. He will do his best but both will drown."

"Oh, Satan! oh, dear Satan!" I cried, with the tears rising in my eyes, "save them! Don't let it happen. I can't bear to lose Nikolaus, he is my loving playmate and friend; and think of Lisa's poor mother!"

I clung to him and begged and pleaded but he was not moved. He made me sit down again and told me I must hear him out.

"I have changed Nikolaus's life and this has changed Lisa's. If I had not done this, Nikolaus would save Lisa, then he would catch cold from his drenching; one of your race's fantastic and desolating scarlet fevers would follow, with pathetic after-effects; for forty-six years he would lie in his bed a paralytic log, deaf, dumb, blind, and praying night and day for the blessed relief of death. Shall I change his life back?"

"Oh no! Oh, not for the world! In charity and pity leave it as it is."

"It is best so. I could not have changed any other link in his life and done him so good a service. He had a billion possible careers but not one of them was worth living; they were charged full with miseries and disasters. But for my intervention he would do his brave deed twelve days from now—a deed begun and ended in six minutes—and get for all reward those forty-six years sorrow and suffering I told you of. It is one of the cases I was thinking of awhile ago when I said that sometimes an act which brings the actor an hour's happiness and self-satisfaction is paid for—or punished—by years suffering."

I wondered what poor little Lisa's early death would save her from. He answered the thought:

"From ten years of pain and slow recovery from an accident, and then from nineteen years' pollution, shame, depravity, crime, ending with death at the hands of the executioner. Twelve days hence she will die; her mother would save her life if she could. Am I not kinder than her mother?"

"Yes—oh, indeed yes, and wiser."

"Father Peter's case is coming on presently. He will be acquitted, through unassailable proofs of his innocence."

"Why, Satan, how can that be? Do you really think it?"

"Indeed, I know it. His good name will be restored and the rest of his life will be happy."

"I can believe it. To restore his good name will have that effect."

"His happiness will not proceed from that cause. I shall change his life that day, for his good. He will never know his good name has been restored."

In my mind—and modestly—I asked for particulars but Satan paid no attention to my thought. Next my mind wandered to the astrologer, and I wondered where he might be.

"In the moon," said Satan, with a fleeting sound which I believed was a chuckle. "I've got him on the cold side of it, too. He doesn't know where he is and is not having a pleasant time; still, it is good enough for him, a good place for his star studies. I shall need him presently; then I shall bring him back and possess him again. He has a long and cruel and odious life before him but I will change that, for I have no feeling against him and am quite willing to do him a kindness. I think I shall get him burned."

He had such strange notions of kindness! But angels are made so and do not know any better. Their ways are not like our ways, and besides, human beings are nothing to them; they think they are only freaks. It seems to me odd that he should put the astrologer so far away; he could have dumped him in Germany just as well, where he would be handy.

"Far away?" said Satan. "To me no place is far away; distance does not exist for me. The sun is less than a hundred million miles from here and the light that is falling upon us has taken eight minutes to come, but I can make that flight, or any other, in a fraction of time so minute that it cannot be measured by a watch. I have but to think the journey and it is accomplished."

I held out my hand and said, "The light lies upon it; think it into a glass of wine, Satan."

He did it. I drank the wine.

"Break the glass," he said.

I broke it.

"There—you see it is real. The villagers thought the brass balls were magic stuff and as perishable as smoke. They were afraid to touch them. You are a curious lot—your race. But come along; I have business. I will put you to bed." Said and done. Then he was gone, but his voice came back to me through the rain and darkness saying, "Yes, tell Seppi, but no other."

It was the answer to my thought.

Chapter 8

Sleep would not come. It was not because I was proud of my travels and excited about having been around the big world to China, and feeling contemptuous of Bartel Sperling, "the traveler," as he called himself, and looked down upon us others because he had been to Vienna once and was the only Eseldorf boy who had made such a journey and seen the world's wonders. At another time that would have kept me awake but it did not affect me now. No, my mind was filled with Nikolaus, my thoughts ran upon him only, and the good days we had seen together at romps and frolics in the woods and the fields and the river in the long summer days, and skating and sliding in the winter when our parents thought we were in school. And now he was going out of this young life, and the summers and winters would come and go, and we others would rove and play as before, but his place would be vacant; we should see him no more. Tomorrow he would not suspect but would be as he had always been, and it would shock me to hear him laugh and see him do lightsome and frivolous things, for to me he would be a corpse, with waxen hands and dull eyes, and I should see the shroud around his face; and next day he would not suspect, nor the next, and all the time his handful of days would be wasting swiftly away and that awful thing coming nearer and nearer, his fate closing steadily around him and no one knowing it but Seppi and me. Twelve days—only twelve days. It was awful to think of. I noticed that in my thoughts I was not calling him by his familiar names, Nick and Nicky, but was speaking of him by his full name, and reverently, as one speaks of the dead. Also, as incident after incident of our comradeship came thronging into my mind out of the past, I noticed that they were mainly cases where I had wronged him or hurt him, and they rebuked me and reproached me and my heart was wrung with remorse, just as it is when we remember our unkindnesses to friends who have passed beyond the veil and we wish we could have them back again, if only for a moment, so that we could go on our knees to them and say, "Have pity and forgive."

Once when we were nine years old he went a long errand of nearly two miles for the fruiterer, who gave him a splendid big apple for reward, and he was flying home with it, almost beside himself with astonishment and delight, and I met him, and he let me look at the apple, not thinking of treachery, and I ran off with it, eating it as I ran, he following me and begging, and when he overtook me I offered him the core, which was all that was left, and I laughed. Then he turned away, crying, and said he had meant to give it to his little sister. That smote me, for she was slowly getting well of a sickness and it would have been a proud moment for him, to see her joy and surprise and have her caresses. But I was ashamed to say I was ashamed and only said something rude and mean, to pretend I did not care, and he made no reply in words but there was a wounded look in his face as he turned away toward his home which rose before me many times in after years, in the night, and reproached me and made me ashamed again. It had grown dim in my mind, by and by, then it disappeared; but it was back now, and not dim.

Once at school, when we were eleven, I upset my ink and spoiled four copybooks and was in danger of severe punishment, but I put it upon him and he got the whipping.

And only last year I had cheated him in a trade, giving him a large fishhook which was partly broken through for three small sound ones. The first fish he caught broke the hook, but he did not know I was blamable and he refused to take back one of the small hooks which my conscience forced me to offer him, but said, "A trade is a trade; the hook was bad but that was not your fault."

No, I could not sleep. These little shabby wrongs upbraided me and tortured me, and with a pain much sharper than one feels when the wrongs have been done to the living. Nikolaus was living but no matter; he was to me as one already dead. The wind was still moaning about the caves, the rain still pattering upon the panes.

In the morning I sought out Seppi and told him. It was down by the river. His lips moved but he did not say anything, he only looked dazed and stunned, and his face turned very white. He stood like that a few moments, the tears welling into his eyes, then he turned away and I locked my arm in his and we walked along thinking, but not speaking. We crossed the bridge and wandered through the meadows and up among the hills and the woods, and at last the talk came and flowed freely, and it was all about Nikolaus and was a recalling of the life we had lived with him. And every now and then Seppi said, as if to himself:

"Twelve days!—less than twelve days."

We said we must be with him all the time; we must have all of him we could; the days were precious now. Yet we did not go to seek him. It would be like meeting the dead and we were afraid. We did not say it but that was what we were feeling. And so it gave us a shock when we turned a curve and came upon Nikolaus face to face. He shouted, gaily:

"Hi-hi! What is the matter? Have you seen a ghost?"

We couldn't speak but there was no occasion; he was willing to talk for us all, for he had just seen Satan and was in high spirits about it. Satan had told him about our trip to China, and he had begged Satan to take him a journey and Satan had promised. It was to be a far journey, and wonderful and beautiful, and Nikolaus had begged him to take us too, but he said no, he would take us some day, maybe, but not now. Satan would come for him on the 13th and Nikolaus was already counting the hours, he was so impatient.

That was the fatal day. We were already counting the hours, too.

We wandered many a mile, always following paths which had been our favorites from the days when we were little, and always we talked about the old times. All the blitheness was with Nikolaus; we others could not shake off our depression. Our tone toward Nikolaus was so strangely gentle and tender and yearning that he noticed it and was pleased, and we were constantly doing him deferential little offices of courtesy and saying, "Wait, let me do that for you," and that pleased him, too. I gave him seven fishhooks—all I had—and made him take them, and Seppi gave him his new knife and a humming-top painted red and yellow—atonements for swindles practiced upon him formerly, as I learned later, and probably no longer remembered by Nikolaus now. These things touched him and he could not have believed that we loved him so, and his pride in it and gratefulness for it cut us to the heart, we were so undeserving of them. When we parted at last he was radiant, and said he had never had such a happy day.

As we walked along homeward, Seppi said, "We always prized him but never so much as now, when we are going to lose him."

Next day and every day we spent all of our spare time with Nikolaus, and also added to it time which we (and he) stole from work and other duties, and this cost the three of us some sharp scoldings and some threats of punishment. Every morning two of us woke with a start and a shudder, saying as the days flew along, "Only ten days left;" "only nine days left;" "only eight;" "only seven." Always it was narrowing. Always Nikolaus was gay and happy and always puzzled because we were not. He wore his invention to the bone trying to invent ways to cheer us up but it was only a hollow success; he could see that our jollity had no heart in it and that the laughs we broke into came up against some obstruction or other and suffered damage and decayed into a sigh. He tried to find out what the matter was, so that he could help us out of our trouble or make it lighter by sharing it with us; so we had to tell many lies to deceive him and appease him.

But the most distressing thing of all was that he was always making plans and often they went beyond the 13th! Whenever that happened it made us groan in spirit. All his mind was fixed upon finding some way to conquer our depression and cheer us up; and at last, when he had but three days to live he fell upon the right idea and was jubilant over it—a boys-and-girls' frolic and dance in the woods, up there where we first met Satan, and this was to occur on the 14th. It was ghastly, for that was his funeral day. We couldn't venture to protest; it would only have brought a "Why?" which we could not answer. He wanted us to help him invite his guests and we did it—one can refuse nothing to a dying friend. But it was dreadful, for really we were inviting them to his funeral.

It was an awful eleven days; and yet, with a lifetime stretching back between today and then, they are still a grateful memory to me, and beautiful. In effect they were days of companionship with one's sacred dead and I have known no comradeship that was so close or so precious. We clung to the hours and the minutes, counting them as they wasted away and parting with them with that pain and bereavement which a miser feels who sees his hoard filched from him coin by coin by robbers and is helpless to prevent it.

When the evening of the last day came we stayed out too long; Seppi and I were in fault for that; we could not bear to part with Nikolaus; so it was very late when we left him at his door. We lingered near awhile, listening and that happened which we were fearing. His father gave him the promised punishment and we heard his shrieks. But we listened only a moment, then hurried away remorseful for this thing which we had caused. And sorry for the father, too, our thought being, "if he only knew—if he only knew!"

In the morning Nikolaus did not meet us at the appointed place, so we went to his home to see what the matter was. His mother said:

"His father is out of all patience with these goings-on and will not have any more of it. Half the time when Nick is needed he is not to be found; then it turns out that he has been gadding around with you two. His father gave him a flogging last night. It always grieved me before and many's the time I have begged him off and saved him, but this time he appealed to me in vain, for I was out of patience myself."

"I wish you had saved him just this one time," I said, my voice trembling a little, "it would ease a pain in your heart to remember it some day."

She was ironing at the time and her back was partly toward me. She turned about with a startled or wondering look in her face and said, "What do you mean by that?"

I was not prepared and didn't know anything to say; so it was awkward, for she kept looking at me; but Seppi was alert and spoke up:

"Why, of course it would be pleasant to remember, for the very reason we were out so late was that Nikolaus got to telling how good you are to him and how he never got whipped when you were by to save him, and he was so full of it and we were so full of the interest of it that none of us noticed how late it was getting."

"Did he say that? Did he?" and she put her apron to her eyes.

"You can ask Theodor—he will tell you the same."

"It is a dear, good lad, my Nick," she said. "I am sorry I let him get whipped; I will never do it again. To think—all the time I was sitting here last night, fretting and angry at him, he was loving me and praising me! Dear, dear, if we could only know! Then we shouldn't ever go wrong, but we are only poor, dumb beasts groping around and making mistakes. I sha'n't ever think of last night without a pang."

She was like all the rest; it seemed as if nobody could open a mouth in these wretched days without saying something that made us shiver. They were "groping around," and did not know what true, sorrowfully true things they were saying by accident.

Seppi asked if Nikolaus might go out with us.

"I am sorry," she answered, "but he can't. To punish him further, his father doesn't allow him to go out of the house today."

We had a great hope! I saw it in Seppi's eyes. We thought, "If he cannot leave the house, he cannot be drowned." Seppi asked, to make sure:

"Must he stay in all day or only the morning?"

"All day. It's such a pity, too; it's a beautiful day and he is so unused to being shut up. But he is busy planning his party and maybe that is company for him. I do hope he isn't too lonesome."

Seppi saw that in her eye which emboldened him to ask if we might go up and help him pass his time.

"And welcome!" she said, right heartily. "Now I call that real friendship, when you might be abroad in the fields and the woods, having a happy time. You are good boys, I'll allow that, though you don't always find satisfactory ways of improving it. Take these cakes—for yourselves—and give him this one, from his mother."

The first thing we noticed when we entered Nikolaus's room was the time—a quarter to 10. Could that be correct? Only such a few minutes to live! I felt a contraction at my heart. Nikolaus jumped up and gave us a glad welcome. He was in good spirits over his plannings for his party and had not been lonesome.

"Sit down," he said, "and look at what I've been doing. And I've finished a kite that you will say is a beauty. It's drying in the kitchen; I'll fetch it."

He had been spending his penny savings in fanciful trifles of various kinds, to go as prizes in the games, and they were marshaled with fine and showy effect upon the table. He said:

"Examine them at your leisure while I get mother to touch up the kite with her iron if it isn't dry enough yet."

Then he tripped out and went clattering downstairs, whistling.

We did not look at the things; we couldn't take any interest in anything but the clock. We sat staring at it in silence, listening to the ticking, and every time the minute-hand jumped we nodded recognition—one minute fewer to cover in the race for life or for death. Finally Seppi drew a deep breath and said:

"Two minutes to ten. Seven minutes more and he will pass the death-point. Theodor, he is going to be saved! He's going to—"

"Hush! I'm on needles. Watch the clock and keep still."

Five minutes more. We were panting with the strain and the excitement. Another three minutes, and there was a footstep on the stair.

"Saved!" And we jumped up and faced the door. The old mother entered, bringing the kite. "Isn't it a beauty?" she said. "And, dear me, how he has slaved over it—ever since daylight, I think, and only finished it awhile before you came." She stood it against the wall and stepped back to take a view of it. "He drew the pictures his own self, and I think they are very good. The church isn't so very good, I'll have to admit, but look at the bridge—any one can recognize the bridge in a minute. He asked me to bring it up. . . . Dear me! it's seven minutes past ten, and I—"

"But where is he?"

"He? Oh, he'll be here soon; he's gone out a minute."

"Gone out?"

"Yes. Just as he came downstairs little Lisa's mother came in and said the child had wandered off somewhere, and as she was a little uneasy I told Nikolaus to never mind about his father's orders—go and look her up. . . . Why, how white you two do look! I do believe you are sick. Sit down; I'll fetch something. That cake has disagreed with you. It is a little heavy but I thought—"

She disappeared without finishing her sentence, and we hurried at once to the back window and looked toward the river. There was a great crowd at the other end of the bridge and people were flying toward that point from every direction.

"Oh, it is all over—poor Nikolaus! Why, oh, why did she let him get out of the house!"

"Come away," said Seppi, half sobbing, "come quick—we can't bear to meet her; in five minutes she will know."

But we were not to escape. She came upon us at the foot of the stairs, with her cordials in her hands, and made us come in and sit down and take the medicine. Then she watched the effect and it did not satisfy her; so she made us wait longer, and kept upbraiding herself for giving us the unwholesome cake.

Presently the thing happened which we were dreading. There was a sound of tramping and scraping outside and a crowd came solemnly in, with heads uncovered, and laid the two drowned bodies on the bed.

"Oh, my God!" that poor mother cried out, and fell on her knees, and put her arms about her dead boy and began to cover the wet face with kisses. "Oh, it was I that sent him, and I have been his death. If I had obeyed and kept him in the house, this would not have happened. And I am rightly punished; I was cruel to him last night, and him begging me, his own mother, to be his friend."

And so she went on and on, and all the women cried and pitied her, and tried to comfort her, but she could not forgive herself and could not be comforted, and kept on saying if she had not sent him out he would be alive and well now, and she was the cause of his death.

It shows how foolish people are when they blame themselves for anything they have done. Satan knows, and he said nothing happens that your first act hasn't arranged to happen and made inevitable, and so of your own motion you can't ever alter the scheme or do a thing that will break a link. Next we heard screams, and Frau Brandt came wildly plowing and plunging through the crowd with her dress in disorder and hair flying loose, and flung herself upon her dead child with moans and kisses and pleadings and endearments; and by and by she rose up almost exhausted with her outpourings of passionate emotion, and clenched her fist and lifted it toward the sky and her tear-drenched face grew hard and resentful, and she said:

"For nearly two weeks I have had dreams and presentiments and warnings that death was going to strike what was most precious to me, and day and night and night and day I have groveled in the dirt before Him praying Him to have pity on my innocent child and save it from harm—and here is His answer!"

Why, He had saved it from harm—but she did not know.

She wiped the tears from her eyes and cheeks, and stood awhile gazing down at the child and caressing its face and its hair with her hands; then she spoke again in that bitter tone, "But in His hard heart is no compassion. I will never pray again."

She gathered her dead child to her bosom and strode away, the crowd falling back to let her pass and smitten dumb by the awful words they had heard. Ah, that poor woman! It is as Satan said, we do not know good fortune from bad and are always mistaking the one for the other. Many a time since I have heard people pray to God to spare the life of sick persons, but I have never done it.

Both funerals took place at the same time in our little church next day. Everybody was there, including the party guests. Satan was there too; which was proper, for it was on account of his efforts that the funerals had happened. Nikolaus had departed this life without absolution and a collection was taken up for masses, to get him out of purgatory. Only two-thirds of the required money was gathered and the parents were going to try to borrow the rest, but Satan furnished it. He told us privately that there was no purgatory but he had contributed in order that Nikolaus's parents and their friends might be saved from worry and distress. We thought it very good of him but he said money did not cost him anything.

At the graveyard the body of little Lisa was seized for debt by a carpenter to whom the mother owed fifty groschen for work done the year before. She had never been able to pay this and was not able now. The carpenter took the corpse home and kept it four days in his cellar, the mother weeping and imploring about his house all the time; then he buried it in his brother's cattle-yard without religious ceremonies. It drove the mother wild with grief and shame and she forsook her work and went daily about the town, cursing the carpenter and blaspheming the laws of the emperor and the church, and it was pitiful to see. Seppi asked Satan to interfere but he said the carpenter and the rest were members of the human race and were acting quite neatly for that species of animal. He would interfere if he found a horse acting in such a way, and we must inform him when we came across that kind of horse doing that kind of a human thing, so that he could stop it. We believed this was sarcasm, for of course there wasn't any such horse.

But after a few days we found that we could not abide that poor woman's distress, so we begged Satan to examine her several possible careers and see if he could not change her, to her profit, to a new one. He said the longest of her careers as they now stood gave her forty-two years to live and her shortest one twenty-nine, and that both were charged with grief and hunger and cold and pain. The only improvement he could make would be to enable her to skip a certain three minutes from now, and he asked us if he should do it. This was such a short time to decide in that we went to pieces with nervous excitement and before we could pull ourselves together and ask for particulars he said the time would be up in a few more seconds; so then we gasped out, "Do it!"

"It is done," he said, "she was going around a corner; I have turned her back; it has changed her career."

"Then what will happen, Satan?"

"It is happening now. She is having words with Fischer, the weaver. In his anger Fischer will straightway do what he would not have done but for this accident. He was present when she stood over her child's body and uttered those blasphemies."

"What will he do?"

"He is doing it now—betraying her. In three days she will go to the stake."

We could not speak; we were frozen with horror, for if we had not meddled with her career she would have been spared this awful fate. Satan noticed these thoughts, and said:

"What you are thinking is strictly human-like—that is to say, foolish. The woman is advantaged. Die when she might, she would go to heaven. By this prompt death she gets twenty-nine years more of heaven than she is entitled to and escapes twenty-nine years of misery here."

A moment before we were bitterly making up our minds that we would ask no more favors of Satan for friends of ours, for he did not seem to know any way to do a person a kindness but by killing him, but the whole aspect of the case was changed now and we were glad of what we had done and full of happiness in the thought of it.

After a little I began to feel troubled about Fischer, and asked, timidly, "Does this episode change Fischer's life-scheme, Satan?"

"Change it? Why, certainly. And radically. If he had not met Frau Brandt awhile ago he would die next year, thirty-four years of age. Now he will live to be ninety and have a pretty prosperous and comfortable life of it, as human lives go."

We felt a great joy and pride in what we had done for Fischer and were expecting Satan to sympathize with this feeling, but he showed no sign and this made us uneasy. We waited for him to speak but he didn't; so, to assuage our solicitude we had to ask him if there was any defect in Fischer's good luck. Satan considered the question a moment, then said, with some hesitation:

"Well, the fact is, it is a delicate point. Under his several former possible life-careers he was going to heaven." We were aghast. "Oh, Satan! and under this one—"

"There, don't be so distressed. You were sincerely trying to do him a kindness; let that comfort you."

"Oh, dear, dear, that cannot comfort us. You ought to have told us what we were doing, then we wouldn't have acted so."

But it made no impression on him. He had never felt a pain or a sorrow and did not know what they were, in any really informing way. He had no knowledge of them except theoretically—that is to say, intellectually. And of course that is no good. One can never get any but a loose and ignorant notion of such things except by experience. We tried our best to make him comprehend the awful thing that had been done and how we were compromised by it, but he couldn't seem to get hold of it. He said he did not think it important where Fischer went to; in heaven he would not be missed, there were "plenty there." We tried to make him see that he was missing the point entirely, that Fischer, and not other people, was the proper one to decide about the importance of it, but it all went for nothing; he said he did not care for Fischer—there were plenty more Fischers.

The next minute Fischer went by on the other side of the way and it made us sick and faint to see him, remembering the doom that was upon him, and we the cause of it. And how unconscious he was that anything had happened to him! You could see by his elastic step and his alert manner that he was well satisfied with himself for doing that hard turn for poor Frau Brandt. He kept glancing back over his shoulder expectantly. And, sure enough, pretty soon Frau Brandt followed after, in charge of the officers and wearing jingling chains. A mob was in her wake, jeering and shouting, "Blasphemer and heretic!" and some among them were neighbors and friends of her happier days. Some were trying to strike her, and the officers were not taking as much trouble as they might to keep them from it.

"Oh, stop them, Satan!" It was out before we remembered that he could not interrupt them for a moment without changing their whole after-lives. He puffed a little puff toward them with his lips and they began to reel and stagger and grab at the empty air; then they broke apart and fled in every direction, shrieking, as if in intolerable pain. He had crushed a rib of each of them with that little puff. We could not help asking if their life-chart was changed.

"Yes, entirely. Some have gained years, some have lost them. Some few will profit in various ways by the change, but only that few."

We did not ask if we had brought poor Fischer's luck to any of them. We did not wish to know. We fully believed in Satan's desire to do us kindnesses but we were losing confidence in his judgment. It was at this time that our growing anxiety to have him look over our life-charts and suggest improvements began to fade out and give place to other interests.

For a day or two the whole village was a chattering turmoil over Frau Brandt's case and over the mysterious calamity that had overtaken the mob, and at her trial the place was crowded. She was easily convicted of her blasphemies, for she uttered those terrible words again and said she would not take them back. When warned that she was imperiling her life, she said they could take it in welcome, she did not want it, she would rather live with the professional devils in perdition than with these imitators in the village. They accused her of breaking all those ribs by witchcraft, and asked her if she was not a witch? She answered scornfully:

"No. If I had that power would any of you holy hypocrites be alive five minutes? No; I would strike you all dead. Pronounce your sentence and let me go; I am tired of your society."

So they found her guilty and she was excommunicated and cut off from the joys of heaven and doomed to the fires of hell; then she was clothed in a coarse robe and delivered to the secular arm, and conducted to the marketplace, the bell solemnly tolling the while. We saw her chained to the stake and saw the first film of blue smoke rise on the still air. Then her hard face softened and she looked upon the packed crowd in front of her and said, with gentleness:

"We played together once, in long-agone days when we were innocent little creatures. For the sake of that, forgive you."

We went away then and did not see the fires consume her, but we heard the shrieks, although we put our fingers in our ears. When they ceased we knew she was in heaven, notwithstanding the excommunication, and we were glad of her death and not sorry that we had brought it about.

One day, a little while after this, Satan appeared again. We were always watching out for him, for was never very stagnant when he was by. He came upon us at that place in the woods where we had first met him. Being boys, we wanted to be entertained; we asked him to do a show for us.

"Very well," he said, "would you like to see a history of the progress of the human race?—its development of that product which it calls civilization?"

We said we should.

So, with a thought, he turned the place into the Garden of Eden, and we saw Abel praying by his altar; then Cain came walking toward him with his club, and did not seem to see us, and would have stepped on my foot if I had not drawn it in. He spoke to his brother in a language which we did not understand; then he grew violent and threatening, and we knew what was going to happen and turned away our heads for the moment; but we heard the crash of the blows and heard the shrieks and the groans; then there was silence and we saw Abel lying in his blood and gasping out his life, and Cain standing over him and looking down at him, vengeful and unrepentant.

Then the vision vanished and was followed by a long series of unknown wars, murders, and massacres. Next we had the Flood, and the Ark tossing around in the stormy waters, with lofty mountains in the distance showing veiled and dim through the rain. Satan said:

"The progress of your race was not satisfactory. It is to have another chance now."

The scene changed and we saw Noah overcome with wine.

Next, we had Sodom and Gomorra, and "the attempt to discover two or three respectable persons there," as Satan described it. Next, Lot and his daughters in the cave.

Next came the Hebraic wars, and we saw the victors massacre the survivors and their cattle, and save the young girls alive and distribute them around.

Next we had Jael, and saw her slip into the tent and drive the nail into the temple of her sleeping guest, and we were so close that when the blood gushed out it trickled in a little, red stream to our feet, and we could have stained our hands in it if we had wanted to.

Next we had Egyptian wars, Greek wars, Roman wars, hideous drenchings of the earth with blood, and we saw the treacheries of the Romans toward the Carthaginians, and the sickening spectacle of the massacre of those brave people. Also we saw Caesar invade Britain—"not that those barbarians had done him any harm, but because he wanted their land, and desired to confer the blessings of civilization upon their widows and orphans," as Satan explained.

Next, Christianity was born. Then ages of Europe passed in review before us and we saw Christianity and Civilization march hand in hand through those ages, "leaving famine and death and desolation in their wake, and other signs of the progress of the human race," as Satan observed.

And always we had wars, and more wars, and still other wars—all over Europe, all over the world. "Sometimes in the private interest of royal families," Satan said, "sometimes to crush a weak nation; but never a war started by the aggressor for any clean purpose—there is no such war in the history of the race."

"Now," said Satan, "you have seen your progress down to the present, and you must confess that it is wonderful—in its way. We must now exhibit the future."

He showed us slaughters more terrible in their destruction of life, more devastating in their engines of war, than any we had seen.

"You perceive," he said, "that you have made continual progress. Cain did his murder with a club; the Hebrews did their murders with javelins and swords; the Greeks and Romans added protective armor and the fine arts of military organization and generalship; the Christian has added guns and gunpowder; a few centuries from now he will have so greatly improved the deadly effectiveness of his weapons of slaughter that all men will confess that without Christian civilization war must have remained a poor and trifling thing to the end of time."

Then he began to laugh in the most unfeeling way, and make fun of the human race, although he knew that what he had been saying shamed us and wounded us. No one but an angel could have acted so; but suffering is nothing to them, they do not know what it is, except by hearsay.

More than once Seppi and I had tried in a humble and diffident way to convert him, and as he had remained silent we had taken his silence as a sort of encouragement; necessarily, then, this talk of his was a disappointment to us, for it showed that we had made no deep impression upon him. The thought made us sad and we knew then how the missionary must feel when he has been cherishing a glad hope and has seen it blighted. We kept our grief to ourselves, knowing that this was not the time to continue our work.

Satan laughed his unkind laugh to a finish; then he said: "It is a remarkable progress. In five or six thousand years five or six high civilizations have risen, flourished, commanded the wonder of the world, then faded out and disappeared, and not one of them except the latest ever invented any sweeping and adequate way to kill people. They all did their best—to kill being the chiefest ambition of the human race and the earliest incident in its history—but only the Christian civilization has scored a triumph to be proud of. Two or three centuries from now it will be recognized that all the competent killers are Christians; then the pagan world will go to school to the Christian—not to acquire his religion, but his guns. The Turk and the Chinaman will buy those to kill missionaries and converts with."

By this time his theater was at work again, and before our eyes nation after nation drifted by, during two or three centuries, a mighty procession, an endless procession, raging, struggling, wallowing through seas of blood, smothered in battle-smoke through which the flags glinted and the red jets from the cannon darted, and always we heard the thunder of the guns and the cries of the dying.

"And what does it amount to?" said Satan, with his evil chuckle. "Nothing at all. You gain nothing; you always come out where you went in. For a million years the race has gone on monotonously propagating itself and monotonously reperforming this dull nonsense—to what end? No wisdom can guess! Who gets a profit out of it? Nobody but a parcel of usurping little monarchs and nobilities who despise you; would feel defiled if you touched them; would shut the door in your face if you proposed to call; whom you slave for, fight for, die for, and are not ashamed of it but proud; whose existence is a perpetual insult to you and you are afraid to resent it; who are mendicants supported by your alms, yet assume toward you the airs of benefactor toward beggar; who address you in the language of master to slave and are answered in the language of slave to master; who are worshipped by you with your mouth, while in your heart—if you have one—you despise yourselves for it. The first man was a hypocrite and a coward, qualities which have not yet failed in his line; it is the foundation upon which all civilizations have been built. Drink to their perpetuation! Drink to their augmentation! Drink to—" Then he saw by our faces how much we were hurt and he cut his sentence short and stopped chuckling, and his manner changed. He said, gently: "No, we will drink one another's health, and let civilization go. The wine which has flown to our hands out of space by desire is earthly, and good enough for that other toast; but throw away the glasses, we will drink this one in wine which has not visited this world before."

We obeyed, and reached up and received the new cups as they descended. They were shapely and beautiful goblets but they were not made of any material that we were acquainted with. They seemed to be in motion, they seemed to be alive, and certainly the colors in them were in motion. They were very brilliant and sparkling and of every tint, and they were never still, but flowed to and fro in rich tides which met and broke and flashed out dainty explosions of enchanting color. I think it was most like opals washing about in waves and flashing out their splendid fires. But there is nothing to compare the wine with. We drank it, and felt a strange and witching ecstasy as of heaven go stealing through us, and Seppi's eyes filled and he said worshipingly:

"We shall be there some day, and then—"

He glanced furtively at Satan, and I think he hoped Satan would say, "Yes, you will be there some day," but Satan seemed to be thinking about something else and said nothing. This made me feel ghastly, for I knew he had heard; nothing, spoken or unspoken, ever escaped him. Poor Seppi looked distressed and did not finish his remark. The goblets rose and clove their way into the sky, a triplet of radiant sundogs, and disappeared. Why didn't they stay? It seemed a bad sign, and depressed me. Should I ever see mine again? Would Seppi ever see his?

Chapter 9

It was wonderful, the mastery Satan had over time and distance. For him they did not exist. He called them human inventions and said they were artificialities. We often went to the most distant parts of the globe with him and stayed weeks and months, and yet were gone only a fraction of a second, as a rule. You could prove it by the clock. One day when our people were in such awful distress because the witch commission were afraid to proceed against the astrologer and Father Peter's household, or against any, indeed, but the poor and the friendless, they lost patience and took to witch-hunting on their own score, and began to chase a born lady who was known to have the habit of curing people by devilish arts, such as bathing them, washing them, and nourishing them instead of bleeding them and purging them through the ministrations of a barber-surgeon in the proper way. She came flying down, with the howling and cursing mob after her, and tried to take refuge in houses, but the doors were shut in her face. They chased her more than half an hour, we following to see it, and at last she was exhausted and fell and they caught her. They dragged her to a tree and threw a rope over the limb, and began to make a noose in it, some holding her, meantime, and she crying and begging and her young daughter looking on and weeping, but afraid to say or do anything.

They hanged the lady and I threw a stone at her, although in my heart I was sorry for her, but all were throwing stones and each was watching his neighbor, and if I had not done as the others did, it would have been noticed and spoken of. Satan burst out laughing.

All that were nearby turned upon him, astonished and not pleased. It was an ill time to laugh, for his free and scoffing ways and his supernatural music had brought him under suspicion all over the town and turned many privately against him. The big blacksmith called attention to him now, raising his voice so that all should hear, and said:

"What are you laughing at? Answer! Moreover, please explain to the company why you threw no stone."

"Are you sure I did not throw a stone?"

"Yes. You needn't try to get out of it; I had my eye on you."

"And I—I noticed you!" shouted two others.

"Three witnesses," said Satan: "Mueller, the blacksmith; Klein, the butcher's man; Pfeiffer, the weaver's journeyman. Three very ordinary liars. Are there any more?"

"Never mind whether there are others or not, and never mind about what you consider us—three's enough to settle your matter for you. You'll prove that you threw a stone or it shall go hard with you."

"That's so!" shouted the crowd, and surged up as closely as they could to the center of interest.

"And first you will answer that other question," cried the blacksmith, pleased with himself for being mouthpiece to the public and hero of the occasion. "What are you laughing at?"

Satan smiled and answered, pleasantly: "To see three cowards stoning a dying lady when they were so near death themselves."

You could see the superstitious crowd shrink and catch their breath, under the sudden shock. The blacksmith, with a show of bravado, said:

"Pooh! What do you know about it?"

"I? Everything. By profession I am a fortune-teller and I read the hands of you three—and some others—when you lifted them to stone the woman. One of you will die tomorrow week; another of you will die tonight; the third has but five minutes to live—and yonder is the clock!"

It made a sensation. The faces of the crowd blanched, and turned mechanically toward the dock. The butcher and the weaver seemed smitten with an illness but the blacksmith braced up and said, with spirit:

"It is not long to wait for prediction number one. If it fails, young master, you will not live a whole minute after, I promise you that."

No one said anything; all watched the clock in a deep stillness which was impressive. When four and a half minutes were gone the blacksmith gave a sudden gasp and clapped his hands upon his heart, saying, "Give me breath! Give me room!" and began to sink down. The crowd surged back, no one offering to support him, and he fell lumbering to the ground and was dead. The people stared at him, then at Satan, then at one another, and their lips moved but no words came. Then Satan said:

"Three saw that I threw no stone. Perhaps them are others; let them speak."

It struck a kind of panic into them and, although no one answered him, many began to violently accuse one another, saying, "You said he didn't throw," and getting for reply, "It is a lie, and I will make you eat it!" And so in a moment they were in a raging and noisy turmoil, and beating and banging one another, and in the midst was the only indifferent one—the dead lady hanging from her rope, her troubles forgotten, her spirit at peace.

So we walked away, and I was not at ease but was saying to myself, "He told them he was laughing at them but it was a lie—he was laughing at me."

That made him laugh again, and he said, "Yes, I was laughing at you, because, in fear of what others might report about you, you stoned the woman when your heart revolted at the act—but I was laughing at the others, too."

"Why?"

"Because their case was yours."

"How is that?"

"Well, there were sixty-eight people there, and sixty-two of them had no more desire to throw a stone than you had."

"Satan!"

"Oh, it's true. I know your race. It is made up of sheep. It is governed by minorities, seldom or never by majorities. It suppresses its feelings and its beliefs and follows the handful that makes the most noise. Sometimes the noisy handful is right, sometimes wrong; but no matter, the crowd follows it. The vast majority of the race, whether savage or civilized, are secretly kindhearted and shrink from inflicting pain, but in the presence of the aggressive and pitiless minority they don't dare to assert themselves. Think of it! One kindhearted creature spies upon another, and sees to it that he loyally helps in iniquities which revolt both of them. Speaking as an expert, I know that ninety-nine out of a hundred of your race were strongly against the killing of witches when that foolishness was first agitated by a handful of pious lunatics in the long ago. And I know that even today, after ages of transmitted prejudice and silly teaching, only one person in twenty puts any real heart into the harrying of a witch. And yet apparently everybody hates witches and wants them killed. Some day a handful will rise up on the other side and make the most noise—perhaps even a single daring man with a big voice and a determined front will do it—and in a week all the sheep will wheel and follow him, and witch-hunting will come to a sudden end.

"Monarchies, aristocracies, and religions are all based upon that large defect in your race—the individual's distrust of his neighbor, and his desire, for safety's or comfort's sake, to stand well in his neighbor's eye. These institutions will always remain and always flourish, and always oppress you, affront you, and degrade you, cause you will always be and remain slaves of minorities. There was never a country where the majority of the people were in their secret hearts loyal to any of these institutions."

I did not like to hear our race called sheep and said I did not think they were.

"Still, it is true, lamb," said Satan. "Look at you in war—what mutton you are, and how ridiculous!"

"In war? How?"

"There has never been a just one, never an honorable one—on the part of the instigator of the war. I can see a million years ahead and this rule will never change in so many as half a dozen instances. The loud little handful—as usual—will shout for the war. The pulpit will—warily and cautiously—object—at first; the great, big, dull bulk of the nation will rub its sleepy eyes and try to make out why there should be a war and will say, earnestly and indignantly, "It is unjust and dishonorable and there is no necessity for it." Then the handful will shout louder. A few fair men on the other side will argue and reason against the war with speech and pen, and at first will have a hearing and be applauded, but it will not last long; those others will outshout them, and presently the anti-war audiences will thin out and lose popularity. Before long you will see this curious thing: the speakers stoned from the platform, and free speech strangled by hordes of furious men who in their secret hearts are still at one with those stoned speakers—as earlier—but do not dare to say so. And now the whole nation—pulpit and all—will take up the war cry and shout itself hoarse, and mob any honest man who ventures to open his mouth, and presently such mouths will cease to open. Next the statesmen will invent cheap lies, putting the blame upon the nation that is attacked, and every man will be glad of those conscience-soothing falsities and will diligently study them, and refuse to examine any refutations of them, and thus he will by and by convince himself that the war is just and will thank God for the better sleep he enjoys after this process of grotesque self-deception."

Chapter 10

Days and days went by now, and no Satan. It was dull without him. But the astrologer, who had returned from his excursion to the moon went about the village, braving public opinion and getting a stone in the middle of his back now and then when some witch-hater got a safe chance to throw it and dodge out of sight. Meantime two influences had been working well for Marget. That Satan, who was quite indifferent to her, had stopped going to her house after a visit or two had hurt her pride, and she had set herself the task of banishing him from her heart. Reports of Wilhelm Meidling's dissipation brought to her from time to time by old Ursula had touched her with remorse, jealousy of Satan being the cause of it; and so now, these two matters working upon her together, she was getting a good profit out of the combination—her interest in Satan was steadily cooling, her interest in Wilhelm as steadily warming. All that was needed to complete her conversion was that Wilhelm should brace up and do something that should cause favorable talk and incline the public toward him again.

The opportunity came now. Marget sent and asked him to defend her uncle in the approaching trial, and he was greatly pleased and stopped drinking and began his preparations with diligence. With more diligence than hope, in fact, for it was not a promising case. He had many interviews in his office with Seppi and me and threshed out our testimony pretty thoroughly, thinking to find some valuable grains among the chaff, but the harvest was poor, of course.

If Satan would only come! That was my constant thought. He could invent some way to win the ease, for he had said it would be won, so he necessarily knew how it could be done. But the days dragged on and still he did not come. Of course I did not doubt that it would win and that Father Peter would be happy for the rest of his life, since Satan had said so; yet I knew I should be much more comfortable if he would come and tell us how to manage it. It was getting high time for Father Peter to have a saving change toward happiness, for by general report he was worn out with his imprisonment and the ignominy that was burdening him, and was like to die of his miseries unless he got relief soon.

At last the trial came on and the people gathered from all around to witness it, among them many strangers from considerable distances. Yes, everybody was there except the accused. He was too feeble in body for the strain. But Marget was present, and keeping up her hope and her spirit the best she could. The money was present, too. It was emptied on the table, and was handled and caressed and examined by such as were privileged.

The astrologer was put in the witness-box. He had on his best hat and robe for the occasion.

Question. You claim that this money is yours?

Answer. I do.

Q. How did you come by it?

A. I found the bag in the road when I was returning from a journey.

Q. When?

A. More than two years ago.

Q. What did you do with it?

A. I brought it home and hid it in a secret place in my observatory, intending to find the owner if I could.

Q. You endeavored to find him?

A. I made diligent inquiry during several months, but nothing came of it.

Q. And then?

A. I thought it not worth while to look further, and was minded to use the money in finishing the wing of the foundling-asylum connected with the priory and nunnery. So I took it out of its hiding-place and counted it to see if any of it was missing. And then—

Q. Why do you stop? Proceed.

A. I am sorry to have to say this but just as I had finished and was restoring the bag to its place, I looked up and there stood Father Peter behind me.

Several murmured, "That looks bad," but others answered, "Ah, but he is such a liar!"

Q. That made you uneasy?

A. No, I thought nothing of it at the time, for, Father Peter often came to me unannounced to ask for a little help in his need.

Marget blushed crimson at hearing her uncle falsely and impudently charged with begging, especially from one he had always denounced as a fraud, and was going to speak but remembered herself in time and held her peace.

Q. Proceed.

A. In the end I was afraid to contribute the money to the foundling-asylum, but elected to wait yet another year and continue my inquiries. When I heard of Father Peter's find I was glad and no suspicion entered my mind; when I came home a day or two later and discovered that my own money was gone I still did not suspect until three circumstances connected with Father Peter's good fortune struck me as being singular coincidences.

Q. Pray name them.

A. Father Peter had found his money in a path—I had found mine in a road. Father Peter's find consisted exclusively of gold ducats—mine also. Father Peter found eleven hundred and seven ducats—l exactly the same.

This closed his evidence, and certainly it made a strong impression on the house; one could see that.

Wilhelm Meidling asked him some questions, then called us boys, and we told our tale. It made the people laugh, and we were ashamed. We were feeling pretty badly, anyhow, because Wilhelm was hopeless, and showed it. He was doing as well as he could, poor young fellow, but nothing was in his favor, and such sympathy as there was was now plainly not with his client. It might be difficult for court and people to believe the astrologer's story, considering his character, but it was almost impossible to believe Father Peter's. We were already feeling badly enough, but when the astrologer's lawyer said he believed he would not ask us any questions—for our story was a little delicate and it would be cruel for him to put any strain upon it—everybody tittered and it was almost more than we could bear. Then he made a sarcastic little speech and got so much fun out of our tale, and it seemed so ridiculous and childish and every way impossible and foolish, that it made everybody laugh till the tears came; and at last Marget could not keep up her courage any longer but broke down and cried, and I was so sorry for her.

Now I noticed something that braced me up. It was Satan standing alongside of Wilhelm! And there was such a contrast!—Satan looked so confident, had such a spirit in his eyes and face and Wilhelm looked so depressed and despondent. We two were comfortable now, and judged that he would testify and persuade the bench and the people that black was white and white black, or any other color he wanted it. We glanced around to see what the strangers in the house thought of him, for he was beautiful, you know—stunning, in fact—but no one was noticing him; so we knew by that that he was invisible.

The lawyer was saying his last words; and while he was saying them Satan began to melt into Wilhelm. He melted into him and disappeared; and then there was a change, when his spirit began to look out of Wilhelm's eyes.

That lawyer finished quite seriously, and with dignity. He pointed to the money and said:

"The love of it is the root of all evil. There it lies, the ancient tempter, newly red with the shame of its latest victory—the dishonor of a priest of God and his two poor juvenile helpers in crime. If it could but speak, let us hope that it would be constrained to confess that of all its conquests this was the basest and the most pathetic."

He sat down. Wilhelm rose and said:

"From the testimony of the accuser I gather that he found this money in a road more than two years ago. Correct me, sir, if I misunderstood you."

The astrologer said his understanding of it was correct.

"And the money so found was never out of his hands thenceforth up to a certain definite date—the last day of last year. Correct me, sir, if I am wrong."

The astrologer nodded his head. Wilhelm turned to the bench and said:

"If I prove that this money here was not that money, then it is not his?"

"Certainly not; but this is irregular. If you had such a witness it was your duty to give proper notice of it and have him here to—" He broke off and began to consult with the other judges. Meantime that other lawyer got up excited and began to protest against allowing new witnesses to be brought into the case at this late stage.

The judges decided that his contention was just and must be allowed.

"But this is not a new witness," said Wilhelm. "It has already been partly examined. I speak of the coin." "The coin? What can the coin say?"

"It can say it is not the coin that the astrologer once possessed. It can say it was not in existence last December. By its date it can say this."

And it was so! There was the greatest excitement in the court while that lawyer and the judges were reaching for coins and examining them and exclaiming. And everybody was full of admiration of Wilhelm's brightness in happening to think of that neat idea. At last order was called and the court said:

"All of the coins but four are of the date of the present year. The court tenders its sincere sympathy to the accused, and its deep regret that he, an innocent man, through an unfortunate mistake, has suffered the undeserved humiliation of imprisonment and trial. The case is dismissed."

So the money could speak, after all, though that lawyer thought it couldn't. The court rose and almost everybody came forward to shake hands with Marget and congratulate her, and then to shake with Wilhelm and praise him; and Satan had stepped out of Wilhelm and was standing around looking on full of interest, and people walking through him every which way, not knowing he was there. And Wilhelm could not explain why he only thought of the date on the coins at the last moment, instead of earlier; he said it just occurred to him all of a sudden, like an inspiration, and he brought it right out without any hesitation, for, although he didn't examine the coins, he seemed, somehow, to know it was true. That was honest of him, and like him; another would have pretended he had thought of it earlier and was keeping it back for a surprise.

He had dulled down a little now; not much, but still you could notice that he hadn't that luminous look in his eyes that he had while Satan was in him. He nearly got it back, though, for a moment when Marget came and praised him and thanked him and couldn't keep him from seeing how proud she was of him. The astrologer went off dissatisfied and cursing, and Solomon Isaacs gathered up the money and carried it away. It was Father Peter's for good and all, now.

Satan was gone. I judged that he had spirited himself away to the jail to tell the prisoner the news, and in this I was right. Marget and the rest of us hurried thither at our best speed, in a great state of rejoicing.

Well, what Satan had done was this: he had appeared before that poor prisoner, exclaiming, "The trial is over, and you stand forever disgraced as a thief—by verdict of the court!"

The shock unseated the old man's reason. When we arrived, ten minutes later, he was parading pompously up and down and delivering commands to this and that and the other constable or jailer, and calling them Grand Chamberlain, and Prince This and Prince That, and Admiral of the Fleet, Field Marshal in Command, and all such fustian, and was as happy as a bird. He thought he was Emperor!

Marget flung herself on his breast and cried, and indeed everybody was moved almost to heartbreak. He recognized Marget but could not understand why she should cry. He parted her on the shoulder and said:

"Don't do it, dear; remember, there are witnesses, and it is not becoming in the Crown Princess. Tell me your trouble—it shall be mended; there is nothing the Emperor cannot do." Then he looked around and saw old Ursula with her apron to her eyes. He was puzzled at that, and said, "And what is the matter with you?'

Through her sobs she got out words explaining that she was distressed to see him—"so." He reflected over that a moment, then muttered, as if to himself, "A singular old thing, the Dowager Duchess—means well, but is always snuffling and never able to tell what it is about. It is because she doesn't know." His eyes fell on Wilhelm. "Prince of India," he said, "I divine that it is you that the Crown Princess is concerned about. Her tears shall be dried; I will no longer stand between you; she shall share your throne; and between you you shall inherit mine. There, little lady, have I done well? You can smile now—isn't it so?"

He petted Marget and kissed her, and was so contented with himself and with everybody that he could not do enough for us all but began to give away kingdoms and such things right and left, and the least that any of us got was a principality. And so at last, being persuaded to go home, he marched in imposing state; and when the crowds along the way saw how it gratified him to be hurrahed at, they humored him to the top of his desire, and he responded with condescending bows and gracious smiles and often stretched out a hand and said, "Bless you, my people!"

As pitiful a sight as ever I saw. And Marget, and old Ursula crying all the way.

On my road home I came upon Satan and reproached him with deceiving me with that lie. He was not embarrassed but said, quite simply and composedly:

"Ah, you mistake; it was the truth. I said he would be happy the rest of his days and he will, for he will always think he is the Emperor and his pride in it and his joy in it will endure to the end. He is now, and will remain, the one utterly happy person in this empire."

"But the method of it, Satan, the method! Couldn't you have done it without depriving him of his reason?"

It was difficult to irritate Satan but that accomplished it.

"What an ass you are!" he said. "Are you so unobservant as not to have found out that sanity and happiness are an impossible combination? No sane man can be happy, for to him life is real and he sees what a fearful thing it is. Only the mad can be happy, and not many of those. The few that imagine themselves kings or gods are happy, the rest are no happier than the sane. Of course, no man is entirely in his right mind at any time but I have been referring to the extreme eases. I have taken from this man that trumpery thing which the race regards as a Mind, I have replaced his tin life with a silver gilt fiction; you see the result—and you criticize! I said I would make him permanently happy and I have done it. I have made him happy by the only means possible to his race—and you are not satisfied!" He heaved a discouraged sigh, and said, "It seems to me that this race is hard to please."

There it was, you see. He didn't seem to know any way to do a person a favor except by killing him or making a lunatic out of him. I apologized, as well as I could, but privately I did not think much of his processes—at that time.

Satan was accustomed to say that our race lived a life of continuous and uninterrupted self-deception. It duped itself from cradle to grave with shams and delusions which it mistook for realities, and this made its entire life a sham. Of the score of fine qualities which it imagined it had and was vain of, it really possessed hardly one. It regarded itself as gold, and was only brass. One day when he was in this vein he mentioned a detail—the sense of humor. I cheered up then, and took issue. I said we possessed it.

"There spoke the race!" he said, "always ready to claim what it hasn't got and mistake its ounce of brass filings for a ton of gold-dust. You have a mongrel perception of humor, nothing more; a multitude of you possess that. This multitude see the comic side of a thousand low-grade and trivial things—broad incongruities, mainly; grotesqueries, absurdities, evokers of the horse-laugh. The ten thousand high-grade comicalities which exist in the world are sealed from their dull vision. Will a day come when the race will detect the funniness of these juvenilities and laugh at them—and by laughing at them destroy them? For your race, in its poverty, has unquestionably one really effective weapon—laughter. Power, money, persuasion, supplication, persecution—these can lift at a colossal humbug—push it a little—weaken it a little, century by century, but only laughter can blow it to rags and atoms at a blast. Against the assault of laughter nothing can stand. You are always fussing and fighting with your other weapons. Do you ever use that one? No, you leave it lying rusting. As a race, do you ever use it at all? No, you lack sense and the courage."

We were traveling at the time and stopped at a little city in India and looked on while a juggler did his tricks before a group of natives. They were wonderful but I knew Satan could beat that game, and I begged him to show off a little and he said he would. He changed himself into a native in turban and breech-cloth, and very considerately conferred on me a temporary knowledge of the language.

The juggler exhibited a seed, covered it with earth in a small flower-pot, then put a rag over the pot; after a minute the rag began to rise; in ten minutes it had risen a foot; then the rag was removed and a little tree was exposed, with leaves upon it and ripe fruit. We ate the fruit and it was good. But Satan said:

"Why do you cover the pot? Can't you grow the tree in the sunlight?"

"No," said the juggler, "no one can do that."

"You are only an apprentice; you don't know your trade. Give me the seed. I will show you." He took the seed and said, "What shall I raise from it?"

"It is a cherry seed; of course you will raise a cherry."

"Oh no; that is a trifle; any novice can do that. Shall I raise an orange-tree from it?"

"Oh yes!" and the juggler laughed.

"And shall I make it bear other fruits as well as oranges?"

"If God wills!" and they all laughed.

Satan put the seed in the ground, put a handful of dust on it, and said, "Rise!"

A tiny stem shot up and began to grow, and grew so fast that in five minutes it was a great tree, and we were sitting in the shade of it. There was a murmur of wonder, then all looked up and saw a strange and pretty sight, for the branches were heavy with fruits of many kinds and colors—oranges, grapes, bananas, peaches, cherries, apricots, and so on. Baskets were brought and the unlading of the tree began, and the people crowded around Satan and kissed his hand and praised him, calling him the prince of jugglers. The news went about the town and everybody came running to see the wonder—and they remembered to bring baskets, too. But the tree was equal to the occasion; it put out new fruits as fast as any were removed; baskets were filled by the score and by the hundred, but always the supply remained undiminished. At last a foreigner in white linen and sun-helmet arrived and exclaimed, angrily:

"Away from here! Clear out, you dogs; the tree is on my lands and is my property."

The natives put down their baskets and made humble obeisance. Satan made humble obeisance, too, with his fingers to his forehead, in the native way, and said:

"Please let them have their pleasure for an hour, sir—only that, and no longer. Afterward you may forbid them, and you will still have more fruit than you and the state together can consume in a year."

This made the foreigner very angry and he cried out, "Who are you, you vagabond, to tell your betters what they may do and what they mayn't!" and he struck Satan with his cane and followed this error with a kick.

The fruits rotted on the branches, and the leaves withered and fell. The foreigner gazed at the bare limbs with the look of one who is surprised, and not gratified. Satan said:

"Take good care of the tree, for its health and yours are bound together. It will never bear again but if you tend it well it will live long. Water its roots once in each hour every night—and do it yourself; it must not be done by proxy, and to do it in daylight will not answer. If you fail only once in any night, the tree will die, and you likewise. Do not go home to your own country any more—you would not reach there; make no business or pleasure engagements which require you to go outside your gate at night—you cannot afford the risk; do not rent or sell this place—it would be injudicious."

The foreigner was proud and wouldn't beg but I thought he looked as if he would like to. While he stood gazing at Satan we vanished away and landed in Ceylon.

I was sorry for that man; sorry Satan hadn't been his customary self and killed him or made him a lunatic. It would have been a mercy. Satan overheard the thought, and said:

"I would have done it but for his wife, who has not offended me. She is coming to him presently from their native land, Portugal. She is well but has not long to live and has been yearning to see him and persuade him to go back with her next year. She will die without knowing he can't leave that place?"

"He won't tell her?"

"He? He will not trust that secret with any one; he will reflect that it could be revealed in sleep, in the hearing of some Portuguese guest's servant some time or other."

"Did none of those natives understand what you said to him?"

"None of them understood but he will always be afraid that some of them did. That fear will be torture to him, for he has been a harsh master to them. In his dreams he will imagine them chopping his tree down. That will make his days uncomfortable—I have already arranged for his nights."

It grieved me, though not sharply, to see him take such a malicious satisfaction in his plans for this foreigner.

"Does he believe what you told him, Satan?"

"He thought he didn't but our vanishing helped. The tree where there had been no tree before—that helped. The insane and uncanny variety of fruits—the sudden withering—all these things are helps. Let him think as he may, reason as he may, one thing is certain, he will water the tree. But between this and night he will begin his changed career with a very natural precaution—for him."

"What is that?"

"He will fetch a priest to cast out the tree's devil.

You are such a humorous race—and don't suspect it."

"Will he tell the priest?"

"No. He will say a juggler from Bombay created it and that he wants the juggler's devil driven out of it, so that it will thrive and be fruitful again. The priest's incantations will fail; then the Portuguese will give up that scheme and get his watering-pot ready."

"But the priest will burn the tree. I know it; he will not allow it to remain."

"Yes, and anywhere in Europe he would burn the man, too. But in India the people are civilized and these things will not happen. The man will drive the priest away and take care of the tree."

I reflected a little, then said, "Satan, you have given him a hard life, I think."

"Comparatively. It must not be mistaken for a holiday."

We flitted from place to place around the world as we had done before, Satan showing me a hundred wonders, most of them reflecting in some way the weakness and triviality of our race. He did this now every few days—not out of malice—I am sure of that—it only seemed to amuse and interest him, just as a naturalist might be amused and interested by a collection of ants.

Chapter 11

For as much as a year Satan continued these visits but at last he came less often, and then for a long time he did not come at all. This always made me lonely and melancholy. I felt that he was losing interest in our tiny world and might at any time abandon his visits entirely. When one day he finally came to me I was overjoyed, but only for a little while. He had come to say good-bye, he told me, and for the last time. He had investigations and undertakings in other corners of the universe, he said, that would keep him busy for a longer period than I could wait for his return.

"And you are going away, and will not come back any more?"

"Yes," he said. "We have comraded long together, and it has been pleasant—pleasant for both; but I must go now, and we shall not see each other any more."

"In this life, Satan, but in another? We shall meet in another, surely?"

Then, all tranquilly and soberly, he made the strange answer, "*There is no other.*"

A subtle influence blew upon my spirit from his, bringing with it a vague, dim, but blessed and hopeful feeling that the incredible words might be true—even *must* be true.

"Have you never suspected this, Theodor?"

"No. How could I? But if it can only be true—" "It is true."

A gust of thankfulness rose in my breast but a doubt checked it before it could issue in words, and I said, "But—but—we have seen that future life—seen it in its actuality, and so—"

"It was a vision—it had no existence."

I could hardly breathe for the great hope that was struggling in me. "A vision?—a vi—"

"*Life itself is only a vision, a dream.*"

It was electrical. By God! I had had that very thought a thousand times in my musings!

"*Nothing* exists; all is a dream. God—man—the world—the sun, the moon, the wilderness of stars—a dream, all a dream; they have no existence. *Nothing exists save empty space—and you!*"

"I!"

"And you are not you—you have no body, no blood, no bones, you are but a *thought.* I myself have no existence; I am but a dream—your dream, creature of your imagination. In a moment you will have realized this, then you will banish me from your visions and I shall dissolve into the nothingness out of which you made me. . . .

"I am perishing already—I am falling—I am passing away. In a little while you will be alone in shoreless space, to wander its limitless solitudes without friend or comrade forever—for you will remain a *thought*, the only existent thought, and by your nature inextinguishable, indestructible. But I, your poor servant, have revealed you to yourself and set you free. Dream other dreams, and better!

"Strange! that you should not have suspected years ago—centuries, ages, eons, ago!—for you have existed, companionless, through all the eternities. Strange, indeed, that you should not have suspected that your universe and its contents were only dreams, visions, fiction! Strange, because they are so frankly and hysterically insane—like all dreams: a God who could make good children as easily as bad, yet preferred to make bad ones; who could have made every one of them happy, yet never made a single happy one; who made them prize their bitter life, yet stingily cut it short; who gave his angels eternal happiness unearned, yet required his other children to earn it; who gave his angels painless lives, yet cursed his other children with biting miseries and maladies of mind and body; who mouths justice and invented hell—mouths mercy and invented hell—mouths Golden Rules, and forgiveness multiplied by seventy times seven, and invented hell; who mouths morals to other people and has none himself; who frowns upon crimes, yet commits them all; who created man without invitation, then tries to shuffle the responsibility for man's acts upon man, instead of honorably placing it where it belongs, upon himself; and finally, with altogether divine obtuseness, invites this poor, abused slave to worship him! . . .

"You perceive, *now*, that these things are all impossible except in a dream. You perceive that they are pure and puerile insanities, the silly creations of an imagination that is not conscious of its freaks—in a word, that they are a dream, and you the maker of it. The dream-marks are all present; you should have recognized them earlier.

"It is true, that which I have revealed to you; there is no God, no universe, no human race, no earthly life, no heaven, no hell. It is all a dream—a grotesque and foolish dream. Nothing exists but you. And you are but a *thought*—a vagrant thought, a useless thought, a homeless thought, wandering forlorn among the empty eternities!"

He vanished and left me appalled, for I knew, and realized, that all he had said was true.